Heartwarming praise for ENCHANTRESS

"Her books are compelling, her characters intriguing, and her plots ingenious."

—Debbie Macomber

"With a deft hand and lyrical prose, Jackson spins a spellbinding tapestry of Medieval Wales, drawing the reader ever deeper into the vibrant drama enacted by richly crafted characters."

—*Romantic Times*

"Lots of action, romance, and atmosphere; not to be missed!"

—Linda Lael Miller, bestselling author of *Shotgun Bride*

. . . and acclaim for LISA JACKSON's previous national bestselling fiction

"What a natural talent! Jackson delve[s] deeply into her characters' motivations, lives, loves, and hidden secrets . . . and boy, does it work!"

—*Literary Times*

"Heart-stopping. . . . Don't miss it!"

—*Old Book Barn Gazette*

"Superb! Lisa Jackson has outdone herself. . . . Highly recommended."

—*Reader to Reader Reviews*

"When it comes to pro_____
Ms. Jackson certainl_____

"[S]pine-tingling. . .

—*T*

LISA JACKSON

Enchantress

POCKET STAR BOOKS

New York   London   Toronto   Sydney   Singapore

A Pocket Star Book published by
POCKET BOOKS, a division of Simon & Schuster, Inc.
1230 Avenue of the Americas, New York, NY 10020

Copyright © 1993 by Susan Crose

Originally published as a mass market paperback in 1993 by
Pocket Books

ISBN: 0-7434-8091-0

This Pocket Books paperback printing December 2003

10   9   8   7   6   5   4   3   2   1

POCKET STAR BOOKS and colophon are registered trademarks
of Simon & Schuster, Inc.

Illustration by Alan Ayers; Hand Lettering by Dave Gatti

Manufactured in the United States of America

For information regarding special discounts for bulk purchases,
please contact Simon & Schuster Special Sales at 1-800-456-6798
or business@simonandschuster.com.

Enchantress

Prologue

Llanwynn, Wales
Spring 1286

"Help me, Lord." Morgana of Wenlock held her chin high, facing the tempestuous wind that shrieked over Wales from the north. Cold and bitter, the sea's breath battered her small body as she stood proudly, like a tiny soldier braced for battle in the tide pools. On other days laughter danced in her sea green eyes and a devilish smile played upon her lips, but not today, not when she sensed that the fates in all their fury had turned against her family and Tower Wenlock.

Today she reluctantly accepted her fate and prayed for a vision—a vision that would put her uneasy mind to rest.

There were those who doubted her, of course. Those who laughed. Aye, and she herself had denied the visions that had crept into her mind since she was a small girl. *Why me?* she'd asked, dutifully praying until her legs ached from kneeling on the cold stone floor of the chapel. *O Lord, why me?* God hadn't answered, turning a deaf ear on her prayers. Finally, when she could pray no longer, she'd unwillingly accepted her grandmother's declaration that her gift was God's will. In Morgana's opinion even God could make mistakes occasionally, and she would just have to accept her destiny. Still, she'd begged for God's guidance and forgiveness for her blasphemy in questioning him—just in case her gift wasn't an error on his part.

As she faced the fierce wind, bitter gusts whipped strands of her black hair in front of her eyes. Rain lashed at her cheeks and peppered the sea that swirled and eddied around her shivering legs.

Closing her eyes, Morgana drank in the smell of salt and brine, and touched the necklace of shells at her throat, closing her mind to the frigid water that threatened to congeal her blood and turn her toes to ice.

She waited, forcing back the cold, hoping that the voice would come, and quickly, praying it would speak to her as it had in the past. Last night she had been restless, unable to sleep, and always after such a night she was able to talk to the wind, to see through a window into the future.

"I am ready." Her words were drowned by the thunder of the powerful ocean. "Tell me. What is to come?"

The voice was soft, rolling on the surf. *There will be death. It comes to the House of Wenlock from the north.*

Her heart began to pound, and she shivered violently. "When?" she asked bravely, not wanting to know.

Soon.

"Who brings it?"

You bring it upon yourselves.

Oh, God. "Tell me more—so that I can prepare," she beseeched the voice, her fingers clenching anxiously in the folds of her tunic. "Please—who will cause this death?" she cried, her throat tight with fear as she strained to listen. But the voice of the wind disappeared, and the vision that was left was blurred—the image of a tall man, a warrior, on horseback. His crest was hidden, and his sword was raised high over his head as if he were about to slay an enemy.

That enemy was her family! She saw the unsuspecting faces of those she loved—her father, mother, sister, and brother—all naively trusting this foe who seemed a friend, who hailed from the north.

"Please, God, no." Morgana trembled, her hand closing on the dagger at her waist. She would not accept death so easily, nor would she allow this horrid warrior on his giant black steed to take the lives of those she loved. She had God on her side, didn't she? Were not her visions proof that he wanted to warn her? To prepare her so that she could defend her family?

In her mind's eye she saw the warrior swing his sword downward, cleaving the air that surrounded the faces of her brother and sister. "No!" she cried. "You will not win!" She drew her dagger, holding it aloft. The terrible visage of the death warrior swam for a minute in her mind, then slowly rippled away. "Leave us be," she ordered, hoping the formidable knight could hear her.

Knees as weak as Cook's blood pudding, Morgana opened her eyes. The day had grown as dark as night. The storm from the north raged savagely, as if the devil warrior had truly heard her. Thunder rumbled across the high cliffs, and lightning scorched the sky, sending Tower Wenlock, mounted high on the ridge, into stark relief.

Wolf growled. He paced along the shoreline, his paws wet, his gold eyes like liquid fire as he stared at her. The thick gray and black hair on the back of his neck was raised, as if he, too, had seen the vision.

Morgana ran through the shallow water, splashing sand and foam upon the hem of her white tunic, and Wolf followed. She paused only to draw a three-fingered rune in the wet sand with a stick. As the sea lapped over her symbol of protection, she tossed the stick aside, knelt, and quickly whispered a prayer for safety.

Her horse, a dappled mare, snorted and pranced, neighing in terror.

"Shhh, Phantom. 'Tis but the wind . . . all is well," Morgana lied, running to the skittish animal. She patted the horse's sleek neck and fumbled with the sodden leather reins.

Finally the cursed knots unraveled. Morgana climbed onto a log and hopped lithely astride the mare's wet back. "Ha!" she cried, bare heels digging into Phantom's smooth sides.

Her game little mare whirled on her back legs, then broke into a gallop, hurtling along the water's edge toward the path leading to Tower Wenlock. Wolf raced close behind, as he had from the day Morgana had found him abandoned in the forest near the castle.

Skirts bunched up, Morgana wound her fingers in the mare's coarse mane as the little horse's hooves pounded the wet sand and the wind, streaming past, stung her eyes.

There will be death. It comes to the House of Wenlock from the north.

Morgana shivered, but not from the cold. Never before had she heard such an ominous message, but never before had Castle Wenlock been so weak. "It will not happen," she vowed, thinking of her family. "There will be no death in the tower." The danger from the north would be defeated.

Gray ears flattened against her head, hooves striking stones, the mare turned onto the path that wound up the cliff face.

Morgana leaned forward. "Do not fear, Phantom," she urged the game little horse. "We will warn them. And this time you and I and Wolf, we will thwart the fates!"

One

Castle Abergwynn, North Wales
May 1286

s God is my witness, I'll not stop until I find my boy!" Garrick, son of Maginnis and baron of all of Abergwynn, slid from his mud-splattered mount, his boots sinking into the wet earth of the inner bailey. His clothes were grimy, his hair unruly, his beard in need of cutting—evidence of days of riding and searching and finding nothing. Nothing! Not one bloody trace of the boy or the nurse.

A scowl as dark as the thunderclouds gathering over the north tower creased his face, his harsh features ruthless and set. Tossing wet hair from his eyes, he swore a silent oath at the fates, or God, he didn't care which.

His knights, brave souls who had ridden with him on his luckless quest, dismounted, avoiding him, leading their horses to the stable. Loyal men, they knew when to leave their lord to his foul moods. This was the foulest, blackest humor ever to have darkened his soul.

Only George, an ungainly boy of barely fourteen summers, whose skin was pockmarked and reddened, dared speak, and this was only because, as Garrick's vassal, he had no choice. "I will see to your steed, my lord," he squeaked out, snatching the rain-swollen reins from Garrick's gloved hand.

Barely hearing the boy, Garrick strode forward, shoulders hunched against the wind, but head unbowed. He would not be broken. He would not fail. As long as there was some trace of breath in his body, he would search for his son. For the first time in his life he didn't care about his destrier, his castle, or his lands. All that mattered was Logan.

With a rattle of heavy chains, the portcullis clanged down, sealing off the castle, as if anything worth protecting remained inside. Garrick snorted at his own vanity. How prideful he'd been. How he'd found pleasure in the thick stone walls, the massive towers, the curtain wall wide and long enough to stand his entire army. God's teeth, what a fool he'd been, thinking this castle, this miserable fortress, was so valuable!

Glaring up at the slate-dark heavens, he muttered a curse to a God who had not only taken his wife away from him three years ago but had now stolen his boy as well.

As if in answer, lightning streaked the sky, a jagged sizzle that flashed white against the square northern tower. Thunder clapped mockingly over the land, as if God himself were laughing.

Garrick threw back his head, and rain drizzled down his neck and face, leaving cold droplets to run beneath his shirt. "I'll find him. By all that is holy and that which is not, I'll find my boy or die trying!"

Again thunder cracked.

Angrily Garrick stalked through the mud to the great hall at the far corner of the inner bailey. Castle Abergwynn was perched high on a cliff. On three sides the fortress stood atop sheer cliffs that fell a hundred feet to treacherous rocks and raging surf. Yet even the thick stone barricades hadn't been protection enough to save his son from harm.

Walking briskly through the forebuilding he didn't bother pausing at the chapel. Let Friar Francis stew in his own sanctimonious juices. Though Garrick heard the chaplain murmuring prayers, he wasn't in the mood to face a man of God, and he'd prayed enough as it was. What good had it done? Had God seen fit to lead him to his son? No! His boots rang sharply against the stone steps as he climbed toward the great hall, his pride, his home, and now not much more than an empty, dark chamber with no laughter, no warmth, no quick little footsteps.

He strode to the hearth and warmed his hands, though the coldness would never leave his heart. Servants, accustomed to his black moods, made themselves scarce, finding work elsewhere. Smoke from the hearth curled lazily upward and out through the few recessed windows, leaving a layer of soot on the stone walls.

The dogs that had been with Garrick, as if sensing their master's mood, slunk into the shadows, growling over a bone or scrap of meat that had fallen into the rushes. Garrick shouted at the hounds until they lay quietly in the corner, their ever-vigilant eyes turned toward him.

It had been ten days since he'd last seen Logan, his son, and although Garrick was lord of the manor, baron of Abergwynn, he was frightened that he would never lay eyes upon his boy again. Curse and rot the souls of those who would steal his child! Blood would surely be spilled if any harm came to Logan.

Scurrying footsteps stirred the rushes covering the floor. Garrick didn't bother looking up.

"You're back, m'lord!" the plump woman servant, Cailin,

exclaimed. "Did you find . . ." But her voice trailed off when she noticed his grim expression. Quickly she crossed her ample bosom before disappearing in the direction of the kitchen.

"Garrick!" Ware's voice echoed off the heavy timbers supporting the high ceiling. Garrick's head snapped up, and he narrowed his eyes against the smoke from the fire as his younger brother, his shoulders square, his blue eyes bright, his chin thrust forward defiantly, climbed down the curved staircase toward the great hall. A good-looking lad, Ware would soon be a man. His chest was thick, his pride great, though he had not yet seen his first battle.

"There's been no word?" Garrick growled, knowing the answer before the question passed his lips.

"No." Ware stood before him, his arrogance visible in the angle of his head.

"No ransom demands?"

"None."

Garrick's jaw hardened, and his eyes turned flinty gray. "The knights who guarded Logan. Have they told you nothing else?"

"Nothing, Garrick." Ware's eyes slid away from the power of his older brother's gaze, and his skin seemed to lose some of its dark color.

Garrick's mouth twisted downward. The boy had no stomach for lashings, and in truth, neither did Garrick. Yet sometimes he had no choice but to beat the truth from those whose loyalty was in doubt. "Did Strahan use every means of making them remember?"

Ware grimaced, as if he were holding on to the contents of his stomach at the memory. "Aye," he whispered, his teeth clenched. "When it was over, they pledged their fealty yet again. They are loyal men, Garrick. You did them an injustice. 'Tis not their fault that Logan wandered off, perhaps over the cliffs—"

A massive hand clenched over the front of Ware's tunic, and Garrick yanked hard, lifting his brother off his feet and forcing Ware to meet his gaze. "I blame no one but myself," he muttered, "but I must know that my men were not a part of this treasonous plot to capture my son."

Ware, true to his Maginnis spirit, lifted his chin and met Garrick's gray eyes rebelliously. "Perhaps it was not treason. Mayhap the child ambled off, his nursemaid after him, and they both lost themselves in the forest. They could have drowned in the river or fallen from the cliffs into the sea—"

"Nay!" Garrick snarled, shaking his brother yet again. "No bodies have been found. I will not believe Logan to be dead. The boy did not wander off." He dropped Ware to his feet and turned back to the fire, hoping the red-gold flames would stave off the cold that had seeped into his soul. "There is still much unrest here. Though Edward is king, there are those who would see him dead and spit on his grave. Since they cannot reach him, they test the very spirit of all those who are loyal to Longshanks. 'Tis not many winters since Llywelyn was killed, less time since the rebellion failed." Garrick rubbed his chin. "Make no mistake, the rebellion is not yet over. It still simmers in the hearts of Welshmen." His nostrils flared in anger. "Aye," he muttered, "and those who were loyal to Llywelyn will stop at nothing to rid themselves of Edward. They would take the life of a child for their cause."

"So you think the culprits be Welshmen?"

Wearily Garrick shook his head and clenched his fists as

if closing his hands around the throat of one of Logan's abductors. "If only I knew."

Ware glanced at the fire. "What of the guards who were to watch Logan?"

"Banish them."

"But—"

"Banish them, I say!" Garrick ordered savagely. "Let them know they are lucky to leave with their lives!"

"You're making a mistake."

The insolent pup. Garrick glowered at his younger brother. "I am baron of this castle. I shall do as I please."

"Yes, m'lord," Ware replied, mockery filling his voice as the door to the castle creaked open and footsteps rang on the stairs to the great hall. Garrick was in no mood for idle conversation. Strahan of Hazelwood, Garrick's cousin and most trusted knight, entered.

Tall and broad-shouldered, with a nose that hooked and eyes as brown as the robes of an almsman, Strahan bore little resemblance to his cousins. One look at Garrick and he frowned. "You did not find Logan."

Beneath his wet tunic, Garrick's shoulders bunched. "No."

"Perhaps now you will consider my suggestion."

Garrick scowled darkly and ground his back teeth together. "You are speaking of the witch."

"She is not a witch but a sorceress—one who talks to the wind," Strahan explained.

"Then she is daft."

"She has found others who were lost," Strahan argued. "Logan's trail is no longer fresh. Even the dogs know not where to look."

Garrick couldn't argue the point. His jaw grew tight, and

he threw an angry glare at the dogs lying restlessly in the shadows. Strahan spoke the truth. Logan and his nurse-maid, Jocelyn, had been missing too long already. Each day that passed increased the chances that Garrick would never see his son again.

"Have you any other plan?" Strahan pressed.

Garrick shoved his wet hair from his face, leaving a streak of mud on his forehead. "I have sent spies to Castle Pennick and Castle Hawarth, whose barons once allied themselves with the rebellion. My men will mingle with the peasants and servants and learn what they can." His nostrils flared. "If the barons have done my son harm," he pledged, his deep voice ringing to the crossbeams overhead, "they will pay with their lives."

"What if your men find nothing?" Strahan asked.

Garrick felt cornered, but he had no choice. As Strahan had pointed out, he would be soon out of options. "If Calvert and Trent return with naught, I shall seek out the witch." The thought of a sorceress—a woman with a talent for magic and the black arts—bothered him. Though he was not deeply religious, he did not like going against God. Noticing Cailin sweeping the rushes, he growled at her to bring him a cup of ale. When her eyebrows sprang upward in surprise, he barked still louder, and soon she returned with a silver cup for each of the men near the fire. Garrick drained his in a single swallow.

He considered what the chaplain might say if he did indeed go forth in quest of a witch, then decided he didn't really give a bloody damn what the good man thought. Leave Friar Francis to his useless prayers. It was time for swords.

* * *

Calvert returned at nightfall. His face was white, and his shoulders slumped as he approached Lord Garrick, who was seated at the trestle table in the great hall. Kneeling before his baron, Calvert said, "I have failed, my lord."

Garrick motioned for him to stand.

"I found no trace of Master Logan at Castle Pennick." Calvert, a short man with a bulbous nose and red eyebrows, struggled to his feet.

"You questioned all the servants?" Garrick asked, his spirits sinking ever deeper.

"Aye, and some of the soldiers whose tongues were loosened with ale."

"Know they nothing?"

Calvert shook his head. "If the boy is at Pennick, he is hidden deep and the secret is kept only by the baron and his most trusted knights."

Garrick turned this over in his mind. He had often met the lord of Pennick Keep, Nelson Rowley. "I think not. Rowley is known to brag. Had he my son, his entire castle would know it," he surmised. "Aye, and Rowley would have made the fact known to me as well." Garrick's eyes focused again on his knight. "You have done well, Calvert. You may take your leave."

Ignoring the pheasant and shoulder of venison on his trencher, Garrick glanced from Strahan to Ware. "We will wait for Trent and see what says he about Castle Hawarth."

Strahan nodded, his dark eyes glinting a bit. "A wise decision."

Ware didn't agree, and his gaze challenged that of his older brother, but he held his tongue and bit off a healthy chunk of meat.

* * *

The next morning as Garrick was walking to the stables, the sentinel's voice rang through the yard. "Sir Trent approaches!" Garrick braced himself. With dread thundering through his brain, he ran to the outer bailey.

Trent's lathered stallion galloped into the yard, the man astride huddled far over the neck of his steed.

Garrick reached the war-horse as the mighty beast slid to a stop and Trent, reins and bits of mane clutched in his fingers, toppled onto the ground.

"See to the horse," Garrick commanded the stableboy as he knelt down and gathered Sir Trent into his arms. Blood stained the knight's shirt and encrusted the corners of his mouth.

George gulped. "He—he is not—"

"Quiet!" Garrick said. He glanced up at Roger, a young page who had run from the great hall. "Summon the priest!" he ordered the boy, fearing that Trent's end was near and he should receive last rites. Garrick lifted the young knight and carried him toward the castle as George, wide-eyed, led Trent's horse toward the stables.

Trent groaned in Garrick's arms, his body convulsing in pain.

"Hold steady," Garrick said gently, though he felt the life draining out of his young charge. He'd been foolish to send one man on so dangerous a mission.

"Master Logan is not at Castle Hawarth—nor is the maid Jocelyn." Trent swallowed with difficulty. His breath rasped and rattled in his lungs.

"Get him some water and have a bed made ready," Garrick ordered Cailin as he carried Trent through the hallway. "Shh, man, hold on to your strength."

"I'll tend to him, my lord," Cailin whispered gravely. "Until Lady Clare returns . . ."

Desperate, Trent grasped Garrick's shirt and whispered in a breath-starved voice, "I was caught by Lord McBrayne."

"Hush, Trent. 'Tis time to save your strength—"

"Nay, my lord, listen," Trent cried, his face twisted in agony, his bloodless lips sucking in air. "I was with a wench in the House of McBrayne. She knew naught of a captured boy."

"Osric McBrayne found you—lying with a wench?" Garrick asked as a white-faced page scurried forward, offering a cup of water.

"Aye," Trent admitted, his eyes glazing.

Garrick scowled as the page forced the cup to Trent's lips. Water drizzled down the knight's dirty, beard-darkened chin. "We will talk more when you are stronger."

"Nay! Now!" Trent insisted, slapping the cup anxiously away as his fingers grappled over Garrick's tunic. "I spoke with others, too—soldiers with loose tongues, craftsmen . . . freemen, and peasants." He struggled, words coming hard to his cracked lips. "None knew of the boy . . . none."

"And still McBrayne did this to you?" Garrick whispered, rage tearing through his soul.

"Aye . . . He said he would have no spies from the House of Maginnis in . . ." Trent's last rattling breath tore through his lungs and he slumped in Garrick's arms as the priest rushed through the huge oaken door.

" 'Tis too late, Father," Garrick stated flatly. "He's gone."

"Let me have him, my lord," Strahan said, wresting Trent's body from Garrick's unwilling arms. Pain knifed through Garrick's heart, for he cared for his men and he felt a blinding stab of guilt for having sent so loyal a knight to his death. His fists clenched, and he swore furiously despite the chaplain's look of reproach.

Ware, who stood near the stairs, had heard the entire conversation. His young face was lined, his eyes dark and threatening. "Will there be war with Castle Hawarth and McBrayne?"

"Not yet."

"But Trent—"

"Trent's death is my fault," Garrick said heavily, his soul as dark as midnight. Trent, trustworthy Trent, was gone. Killed because of Garrick's blind obsession with finding his son. He was lucky Calvert had survived.

He glanced down at his hands, still sticky and soiled by Trent's blood.

Mindful that his men were watching, he strode to the table where less than a fortnight ago his child had eaten with him. He took the towel offered him by a page and scrubbed his hands, revenge burning hot in his mind.

If there were any servants about, they had vanished to safety, although a cup of ale was waiting. Dropping into his chair, Garrick leaned forward and braced his forehead against his fists. For the first time he considered the possibility that Logan and his nursemaid might be dead.

Squeezing his eyes shut, he told himself to be strong, to accept the fate that God had dealt him, but his jaw grew tight with anger and his soul sick with misery. What kind of a test was God giving him? How much longer would he suffer the pain of not knowing what had happened to his only son?

Hearing the scrape of a boot, he reached instinctively for his sword and swung his head around, only to find Strahan, his face set, standing rigid on the other side of the table.

"What is it?" Garrick demanded.

" 'Tis time to put this matter to rest," he said.

One of Garrick's dark brows inched upward. "Now you are giving orders?"

Strahan's lips tightened. "Not orders, my lord. Advice."

"Aye, and I need advice now, do I?"

"I think so, yes."

"Strong words, cousin."

Strahan didn't back down. "The men are ready to ride."

"Ahh." Garrick stretched his long legs under the table. "To Castle Wenlock and the witch."

"The sorceress—and even she does not deign to call herself such."

Garrick's eyes narrowed on his cousin. He motioned with his fingers. "And tell me of this woman—of her powers."

A gleam appeared in Strahan's sod-dark eyes. "She is the elder daughter of Daffyd of Wenlock and a beauty at that. Her grandmother, Enit, is supposedly a Welsh witch, and rumor has it that Morgana has inherited her powers."

"But you claimed she wasn't a witch."

"They say she can see into the future. She hears the fates speaking in the wind."

Garrick snorted disdainfully, then swallowed most of the ale in his cup. "I do not believe in witchcraft or sorcery or talking to the wind."

"Aye, you are a God-fearing man," Strahan said with more than a little mockery.

Garrick slid him a cold glance. "You doubt my convictions?"

Strahan shook his head. "I only want to help you find Logan."

"If the witch refuses to help?"

"She cannot. You are her lord."

Garrick studied his cousin. He sensed that Strahan wasn't being completely honest with him. Though Strahan was his most skilled knight, he was as shrewd as he was loyal. He'd often made his ambitions known and was anxious to possess the castle and lands that Garrick had promised would someday be his. As soon as Logan was found, it would be time to give Strahan his due, Garrick thought. "The witch's father may protest the taking of his daughter."

Strahan's lips slid into a sly smile. "I am prepared to marry Morgana of Wenlock."

"Are you? Even though you think her a devil-woman? What kind of a wife would she make?" Garrick asked, amused. He took another swallow of ale. "During your first argument she might become angry and curse you, causing your member to shrivel or your hair to fall out."

Strahan caught his cousin's humor and laughed heartily. "Nay, cousin. I will keep the witch so satisfied that she will use her powers only to keep me in her bed."

"Then she must truly be a sorceress," Garrick replied, as he knew his cousin's need for the company of women.

Strahan propped one booted foot on a bench and leaned forward, closer to Garrick. "I want this woman, Garrick. I met her only once, but I have not forgotten her. She will find your son for you."

Garrick had no choice. Remaining at the castle, waiting, was doing no good, and he could not bear to sit idly by as time passed—time that might mean his son's life.

"If I go, you and Ware must remain here to defend the castle. There may be word of Logan, and Lady Clare will need protection, though I doubt she'll want it," Garrick said, frowning as he considered his strong-willed sister. Even now she wasn't on the castle grounds but had gone to visit someone who'd been taken ill in the village. Against her judgment, however, she had taken two of the baron's best knights with her. "Keep my sister safe," he muttered to his cousin.

"As you wish," Strahan agreed, though his eyes clouded a bit and Garrick suspected that his cousin might have his own reasons for wishing to go on the journey. He was obviously taken with this witchwoman, though why he had not mentioned her before was a mystery. It had been three winters since Strahan had ridden to Tower Wenlock, and at that time, his visit had been brief, only to assure Garrick that Daffyd of Wenlock was loyal to Edward.

Garrick rubbed the stubble on his chin in frustration. If indeed this Welsh witch could help him locate his son, then nothing else mattered. He would use her.

And if she couldn't find Logan, he'd have the satisfaction of proving her a fraud, though in truth it mattered naught. Whether she be witch or woman wasn't his concern. All that mattered was that he find Logan.

He took a long swallow of ale and felt a welcoming warmth in the cold pit of his stomach. But the pleasure of drink did not ease his mind. For the first time in his life, Baron Garrick, son of Maginnis, felt absolutely powerless.

After draining his cup, he slammed it onto the table. "We ride at dawn."

Two

"I don't know why you allow her to speak like a heathen, Father," Glyn complained. Morgana's family was eating supper at the large trestle table in the great hall of Tower Wenlock. As usual, Glyn was casting her sister dark looks.

"I'm not a heathen," Morgana insisted. From the corner Wolf growled low in his throat.

Glyn visibly jumped. "Keep that beast away from me!" She wrinkled her pert little nose and tossed her head, golden curls falling past her shoulders. "There is gossip of her, Father. The servants say she thinks she's a witch or a man—but that she most certainly isn't a lady."

Daffyd of Wenlock sighed. "I will hear no more against your sister, Glyn." He glanced at his son and frowned. "You, Cadell, finish your food. 'Tis a sin to waste it."

"Would God strike me dead?" Morgana's fourteen-year-old brother straightened, but his blue eyes lost none of their mischievous luster.

"Nay, but I would punish you and well," Daffyd bit out.

Cadell immediately took interest in his trencher and the brawn thereon.

However, Glyn frowned sullenly. "But Morgana hunts rabbits and chants spells and talks to the wind."

Morgana lifted a dark brow. "Pray tell, sister, what do you do?"

"I am a lady. I sew, and I pray to the holy saints," Glyn replied, lifting her chin.

"Do you, now?" Morgana remarked. "Then perhaps you should pray to the saints that my aim is true and that when I use my arrows on rabbits and quail I do not miss my mark and strike you by mistake," Morgana said, smiling inside when she saw her sister's face drain of color.

"Morgana!" Daffyd muttered. "I'll not have that kind of talk at my table."

"Nor will I," her mother added, sending a knowing look at her elder daughter. Meredydd knew that Morgana's sharp tongue was partially her fault. Because she loved Morgana's spirit, her love of nature, her ability to defend herself, Meredydd had allowed her firstborn daughter to ignore convention, much to her husband's chagrin, though even Daffyd had trouble denying his elder daughter. Meredydd feared that Morgant—or Morgana, as she insisted upon being called— would have more than her share of trouble to deal with. What man would want to make her his wife? A wife with a sharp tongue and an outspoken manner was not a blessing to any man. It was well past time for Morgana to consider a husband.

Glyn, on the other hand, excelled at womanly tasks. She knew her place and how to wheedle what she needed from any man. Her fair curls and crystal blue eyes had already enchanted more than one knight from the neighboring castles. Aye, Glyn would marry well, but Morgana . . .

"What is this trouble you've been speaking of?" Daffyd asked his eldest child as he sliced some meat from the ribs of a roasted boar and motioned impatiently at his son, who was trying to escape from the table yet again. As the boy somewhat sullenly slid back onto the bench, Daffyd again looked at his eldest. "Morgana? The trouble?"

" 'Tis trouble and death. From a warrior in the north." Morgana ignored the eggs in jelly on her trencher and addressed her father. "I am certain of it."

"As certain as you are of the voices in the wind?" Glyn asked, clucking her tongue. "Honestly—"

"Do not jest about this, sister," Morgana warned.

Glyn tossed her head prettily and pouted. "We've heard about this trouble all week and we're sick of it. There is no trouble, Father. To the north is Castle Abergwynn."

"Aye," their father agreed. "You are confused, daughter. The war's over; the Welsh rebellion has been put to rest by Edward. Longshanks proved that he is the most powerful, and now we all pay homage to him whether we so wish it or not. 'Tis to the east where our enemies lie."

Glyn, obviously pleased that their father doubted Morgana, grinned prettily. "Perhaps you should chant a spell for us, Morgana, or make the mark of a cock upon the dirt to keep us safe from evil spirits."

"Should I, now?" Morgana's gaze rested on Glyn's fair face. " 'Tis said that the mark of the cock will cause ugly spots on the faces of blond maidens who pretend to be virgins but have already lain with men."

"Morgana!" Meredydd said reproachfully.

Glyn drew in a quick breath, and Morgana, eyebrows lifted, asked, "Would those spots cause you reason to worry, sister?"

"Morgana! Father, hush her tongue!" Glyn screeched.

"That is enough," Daffyd ordered.

"As for evil spirits, the only one in this castle is you!" Morgana mumbled around a mouthful of jellied egg.

"No more!" Daffyd, with a wave of his hand, dismissed both of his daughters as well as his son. "I'll not have my dinner ruined by this petty bickering. Glyn, you are not to keep company with servants and gossip about your sister. And, Morgana"—his eyes, duplicates of her own green orbs, held hers—"you will be kind to your sister." His harsh tone softened. "I will hear more about this trouble when you feel it."

"Aye, Father," Morgana said, willing herself not to shoot a satisfied look in her sister's direction. She, with a quick prayer, left the table and hurried through the great hall with Wolf at her heels.

Outside, the sky was blue and the scent of herbs from the garden wafted on the spring air. Morgana ran across the wet grass of the bailey to one of the huts within the castle walls.

"Berthilde!" she called as she hurried into the darkened interior. The familiar odors of beeswax and tallow enveloped her like a favorite cloak.

An old woman, her back humped with age, her skin wrinkled, smiled when she spied Morgana. "Do not tell me you wish more candles," Berthilde said with a soft laugh, "and keep that beast out of here."

"Wolf, stay!" Morgana ordered, then turned back to Berthilde. "Aye. I need candles, but only four."

"Your father wishes them?"

Morgana shifted from one foot to the other. She did not wish to lie, yet she had to have the scented tapers. "Nay, my mother needs them—for her chamber and the bower."

The old crone lifted her sparse gray eyebrows. "Her chamber is so poorly lit?"

"Aye, on these dark days it is hard for her to see the sewing and embroidering."

Berthilde chuckled and handed Morgana four candles. "Be sure these are not wasted," she warned. "I have to answer to the steward just as he answers to your father. No one within the castle walls, least of all the steward, welcomes Daffyd of Wenlock's wrath!"

"There will be no waste," Morgana assured her quickly.

"Make no mistake," Berthilde said, her watery blue eyes sparkling with suppressed devilment.

She knows, Morgana guessed, *and yet she gives me the candles.* Stuffing the candles into the pouch at her waist, she whistled to Wolf and made her way to the stables, but instead of finding her mare saddled and ready, she found her father, his lips compressed, his eyes cold.

"You have come for your horse," he charged.

There was no reason to lie. "Aye, Father, I wish to go riding."

"Despite the trouble that you say is coming."

She nodded, feeling a blush steal up her neck.

Daffyd glowered at his firstborn. "I think it best if you stay inside the castle walls."

"You would treat me like a prisoner?" she asked, astounded. Never in all her years had her father confined her within the fortress. He had at times asked her not to ride in the woods, told her to stay near the tower, or sent a guard to ride with her, but not once had he forced her to stay inside the walls.

Her father's features softened. "I could never treat you like a prisoner, daughter. You are too like the falcon—free in spirit and body. Yet there is truth in what Glyn says. The servants do speak of you and, yes, even laugh at your expense."

"Even though I have proved myself?" Morgana demanded, her temper beginning to fire as she stood in the half-light of the stables. She stomped her foot angrily, and a horse neighed. "Did they laugh when I found the smith's wife lost in the woods and nigh to deliver his firstborn son? Did they laugh when I foretold the storm that ripped the thatch from the roofs of their huts? Did they laugh when I discovered the wounded soldier and knew him to be a traitor?"

The horses shifted restlessly in their stalls.

"Nay, daughter, they did not laugh."

"But now they mock me, and that is because of Glyn. 'Tis *she* who does not understand that the forces of nature are at one with God! 'Tis *she* who makes fun of that which she does not understand! 'Tis *she* who thinks it is becoming to a woman only to sew and stitch and primp and pray!"

A gray war-horse snorted, and Daffyd took his daughter's arm, leading her from the dusty interior of the stables. "Mayhap Glyn is right," he said sadly.

"But surely—"

"Now, listen, Morgant—and aye, that is what I will call you, as that is your given name!" he added when he saw the protest that was forming on her tongue. "I want no more of your spells or your sorcery. From this time on, I want you to concentrate on acquiring the skills of a lady."

Morgana's eyes became slits. "What of the trouble to the north? Wish you to know no more of it? Would you risk your family, your castle, those vassals who are loyal to you, because Glyn has decided 'tis time I became a lady without vision?"

"You try my patience, daughter!"

"As you try mine, Father." They were outside now, and the armorer, who was dipping mail in barrels of sand and vinegar, glanced at them, only to let his gaze slide away. Several tradesmen, leading horse-drawn carts, were rolling into the bailey.

Morgana knew that she was being disobedient and that

people could overhear their argument. She could see the spark leap in her father's gaze. Though she realized he could be very strict and cruel when he chose to be, she could not hold her tongue. "The servants and your soldiers—aye, even Glyn—seek your protection. Would you deny them?" she demanded in a harsh whisper.

"I will put no more stock in magic and sorcery this day," Daffyd declared. "You, daughter, will not defy me!" To add credence to his strong words, he strode directly to the porter at the gate and gave the order.

Morgana stared at his broad back and silently sent up a prayer for patience. Why, suddenly, was she at odds with the father who had indulged her all her life? Wasn't it he who had taught her how to shoot straight with a bow and arrow? Hadn't Daffyd himself loved God's earth, and hadn't his mother, Enit, been her teacher in the ways of magic? Hadn't he allowed her to keep the wolf pup she'd found alone in the woods when others in the tower had seen the scrawny beast as an evil omen? Even Friar Tobias had crossed himself at the sight of the pup.

She stamped her foot in impatience and stalked back to the castle. She didn't intend to pick up a needle and thread. No, she would wait, but she would do what must be done. "Stay," she whispered to Wolf, scratching him behind the ears and leaving him in the great hall.

She climbed the back stairs to her grandmother's room and found Enit sitting up in bed.

"You are in trouble, child?" Enit asked, barely able to speak, her voice rasping in her lungs. Her hair was so thin and fine that her scalp showed through the sparse strands, and her skin was wrinkled and spotted with age. Her blue eyes were now a milky white, and her vision was failing.

"Father has insisted upon keeping me locked in the castle."

"Ahh—don't tell me." The old woman chuckled, but her laughter ended in a cough. "You have argued with your sister again."

"It is impossible not to!" Morgana said churlishly.

"But Glyn does not understand the powers. So far, of all my son's children, only you have been blessed, though I was nearly a woman before I first noted my gift. But the sight will come to another of Daffyd's children. This *I* have seen."

"The sight, 'tis a curse!" Morgana grumbled. " 'Twould serve Glyn right if she could talk to the wind. Then we'd see just how God-fearing she truly is!"

Enit lifted her frail hands and clucked her tongue. Her skin was nearly translucent, the blood in her veins webbing blue. "A curse you call it, but has not your gift saved us all?"

"Aye," Morgana agreed, sitting on the edge of the bed and taking her grandmother's hand in hers. "But it frightens me," she admitted. " 'Tis so strange and so powerful."

"Be patient, Morgana," the old woman said, and the warmth from her frail body seeped into Morgana's. "Be brave. Trust in your power as you trust in God." Enit closed her eyes. "Aye," she whispered hoarsely, her voice barely audible, her grip surprisingly strong as she clasped Morgana's small hand, "there will be pain, but also great happiness, and that happiness, granddaughter, will be yours—if only you will accept it."

Hours later in the lord and lady's chamber, Daffyd sat on the edge of the bed and nudged off one boot with the toe of the other. His wife, already under the covers, saw his beetled brow and noticed his haggard expression. "You are worried, husband."

He shrugged. Daffyd had never been able to confide in his wife. To him, telling her his troubles was a sign of weakness. "There are always worries."

"Especially when one has a headstrong daughter."

He glanced over his shoulder and snorted. "Two headstrong daughters and one mulish son."

Meredydd laughed. "You would have it no other way."

"Aye, but Glyn is right. I cannot allow the servants to gossip about Morgana." He frowned as he kicked off his second boot. "I have decided it is time she married."

His wife eyed him saucily. "Whom will she marry?"

"That I haven't yet decided. But it will be a lord who can provide us with unity and protection from Osric McBrayne."

"Would it not be better to marry her to one of Osric's sons?" his wife asked, smothering a smile.

Daffyd shook his head, then yanked off his tunic. "I cannot give her to one of my enemies! God's truth, Morgana tries me, but I cannot send her into marriage with a McBrayne." On a heavy sigh, he blew out the candle.

"Good. Because Morgana will not like you picking her mate."

"She has had long enough." He slid beneath the fur coverlet, nestling closer to his wife, feeling the curve of her naked body mold itself against his backside. "She will marry and marry soon. Her marriage will increase the wealth and power of Tower Wenlock," he proclaimed. "I shall speak to Morgana in the morning."

"Saints be with you," Meredydd whispered against his neck.

"That is not all. Cadell will be sent to another castle to learn his manners. He's lingered too long with us as it is. Since he returned from Castle Broxworth where he learned to be a page, he has fallen back on his old slovenly ways." Daffyd felt his wife stiffen. "Don't argue with me about this, woman. 'Tis time for him to become a squire."

"But he's just a boy—"

"Aye, and a bullheaded one."

"Like his father."

"Or his mother."

Meredydd sighed loudly, her breath stirring against the bare skin of his back. Daffyd quickly forgot about wayward children and centered his full attention on the woman who was smoothing her palms over the skin of his abdomen.

Morgana silently slipped from the bed. The room she shared with Glyn was dark. Only moonlight, filtered through a thin layer of fog, drifted through the window and allowed her any vision. The castle was still save for the sounds of Glyn's breathing, a rodent scurrying through the rushes, and the wind whispering outside the walls.

Wolf, amber eyes glowing, raised his head, but Morgana pressed a finger to her lips to quiet him.

Wearing her chemise and tunic, Morgana gathered her pouch, a rope she kept beneath her bed, and her dagger. She tossed her cloak about her shoulders, and carried her boots to the door.

"Where are you going?" Glyn asked, and Morgana, whose eyes had adjusted to the dim light, saw Glyn's crown of blond hair move as she propped herself up on one elbow and yawned.

"I will be back soon."

"You are defying Father."

"I just need some air, sister."

"You lie!"

Morgana could hear the smile in her sister's voice. "I will be back shortly, and I trust that you will not reveal that I am gone," she said patiently, though in truth she wished Glyn would think their conversation a dream and fall quickly to sleep.

"Why shouldn't I? You are out to practice the black arts, are you not?"

There was only one way to keep her quiet. Morgana stole across the room to her sister's bed and, leaning over Glyn, whispered in a crafty voice, "Aye, sister, you have found me out. I go now to do that which is forbidden."

Glyn's eyes grew round in the darkness.

"It would be wise for you to pray," Morgana added, sending up her own silent prayer for forgiveness for teasing her sister.

"Pr-pray for what?"

"That I don't cast a spell upon you—a spell that could maim your beauty? Perhaps blacken your teeth or turn your hair the color of blood?"

Glyn's hand flew to her mouth. "You would not!"

"No, I would not. Unless you do not keep my trust!"

"But Father forbade you!"

"Aye, and he will not know, now, will he?"

"You are wicked, Morgana, and evil! Father will punish you, and if he does not, then God will."

"That is between God and me," Morgana said. "Now, do I have your word?"

Glyn licked her lips and nodded, her pale hair reflecting

silver in the moonglow. "Aye," she whispered. "I will not betray you. Only please do not curse me."

Morgana's patience wore thin with her sister. "I would not." She turned to the dog. "Keep Glyn here, Wolf. See that she escapes not."

Glyn gasped in terror. "Do not leave me alone with—"

"Do not cross the wolf," Morgana ordered her sister. "You yourself have called him a devil dog."

"I will pray for your soul," Glyn promised, trying her best to sound pious, though her voice trembled slightly.

"Do so." But the thought of Glyn's prayers for her only hastened her toward her task. Morgana often thought Glyn's piety was convenient. Her younger sister did not seem so pure, as much as she wished to seem innocent. But Glyn's devotion or lack thereof was not Morgana's concern.

She was careful with the chamber door, for it sometimes creaked as she shoved it open. She glanced along the darkened hall. Running her fingers along the wall and counting her footsteps, she crept down the back steps and out the door to the bailey. The night watchmen were at their posts, but the fog, rolling in from the sea, was on her side as she hid in the shadows. She took the circular stairs in the western tower, where no sentinel stood. The soft leather of her boots barely scratched on the smooth stones as she climbed. At the top of the outer wall, she crouched, secured her rope, then lowered herself slowly, hand over hand, her feet braced on the smooth stones, to the outside and the grounds, which were high over the ocean. Leaving the rope dangling free, she walked carefully along the narrow path that zigzagged down the cliff face, her feet sliding on pebbles, for the way was dark, the fog a wet, misty blanket that clouded her vision as she followed the sound of surf pounding against the shore.

The briny scent of the ocean and the ever-pounding tide usually calmed her, but this night, knowing that she had disobeyed her father, deceived Berthilde, and threatened Glyn, she found no quietude in the sure movement of waves against the sand.

Walking to the edge of the sea, she waited, letting the fog wrap itself around her. The breath of the sea, cold and damp, brushed against her face. Morgana closed her eyes, envisioning the fog enveloping her, swirling counterclockwise, forming a brilliant cocoon, protecting her and Tower Wenlock from the unknown enemy hiding in the mists.

When she opened her eyes again, she was soothed. Kneeling on the sand, she murmured, "Keep us safe, O Lord, from that danger which cometh from the north."

With a stick of driftwood she drew a large circle in the sand. She placed dry tinder and driftwood sticks at the northern, eastern, western, and southern points of the circle, then placed a candle at each point. Using her flint, she carefully lit the candles, allowing the hot wax to drip onto the wood and chanting as she worked. "Nothing from the south can harm Tower Wenlock," she intoned. After lighting the tinder, she watched the fire glow red, grabbed a burning stick, and strode to the westerly point. "Nothing from the west can harm Tower Wenlock." Slowly she advanced to the north, lit the tinder, and said in a louder voice, "Nothing from the north can harm Tower Wenlock," and finally at the easterly point, she intoned, "Nothing from the east can harm Tower Wenlock!" At that point, she ran back to the southerly point. Grabbing another burning stick, she hurled it into the air, sending golden sparks aloft to spray the ground. "Nothing from above can harm the tower." When the stick fell, she picked it up, threw it hard on the ground, and watched the embers flash and sizzle in the fog. "And nothing from below can harm Tower Wenlock!"

Her spell accomplished, she cast her burning stick into the southerly fire and sat cross-legged on the sand in the middle of the circle. She felt the sea air shove her hood from her head and smelled the smoke as the four fires smoldered and burned.

Scarlet coals glowed against the sand. Crossing herself, Morgana began to murmur a prayer. But as she raised her gaze to the heavens, her words froze upon her lips.

Beyond the circle, past the northerly fire, the mist parted and the vision appeared once more.

On the other side of the golden flames that licked skyward stood a warrior, the fiercest she had ever seen. Blood red shadows danced across the angular planes of his face and turned his tunic crimson. His jaw was steady and hard, his black hair wet from the fog. Loose strands fell over eyes the color of steel.

Morgana's breath stopped in her lungs.

"What kind of witch are you?" he demanded, his voice booming over the steady pounding of the surf. "A witch who casts spells and works omens, then crosses herself and starts to pray?"

So he was flesh and blood! He was so huge and dark that the thought that he was mortal was small comfort.

"Nay, I am no witch!"

"A sorceress, then?"

She shook her head, trembling suddenly from the coldness of the night. Her fingers fumbled for the dagger at her waist as she struggled to her feet.

His eyes narrowed, and his lips thinned. "But you are

Morgana of Wenlock, are you not? The one who is sometimes known as Morgant?"

"Aye," she replied, trembling in fear.

He seemed satisfied at that. Crossing his arms over a chest as broad as that of any of her father's finest knights, he commanded, "Come with me, then. I have traveled many miles to find you."

She licked her lips anxiously. So this warrior clad in black was the danger she had heard murmured upon the wind. "Are you from the north?"

"Aye. Garrick of Abergwynn."

"The baron himself?" she asked in disbelief.

"Aye." He motioned to the circle and the four fires smoldering in the night. "What is this? Some devil magic?"

"Nay." She frowned at her useless scratches in the sand. How feebly they had protected her. It was probably these very fires that had caught the fierce one's attention! "This is not magic at all," she said in disgust.

"But you are the one with the powers—the one who can see into the future?"

Morgana evaded him. "Only occasionally, my lord."

"Upon request?"

She shook her head, and the warrior scowled sullenly. He gestured impatiently to the four dying fires. Candle wax sizzled against the embers. "I have no time to tarry. Let us be on our way."

"*Us,* my lord?"

"Aye, Morgana. There is no time to lose. I need you and your powers and will have you serve me."

Morgana's mouth nearly dropped open, but she held it firmly in place, and though this man was no sworn enemy, she slipped her dagger from its sheath. "I cannot leave Tower Wenlock without my father's permission."

His lips twisted. "Did he give his permission for you to steal into the night and light fires upon the beach and cast spells into the wind?"

Morgana wanted to lie, to wipe the smugness from his savage face, but she could not. If he was truly Maginnis, and his crest gave credence to his claim, then she was compelled to obey him. "My father does not know I am here."

"You disobeyed him."

"I tried to protect him. But I have failed."

"Failed?" he repeated, kicking at the sand with his boot and extinguishing the northern fire. "Well, Morgana, you must not fail me."

He advanced upon her, and as he drew closer, she tilted back her head to eye him full in the face, though her knees threatened to buckle. "What is it you wish of me?" she whispered, silently praying that she would not tremble in front of him.

"You must help me find my son."

Three

This is not the way to the tower," she said, half running to keep up with the baron's longer strides as he pulled her across the sand. He'd plucked her dagger from her hand and kicked sand over her fires, then told her that she had no choice in the matter.

"But it is the way to my camp."

"You have your soldiers with you?"

"Aye."

"To attack Wenlock?" Fear rose in the back of her throat.

He stopped, turning to face her in the darkness. "You think I would lay siege to my own vassal's keep?"

"Aye . . . you bring death." She quivered beneath his hand, but thrust her chin forward mutinously.

"I bring no death," he said angrily, tugging at her arm again. "I only want my son."

She didn't believe him. The man was too like the warrior in her vision. Nay, she had made no mistake. Garrick Maginnis was the danger—the death.

They reached the northernmost point of the beach. A black steed minced nervously. Nostrils flared, raven-colored ears pricked forward, one foot anxiously pawing at the sand, the horse snorted and tossed his great head as Garrick approached.

"He trusts no one but me," Garrick said before lifting her as easily as a sack of grain into the saddle.

"I can walk," she said.

"Ah, witch, are you frightened of the beast?" He climbed up behind her.

"Nay. The only beast I fear is man—a warrior from the north who will bring death to my home—and even he does not scare me all that much."

"Why is that?"

She slid a knowing glance over her shoulder. "God and the fates are with me."

"Ha! A witch who believes in God," he mocked, strong arms closing around her as he slapped the reins on the charger's shoulder. The stallion bolted. Morgana nearly lost her balance, but the muscular arm surrounding her waist kept her astride. The steed was swifter than her own mare, and the wind tore at Morgana's hair, stealing her breath and stinging so that she had to blink against the tears that formed in her eyes.

She clutched the stallion's mane and tried to feel neither the front of Garrick's thighs pressed intimately to the backs of her legs nor the apex of his legs so intimately caressing her buttocks. In her fear she ignored the way his body molded itself around hers, making her feel small and womanly for the first time in her life. His breath was hot against the nape of her neck as the horse sped through the mists that lingered on the sand.

They rode up the path that wound through the woods, leaving the sea far behind. The forest closed around them, the light from the moon glimmering through the branches overhead.

Saints be with me, Morgana thought desperately as she spotted the fires of the camp, glowing embers that flashed through the trees. Even if Garrick was honorable, which she doubted, what of his army? She had met many soldiers in her lifetime, but always in the company of her father, behind the secure fortress walls of Tower Wenlock.

Perhaps Glyn had been right, Morgana thought morosely. Perhaps she was being punished for escaping the castle walls.

She frowned in consternation and wished she had not given up her dagger so easily. Now, aside from the fact that Garrick's men thought she was a witch, she had no protection other than her wits. However, men had often proved as superstitious as women—afraid of that which they could not explain. If need be, Morgana would let them think she was a sorceress, a witch empowered to cast horrible spells upon them. They would believe her as easily as Glyn had.

"Who goes there?" a sentry called as the horse galloped into the clearing.

" 'Tis Garrick," the fierce one responded.

The war-horse slid to a stop in the circle of light cast by the fires. Garrick hopped lithely to the ground. Several men surrounded them, and eager gazes sought out Morgana, still astride the sweating steed.

Despite her thudding heart and weak knees, Morgana held her head high and met each lusty gaze with imperious eyes.

The first sentry, a thin knight with a bony face, smiled as his gaze lingered for a hopeful minute on the swell of her breasts before landing full on her face. "Have you a prisoner?" he asked his lord, desire already gleaming in his dark eyes.

"Nay, 'tis the witch herself." Garrick helped her to the ground, his hands spanning her waist.

The sentry's expression changed. His skin turned white, and suspicion darkened his gaze. "If she is not a prisoner—"

"She is my guest and will take us to Wenlock at dawn."

Morgana whirled upon him. "You would keep me here? Nay, I must return to the castle. My father would not be pleased should he find me in the company of soldiers."

"Would your father be pleased if he found you alone on the beach?" Garrick wondered aloud, his eyes silently appraising her. "What kind of father would let his daughter run free near the sea, chanting spells and calling spirits in the middle of the night?"

"A father who believes his daughter wants only to protect his castle," she snapped back. If Garrick thought she really called spirits to help her, so be it. His own belief and fear of the dark arts could prove to be his downfall. Never mind that she practiced no witchcraft—let him think what he would.

"Is Daffyd such a fool to think you can protect Wenlock by the casting of spells?" he asked skeptically.

"My father trusts me." Even as she spoke the words, she felt a pang of guilt. She'd betrayed her father's trust, and in truth he would be furious. Her sire, though usually a calm man, had a biting temper and could sometimes conjure up the most horrid punishments.

"If your castle needs protection, why did Daffyd not send a messenger to me?" Garrick asked. "As he is my vassal, 'tis my duty to protect Tower Wenlock."

"Then you've been sorely lacking in your duty," she replied, and the sentry drew a quick breath between his teeth. Obviously he was not used to hearing impertinence spoken to his lord.

Garrick's expression hardened. "We will discuss this in the morning," he muttered.

"I'll not be held prisoner!"

"Did I not say you were a guest?"

"Then as a guest I would like my dagger back and would appreciate my privacy."

"To run back to the beach and call up your devil spirits?" he mocked. "Nay, you could be harmed. I will see that you are returned to your father safely."

"As part of your duty?" she sneered.

"Yea."

The sentry cast a worried look from his lord to Morgana. "Where will she sleep?"

"In my tent."

"Nay!" she spat out, horrified. What kind of protection was this? Had he taken her for his own lustful pleasure? Furiously she rounded on Garrick. "I'll not warm your bed, my lord."

He smiled then, a rakish slash of white in the darkness. "I'll not harm you."

"And your soldiers?" she asked, glancing at the curious gazes cast her way.

"Nay. They will not want to force themselves past the portal that devil magic guards. I will see to it." To his men he said, "Return to your posts. We have but a few hours until we break camp."

Obediently the men scattered among the fires and tents, casting only a few curious glances over their shoulders at Morgana.

"Where will you sleep?" Morgana asked when she was alone with Garrick and his one stubborn sentry who would not leave.

"At the entrance of my tent, to protect you. As I said, 'tis my duty."

"Curse your duty!"

"No doubt you already have," he said maddeningly.

Motioning quickly to the sentry, he ordered, "Take her to my tent. See that she is given food and water, and post guards on all sides. I shall sleep at the entrance."

"You cannot do this!" she said, desperate to return to Tower Wenlock. She had to warn her father, even if it meant admitting that she had disobeyed him.

"I can and I will. You forget that I am your lord."

The sentry, casting her a worried glance, grabbed hold of her arm and led her to the largest tent in the camp. Though she fought him, he was stronger and his long, gloved fingers dug into the flesh of her arm as she struggled.

"Let me go, you beast."

He didn't respond, and as they reached the tent he grabbed for the flap. Morgana, furious, muttered, "If you value your ability to lie with a woman, you will not touch me, for it is in my power to take away from you that which pleasures you most."

"You speak nonsense, mistress," he replied, but ran a nervous tongue around his lips. Instinctively he touched the apex of his legs, as if to make certain that his male parts were not shriveled.

She arched a wicked black brow. "Be forewarned and do not be foolish enough to make me prove myself."

"Aye, you are from the devil," he muttered, swallowing hard. After ordering several soldiers to guard the tent, he opened the flap and Morgana walked stiffly inside.

She almost grinned at his gullibility. So Garrick Maginnis's proud knights were only fearful men in mail! Perhaps her escape would prove easier than she had imagined. As for the baron—oh, she would love to see his face when he found out that she had duped his soldiers. It took all her effort not to laugh and thereby foil her plan.

If her escape was to work, she would have to be patient and wait until the camp was quiet again—until she could safely slip past the guards and into the forest she had known all her life. Once she was in the privacy of the woods, she could steal quietly back to the beach and run to the castle, where she would shimmy up the rope and wake her father.

She thought guiltily of the rope swinging from the great walls of Wenlock. Unwittingly she had offered enemies easy access to the inside of the castle. Her father, mother, brother—aye, and even Glyn—could be murdered as they slept, because of her foolishness.

"God protect them," she prayed silently, filled with remorse. Oh, if only she could return to the castle safely, she would never again disobey her father! Never! Vowing to change her ways, she lay on a thick pallet in the center of the tent. She closed her eyes and pretended to fall asleep, but in truth she waited, her mind counting off the slow seconds, her breathing slow and even to fool the guards, her body as taut as a bowstring, as the noise in the camp slowly died again.

She didn't doubt that Garrick had positioned himself at the entrance of the tent. She could see his shadow, cast in scarlet by the dying embers of the fire, propped up near the flap. There were men stationed all around, though she couldn't detect a silhouette on the darkened side near the forest.

"Mother Mary, be with me," she said as she prepared to make good her plan. Her throat dry, her heartbeat thundering in her ears, she quickly drew in the dirt a symbol that meant nothing, just to give the lustful sentry something more to dwell fearfully upon. Then, sucking in her breath, she inched noiselessly to the back of the tent, carefully lifted the cloth, and rolled to freedom. The sentry standing guard leaned against a tree, his head nodding forward.

Though fear curdled in her stomach, Morgana smiled to herself. Garrick of Castle Abergwynn had a pitiful army if these sentries were any sample of his strength.

Nearby a horse nickered softly and stamped its hoof. Morgana caught her breath and didn't move. The sentry snorted, but his head nodded back. Fool, Morgana thought. She considered stealing the steed, then tossed the idea aside. It wouldn't do to take from a lord, especially a lord she planned to humiliate by slipping from his grasp. It didn't matter that she only meant to borrow a mount for the night—Baron Maginnis would likely strangle her with his own two hands.

She was better off on foot.

Morgana tucked her feet beneath her and, crouching low in the shadows, scurried silently to the forest's edge. The air was thick with dampness. Fog still clung to the ground, wisping around thickets of oak, alder, and maple. The smell of dank earth and ferns greeted her as she considered Garrick, the mighty warrior, waking up to find that a mere unarmed girl—nay, a witch, as he called her—could elude him and his trained sentries. It warmed her heart a little, though she was tempted to return and retrieve the dagger that the black-hearted devil had stolen from her.

Leaves and branches crunched softly beneath her feet as she hurried toward the sound of the sea. She found the path on which she and Garrick had so recently ridden and, after creeping out of the shadows, broke into a run.

The water was only a short distance away; she could hear

the dull roar of waves crashing against the sand. Only one more corner and . . . She stopped dead in her tracks. Her heart slammed against her ribs. The swirling sea mist parted, revealing the sharp silhouette of a man.

Morgana swallowed back her fear as she realized she had nearly collided with none other than Garrick of Abergwynn. Looming in the night, moonlight illuminating his formidable face, he blocked the path. His eyes flashed silver; his lips were drawn back against his teeth. "Well, witch," he said with quiet menace, "would you leave me so soon? Before you have helped me find my son?"

Morgana wanted to step back but held her ground. "I said I could not help you."

He moved closer as the moon passed behind a cloud. Her skin prickled in apprehension. She considered dashing around him, but knew her attempt to escape would be futile. " 'Tis said you have helped others find their lost kin," he said slowly.

"Aye."

"So you would deny me the same kindness?"

He was so close she could feel the heat from his body, smell the earthy maleness of him. "Nay, I would not," she admitted, "but I know not that I can help you. You do not believe in my gifts."

Even in the darkness she could see his features grow strained. "I have little faith in sorcery and not much more in God." He rubbed an impatient hand around the back of his neck, and his breath whistled slowly from his lungs. "But I must do whatever I can to find my son. If that means I must use whatever powers you possess, so be it."

"And yet you are not afraid of me?"

He barked a short laugh. "Afraid of one so small? Nay, witch Morgant—"

"I am called Morgana."

"Morgana," he repeated, her name rolling easily off his tongue. "I fear only losing my son."

For the first time, Morgana believed him. Few things would daunt a man so strong, but the loss of a child could certainly cripple even the most powerful warrior.

"Has your wife agreed that you should seek me out?"

"My wife is dead, struck down in the birthing of Logan," he said, a quiet rage contorting his face. The forest seemed to darken around them. "The very God you pray to took her in the giving of my son."

"We do not always understand the way God works."

"Aye," Garrick muttered, his eyes gleaming angrily. "Nor do I any longer pay him homage."

"Mayhap that is why he has taken your son."

"This is not God's doing," Garrick snarled. "It is the work of my enemies, and you, Morgana, will help me find out who would steal the boy. Logan is all I have left." Wasting no more time, Garrick grabbed her arm and yanked her roughly back to the camp.

She stumbled several times, but he caught her, dragging her back along the path, uncaring that brambles and twigs plucked at her tunic and snatched at wayward strands of her hair. Oh, if only she had her dagger! She would gladly show him how well she could use it before she escaped to the tower.

As if reading her mind, he glanced at her and smiled grimly. "If you are so anxious to return to your father, we will not wait for dawn. We shall go now."

Together? No! Morgana tried to wrench her arm free, but

the steely fingers would not release her. "I should return alone," she argued.

"Nay. 'Tis time I met with Daffyd and we discussed your journey."

"My journey?" she repeated, suddenly apprehensive.

"To Abergwynn."

Her heart nearly stopped. "Nay, I'll not—"

"You will, my lady," Garrick assured her, his fingers biting into the soft flesh of her upper arm.

"My father will not allow it!" she argued proudly, but felt the cloak of doom settle over her shoulders.

"He has no choice. 'Twould be my guess that Daffyd will gladly wash his hands of you. No doubt he would like to find someone to make a proper lady of you."

"Is that what a baron does—spends his time teaching women to sew and weave?" she taunted.

He laughed at her barb. "Nay, mistress, but there are many at Abergwynn who would do just that. Though, God's truth, Clare has yet to turn a witch into a lady. 'Twill be a challenge for her."

Terror seized Morgana. Castle Abergwynn was several days' ride to the north, far away from the safety of Tower Wenlock. She would know no one there, save this tyrant of a lord who would have her do his bidding on a whim. The thought of his soldiers and their lust-filled gazes turned her blood to ice. Already Morgana did not like or trust Clare. Panic tore at her soul, and her heart began to slam against her chest.

Nay, she would not willingly go to the castle in the north. "I can do much here," she said, hoping to reason with him.

"But much more at Abergwynn. 'Tis from there that Logan was stolen."

"You saw him taken?"

"Nay."

"And what of your guards?"

Garrick glowered down at her. "They know nothing," he muttered, half pushing her into the clearing and calling to the same sentry who had eyed her earlier. "The witch requests to return to Tower Wenlock before the morning. I shall take her there myself. You, Sir Randolph, will secure the camp until dawn at which time you will continue on to the tower."

The sentry nodded curtly. "Aye, my lord."

Morgana couldn't believe her ears. Was this man out of his mind? Baron or no, he couldn't just ride to the castle and expect to be let in at this hour of the night. Aside from the sentries, most of the inhabitants of the castle were fast asleep.

Garrick ordered Randolph to fetch his horse. The knight quickly did his bidding and within seconds, it seemed to Morgana, the black beast came prancing and snorting to them.

The stallion is as impatient as his master, she thought mulishly, sending Garrick a dark look. Oh, if only she could curse this warrior before he wreaked havoc on Tower Wenlock. If only, with a few words and a quick spell, she could banish him back behind the portcullis of Castle Abergwynn!

Garrick muttered commands to Sir Randolph, climbed into his saddle, and hauled Morgana up in front of him. Again his body was cupped around hers, his massive chest pressed hard against her back, his arms strong around her, his hands gripping the reins.

He yanked hard and turned the steed, then headed back to the road leading to Tower Wenlock. Morgana closed her mind to the feel and scent of him. In truth she barely noticed. Her heart was thudding in fear, and her stomach was tied in painful knots as the horse picked his way along the mist-shrouded road.

Saints in heaven, what would her father say?

Four

"'lord, there are visitors!" Geoffrey's voice was muffled by the thick door.

A loud noise—harsh pounding—startled Daffyd from a pleasant sleep. Instinctively he reached for his sword, kept hidden beneath the straw of his mattress.

"Visitors?" he repeated, feeling his wife stir beside him. She found her clothes as Daffyd slipped his tunic over his head and yanked on his hose.

"I will see who—"

"Nay, wife," he said irritably as he opened the door and slipped into the hall where the sentry stood holding a torch. Daffyd, in a foul mood, frowned angrily. "Tell the visitor he must wait until morning."

" 'Tis the baron himself, sir. Garrick of Abergwynn."

Daffyd froze. "The lord?"

"Aye, sir. He has with him Mistress Morgana."

"Morgana?" Daffyd repeated, the cobwebs clearing from his mind. "But she is asleep in her room."

"Nay, she is with the baron and none too happy about it."

Daffyd's rage boiled up from within him as he realized that Morgana had disobeyed him. Lord, but she was stubborn and prideful! "She was not in the castle tonight? She disobeyed me?" he demanded, his incredulity mixed with fury.

The sentry shifted uncomfortably, the flames from his torch casting restless orange shadows against the walls. Obviously the man did not want to speak ill of Morgana.

"Out with it," Daffyd thundered, "or you will be punished as well as she!"

Reluctantly the guard said, "The mistress let herself outside by climbing down a rope that was hung over the castle walls."

Daffyd swore angrily, and his mood grew foul. "If this be so, she will be punished! Give the baron entrance and tell Morgana, if it is really she, to wait for me. And bring me that rope!" Taking a candle from the hallway sconce, he stormed down the long corridor to his daughters' room and threw open the door.

Glyn was scurrying across the rushes to her bed. No doubt she had been eavesdropping. Morgana's bed was empty; her wolf dog paced beneath the window. "By all that is holy, what is wrong with that girl?" he roared, then glared at his younger daughter. "What know you of this?" he demanded suspiciously as he swept one hand toward the empty bed.

In the flickering candlelight, Glyn trembled. "I know nothing, Father."

"Nay?" he countered. "Yet you are awake and can see very clearly that Morgana is not here." His voice grew low and shook. "Mayhap, daughter, you should think again."

Glyn licked her full lips. "She promised to curse me should I tell you."

"I shall punish you if you don't. I promise you, daughter, my punishment will be much more severe than any of Morgana's spells!"

The damned dog growled.

Glyn cowered all the more. Finally, eyes round, she whispered, "Morgana . . . she went off to cast her spells again." Glyn crossed herself speedily. "She swore to cast an evil spell against me should I betray her."

"And you believed her?"

"Aye. Morgana is . . . is not sound, father. Her mind—"

"Ah! She fools even you, though you have grown up with the sprite! 'Tis Enit's fault. I should never have let my mother tell her of the old ways!" Disgust flared his nostrils. "Stay in your bed until morning. Elsewise you'll get the same punishment as she."

Glyn swallowed hard, and her hand, already near her soft lips, touched the edges of her teeth, as if to be sure they were still in her head. In her own way, Glyn was as much trouble as Morgana . . . well, nearly. By the ghost of his father, Daffyd didn't know what to do with his girls!

He strode back to his own room, donned his best tunic, and spoke quickly to his wife. "We have a guest, it seems, the baron himself. Have the servants make the best room ready for him and order the cook to prepare a feast."

Meredydd was already braiding her hair. "Aye," she agreed. "What brings him here?"

"God only knows." Daffyd sighed. "The sentry claims Morgana is with him."

"With the baron?" Meredydd exclaimed.

"Aye." Daffyd made an impatient movement with his hand. "Though I'm not sure why or how. Glyn says Morgana left the castle to cast more of her foolish spells."

"Perhaps she cast a spell for a husband and the baron appeared," Meredydd joked.

"Nay, wife, this is no time for jest," Daffyd nearly barked.

" 'Tis your fault that she has been allowed to run wild and free."

"But not the fault of your mother?" Meredydd asked evenly. "Enit is the one who showed Morgana the powers of nature. As for Morgana's freedom, who taught her to use a bow and arrow and fight with a dagger, hmm?"

"Aye, wife," he admitted, swatting at the air to shove aside her arguments, "that blame 'tis mine."

"Let us not lay blame, husband. Let us only find out what the lord wants and what he has to do with our daughter."

"Aye, I shall find out," he promised, striding to the door as Meredydd found her crimson tunic and began to dress quickly. The baron of Abergwynn was a most handsome man, a widower who had yet to claim a new wife. Perhaps Morgana . . . Meredydd thought as she adjusted a silk belt around her waist. Why not? The girl was beautiful, spirited, and well past the age of marriage.

Meredydd twisted her hair beneath her wimple. 'Twould take a strong man to tame Morgana's spirit and gentle her serpent's tongue. What man would be more likely than the baron himself? With that thought she smiled and decided that Baron Garrick of Abergwynn would be a most welcome guest, a most welcome guest indeed.

Morgana squared her shoulders as her father, his face etched with fury, approached her in the great hall. Firelight and rage gleamed in Daffyd's eyes.

The giant of a man who was the baron stepped closer to her—as if to protect her! Morgana shot him a scathing look. She did not need his protection from her own father.

Daffyd, jaw clenched, turned to the baron. "Welcome

to Tower Wenlock," he said tightly. "I've awakened the servants, and they will offer you food, the best room in the castle, and whatever else you may need."

Garrick's eyes glinted, his lips twisted into a lazy, disarming grin. "I accept your hospitality."

"What's mine is yours." The tension in Daffyd's shoulders eased a bit at the baron's manner. Mayhap there was no trouble at all.

"Are you saying, Daffyd, that I can have anything I would like?"

"Aye. As I am your vassal, all you need do is ask."

Morgana felt the tension in the great hall, and when Garrick's gloved fingers surrounded her shoulder, she held herself firm, refusing to quiver.

A satisfied smile crossed Garrick's face. "Then I thank you, Daffyd," Garrick said, "for all I want is your daughter— Morgana."

Morgana nearly fainted. Her breath lodged in her throat. *Nay! Nay! Nay!* "Father, please—" She heard a rustling on the stairs and watched in horror as her mother descended the steps. Another smaller figure followed her, and Morgana died a thousand horrible deaths as Glyn, her blue eyes shining, crept into the room.

Meredydd's face was flushed, her eyes bright. "Did you hear that, Daffyd?" she asked, smiling at her elder daughter. "The lord has asked that Morgana be his wife."

"No!" Morgana cried instinctively, drawing away from this arrogant man.

"Hush!" her father ordered. "You have no right to speak. Look at you!" He motioned to her scratched and muddy tunic, her tangled black hair. "That you are my daughter brings me only shame!"

"Father!" Morgana cried, her throat closing, her eyes burning when she saw the disdain in Daffyd's eyes.

"You have disobeyed me for the last time, Morgana. As for you"—he cast his eyes on Glyn—"you, too, have disobeyed me this night. Did I not tell you to stay in your room?"

"Aye," Glyn whispered, blushing as she gazed up at Garrick, "but I could not stay away when I knew that the great lord had chosen to visit us." She smiled prettily, dimpling. "Forgive me, Father."

"Let us not talk of this now," Meredydd said swiftly, a smile creasing her pretty face. "You heard Lord Maginnis, Daffyd."

Garrick held up his palm. " 'Tis not my wish to marry your daughter."

"But"—Meredydd gulped, and her hand flew to her throat as she took in Morgana's disheveled appearance—"Morgana is a lady."

Daffyd snorted, and Morgana had to bite her lip to keep from shouting at them all.

Garrick said, "I have no need of a wife. I have but a mission for your daughter. Because of her sorcery and powers I wish Morgana to help me find my son."

Meredydd's smile fell. Her gaze darted from Morgana to Garrick, and Morgana cringed inside when she realized that her mother thought she had lain with the lord—the twigs in her hair, her torn and dirty clothing, the late hour.

"Mother, 'tis not as it seems," Morgana tried to explain.

Her mother said woodenly, "I do not understand."

" 'Tis not my intention to wed Morgana, but to use her powers, if they exist, to find Logan. For this, I am prepared to bargain with you," Garrick said, his handsome face reflecting his silent agony over his son. Morgana did not doubt that he suffered, yet she did not trust this warrior from the north, baron or no. The vision had been too clear. This man promised death for Wenlock.

She drew away from the lord who would be her master and had to fight to keep her sharp tongue from betraying her true feelings. "I will help you, my lord, but I will not leave Tower Wenlock."

Garrick's eyes moved from her face to Daffyd's grave countenance. Did her father also believe that she had lifted her skirts to the baron? Shame caused her cheeks to flame crimson, and Morgana's insides twisted. A glance of understanding passed between the two men, and Morgana realized that her fate had been sealed—by this beast who used but mocked her powers and by a father she had disobeyed. Her voice trembled. "I will not—"

Her father threw her a dark look for her impertinence.

Garrick removed his gloves and, as if there had been no interruption from Morgana, said to Daffyd, "Not only will I pay you well, but I will keep Morgana at Castle Abergwynn for a year and, with the help of my sister, Clare, turn her into a proper lady. Several of my knights would willingly wed her, though she is older than most would prefer. One man has already talked to me of her, and I promised to speak to you."

A yelp escaped her. What man? The lust-filled eyes of Garrick's knights came back to haunt her again, and Morgana could suffer his indignities no longer. "Father, you cannot barter with my life," she said, but even as the words passed her lips, she knew she had no choice in the matter. Her father and the baron could choose her destiny. "By the teeth of the dogs I'll not—"

"Nay," her father commanded. "We will have no chanting of spells or curses within this hall!" He tilted his head up to meet the power of Garrick's gaze. "I will accept your offer," he said, ignoring Morgana's swift intake of breath. "My daughter is wayward and untamed, and I have protected her." His angry gaze swung to Morgana. "But this night she has not only lied and disobeyed me but has also cast off her home, leaving it open to attack." He motioned to his vassal, and the knight tossed a rope onto the floor to tangle in the rushes.

Morgana felt as if her heart had dropped through the smooth stones of the floor. Tears of regret threatened her eyes, though she would not shed even one small drop—not in front of this beast who would take her from her home.

"Did you, Morgana, escape this castle by this rope and leave it dangling unattended?" Daffyd asked, his face florid, his lips white.

She nodded bravely. "Aye."

"Did you know that an enemy could scale the castle walls and take us unawares?"

"I did not think—"

" 'Tis obvious you did not think!" Daffyd roared, his voice rumbling to the timbers overhead. "Did you disobey me?"

"Aye, Father, but 'twas to protect the castle—"

"Enough, daughter!" he said, deeply wounded, his face twisted by rage and disappointment. "You leave me no choice. This will be your punishment. You shall ride with Baron Maginnis whenever he decides to leave, and you will not be welcome back at this tower. You will marry a man the baron chooses for you, and you will not argue! Nor will you ever set foot in Tower Wenlock again!"

Meredydd's face drained of color, and her fingers tightened in the sleeve of her husband's tunic. "Do not do this, Daffyd," she pleaded, her voice a rough whisper. "You are angry now, and you should be, but 'twill fade. Do not cast aside our firstborn. Do not!"

Daffyd shook his head. "Hear you me, Morgana?"

Morgana nodded stonily, unbelieving. Surely her father would forgive her. Yea, she had disobeyed, but this banishment with the lord of Abergwynn from the north? Nay, this could not be happening. In the morning, when Daffyd's anger had passed, he would retract his hastily spoken words. "Banish me if you will, Father," she said bravely, her throat thick, her chin thrust forward, tears beginning to form. "But please be merciful and do not send me to Castle Abergwynn."

Daffyd's mouth opened and closed. " 'Tis the best place for you."

"Nay."

"I will ensure her safety," Garrick said.

"Nay, nay, nay! He is from the north, Father. He will destroy us all!"

Daffyd drew back as if to slap her, but clamped his fist closed and banged it against his open palm instead. "Lord Maginnis is our baron. You will do as he says. If you do not, Morgana, you will be dead to me. Glyn and Cadell will be my only children!"

Morgana gasped as her father motioned to the very sentry who had retrieved her cursed rope. "Take her to her room and see that she escapes not."

"Nay! Father, I beg you—"

"Do not beg, Morgana. 'Tis weak," Daffyd ordered.

Morgana crumbled inside. Her own father, the man she

respected and loved ... Though her soul ached and her pride and love were battered, she tossed back her head and walked stiffly up the stairs.

"Now, Lord Maginnis," she heard her father's voice following her like a ghost up the stairs, "let us rest. Tomorrow we shall talk of payment."

She turned cold as stone inside. Would her father sell her so easily?

Aye, Morgana, have you not endangered this keep you love so dearly?

She nearly stumbled as the sentry flung open her bedroom door. She walked inside, and the door banged shut behind her, echoing like a clap of thunder through the old stone halls. *I am doomed,* she thought desperately, walking to the window and staring out at the familiar castle walls and the gardens she had known all her life. The sun was just beginning to crest the hills to the east. Pale lavender light flooded the valleys, and the morning breeze brought with it the smells of spring—new-sown oats and barley, fresh-turned earth and wildflowers. Wolf, whining, padded over to her, and she stroked his broad head.

Aye, she had been foolish, she thought wretchedly. She had to pay.

But this banishment from that which she loved? How could her adoring father be so harsh?

"I will return," she vowed, sending a prayer to the skies to ask for forgiveness as tears studded her lashes and drizzled from the corners of her eyes. "I shall find Garrick's son, pretend to become a lady, and protect the tower as well."

For if the danger and death were to come from the north, what better way to thwart the fates? Before the death swept down upon Tower Wenlock, Morgana would halt it in the northlands.

Closing her eyes, she felt a breath of wind against her face. *Tell me,* she pleaded silently, her fingers curling in wolf's thick fur. *Tell me how Garrick of Abergwynn will harm us.*

She waited, squeezing her eyes shut, listening for the voice.

Please tell me more of the death and the danger.

She strained to hear as the breeze caught in her hair and rustled through the rushes.

But though she listened a long, long while, the wind said nothing.

Five

God will punish you!"

The door to her room swung open, and Glyn, wearing Meredydd's favorite blue tunic and white mantle, swept into the room.

"He already has."

"Aye, and now mayhap you'll be more devout. You didn't even come to mass this morning," Glyn said, her eyes filled with smug satisfaction.

Morgana cared not what Glyn thought. She'd spent the few hours before dawn in abject misery. As the servants awakened and the familiar noises that were a part of every morning seeped into her room, she'd stood at the window. A cock crowed, and she heard her servant girl, Gwladys, throwing seed to the chickens, clucking at the roosters and hens. As the sun climbed over the hills, Morgana had seen the chaplain scurrying across the bailey. Stableboys had swept the stables, and the smith had begun pounding out horseshoes, his hammer clanging loudly. The laundress had soaked sheets and clothes in a wooden trough near the candlemaker's hut, and old Berthilde had waddled into the shop. Morgana had spent the hours filled with remorse.

Then the soldiers had come bearing the crest of Maginnis. With rustling chain mail, the creak of wagon wheels, the shouts of men, and the continual thud of horses' hooves, Garrick Maginnis's army had arrived and made camp outside the walls of Tower Wenlock. Her home. Her throat clogged when she remembered her father's anger, his hasty words of banishment.

Glancing up at Glyn, she asked hopefully, "Has Father changed his mind?"

"Nay. You are still to be banished." Sighing, Glyn crossed her small bosom and eyed her sister. "God be with you," she said softly. "You will need all of his blessings."

Morgana raised a skeptical eyebrow. Whenever Glyn was in one of her pious moods, there was usually mischief about. "Did God tell you this—that I would need his blessing?"

"Oh, Morgana, I pray for your wretched soul," Glyn said, her face serene, her blond hair and blue eyes adding to her angelic appearance.

"Have your prayers been answered, sister?"

"Indeed they have." Glyn clasped her hands over her bosom, and a mysterious smile toyed with her pink lips. She tossed her hair over her shoulders, inviting Morgana's questions, but Morgana, sick of her sister's convenient piety, ignored her.

"Do you not think the baron is handsome?" Glyn asked, flitting to the cupboard where her tunics and hose were stored. She found a belt of silver silk and wound it around her small waist.

"Handsome? The fierce one?" Morgana shook her head. "He is cruel, not handsome. He brings death to us all. Garrick of Abergwynn is evil."

"Evil?" Glyn repeated, her pretty brow puckering. "Oh, I think not. He was with the chaplain and Father all morning long, and during breakfast he laughed, though not that often, and he oft sent looks of longing at me." She smoothed her hair, tucking a straying lock beneath her wimple, obviously pleased with herself, and though Morgana felt a needle of irritation pierce her skin, she ignored the little pang. "I don't think 'twill be too long before he asks for my hand." Glyn gave a final tug on the belt.

Morgana nearly choked. "Marriage? You would consider marriage to a man who wants nothing but to destroy Tower Wenlock?"

"He has no such intention!"

"You know not of his intentions," Morgana said quickly.

"I know that he is the most handsome, most powerful, and most wealthy baron in all of North Wales."

"So?"

"I know also that he has no wife; so powerful a man needs a wife and children."

"What makes you think he will have you?"

Glyn smoothed the folds of her tunic. "You did not see the looks he cast me as we shared a trencher of venison and gravy! He was captivated by me. Oh, Morgana, it was so romantic! 'Tis God's will that we be wed. I know it."

Morgana could not have been more surprised if Glyn had walked naked into their chamber and begun speaking in a foreign tongue. To be seated next to a baron of Maginnis's rank was unheard of. "But how—"

"As I said, it seems our father is talking very seriously to Lord Garrick." Glyn's eyes slitted, and she seemed very proud of herself, much like the kitchen cat after stealing cream from the cook's pantry. "It would not surprise me if I were betrothed to the baron by evenfall."

Morgana's mouth gaped open, and upon hearing Glyn's tinkling laughter, she snapped her jaw shut. What did she care if Glyn married Maginnis? If the silly goose chose to marry the first handsome lord to walk into Tower Wenlock, then so be it. Glyn deserved the fate she so obviously wanted. As for Morgana, she intended not to wed anyone, particularly a beast from Abergwynn. "Did God tell you that you were the chosen bride of Maginnis?"

Glyn's eyes widened, and she hurriedly crossed herself. "I do not pretend to talk to our Holy Father. Yet God lets His will be known in quiet ways."

"Such as lustful looks over greasy trenchers of meat?"

Glyn lifted her head, and her cheeks flamed scarlet. "You were not there, sister. You did not see the desire in the great lord's eyes. If you had not been so foolish as to disobey Father, and if you had let the baron come here this morning as he had planned, then mayhap you would have been seated beside him and caught his eye." Her gaze slid down Morgana's dirty tunic, and she shook her head slowly from side to side, as if pitying some poor almswoman she'd found in the street. "Though I doubt the lord would want a wretched sinner such as you."

"Careful, Glyn," Morgana warned. "I have not yet lost my powers." She glanced at the window. "Come wind, touch my soul and wrap your cold hands around Sister Glyn's—"

Glyn screeched and ran to the door. "Nay, heathen! Stop it. I'll hear no more of your spells!" she cried, pounding on the oaken planks as the sentry swung the door open. Gathering her skirts, she cast one last frightened look over her shoulder. "You will be punished," she said, lifting her chin stiffly.

"Thank the Lord that you are here to impart God's word and save me!" Morgana tossed back smartly.

"Morgana!" Meredydd, overhearing the last of her daughters' exchange, scowled as she swept into the room.

Glyn lingered in the doorway, but Meredydd motioned for the sentry to close the door. "Now, daughter," she said, dropping on the edge of the bed and eyeing her firstborn's dirty face, tangled hair, and flashing eyes, "I'll not have any disrespect to God or the church. You'll see the chaplain when we're through here, and you'll ask for a penance."

Morgana nearly choked, but she nodded. Oh, what a horrid, horrid day! Things were going from bad to worse.

Meredydd grabbed her eldest by the shoulders and slowly surveyed Morgana. Sighing, she said, "We must work fast. Your father's ordered a feast in the baron's honor for this night, and I have much to do. But first you must ready yourself."

"I'm allowed to partake?" Morgana asked, unbelieving.

Meredydd cast her daughter a knowing look. "If you behave yourself." She pointed a long finger at Morgana's nose. "You are not to chant or call the wind or any such nonsense."

"But is that not what the great baron wants? Is that not why he's here? Because he thinks I'm a sorceress?"

"You shall not display yourself at all, Morgant. Now, I've no time for argument. I've called for Nellwyn to bring up bathwater. We shall wash you, comb your hair, and dress you in your finest tunic." She paused, biting her lower lip as she studied her daughter. "Tell me, last night . . . did he . . . ?"

Horrified by her mother's look Morgana swallowed over a lump of pride in her throat. "No, Mother. I am still a virgin, if that's what you're asking! I would slit my own throat rather than lie with such a man."

Her mother flushed scarlet. "Glyn thinks he's handsome."

Morgana snorted. "Glyn is a fool! She can have him,"

Morgana replied but thought she saw the ghost of a smile on her mother's full lips. What, she wondered, did Meredydd find remotely humorous about this wretched situation?

"So you want a husband for your daughter?" Garrick asked, his eyes narrowing on the man who had sired the witch. Garrick had dealt often with fathers anxious to marry off their daughters who for one reason or another were not able to find suitors. Usually the girl was homely or without dower or disfigured. Not so Morgant of Wenlock. She was a good-looking one, the sorceress. Thick black hair, eyes the color of a dark forest, and lips full and supple, though they always seemed to be drawn into a stubborn pout. Were it not for her sorcery and her sharp tongue, Morgana would have been a woman more desirable than any he'd met in a long, long while.

Daffyd was in a hurry to marry off his eldest, as she, at seventeen, was old for a maiden. No doubt more than one knight had shied away from her because of the cutting edge of her dagger and her razorlike words. Yea, and what man who was not daft himself would want a wife who talked to the spirits? Strahan wanted her, but Strahan, loyal though he was, had always been something of a puzzlement.

Daffyd stroked his chin thoughtfully. "Aye, Morgant needs a husband. Make no mistake, the man must be stronger than most."

"Must he be rich?" Garrick asked, accepting a cup of wine from a fresh-scrubbed maid who averted her eyes and slipped quickly behind a curtain. "Are you seeking a dowry for Morgant?"

Daffyd, a shrewd man, was not a liar. "Yea. She is beautiful and, though stubborn, could become a willing wife who would bear strong sons."

"She's rumored to be a witch. In truth, that's why I'm here."

"Her powers are not of the black arts," Daffyd said quickly, but Garrick noticed the sweat collecting on the upper lip of his host. The sorceress was more trouble than Daffyd would dare admit. Mayhap this castle was in need of gold. He eyed the interior walls, whitewashed and clean, and noticed the painted wool wall hangings as well as the fresh, fragrant rushes on the floor. The linen had been clean, the gardens near the kitchen without weeds. Daffyd of Wenlock was lord of a well-run castle, showing no need of gold, though, from what Garrick had noticed, his army was small.

Daffyd mopped his brow. "God's truth, m'lord, Morgant is as headstrong as Friar Tobias's donkey." He took a swallow of wine. "Though she's much swifter than the friar's mount, she's wayward and needs a strong man who will bend her will to his."

"Is that possible?" Garrick asked, leaning back in his chair and drinking from the silver-rimmed cup he'd been offered. He and Daffyd were alone in the great hall, though Garrick heard the soft sound of servants' footsteps beyond the curtained inner door. Voices drifted through the maze of hallways from the kitchens and tower rooms. He thought of Morgana locked away in her chamber. The witch would no doubt be furious, her tongue as sharp as the knife he'd taken from her.

Daffyd rested the heel of a boot on a bench used during meals. "Morgant is my firstborn, and I love her—aye, too much mayhap. Though she was not a son, even as a small child, she enjoyed doing man things. Meredydd and I should have bent her will at a younger age, but"——he motioned quickly with his hands, dismissing the past——"Morgant was never interested in embroidery or any duties fit for the lady of the house. Not that she couldn't perform them, mind you, had she the need. Nay, it was that her interests were with the archers and the smith and the candlemaker——"

"With witchcraft."

Daffyd scowled. "She is not a witch, Lord Garrick. I say to you on the souls of all my children, she is no witch."

"But I'm in need of a witch right now. Or a woman with the power to find my son. Think you she is able?"

Daffyd was a cunning man. He wasn't about to destroy the good fortune that God had dropped into his lap. For having the baron here, with need of Morgant's powers, was good fortune indeed. Yea, God had smiled on Tower Wenlock this day. Thoughtfully, he scratched his chin. "She has found others," he admitted slowly.

Garrick leaned forward, his wine forgotten. "Has she ever failed?"

Unable to lie, Daffyd nodded. "Only once. Her vision was unclear, and she was unable to find the miller's youngest son, a lad of twelve who, when the miller awoke one morn, was not to be found. Morgant found not a trace of the boy. She insisted she failed because the lad wished not to be discovered. His father whipped him, as the son was lazy, she said, and the boy had run off."

"Say you that she can find only those who want to be discovered?"

Daffyd shrugged. "I know that she has failed but once. If you want to be reunited with your boy, my lord, then Morgant can be of help to you."

"And you are willing to let her go?"

"To you? Of course," Daffyd asked, bowing his head slightly. "All that I have is yours, m'lord."

Garrick guessed that the man was being overly humble, but he didn't care. The Welsh barons were known for their cunning and their treachery. Though Daffyd of Wenlock had never risen against the king and had proved himself a faithful vassal, he might still have ties to the rebellion. True, the uprising had been thwarted, but the cry for independence still echoed through the forests and hills of Wales. The need for freedom from English rule was in the heart of more than one Welsh vassal. Garrick would not be so blind as to trust Daffyd completely. "What about the dower? What price would you have?"

"The gold is insignificant, though it is costly to run a castle and I would lose a fine leader if Morgant leaves." As if reading the skepticism in Garrick's eyes, Daffyd hastened on. "Though she is but a woman, the servants, and aye, even some of the men, trust her wisdom and follow her." He sighed. "Some would probably follow her into battle. They are as loyal as that wolf dog that pads behind her."

"So gold is what you're after."

"Gold would help," Daffyd admitted as he turned his cup between his palms. "But I ask only that Morgant be taught to be a lady, that she be married to a worthy man, and that my other two children, Glyn and Cadell, receive some of the same training—Cadell as a squire and knight, Glyn as a lady."

"At Castle Abergwynn?"

"As you wish."

Garrick turned the request over in his mind. The boy, Cadell, was welcome. Only a few years younger than Ware, Garrick's own brother, Cadell could learn well at Castle

Abergwynn. Glyn could also fit easily into the daily routine of the keep. Surely Lady Clare could mold the younger daughter into a fine lady; Glyn had already shown herself a willing pupil. She'd been overly friendly and soft-spoken at supper, her manners already in evidence. Yea, she would soon make some knight a devout and well-mannered wife. But the witch, she was another matter. Sharp of tongue, quick of wit, and fleet of foot, she was dangerous and spirited, a woman who would not bend easily to any man's way.

Perhaps Strahan had been too hasty in asking for Morgant's hand.

Several others of his men were in need of wives, and more than one would gladly take a woman as beautiful as Morgana. But Sir Randolph had a cruel streak that, though useful in battle, would not bode well for his woman, and Sir Fulton was portly and a clown, a knight who enjoyed ale and bawdy stories and big-bosomed wenches.

Nay, neither would do for Morgant. Strahan had already spoken for her. Garrick had given his word. Strahan was strong enough to handle Morgana, and yea, he had seen a glint of desire in Strahan's eyes when he spoke of her. "If Morgana will help me find my son," Garrick said slowly, his fingers running over the silver rim of the cup he was holding, "then I promise you this: she will marry a knight of my choosing, a good man who will be given his own land and castle. He is my own cousin, Strahan Hazelwood, a loyal follower of our king. He has already inquired of her."

Daffyd grunted. He'd met Strahan. His old eyes gleamed, and he chanced pushing his good fortune a bit. "What of Glyn?"

"She may come to Castle Abergwynn to be taught by

Lady Clare, but I can promise no more. Not until Logan is returned safely."

"What if he is not?" Daffyd asked.

Garrick's mouth turned hard. His hands quit moving along the edge of his cup. "Pray that doesn't happen," he said, his face suddenly dark and forbidding. "I did not come here on a fool's mission. Your daughter must not fail."

"She will not," Daffyd assured his guest, though he rubbed his palms on his breeches as if anxious.

Garrick tossed back his wine and left the empty cup on the table. "There is more you wish?" he asked, beginning to dislike Daffyd of Wenlock.

"Aye, m'lord. As you may have noticed, my soldiers are few, lost to disease last year and in defending our king during the uprising of neighboring lords, especially Osric McBrayne. We are in need of good men to secure this keep and to protect the village. If you could but leave a few of your soldiers—"

"Twenty of my best men shall remain here. But I have learned there may be war with the Scots. If I'm called upon to ride with Edward, I will need my knights."

"And have them you shall, as well as soldiers from Wenlock. Thank you, m'lord," Daffyd said with obvious relief. He vowed his fealty once again, then, standing, offered Garrick a smile. "Now, come, rest a while. Soon we will feast and celebrate our renewed alliance."

Garrick didn't move. His eyes, hard as steel, held the other man's, and his lips barely moved as he spoke. "Know you this, Daffyd of Wenlock. I have traveled long to come here in search of a witch. I will do everything you ask, but now your daughter must not fail me."

Six

Ahh, m'lady, 'ow lovely ye look!" Nellwyn, a gap-toothed girl with freckles and hair the color of flame nodded approvingly at Morgana. She clasped her hands before her chest and sighed.

"Lovely?" Morgana snorted. "I do not feel lovely," she grumbled, refusing to eye herself in the mirror that Meredydd insisted on holding near her face. Her sendal tunic, a lavender color that reminded Morgana of twilight, was trimmed with rabbit fur. Her white mantle was embroidered in hues of pink and rose, and a silver belt was slung around her waist.

For once her dark curls were restrained and trained beneath a wimple.

"No one will recognize you," her mother predicted.

Mayhap that wasn't so bad. Her father might have forgotten his bad mood, and should he see his elder daughter behaving in a ladylike fashion, perhaps he would forget the angry words he'd spoken in such haste. If Morgana could but get Daffyd alone, apologize for her foolishness of the night before, and swear to be obedient in the future, there was a chance her father would forgive her and take away the wretched punishment he'd so quickly meted out.

Glyn slipped through the door and, upon spying Morgana, stopped still and audibly gasped. Morgana felt a surge of vindication when she thought of her reaction to Glyn's announcement that she was to marry Baron Maginnis.

"Morgana?" Glyn said, her throat bobbing a little as she closed her mouth and stared in disbelief at her older sister.

"Aye?" For effect, Morgana lifted her chin just a little more proudly, mimicking a haughty pose she'd often seen when Glyn was in the presence of handsome men. Then quick as a cat springing, she ripped off the wimple. "I'll not wear that binding—"

"As you wish," her mother said, rolling her eyes to the ceiling.

"I—I—" Glyn was still staring at Morgana. She cleared her throat, and Meredydd could not keep the corners of her mouth from twitching upward in an amused smile. "I must get dressed. Already it's late, and I must not keep the baron waiting."

"Of course not," Morgana agreed as her sister fussed about in the cupboard until she finally decided on her blue silk tunic and ermine-edged mantle.

"Come, Nellwyn, help me with my hair," Glyn ordered snappishly, and the maidservant was soon brushing Glyn's hair into a soft golden braid.

Morgana was tired of being held virtual prisoner in her own bedchamber, though she wasn't in the mood for festivities. Not so Glyn, who, spying her reflection, began humming and, when Meredydd wasn't looking, added rouge to her cheeks. " 'Twill be a grand celebration," Glyn predicted. "Father sent word to several neighboring lords, and though they are lesser, they will share in the merriment."

"Is the baron in the mood for festivities?" Morgana asked, thinking of the fierce one and the sorry fact that he still held her dagger in his possession.

"He will be," Glyn said merrily. "There will be musicians and minstrels, and I shall dance with him." She continued talking rapidly, planning the evening ahead, and Morgana, thinking of her future, became more morose. She sat near the window as the sun set and saw the figure of a lone man walking the inner bailey walls. Garrick of Abergwynn, his visage as dark as the approaching night, stalked the courtyard, and his mood did not invite company. Morgana could not imagine him dancing with Glyn or laughing at the antics of jesters or singing or partaking of bawdy stories.

Would he, like so many lords before him, with too much wine in his belly, lie with a kitchen wench? Perhaps Gwladys. She was pretty enough, with her sable hair and full lips, and she had been known to lift her skirts to visiting knights. Though Morgana's mother did not approve of the wenches' behavior when soldiers were about, there was naught she could do.

Besides, the young maids were all too eager, which kept the randy soldiers who visited in fine spirits. The crop of bastards who were born each year were always treated well at Tower Wenlock. When they were old enough, they were given jobs within the castle walls so that they could earn their keep.

Aye, Gwladys or Nellwyn or any of the other women servants would likely lie with a baron of Garrick Maginnis's wealth and power. 'Twould be an honor to share the bed of one who was master of Daffyd of Wenlock.

It bothered Morgana a little to think of some woman lifting her skirts to him, but she closed her mind to those wayward thoughts. What cared she? He could lie with a hundred wenches and 'twould not matter. She saw his shadow pass on the stable walls. He turned suddenly to face her, his head tilted upward, his gaze locking with hers for an instant. Her heart kicked a bit, but she didn't flinch, intent on proving she was not afraid of him or his power. Upon studying his features she halfheartedly agreed with Glyn: the man was handsome in a rugged manner. Even in the purple twilight, she saw the determination in his gaze, knew that he was here only because of his son.

Aye, if he lay with a wench this night, it would be to forget the great melancholy that overcame him when he thought of his boy. She felt as if he had told her this, though she could hardly know his thoughts. But for one instant she felt as if she'd peered into the darkness of his soul.

Unnerved when he didn't swing his gaze away, Morgana, head aloft, moved away from the window and ignored the fact that her heart drummed within her chest and her hands trembled slightly at the thought that soon she would be riding with Baron Maginnis on a long journey to Abergwynn.

"Please, God, no," she whispered silently, but knew in her heart that her father would never turn against his word once he had given it. She was doomed.

Garrick had no appetite, nor did he have any interest in the maids who cast him fond looks or in the music that swelled to the trusses of the great hall. Nay, he wanted only to leave Wenlock with the witch and start the hunt for his son. He took a long swallow of wine and called himself a fool. Morgant had given him no reason to believe that she could help him.

Yea, he'd seen her mumbling words to a stormy sky, scratching a circle in the sand, and stalking around burning candles in the darkness by the sea. God's truth, he'd been captivated by her and her silly antics, watching as the wind tore at her hair and pressed her tunic to her supple figure. With the roar of the sea as an accompaniment, her chants had been somewhat bewitching.

Worse yet, the ride to the camp and later to Wenlock, when he'd had to physically restrain her, had been difficult. Her small body, though tense, had molded itself to his and the roundness of her buttocks had pressed firmly against his crotch, causing an unlikely swelling of his manhood.

He'd hidden his reaction to her, and Morgana, frightened as she was, had not noticed. God's teeth, what was wrong with him? He finished his wine with one swallow and wiped his mouth with the back of his hand. A page, no more than eight, drew close and offered more spirits. Garrick grunted and motioned toward his cup. Obviously nervous, the lad was careful to spill nary a drop, though he did look up when a murmur swept the room and all eyes turned toward the staircase where Morgant of Wenlock slowly descended.

Her appearance gave pause even to Garrick, for this was not the slender girl with the wild hair and swift blade he'd found last night; nay, this female descending the steps was a woman, full grown and beautiful. Her skin was clear, her green eyes fringed by graceful lashes, her small chin thrust forward in defiance. Her black hair curled around her face, restrained only by a braid. Her gown flowed around her, but hugged her bosom, showing off the sculpted shape of her breasts.

Again Garrick felt a stirring in his loins, and he crossed his legs. Fool! He heard a few of his men comment under their breath at the witch's beauty, and more than one lustful glance was cast in her direction.

She would be more trouble than she was worth, Garrick realized, though even he was dumbstruck at her beauty. A journey with an army of randy soldiers was never easy, but with so comely a woman along, the going would be much worse. Men would quarrel, perhaps come to blows, and the maiden herself, too spirited for her own good, would not be easy to handle.

Head aloft, she walked down the stairs while every eye in the great hall was trained on her.

Daffyd, seated next to Garrick, frowned at his daughter's approach. "Were she not so headstrong she would make some man a fine wife. She is beautiful, aye, and as smart as any woman should be. Quick with a dagger and bow, she is an excellent huntress and warrior."

"What needs she of a husband?" Garrick asked, and Daffyd snorted, watching as his firstborn left the great hall and walked toward the chapel where she was to meet with the chaplain and atone for yet another blasphemy against God. Would she were as pious as Glyn, Daffyd thought, as his second daughter strolled slowly down the staircase and entered the great hall. Though Glyn in her own way was headstrong, she, like most women, could be bent. But Morgant—God's blood, the girl was a trial.

Glyn curtsied to Lord Maginnis and took a seat on the bench next to him. She blushed prettily as the baron spoke to her, and Daffyd wondered if Maginnis would ask for her hand. He was in need of a wife to run his castle and bear him an heir. True, there was Maginnis's son, Logan, who, if still alive, would be the rightful heir to Castle Abergwynn and all its fiefdoms, but the boy had been missing for a fortnight, and even with Morgant's help, the chance of finding Logan alive was naught in Daffyd's mind. So why should the baron not marry a fair maid like Glyn? Though not as striking as Morgant, Glyn was certainly beautiful, and at least she knew how to behave! Yea, she would make the baron a dutiful wife.

For the first time since discovering that Morgana had defied him by stealing away from the castle walls, Daffyd of Wenlock smiled.

"Forgive me, Lord, for I have sinned." Morgana knelt at the altar in the chapel, whispering prayers of atonement. The chaplain, a well-fed man with a ring of thick red hair surrounding a bald pate, was a stern believer in God. He clucked his tongue at her confession.

"The Lord God will serve out his own punishment for you, Morgant," he said, then rattled off her penance, leaving Morgana alone in the chapel, the tiny flames of candles flickering against the stone walls, to make her peace with God. Her head bowed, she closed her eyes, asking God to intercede so that she might not have to ride with the baron.

"Any task you give me will be not too great," she murmured, "but please deliver me from the devil from the north."

A quiet cough caused a cold finger of fear to steal up her spine. She licked her lips and caught a glimpse of black hair and a hawkish nose.

"Devil?" he asked, when her prayer-cadence was silent. Maginnis slouched, with one shoulder propped against the door frame.

"Speak ye not of the dark prince in the house of the Lord."

" 'Twas you who spoke of Satan."

"I'll not hear this blasphemy!" she hissed.

"Ah, so now you speak like your sister, telling those around you of God's will."

Morgana rose to her full height, yet still she had to tilt her head back to meet his gaze. Candlelight was reflected in his gray eyes, but Morgana stood firm. "I know not how you act in the chapel at Abergwynn, but here we respect all that is God's."

"By burning candles and chanting to spirits while wading in the sea?" he mocked, the amusement dying in his eyes.

Morgana brushed past him, but he snagged her elbow, spinning her around. Her breath caught in her throat as she slammed against him. He pressed his face close to hers to study her as if she were some odd creature he'd never seen before. The smell of wine was on his breath, and his features were harsh. Panic swept through Morgana. "You're a puzzlement," he said lazily, "and, I suspect, quite treacherous. Were it not for Logan, I would have naught to do with you."

"Then leave me be."

"Unfortunately, it is done. Your father and I have come to an agreement, Morgana. All you must do is live up to your part of the bargain and you will be a wealthy woman, mistress of your own castle, wife to one of my best—"

"No!" Morgana tried to wrench away from him. Oh, if she only had a dagger, she would risk God's wrath and spill this knight's blood in the chapel!

"You have no choice, m'lady."

"You're a beast!"

"So some say."

"And a heathen!"

His lips thinned dangerously, and the fingers around her upper arm were punishing.

The man was pure poison! "How is it, Sir Garrick, that you have been knighted and have pledged your faith in God, yet you mock him? Did you not kneel before the altar and swear to defend God's honor with your very life?"

Garrick's eyes glowed with an angry fire. "God has seen fit to take my wife's life in giving me a son, only to wrest that son from me as well."

"It is his will."

He yanked on her arm and drew her to him, his lips curling in disgust. "Do not speak to me of God's will. It is His will that I find my son and that you help me, witch," he said, and she knew she'd pushed him too far, ignited a temper that was deadly. "So I care not if you are pious or pagan." His breath, sweet with wine, filled the air. "Naught matters save Logan."

"What if I can't help you?"

"Oh, you will, witch, for your father and I have struck a deal. You are to ride with me on the morrow and help me find my son. For this I have promised that you be wed and wed well."

Cold fear slid like ice through Morgana's blood. She knew she should hold her traitorous tongue, but she could not. "Nay, I'll not—"

"Fear not, your future husband is my most honored knight and friend. He will serve you well, and you could do no better than my cousin."

A relative of this black devil's? Never! She tried again to wrench away, and Garrick, as if sensing that he was about to lose control, released her arm. "Have you not already met Sir Strahan?"

The name brought foggy but unwelcome memories into Morgana's mind. "I think not. I know no one by—"

"Strahan of the House of Hazelwood," Garrick said impatiently. "He was here not two summers past."

Morgana's fears crystallized, and her future, already bleak, grew all the darker at the memory of the man to whom her father had so casually betrothed her. "Nay," she whispered, shaking her head and trying to draw away. "I will not."

His features knotted in confusion. "God's teeth, Morgant. Most women would count themselves lucky to be his chosen, and he seems fond of you—" He stopped short, as if he had no reason to explain his decision. "Strahan's better than most who would offer themselves to a woman who deals in magic."

"Then I'll not marry."

"You would defy me?" Again his anger flared.

"Aye, if you force me to marry against my will."

"Who says your will matters?"

"I'll not—"

"You will marry Strahan," Garrick growled, his face drawn taut. "As soon as you find my son." As if he foresaw the protest rising in her throat, he clasped both hands around her arms and pressed his face next to hers. "And you will find my son, Morgant."

"If it's God's will—"

"It's *my* will, witch, and you will make it happen!" he whispered harshly, and again his eyes, in the shadowy chapel, were dark with despair and torment. For a fleeting second Morgana's heart went out to a man who was so obviously wretched with grief. "Logan is not dead," Garrick stated, forcing himself to believe that his boy was still alive, "and you will lead me to him or your vision will indeed come true. All that you love, all this"—he motioned broadly, and she realized that in his darkest desperation, he was dooming the entire castle—"will cease to belong to your family."

"You cannot . . ." But her voice trailed off, for this man could do as he pleased. Her throat closed in upon itself. "So it's true. You are the danger from the north."

Garrick shook his head and drew his lips back against his teeth. "Aye," he said in a deathly quiet voice that was barely audible in the cavernous chapel. "If Logan is not found alive, I swear to you on the blood of my child, I will be the death of all that is Tower Wenlock."

Seven

"Would you like more wine?" Glyn asked with a giggle as she smiled up at Lord Garrick.

Morgana's stomach revolted. She barely tasted the eel pie and the pheasant and was all too aware of the baron seated so close to her at the table. Rather than risk her father's ire for not eating, she carefully slid most of her meal to Wolf, who lay beneath her bench, eyeing each morsel hungrily.

Beneath the sweep of dark lashes, she noticed her father talking and joking with Baron Maginnis, as if his daughter's—aye, his very castle's—fate mattered not to him.

Marriage to Strahan of Hazelwood! Was her father so angry with her that he would marry her off to such a monster? She almost lost the contents of her stomach yet again. Not that Sir Strahan was not handsome—indeed, Glyn had said much about his dark good looks—but he was related to Maginnis, and Morgana believed Strahan's soul to be as black as night.

Maginnis's threat hung over her.

"Morgana, eat," her father ordered, pointing with his knife at the platter of white curd and meat cooked in almonds. " 'Tis your favorite."

"Aye, Father," she said, not wishing to anger Daffyd any further. But the meat balled in her throat and she could barely swallow.

Maginnis cast her a dark look when she set down her own

knife and could eat no more. "The journey to Abergwynn is long, and you will need your strength."

She did not reply, nor did she partake of the celebration. Glyn laughed at the antics of the jesters and jugglers, and as the minstrels made their merry music she danced with more than one handsome knight. But Morgana returned to her chamber where Nellwyn, who claimed to have once been a servant to the king in London, was bustling about, packing tunics, mantles, wimples, and hose. "Aye, 'ow lucky you are, m'lady," Nellwyn prattled. "Such an adventure you'll be 'aving, and with the baron." She sighed and looked dreamily out the window. " 'E's a handsome one, 'e is. I'll wager 'e knows 'ow to pleasure a woman, that one."

"Nellwyn!" Morgana cried. "I care not what he does or whom he does it with."

"Ah, so 'tis true that you're betrothed, and to the baron's cousin, no less."

"So it seems," Morgana bit out, though the very idea settled like lead in her stomach. She would no more marry Strahan of Hazelwood than she would wed the fierce one himself. Nay, when she married, her bridegroom would be a man of her own choosing, and Sir Strahan, from what she had seen of him, would not a good husband and father make.

She had spied him when she was barely fourteen. A band of Maginnis's soldiers had rested at Tower Wenlock for the night. Strahan, the leader, had shown interest in her even then. He'd smiled at her during dinner, joked with her openly, and ignored Glyn's attempts to turn his attention away from Morgana.

Glyn, in an attempt to undermine his interest in her older sister, had mentioned that Morgana was a sorceress and that she spent hours talking to the wind. Sir Strahan at first had been amused. "Bewitch me, then, sorceress," he'd said, catching her in the garden picking herbs that afternoon. The roses had been in bloom, adding fragrance to the air, and bees from the hives near the kitchen had buzzed within the bailey walls.

"I'm not a sorceress," Morgana told him.

" 'Tis said you talk to the wind and that the wind answers."

Curse Glyn for her wagging tongue! Morgana ignored the comment and went about digging herbs with her knife, the blade gleaming in the hot sun. But Strahan lingered and seated himself on a garden bench beneath a mulberry tree. With one leg drawn up, he pretended to polish his sword with a cloth, though Morgana felt his gaze heavy upon her as he watched her work.

"Some of your father's knights claim you may be a witch."

"Do I look like a witch, Sir Strahan?" she asked, stopping her digging to stare him full in the face. A breeze came up, tugging her hair away from the wimple and blowing some black strands in front of her eyes. She saw it then, the desire that darkened Strahan's gaze and curled the corners of his mouth.

Wolf, lying in the shade of the mulberry, growled, showing black lips, but Strahan took no notice of the dog. He sheathed his sword, very slowly, his eyes never leaving Morgana's as the blade slid silently into its scabbard. "Nay, you are a beautiful maid, perhaps the most beautiful in all of Wales."

Morgana was not flattered. "Then mayhap you should believe your eyes and not the gossip of my father's men." She plunged her dagger into the dry earth, intent on her task, but Strahan was not to be neglected.

Standing, he dusted off his hands. "Glyn tells me you

hunt and shoot an arrow as straight as do any of your father's soldiers."

She saw no reason to lie about her talents. In truth, she would exaggerate her skill to scare the knight off. "Aye."

"Also, that you are . . . quick with your dagger."

She fingered her knife. "If need be."

Dropping to one knee, he leaned close to her, his breath fanning her ear. "Then tell me, can you see what will be?" he asked eagerly, excitement showing on his hard features. "Can you tell what will happen next year or the next?"

Morgana stopped digging. "Nay."

"But you have found lost ones, warned the townspeople of storms, and even discovered a traitor."

She didn't respond. Sweat inched its way down her back and oiled her palms, making digging more difficult under Strahan's watchful eyes.

"Did you warn of an attack on the village?"

Again she kept her eyes lowered.

"A talent for seeing what will come is of great value, Morgana," he said very deliberately. "Is that why you are not yet betrothed, because the dowry your father wants for you is high?"

She lifted her head then and felt the anger burning in her gaze. "I have not yet married as I have not yet found a man who suits me," she told him, placing the herbs in a cloth bag and slinging it over her shoulder.

A hard smile crossed Strahan's lips. "Your father gives you say in who will be your husband?"

"My father wants me to be happily wed." That was perhaps a mild lie, but it seemed necessary to bend the truth a little. Sir Strahan was a clever man, but something about him drew the muscles of her back into a knot.

"What kind of man would you have?" he asked, keeping his voice low so that Gwladys, who was telling the other servants how to lay out the sheets to dry, would not overhear his words.

Morgana arched a fine dark brow and said, "A man who does not talk too much, a man who would not treat me like a servant, and a man who would not bother me with silly gossip."

His lips thinned into an evil smile that caused fear to settle in her throat. "I think m'lady that what you need is a husband who would tame your wild spirit."

The knot in the small of her back tightened still further.

"A man who would use your powers for the benefit of his castle and king, a man who would enjoy your beauty and teach you how to use your sharp tongue to his advantage." He touched her then, one long finger tracing the slope of her cheek to linger at the corner of her mouth. His gaze, narrowing, moved even farther down to rest at the swell of her breasts. Though she was fully dressed, Morgana felt as naked as a newborn babe. "A man who would show you the art of loving . . . the secrets of passion."

"I need no man, Sir Strahan," she assured him, standing quickly, turning on her heel, and marching stiffly back to the kitchen while the sound of his mocking laughter followed her into the castle.

That very night, unable to sleep, she crept toward the kitchen, but as she rounded a corner, Morgana spied Sir Strahan in the hallway with Springan, a red-haired maid of sixteen who served Meredydd. The girl was pushed hard against the wall, her skirts aloft, and Strahan was pressing his body rigidly against hers. At first Morgana thought he was forcing himself upon her, and she wanted to call the guard, but the maid closed her eyes, her head lolled back, and her arms encircled Strahan's neck. "Please, oh, please," she murmured as they slid as one down the wall to the stone floor. Springan's red curls fanned out around her head, and Strahan buried his face in her neck, one hand reaching beneath her skirt.

Morgana's stomach roiled, and she started to step away, but not before Strahan, lowering himself over the maid, caught a glimpse of her. He smiled his wicked grin. Then, as if he enjoyed knowing that Morgana was watching them, he bent to kiss Springan with renewed passion, and the maid-servant moaned—in pain or in ecstasy, Morgana knew not which.

Her heart beating as fast as doves' wings, Morgana stumbled along the hallway, racing to her bedchamber and wishing she had not spied the act of lovemaking. She knew how babies were conceived as well as how they were delivered—anyone living with the animals in the castle knew how they bred—but she'd never before witnessed the act of lovemaking between a man and a woman, and she had been disgusted by the display.

The next morning Sir Strahan sat at the table with Morgana, sharing a trencher of bread with her, and his eyes gleamed with devilment, though he spoke not a word about his display with Springan. Even when the maid appeared to clear the table and offered to polish his sword, Strahan did not look much at her or give her a smile. Indeed, it was as if she were no different from any other servant, though Springan's eyes betrayed her. As she went about her chores, her gaze followed Sir Strahan, and the looks she cast Morgana were murderous.

Fool, Morgana had thought as Strahan and his men left the following morning.

When Springan's bastard had arrived nine months later, the girl had refused to name the father, but Morgana knew the dark-eyed baby had been sired by Strahan of Hazelwood.

Now Morgana was to marry the cur. The thought was revolting, and she swore to herself that she'd find a way out of this betrothal. Her father had refused to listen to her arguments, and her mother, usually her ally, had stiffly informed her that it was well past time she was wed, that a cousin of the baron's was certainly a good man, and that Garrick of Abergwynn himself had promised that Morgana would become the lady of a fine castle in the north, which he planned to give to Strahan upon their marriage. So it mattered not what Morgana wanted.

As for Springan's two-year-old, Morgana had held her tongue about the babe's father. Springan was a good and loyal servant, and though she'd made a mistake with Strahan, she was not the first young maid to have her head turned by a handsome knight and thereafter bear his child.

But the thought of marrying Strahan was, in Morgana's mind, a curse, as if God himself had decided she must be punished for her lack of devotion. "Leave me now," she commanded Nellwyn, but the maid took no notice.

" 'Twas Sir Daffyd 'imself who told me to pack your things for your journey. I cannot disobey 'im. I'll only be a little while." She folded some more of Morgana's belongings and then, balancing the large bundle, left Morgana to her thoughts.

Morgana knelt beside the bed and hung her head. "Deliver me, Lord. Help me find a way to escape this fate. Do not tie me to a cruel man, and please protect all that is

Tower Wenlock." Her heart pounded with dread as she remembered Garrick's words in the chapel. If she failed in her task, he would seek revenge against her home and family. Why, oh, why, had she taunted him? He was a harsh man, a powerful man, a man one did not defy.

"I will miss you, child," Enit whispered as Morgana entered her grandmother's chamber. Enit looked frailer than ever, her skin thin as parchment as she lay under a fur comforter.

"Aye, and I will miss you." Morgana, her heart heavy, sat on the edge of the bed, taking the older woman's hands in hers. Though bony and thin, Enit's hands were still strong.

"Something is bothering you."

"Aye."

"What is it, Morgana?"

A chill of premonition caused gooseflesh to rise on her skin. "What if I fail, Grandmother? What if I cannot find the child of Maginnis? What if he is already dead?"

"You cannot change what has happened, but mayhap you can steer the course of the fates in a new direction."

"I think not."

Enit patted Morgana's hands with the patience of the elderly. "Follow your heart, child."

"My heart does not belong to Castle Abergwynn or to the baron and especially not to Sir Strahan."

Enit smiled, a small mysterious grin that twisted her thin lips. Her cloudy eyes seemed to sparkle again. "Your mother says you are to be his bride."

"Never!" Morgana said. "I'd rather die."

To her surprise Enit chuckled softly, then began coughing. "Go, child," she said, her body racked with a fit that was squeezing the life from her. "Your destiny lies to the north, with Maginnis."

"Nay, I—"

"I have seen it," Enit said softly as Morgana reached for a cup of water and honey and held it to her grandmother's lips.

"You've seen what?"

Enit waved her favorite grandchild away. "Trust in your visions. Do what you must. If marriage to Strahan of Hazelwood is your destiny, you must accept it."

"Never!" Morgana cried.

"Do not fret." Enit patted Morgana's hand. Her fingers were cool. "Marriage to Hazelwood is the only answer."

Morgana's insides turned to ice.

"God bless you, Morgana, and listen to the wind, for 'twill be your friend."

Morgana crossed her arms churlishly over her chest and fought back her rising dread of the future. "The wind speaks not to me these days."

"It will."

Morgana wasn't convinced. "If I fail in this task . . . ?"

"Fear not. The fates are with you. When I see you next, your path will be clear, and I will help you . . ." Enit's paper-thin eyelids lowered, and Morgana knew she might never see her grandmother alive again. She trembled inside for Enit with her sorcery, quick laughter, and soft touch. Enit had been Morgana's best friend for all her seventeen years. She kissed the old woman's forehead and offered a prayer that her grandmother not be taken just yet.

"Morgana?" Meredydd's voice floated through the darkness. " 'Tis time you were abed," she said, entering the chamber. "You're to leave early in the morning. Come on, off with you now." She shooed Morgana out of Enit's chamber and along the hallway, pausing only to kiss her firstborn lightly on the cheek at the doorway of the chamber belonging to Morgana and Glyn. "No pranks, now," she said, glancing at the sentries who still guarded the chamber door, as Morgana's father insisted.

"Does Father think I will try to escape?" Morgana asked.

Meredydd chuckled. "He is only being careful."

Morgana stepped toward her bedchamber, but her mother's fingers caught the sleeve of her tunic. "Maginnis brought some of the boy's things and has placed them in your room."

"But—"

"He knows that you have found others after touching their clothes or something they valued." Meredydd's face looked pale in the moving light from the sconces still burning in the hallway.

"Mother, I don't know if I can—"

"Hush! You can and you will," Meredydd said, sealing her lips firmly. "All these years you have been a willful, strong-minded child, and I have let you run free. But now 'tis time to become a woman—a lady."

"As well as a sorceress," Morgana said sullenly. "Many's the time you have told me to forsake my powers and—"

Meredydd's fingers found the flesh of Morgana's upper arm. " 'Tis too late. Now use the powers God has granted you and help the baron find his son!" She released her grip and shook her head, her voice softening a little. "Oh, child, how you try my patience." Sighing, she whispered, "Good night, Morgana. Sleep well."

"But find the boy," Morgana couldn't help muttering under her breath.

"Above all else." Grasping her tunic around her as if she felt a chill, Meredydd hurried along the hallway to her own chamber.

It wasn't that she didn't want to find Logan, Morgana thought as she hastened into her room. She started when the heavy door clunked as it closed behind her. If she could conjure the boy up this very instant, she would do just that. But 'twas not as easy as casting a spell and making the child appear.

She kicked her boots against the wall. Glyn, sleeping peacefully, snorted at the sound, but didn't wake up, as if she were indeed resting with the guiltless conscience of a saint. Perhaps she was more God-fearing than Morgana believed.

On the foot of Morgana's bed lay a bundle of clothing and a toy, a chunk of wood whittled into the shape of a boat. Morgana ran her fingers over the tiny ship. So this little piece of yew had belonged to Maginnis's lad. Oh, that she could reach him. Was it even possible? Well, why not try? She walked to the open window and felt the breath of the wind against her face. Closing her eyes, she held the smooth toy to her chest and forced her mind to be free. "Logan, please call to me," she whispered, but she heard no response, nor did she see even a faint image. "Please," she called again, knowing in her heart that her attempt was futile. Again she waited and again heard nothing.

Still clutching the toy, she knelt by her bed and sent up a small prayer before sliding between the linen sheets and closing her eyes. She didn't want to sleep, for sleep would bring the morning, and too many worries spun round in her head. To calm herself, she absently rubbed the tiny ship's bow. Finally she dozed, and the old, familiar sounds of

Tower Wenlock—the mice scurrying through the rushes, the wind whispering through the inner bailey, the soft tread of sentries on the tower walls—soothed her into sleep.

How long she dozed, she knew not. The moon, hidden by thick clouds, cast only shadowy light through the window as she opened her eyes and heard the crying . . . a child's frightened wail.

Morgan rose slowly. She heard Glyn's even breathing and the rush of wind as it passed through the open window. In the distance an owl hooted softly, and the fragrance of lilacs from the garden swept into the bedchamber.

Grabbing for the dagger she no longer had, Morgana rose, the skin on the back of her neck prickling in fear. Oh, that she hadn't lost her knife to Maginnis! As she stood, something tumbled to the floor with a sharp thunk. Morgana jumped before realizing that she'd knocked the toy ship into the rushes.

From the foot of the bed Wolf growled low in his throat, and Morgana froze. Who or what had disturbed her? She glanced around the chamber, but even in the dark, she could see that all was well. Glyn was snoring softly, sleeping with the peace of the self-righteous, and the door to the chamber was shut. Morgana's boots were just where she'd cast them.

She stole to the window where cool wind caressed her face and blew her hair out of her eyes. From the sill she surveyed the darkened bailey, seeing the shifting shadows on the grass, reflections of thick clouds moving slowly across the moon. The sentries were posted, alert as they walked with the extra guards Maginnis had brought to the castle.

She felt his presence, knew that the baron was somewhere in the bailey. Did the man never sleep? Squinting, she

stared into the darkened corners, trying to see her enemy—
the man who had betrothed her to that snake Hazelwood.

She was about to turn back to bed when she heard the
crying again. Soft. Filled with terror.

Closing her eyes, she concentrated only on the noise,
hoping for a vision, for she suspected that the pitiful sound
belonged to Maginnis's son.

"Where are you?" Morgana whispered.

But the noise died to a pitiful sob, then faded.

"I can help. Please . . ."

The sound was gone and Morgana, her flesh chilled,
opened her eyes to see an owl circling above the well.
Perhaps she'd only heard the cry of a night bird stalking
prey.

"God help me," she prayed. "And be with the baron's son."

Garrick couldn't sleep. Too much time had been wasted
already, and the thought of spending hours doing nothing
to find his boy grated on him.

This entire trip was a fool's journey. The witch, if so she
was, could be more trouble than she was worth. As for her
powers, Garrick had seen no evidence of them. In fact, what
he had witnessed was a spoiled daughter who acted like a
man, took no interest in womanly duties, and possessed the
tongue of a harpy.

He kicked at the dirt in the inner bailey, relying on the
poor moonlight to be his guide when he heard a night bird
swooping down from the heavens. He glanced up, and his
gaze was snagged by the figure of a woman in a high
window of the tower. He had no doubt the woman was
Morgana. Her skin was as pale as alabaster and her hair,
long and flowing, caught in the breeze. His heart kicked.

Who was this woman? Enchantress? Witch? Sorceress? Or was she just a beautiful woman whom his cousin Strahan had tricked him into fetching for him?

He couldn't help wondering, as he stared up at her in the moonlight, aware of her ethereal beauty, if he hadn't been played for a fool.

Eight

Damned tough skin," Cook muttered, her fleshy arms straining at her task as she flayed an eel. A fire burned hot in the pit, and dried spices and iron pots hung from the ceiling. The eel was strung from a nail in the rafter, the slippery skin nearly pulled off, the innards cast aside.

"Well, m'lady, up early, ain't ye?" Cook asked, exposing the few teeth she had left as she smiled over her shoulder at Morgana. A hefty woman who liked her own fare, Cook had always allowed her in the kitchen, perhaps because Morgana was quick with an arrow and oft brought in a fat pigeon or pheasant when other bowmen had failed. "Y're soon off on a great adventure." Cook chuckled, her great shoulders shaking, as she washed the meat clear with water, then chopped savory, thyme, marjoram, and parsley into the yolks of hard-cooked eggs. She glanced up from her work and scowled. "Gwladys! Mind the fire now, will ye?" Clucking her tongue she took the long fish from its hook, laid it open on the scarred table, and stuffed her egg and herb concoction into the eel's slit belly. "Well, we'll be missin' ye, m'lady"—she frowned at Wolf as he positioned himself at the door of the kitchen, ears pricked forward, his tongue licking his black lips—"though I won't mind that beast stayin' away from me fires!" With skilled hands she yanked the eel's skin back onto its flesh and sewed the cavity closed. "Here, Gwladys, it's ready to roast. Mind ye don't set the spit too low. I'll not be servin' the great lord burned fish!" With one eye on the younger woman as Gwladys hoisted the eel over the fire, Cook wiped her hands, then glanced again at Morgana. "I've somethin' for ye, m'lady." She motioned to a drawer and took out a sack. "My best herbs, those that you won't be findin' at Abergwynn, I'll wager, and old Berthilde stopped by with some candles, as she knows ye've a use for them." The cloth sack smelled of tangy herbs and beeswax. "Ah, but we'll be missin' ye," she added, smiling though her gaze shimmered a bit. "Curse the damned pepper," she muttered, swiping at her eyes. "Gives a woman fits. 'Ere ye go, now, take these with ye. Ye'll be needin' 'em for findin' the boy, unless I miss my guess."

"M'lady," a sweet voice chanted, and Morgana turned to find Springan, her small boy in tow, scurrying through the door toting a load of firewood. Sourly, she dropped the sticks into a bin and dusted her hands of the dirt and moss. "Sir Daffyd has given me the honor of becoming your maid," she announced, her eyes slitting a bit.

"My maid?" Morgana repeated, stunned. "But I've no need of a maid."

"At Abergwynn." Springan's smile was meant to be friendly, but she let her eyelids fall to hide her true expression. "I thought you knew. 'Tis your mother's gift to you."

"Do you want to go with me to Abergwynn?" Morgana asked.

"Aye."

"But what of Lind? Is he not too young to make the journey with soldiers?" Morgana asked, surprised that the young mother would leave her son and the comfort of Tower Wenlock to risk the unknown at Abergwynn. Here her boy would be accepted as part of the household, but at the castle of Maginnis . . . ?

"Lind will follow later," Springan replied without much concern. "When we are settled at the castle." She reached down and picked the boy up, resting him on one rounded hip.

"Aye, and I'll be takin' care of the lad until he leaves for Abergwynn," Gwladys piped up as the eel began to sizzle over the fire.

"Well, see that you sweep the rushes here and clean this place before ye leave," Cook ordered Springan, shaking her head as she began gutting chickens. Springan managed a cold smile and took her boy outside.

A premonition of dread tickled Morgana's scalp. Springan, though loyal, was known for her temper and stubborn streak. She had been in several fights with the other maids. Her being at Abergwynn could only spell trouble.

There was no time for long good-byes. As Morgana rode through the gates of Tower Wenlock, she glanced over her shoulder and saw the members of her family clustered near the steps of the great hall. Her chin wobbled slightly, but she waved and straightened in the uncomfortable saddle. Wolf, who had not left her side ever since the soldiers arrived, had been forbidden to go with her. Her father and the baron were adamant; she was allowed her horse, her clothes, some jewelry, and the servant girl, Springan. All else remained at Wenlock.

Morgana held no illusions as to Springan's intentions. She left her babe with the cook and, under the guise of servitude, lowered her lashes around her lady. But Morgana had caught the gleam of hatred in Springan's eyes when her father announced that she was to wed Sir Strahan.

Springan, on an aging brown hack, rode at the rear of the company near a cart carrying the supplies, and Morgana ignored the murderous looks she felt cast her way by the girl. Springan wasn't Morgana's only enemy. Many in this company of men would just as soon see her dead as have to deal with her. The sentry she had once duped, Sir Henry, oft sent her glares full of pure hatred, and the other men, though somewhat fearful of her powers, were either lusty individuals whose looks indicated they'd like to lie with her, or skeptics who snorted at the thought of this fool's journey to fetch a witch for Sir Strahan's bride.

Morgana had heard the whispers, knew that though the men feared and loved their leader, some thought he'd lost his mind when he lost his son.

Wolf, who had been leashed near the stables, sent up a baleful howl as Morgana disappeared from his sight and the portcullis clanged down behind the company. Her throat closed as she thought about never returning to Tower Wenlock, never seeing her grandmother again, never running in the surf with the dog playfully barking and splashing with her.

Wolf howled shrilly again, and Morgana's very soul seemed to tear.

"Christ's blood! What was that?" one skinny young soldier asked as he whipped his head around.

"The witch's cur" was the short reply, given by a soldier whose teeth had all but rotted away.

"But it sounded—"

"Aye, like a cry from a soul who's been damned."

The thin soldier crossed himself quickly and licked his lips. "I only hope Sir Garrick knows what he's doing."

"Has he not been good to you?"

"Aye, but the witch, she threatened to curse Sir William's manhood."

The black-toothed one laughed. "I'd say she failed, for I saw William with the cook's maidservant only last night. From the sounds of pleasure coming from the wench, I doubt the curse took."

"But to have her here with us, with Lord Garrick—"

"Shut your mouth and ride. 'Tis not for you to question," the older man said sharply.

Morgana, overhearing the conversation, held her head high and, taking advantage of the situation, lifted one crafty dark brow and chanted some meaningless words under her breath.

The skinny soldier jumped, and his horse responded by attempting to bolt.

Phantom, in the company of unfamiliar horses, side-stepped and snorted, tossing her mane and tail as Morgana tried to keep pace with the double file of soldiers on sturdier mounts. They traveled along the road and through the woods, the very same path on which Lord Garrick had forced her to ride with him only two nights before. In the name of Mary, had it been but two days since the course of her life had changed and she'd been forced to ride with the savage one?

The forest that surrounded Tower Wenlock was thick and lush, filled with game. Morgana had once loved this thicket of trees with all her heart, and the wildflowers and warm earth had always brought her joy. But now the woods seemed gloomy and dark. Fog from the sea still rolled among the black trunks, and even the new foliage, dripping with morning dew, seemed darker than the usual green of spring.

Morgana watched Lord Garrick, riding at the front of the company. He sat tall in the saddle, and because of his height combined with the size of his destrier, he towered a full head above most of his men. He rode bareheaded, his black hair damp from the mist, his lips pressed into a line of steel. She wondered if he ever laughed, but doubted he found much merriment in life, especially since the disappearance of his child.

The road curved, and the horses plodded through the mud. One stallion, ridden by Sir Randolph, sidestepped. Phantom lifted her head, her nostrils extended, and, snorting, gathered herself as if to bolt. "Not now!" Morgana whispered. In truth, she too wanted to flee this harsh band of soldiers, but the time was not ripe. She could not leave until she'd tried to find the baron's boy, but as soon as the lad was discovered, alive or dead, Morgana would escape and flee far to the south.

She thought sadly of her home, where she was not wanted, but she doubted that Maginnis would direct his wrath at her father once she had accomplished her mission. She was determined not to marry Sir Strahan, even if she had to hide in the forests and villages for the rest of her life.

What kind of life would she have? A lady thrown out of her own father's castle? A sorceress whose powers some believed bordered on the dark arts? A woman who had defied the baron of Abergwynn, a handpicked vassal of the king? If and when Lord Garrick ever caught up with her, he would have no choice but to try her and see that she was hanged as a witch. *If* she got caught. That, she swore, would never happen. Should she have to leave Wales, she might as well leave all of that which was called England. By the eye of the raven, there seemed no way out of this mess.

Again Phantom lunged, and Morgana pulled back hard on the reins.

"It seems your horse is spirited, m'lady," said a knight riding on a huge white destrier with several battle scars showing upon its flanks. That soldier was a cruel one, Morgana guessed, the one whose eyes always seemed to flame when he looked at her, the one whose mouth twisted like an evil serpent when his gaze traveled lower than her chin.

"Spirited?" Another knight, the heavy one known as Fulton, asked in a loud hiss. "Or besieged by spirits?"

A ripple of laughter waved through those riding closest to her, and Lord Garrick sent a chilling glance in her direction. "Enough," he commanded and the laughter died, but not before Morgana caught the twitch of his own thin lips, as if he'd been amused by the joke at her expense.

Bastard.

"We will bide our time," she whispered to Phantom. But she could not fail. Her family's very lives depended upon her and her stupid powers. Oh, that they would work quickly, that she would find Logan and restore whatever peace the baron had once felt. Then mayhap he would set her free.

If not, she would escape him and the doom of the marriage he had arranged for her. Her grandmother's prediction, that she was destined to marry Strahan, echoed through her head. Never! Never! Never!

They rode without break until evenfall, when they reached a clearing in the trees. There the soldiers quickly dismounted, leaving their horses in the care of the youngest rider, a boy known as George, who also looked after Phantom. "Keep your eyes on this one," Garrick commanded the boy in Morgana's presence. " 'Twould be a shame if Lady Morgana's horse escaped."

"I will guard it with my very life," the boy replied earnestly.

With a few quick commands to his men, Garrick approached Morgana and relieved the sentry whose job it was to watch her. "I'll see to the lady," he told the man. "You make sure her servant girl is taken care of." Noticing the smile tugging at the corners of the big knight's mouth, he added, "And no harm is to be done to her. The men are to keep their distance. She is Lady Morgana's maid, and she's to be treated well." Garrick's eyes narrowed on the man, who was but an inch shorter than he. "Do you understand, Sir Marsh?"

"I will see to her personally."

"She's to sleep in my tent. With the lady."

Morgana made a sound of protest. Sleep in the same tent with Garrick? Did he not remember the last time, when she had slipped from his shelter and—

"This time you will stay where you are put, m'lady," he said, as if reading her thoughts.

"I'll not be ordered about and—"

"See to the servant girl," Garrick ordered Sir Marsh. Turning swiftly, he grabbed Morgana's arm and guided her away from the clearing where his men had quickly set to work, staking tents, building a fire, posting guards, and unloading the wagon of supplies needed for the evening meal.

She tried to wrench away, but her attempt to escape was futile, for his fingers were as strong as the steel in his sword. His strides were long and swift, his mouth set, and she had to run to keep up with him. "What are you doing? Where are you taking me?" she demanded, keeping her voice low as twigs snapped beneath her feet. The path was crooked and not well traveled, and puddles had collected where the carpet of moss and leaves had been scraped to bare mud.

"Let go of me!" Again she yanked, but his expression only turned harsher. His grip was punishing as the trail widened and the trees gave way to the banks of a shallow creek. Clear water splashed over time-smoothed stones, and ferns grew along the earthy shore.

"It's been a long ride. I thought you might want to wash," Garrick said, "or relieve yourself."

"You're too kind," she mocked, rubbing her arm as he released her. Though she was grateful that he was concerned for her needs, she didn't like the way he bullied her.

"You try a man's patience, witch," he said as she watched the silver flash of a fish as it swam beneath the surface.

"As you try that of a woman!"

Garrick leaned against the rough bark of an oak tree and crossed his arms over his chest. "Would you prefer to have Sir Randolph guard you? He has offered his services."

Morgana swallowed hard. Randolph's lechery was evident in his evil glances, but she had kept him away by chanting words that meant nothing and by threatening to curse him. But how long, without proof, would he believe in her powers?

Garrick propped one boot against the flat top of a large boulder near the creek. "Randolph is not the only knight who has shown interest in you, but as you are promised to Sir Strahan, and as you have a duty to fulfill to me, I see no reason to let anyone but myself be your guard."

"I'm flattered, m'lord," she said, unable to hide the trace of sarcasm in her words and wishing she could control her tongue.

"Aye. Well you should be." His eyes glinted a little, as if he were joking with her. "Now get on with it." He motioned toward the stream. "We have not much time."

"Think you, I'll—" But her protests died as he turned his back to her and waited. She slipped between the bushes to a protected spot near the creek and accepted his offer of privacy. The grime of the journey was thick on her skin, and she took a few minutes to comb her hair and to wash her face and hands. She thought fleetingly of escape. With her agility, she could quickly cross the stream on the flat rocks that protruded above the rush of water. But without Phantom, how far would she get? Where would she go? Back to Tower Wenlock, wherefrom she'd been banished? Or to Castle Pennick and Lord Rowley, the old man who had more than willingly offered to marry her to strengthen his ties with the house of Wenlock? The thought of marrying a man who was older than her father made her shudder. Even Sir Strahan would be better than Nelson Rowley.

"Morgana?" Garrick's voice was filled with irritation.

Morgana hurried, hating the fact that she jumped when he called for her.

She appeared from a copse of oak, and Garrick, though angry, was taken again by her beauty. She'd removed her wimple, and her hair fell down her back in tangled raven-colored waves. Her cheeks were fresh-scrubbed and red from the cold water she'd splashed upon her face. Her eyes were large and starred by the drops of water that still clung like dewdrops to her thick lashes.

Garrick's gut knotted at the sight of her. "You take too long," he said gruffly, still rocked by the simple beauty of this woman.

"Just doing your bidding," she said saucily. Turning, she

started up the path, but again Garrick grabbed hold of her arm. This time she yanked it back and whirled upon him. "I'll not be letting you lead me like a blind horse!" she said, her cheeks flaming. "I can find my way back to the camp alone!"

He couldn't help but admire her courage, and he wondered at the wisdom of his next move. "I wanted but to return this." He held out her dagger.

"You would trust me with this?" Her anger seemed to melt before him.

"Trust?" He shook his head slowly and eyed the thin blade. In truth, he'd not been comfortable with the dagger since taking it from Morgana. "You may need it. We cross through lands that are not happily ruled by Edward." He handed her the knife, and Morgana wrapped her fingers familiarly around the hilt.

"You think I won't use this against you?" she asked.

He rubbed his chin, and his gaze turned thoughtful, his handsome face pensive. "I think many things of you, Morgana of Wenlock. Some good. Some bad. But in all that I have seen of you, aside mayhap from leaving your father's castle vulnerable with your rope, you are not a fool."

She snorted. "Yet I am on this fool's mission with you."

His jaw clenched and anger flared his nostrils, but he held his tongue. Motioning her ahead, he said, " 'Tis time we were back in camp, and unless you want to be led like a blind horse, you'd better start walking."

She glanced at his face, searching for a trace of humor. A glimmer of amusement flickered in his gray gaze but was quickly disguised beneath his stony countenance. So the fierce one had more depth to him than she'd first thought. Surprisingly, she was pleased and chastised herself silently for being a dunce. So the man had a sense of humor. So what? Rather than risk angering him further—for he could easily take back her precious knife—she turned quickly and started along the path, ducking the low-hanging branches and carefully skirting the puddles. She sheathed her dagger, and it rode along her hip comfortably.

At the camp, the fire was burning bright. Several rabbits and quail sizzled on the spit, and the scent of smoke wafted through the forest. The tents were arranged near the perimeter of the clearing, and soldiers milled about. Some polished swords; others talked and laughed while drinking ale; still others were playing a game of throwing knives in the red shadows of the campfire.

The horses were tethered and fed, and sentries, more alert than the one who had let Morgana slip out of Garrick's tent the night she'd met the great lord, guarded the site, their eyes moving slowly over the closing darkness of the woods.

Garrick led Morgana to his tent. She spent the evening with Springan, who spoke little. They were brought food and wine while a guard sat near the entrance of the tent and Morgana had little doubt that others, perhaps two or three, were posted to the rear. She chewed scorched rabbit thoughtfully. Surely Garrick was the death from the north, unless her vision had lied. Aye, he had vowed vengeance on her family should she fail in her mission. Yet he had trusted her with her dagger.

Springan seemed near sulking as she sat on the edge of the pallet.

Morgana, from boredom, tried to speak to the girl. "Missing Lind, are you?" she asked, shoving her trencher aside.

Springan shrugged. "A little."

"Gwladys will be good to him."

Springan didn't comment, pretending interest in her food and not looking up from her meal.

The time passed slowly, and when Springan took the remainder of food to the guard, Morgana walked to the door of the tent.

"Orders are that you are to stay inside, m'lady," the guard, Marsh, insisted. He offered her a wide toothless grin that turned Morgana's insides cold. A scar ran down the length of his cheek and was testament to the battles he'd fought.

Morgana clamped her teeth together—to tamp down her fear and try to still her tongue. During all her seventeen years she'd been allowed to run free and do as she wished, but ever since the horrid vision and meeting Garrick of Abergwynn, she'd been held captive, first by her own father and now by the bloody lord himself. "Tell Lord Garrick I wish to stretch my legs," she commanded coolly.

The big man frowned, and his beard-roughened face took on a stern expression. "You are to stay in the tent, m'lady."

Morgana took a step closer to the huge man and thought of the dagger in her belt. "And if I don't?"

"The baron will not be happy."

"I care not whether he is happy or sad. I need to stretch my legs, and if you don't let me pass, I'll be forced to change your mind," she said sweetly.

Marsh smothered a smile, but clucked his tongue. "I know of your dagger, but I'm not afeared of it."

Morgana tilted back her head, looking the huge man square in the eye. "It's not a blade I'll be needing," she said in a low voice, hoping this large man would prove as superstitious as his fellow knights. "By the skin of the toad and the wing of the bat—"

"Enough!" Garrick, seeing the crafty smile playing upon Morgana's lips, strode to his tent. " 'Tis time we slept. You," he ordered the sorceress, "shall sleep here"—he pointed to a pallet thick with furs near the center of the tent—"and you, servant woman, will sleep near the flap."

Morgana eyed the largest bundle of furs tossed on a pallet bare inches from the one he had named as her bed.

"I shall sleep next to you, witch, to make sure you don't chant and disappear before you have fulfilled your promise."

"I'll not sleep next to you!"

"You've no choice," Garrick commanded. "You rest on your own pallet or I'll see that you share mine." His eyes were as dark as night, his lips thin with anger at being contradicted in front of his men. Several of the knights were close enough to the flap of the tent to hear the exchange, and Marsh, still planted firmly at the entrance, could not help but overhear the argument. Morgana guessed few defied Garrick of Abergwynn, yet she refused to back down.

"Have it your way," he said before Morgana could respond. He threw an angry glance at the guard. "Sir Marsh, take Springan outside to wash herself. Do not return until I say."

Morgana's throat froze as her plight became clear. Obviously the baron intended to punish her. "Nay . . ." she whispered.

"Do as I say!" Garrick snapped, and the guard grabbed Springan's arm, drawing her outside the tent and letting the flap close. Inside, the air was close, the darkness permeated only by the red glow of the fire without.

Morgana shivered, feeling his presence, watching as he moved slowly around her, circling her as a wolf might stalk its prey.

"Dare you defy me in front of my men?" he growled, his voice as low as the sound of surf rumbling to the shore.

The hair on the back of Morgana's neck lifted. "I did not—"

"Dare you argue with me?"

She stood, braced, waiting, sure that he might strike her at any moment. "But I—"

"Dare you chant silly, meaningless words to frighten my men and mock them?"

He quit moving. His bootsteps were hushed, and he was standing behind her, so close that she could smell him, could feel his breath, hot as dragon's fire, against her neck.

"You try my patience, witch, and I'll not allow this farce to continue. My men have pledged their fealty to me! They are loyal and—"

"You do not own me, Lord Garrick!"

"Do I not?" he returned, and she trembled at the taunting sound of his words. "Edward has given me these lands and all that which is upon them. Aye, in truth, they are partly his, but he would not argue that all that is Wenlock, including the people therein, belongs to me."

"Nay, you do not—"

"Unless I have harmed you, I can do what I will."

Merciful God. She reached instinctively for her dagger, but a hand, large and calloused, folded quickly over her wrist, clamping hard over her skin and drawing her back against him so swiftly that her breath caught in her lungs. Her spine pressed against his abdomen, and though she tried to move, her buttocks were slammed against his rigid thighs. Steel muscles bound her to him, as his other arm surrounded her, holding her fast, his fingers splayed beneath her breasts.

She dared not move. Never had she been held so close by a man and certainly not with the savage power she felt in the coil of his muscles.

"I did not give you back your dagger so that you could use it against me," he snarled against the nape of her neck, and she quivered in fear.

She swallowed back a hot retort, though a thousand sharp words spun through her mind. Lord, please let me get through this, she prayed in terror-riddled silence. The vision had been right. The danger was from this horrid knight.

"What? No incantations?" he mocked. When he let his one hand slip lower, beneath her hip-slung belt, she tensed. Did the beast mean to take her? But his fingers, hot through her tunic, did not probe her legs. Instead they found their way to her dagger and unsheathed the silvery blade. He held the knife in front of her nose. "This is yours, m'lady, but since you must now sleep with me, I think it best kept in my hand." Turning his head toward the door, he barked, "Bring in the servant girl and prepare the camp for the night."

Springan, eyes round with fear, crawled back inside, and Morgana wished she could indeed chant a spell and disappear. A tiny smile tugged at the corners of Springan's mouth when the servant girl discovered her lady in the arms of Garrick of Abergwynn.

"Turn your back to us and sleep," Garrick ordered sharply. Springan spun quickly and slid beneath the furs on her pallet, her face to the wall of the tent. Garrick folded his knees, and together he and the witch tumbled onto his pallet. "Now," he said in a voice as low as death, "push me no further, woman, and taunt me no more in front of my men, or I will be forced to find other means of making you bend to my will."

nine

"Let me go," she commanded in a whisper that was rough and frantic.

"You'll stay here. With me." Garrick seldom doubted the wisdom of his decisions, but this time he knew he'd made a vast mistake. Lying with Morgana tucked against him had been a horrible error in judgment. The woman was betrothed to Strahan, by Garrick's own word, and yet here he was, one arm tucked around her waist, another gripping her right hand. She was rigid in his arms, her breathing shallow, showing her fear. She smelled of lilacs and spring, and his fingertips felt the beat of her pulse on the inside of her wrist.

"I'll not lie with you."

"You'll rest, little one. That is all."

"I cannot rest with you holding me prisoner. Release me!" She struggled, but her arms, though strong, were no match for his.

He almost chuckled. Who was this tiny woman who snarled orders like a king? Did she really think she could best him? He smiled in the darkness at the challenge. "Release you? And have you slit my throat? I think not."

"You have no right!" He felt her tense, then straighten. Her heel connected painfully with his shin.

His breath whistled through his teeth. "Do not test me, witch."

"I'll not lie here on your bed and—oooh!"

He swung one leg over hers, pinning her to the pallet. Still holding fast to her arms, he leaned over her. In the tent's dark interior he could barely make out the features of her small face, but he saw her eyes—round, reflecting the golden illumination from the filtered firelight, sizzling like lightning. When his gaze shifted lower, he noticed that her tiny mouth was pursed, her full lips drawn together, and he wondered if she had the nerve to spit at him.

"Unhand me," she warned.

He didn't respond, just shifted his weight slightly. He felt every point where their bodies touched. His leg, though covered with a coarse legging, fit perfectly inside hers, and even as she tried to squirm away, he held her fast. Her hair streamed out over the furs. Night-black curls gleamed as they framed a face so small and enchanting he could think of nothing save kissing her.

Nervously she licked her lips, and as he watched the silken path of her tongue, he felt his manhood rise, stiff and full, pressing hard against his clothes, betraying him.

"What?" he finally asked when she stopped moving beneath him. Aside from the rise and fall of her breasts, she was still. "No chants? No spells? No talking to the wind?"

She swallowed hard but did not reply. Her gaze locked with his, and deep inside, he suppressed a groan. The ache between his legs tormented him. Not since his beloved wife, Astrid, had he wanted a woman more . . . and perhaps this passion he felt for the witch, this forbidden desire, was even more intense than his faded memories of Astrid. Caught between anger and awe, he became the same kind of beast as many of his men, wanting to feel her supple body yield to his, wanting to feel her hips rise to greet his manhood and hear that soft whoosh of her breath as he entered her. He wanted her to pulse around him, to writhe anxiously beneath him, to buck upward in silent invitation, to—

"Do not mock me, m'lord," she whispered on a ragged breath.

His wild, humiliating fantasies were brought up short. "Why not?" he demanded in a voice that was rougher than usual. "I brought you on this journey for your skill with magic. Prove to me that you're not a fraud."

"And what would you wish? That I turn your hands into hooves? That I cause the fire to rise up and devour your tents? That I turn a beetle into a war-horse? What?"

Gazing down at her, seeing the glimmer of humor in her eyes as she openly ridiculed him, Garrick felt foolish. He flung his knee from between her legs, and still holding on to her wrists, he cursed the fates that had brought him to this. "On Logan's soul, woman, all I want from you is help in finding my son," he said, unwilling to admit how his body cried out for hers.

Morgana shivered, but not from the cold. "I will try," she said, grateful that he was no longer poised above her, that his gray gaze was no longer searching hers. Her heart had begun to beat rapidly, as if she'd been running and was out of breath, and the feel of his leg pressing against the inside of her thigh had caused a heat to race like wildfire through her blood.

Aye, she'd felt fear of this man, but there had been a new emotion swirling through her heart, and she'd been spellbound by his face, so close to hers, his hands surrounding her fingers, the pressure of his hip against her thigh. Her throat dry, she didn't move, but the scent of him, male and leather, forest and sweat, was everywhere, and the touch of his hands, warm and firm, made sleep impossible.

She closed her eyes, wishing for the oblivion of slumber, wishing for morning, wishing she'd never met the man who held her prisoner.

For the rest of the journey to Abergwynn, Morgana held her tongue. Garrick insisted she ride next to him, and amid the hidden smiles of the men and their knowing gazes, she sat in the hated saddle, her back stiff with as much pride as she could muster. Obviously the men thought she had lain with their lord. Though her cheeks turned crimson when she caught the shrewd glances of Garrick's most trusted warriors, she let the men think what they would. Professing her virtue would do no good. Besides, her soiled name might prove helpful, for certainly Sir Strahan would not want a woman who was no longer a virgin.

Only three people knew the truth—Morgana, Lord Garrick, and Springan, all of whom had shared the tent. Springan, however, could have slept part of the time, thinking that while she dozed Garrick had taken Morgana, when, in truth, he'd shown no interest in her whatsoever.

Morgana had not slept a wink as she lay rigid next to the man who held her dagger in one hand and her wrist in the other while snoring softly—as if he didn't have a care in the world! She was jealous of the rest he could so easily attain.

When she'd dared move her hand away from his as they stretched out upon the pallet, he'd half awakened and dragged her nearer to his warm body, so she'd forced herself to lie without moving a muscle, her sleepless body aching, her eyes burning for lack of rest.

In the morning, of course, the soldiers had attributed the

dark circles under her eyes and her weary posture to the belief that their lord and master had spent hours pleasuring her, teaching her the art of lovemaking. That scandalous thought brought fresh color to her face.

She'd thought about what it would be like to lie with him. Aye, trying to rest with her body so close to his, hearing the soft sounds of his breathing, and feeling his leg brush against hers had caused her silly heart to beat much too rapidly. She'd imagined his callused hands against her bare skin more than once and had been ashamed at the stirrings deep within her at the turn of her thoughts.

The knights' belief that she was Garrick's lover served another purpose, however. None of the men dared send her lust-filled glances any longer. The soldiers kept their distance from her, for which she was thankful, though she had trouble lifting her head proudly, knowing that they thought she was no better than a common wench.

Let them think what they would, she decided as she rode and tried to keep her eyelids from drifting downward. Her muscles throbbed from lack of rest, her fingers were nearly useless on the reins. Above the odor of horses, dirt, and sweaty men, she smelled the sea-scent in the air, for though the road between Abergwynn and Wenlock wound through forest and valley, the rutted lane was never far from the ocean.

They rode through the forest and rolling meadows and on the third day passed through a small village, where shopkeepers and almsmen alike smiled and cheered as Garrick's men guided their mounts along the narrow streets. The horses' hooves rang on the cobblestones, and the smell of smoke and refuse drifted over the pervasive scent of horseflesh. Morgana lifted her chin, but caught more than one interested stare cast in her direction. It was not often a woman rode beside the baron, she realized, and she wondered how many of the townspeople thought she spent her hours dabbling in the black arts.

She noticed a cat slink down an alley, and a group of children who had been stalking the animal pulled up short to stand at the corner and gape, their attention now riveted to the procession. Several of the older boys laughed and pointed at Morgana, and one sly little girl drew back in horror at the sight of her.

So that was how it was going to be, Morgana thought sadly.

On the upper floors of the shops, shutters were thrown open, letting out the smell of roasting meat and the cries of babies as women and small children stared down at Baron Garrick and his soldiers.

On the street, men laughed and clapped each other on the back. So Garrick, the beast of Abergwynn, was loved by those whom he guarded. The dirt-smudged faces of small boys and the toothless grins of stooped and crippled ancients attested to his popularity.

A scrawny boy, prodded by his peers at the corner near the bakery, broke apart from the group while his friends stood by and watched his thin body move through the crowd toward the soldiers. Several of the boys glanced up at Morgana, and their eyes shone with malevolence. No good would come of this, Morgana thought as the boy wove his way among the onlookers and ran into the street. Freckles were sprayed across his nose, his hair was lank and in need of washing, and his eyes were as blue as a summer lake.

"It's the witch! She's here!" he cried, pointing a grubby little finger at Morgana.

Garrick pulled hard on his mount's reins, and his horse stopped, forcing each soldier to rein in his horse until the entire company drew up short. Morgana wished she could sink beneath the cobblestones, but instead lifted her chin slightly. Phantom sidestepped, and a few other horses snorted, breaking the silence that the small boy's proclamation had caused. "I'm not a—"

"Witch! Witch! Drinks the blood of babes! Witch! Witch! Eats the eyes of knaves! Witch! Witch! Burns the skin of—"

"Tommy!" A thin woman wearing a dusty red kerchief over her hair raced through the shuffling throng. Her gaunt face was twisted in horror as she stretched her thin arms out toward her child. Scooping the boy up, she held him to her chest and stared up at Garrick with cold fear in her eyes. "I'm sorry, m'lord," she whispered. Her lower lip trembled until she clamped it between her front teeth.

The town, boisterous only moments before, had become hushed. In the distance a chicken squawked, but the merry villagers were now sober, all eyes trained on Morgana. Tommy's comrades quickly dispersed, breaking apart and running down separate paths lest they incur the baron's wrath.

"Bring me the boy," Garrick said, and the woman, shivering visibly, did as she was told.

"Do not punish him," Morgana whispered, though her insides were twisted, her heart stone cold from the wretched chant he'd aimed at her. Nonetheless, he was just a boy, believing the horrid stories that no doubt had been grist for the gossip mill ever since Garrick had announced he would be riding to Wenlock. Gossip was known to breed within castle walls before racing along its cruel path to the villages and towns of the countryside. The boy, spurred on by his friends, was but repeating what he'd heard.

Behind Garrick, several soldiers coughed, as if to disguise the urge to laugh aloud, though Morgana found the situation far from humorous.

Garrick bent low on his horse and hauled the boy into the saddle with him. His features harsh, he studied the white-faced lad.

Tommy's mother lifted her arms in quiet supplication. "M'lord, please. Show mercy."

"Tommy, is it?" Garrick asked, his stern face softening slightly as he thought of his own son. This mud-splattered urchin with the unruly hair was not so unlike Logan. Garrick's throat grew thick, and the swift justice he wanted to inflict on the boy melted.

"Aye, and it's Tom I'm likin' to be called," the boy said with more than a trace of defiance.

Morgana sent up a quiet prayer for the child.

"Tom, then. This *lady* is Lady Morgana of Wenlock," Garrick advised the boy.

"The witch," Tommy replied, unintimidated by the lord who balanced him on the shoulders of his huge horse.

"Where did you hear that?"

Tommy shrugged his thin shoulders. "Ev'ybody says y're out lookin' for a witch to conjure up your son."

Tommy's mother moaned softly. Morgana thought the woman might faint into the arms of the butcher who, wearing his blood-spattered apron, stood behind her.

"Do they, now?" Garrick's jaw hardened, and his eyes narrowed on the boy. The silence in the town, interrupted only by the shuffling of the horses' hooves and the occasional bark of a dog, was oppressive. Morgana wished she could do something. "Say they anything else?" Garrick asked.

"That she drinks blood when the moon is full and eats live rats, and if she touches you at midnight—" Tommy stopped suddenly, catching a swift look from his mother.

"Yes? What happens if she touches you at midnight?"

"Your throat will close and you'll swallow yer own tongue."

Garrick's own throat clenched, and Morgana was afraid he might shake the child senseless. She knew the power of his hands, how cruel they could be. Instead, the great lord suppressed a smile. "I think you should apologize to the lady."

"But Mum says—"

"Apologize," Garrick ordered, and the boy, casting a glance at his frightened mother, suddenly understood his plight. He swallowed hard and anxiously licked his lips. "Sorry," he mumbled, stealing a totally unrepentant glance at Morgana.

"Please, Lord Garrick, he is only a child. Do him no harm," the mother beseeched. She threw herself to her knees in front of Garrick's war-horse. The steed stomped and tossed back his head.

"Yea, and he's a boy who needs to learn some manners," Garrick replied, turning his attention back to the boy. "So, Tommy, you are to come to the castle each day at dawn until I relieve you of your duties. You are to work until nightfall helping the grooms clean the stables. And your friends must come with you."

"But"—Tommy looked frantically at the now-vacant corner—"I have no friends."

"So it appears." Garrick forced the urchin to stare straight into his harsh gaze. "But they were into this mischief as much as you were. Tell them I recognized them, and if Ralph, the smith's son, and the thatcher's daughter, Mary, and the others don't show up with you, they'll have a much harsher punishment to face the next day."

"But—" Tom whispered, his throat working at the thought of confronting his cohorts in crime.

"Tell them, Tommy Jackson." With a severe scowl, he lifted the boy off the horse's shoulders and, with powerful arms, dropped him softly onto the road. "And if you show disrespect to Lady Morgana in the future, I shall be forced to find a more severe punishment."

"He'll be more than respectful." Tommy's mother wrapped her skinny arms around her son.

"See that he is." Garrick shoved his heels into his steed's sides, and the horse moved forward, leading the double file of soldiers through the main street of the village. The townspeople were now quiet, but their eyes followed Morgana as she rode stiffly on Phantom. From the corner of her eye, she saw the looks cast her way: the wary, resentful stares sent her by mothers shooing their children inside the buildings lining the street; the raised eyebrows and smirks of the older boys; the appraising glances of the men with lopsided grins dominating ruddy complexions. Yea, she'd been branded by them all.

The villagers thought her a witch and surely would alert the church officials. For the first time, Morgana knew fear. At Wenlock her powers and visions were known to the chaplain, as was her devotion to God. The chaplain often spoke of her visions as the light of God, though Friar Tobias seemed inclined to believe that finding the smith's son and predicting a savage storm was not a gift from God but, more likely, pure luck.

Here at Abergwynn, however, she would have to confront a new chaplain, and perhaps several monks as well, and convince them of her piety while all around, the towns-people, freemen, and servants in the castle would be looking to Morgana for amusement, or worse. Oh, cursed, cursed visions that had brought her here!

Through the town and past rolling fields of oats and wheat they rode. Morgana barely noticed the long stalks of grain bending before the wind, nor did she see the shimmering silky green waves of uncut hay nor the wildflowers heavy with blossoms along the roadside. No, she stared ahead to the rise in the land and the castle that stood thereon. Three times larger than Tower Wenlock, the fortress rose from the very cliffs on which it was mounted. Stone walls, thick enough to drive a cart atop, guarded the inner ward, and massive towers and battlements soared higher still, providing a falcon's view of the surrounding lands.

From the highest tower, atop a pole, a large blue and gold banner snapped in the breeze, proclaiming to all that this castle and the surrounding forests, fields, and towns all belonged to Lord Garrick Maginnis, baron of Abergwynn.

"God help me," she whispered.

Ten

cannot believe you would be so foolish!" Clare Maginnis whirled on her heel to face her brother, her palms turned toward the rafters of the great hall, while servants scurried into the room, preparing the table for a feast to celebrate Garrick's return, and Ware pretended no interest in the conversation. "You went all the way to Wenlock in Llanwynn in search of a . . . a . . ."

"Sorceress." Garrick was tired of his sister's theatrics. Clare had, since childhood, known how to create drama in the most ordinary of situations, and this . . . Well, she was reveling in what she considered her brother's foolishness.

"A sorceress," she repeated. "And what, pray tell, do we need of a sorceress?"

Garrick's patience was as thin as lambskin. "For Logan," he whispered harshly. "You know why I brought Morgana here."

"I only heard from Strahan," she said, her eyes blazing. "By the time I heard the news, you were gone!"

Garrick ignored her fury and asked the question that was uppermost in his mind. "There has been no word of Logan, has there?"

"None," Clare admitted, glancing at her younger brother. Ware brushed a fleck of dirt from his boot and, frowning, wagged his head. "But this—this girl . . . she cannot hope to find Logan." Clare, her anger and taste for drama spent, walked closer to Garrick and placed a soft hand on his shoulder. "Accept God's will, Garrick. Know that Logan has joined his mother—"

"Nay!" Garrick swept his sister's fingers from his tunic and stepped quickly away from her. "He's *not* dead, and I'll hear no more of this talk. Morgana is here to help me find the boy. She is betrothed to Strahan."

Clare's brows lifted a fraction. "To Strahan?" she repeated, though Garrick knew that his announcement came as no surprise to her. She rubbed her hands against her arms as if she felt cold, then motioned impatiently to a servant who had entered the great hall. The girl turned swiftly and hurried down the hallway toward the kitchen.

"Aye, you know that Strahan asked for her hand and I agreed."

"Mmm." Clare plucked absently at her robe and didn't meet Garrick's eyes. "Did you also agree to bed her?"

Ware sucked in his breath, and Garrick's patience snapped. With the speed of a striking snake, he crossed the small space between them and towered over his sister, but Clare didn't back down an inch. She met his glower with a defiant glare of her own.

Garrick growled, "I did not steal her virginity, sister, though I see not why I have to defend my actions to you. Aye, she slept in my tent, next to me, so that I could prevent her escape, but—"

"Escape? Was she a prisoner?"

"God's blood! Why should I explain these things to you?"

"She came of her own will?"

Garrick muttered a curse under his breath. Clare would be the bloody death of him. Always the questions, always the demands—oh, but if he could marry her off and send her to some remote edge of his lands! Her marriage had ended tragically, and would that he could find a new husband for her. "I have no time for arguments!" he thundered as Strahan approached. His cousin's face was murderous, and Garrick knew in an instant that he, too, had heard the gossip surrounding Garrick's journey home with the witch.

"A word, m'lord?" Strahan asked curtly.

Garrick motioned for Clare and his brother to leave, though both, bullheaded as they were, took their time about slipping through the curtains. Waving Strahan into a chair by the fire, he called to a page and ordered ale. His head began to pound, and he wondered, not for the first time, if Morgana of Wenlock was more anguish than she was worth. "Was there trouble while I was gone?"

"Nothing serious. A lad of fourteen was caught hunting deer in the forest, and the steward was concerned about some missing sugar and accused the cook of being careless, but all else was well." Strahan made an impatient movement with his hands, as if to clear the air of the petty issues. "As you've probably heard, there was no word of Logan."

"Aye." Garrick's black mood darkened. An ache settled into his heart, and he wondered if ever he would see his boy again. Was he, as everyone seemed to think, chasing a fool's dream? Why could he not concede that his son was gone, delivered to God?

Wearily he accepted a cup of ale from a spotty-faced page and let his dark thoughts swirl in his mind as he drained the mazer. Someone had betrayed him. Someone had taken the boy. Whether Logan was alive or dead, that traitor would be found out. And he would pay with his very life.

"Garrick?"

He glanced up at Strahan and noticed the thin white lines surrounding his cousin's mouth. "You wish to speak of Morgana," Garrick said, resting a heel on the hearth and letting the warmth of the fire seep into his bones.

"Aye."

"She will be your bride. Daffyd of Wenlock agreed, and I promised to pay a small dowry. As a wedding gift I'll give you Castle Brynwydd and the lands thereabout. I know 'tis not so grand as Hazelwood, but 'tis the best I can offer."

Strahan's eyes clouded at the mention of his lost home. "You're too generous."

"I think not. You'll be paying a price yourself when you marry the witch." He tried to make light of the subject, but his already black mood coupled with the thought of Morgana marrying Strahan only caused his spirits to sink still lower. What should he care whom the sorceress married, once she'd found Logan? She was nothing but trouble, that one, and though her beauty was disturbing, she would give a man little but grief.

"I know how to handle a woman," Strahan said, motioning for more ale. He seemed satisfied, his eyes gleaming, his smile crooked and dashing. "Morgana will be no different from the others. Should she displease me, I'll teach her obedience."

Garrick's fingers curled tightly over his cup. "You'll not lay a hand on her, Strahan, no matter what she does."

Strahan's nostrils flared a bit. "I have never struck a lady."

"Or a wench?" Garrick asked.

Strahan shrugged. "I remember not."

Strahan's gaze was steady, and Garrick did not know him to lie. Yet, of late, Garrick had felt some doubts about his cousin. Strahan seemed tense and quick to anger. Ever since

Logan's disappearance the entire castle had been on edge, as if the inhabitants had adopted the gloomy anger that had surrounded Garrick himself.

Strahan rubbed his jaw slowly. "There are rumors that Morgana slept in your tent."

"Aye. I did not want to return empty-handed." He told Strahan about finding Morgana by the sea and of her attempts to outwit him. "I wanted to bring her safely here, and so she and her servant girl slept in my tent."

An unspoken question lingered in Strahan's eyes, and Garrick said quietly, "Believe no gossip, Strahan. Morgana's virtue was safe with me."

The tension drained out of Strahan's shoulders, and he smiled again, showing a flash of white teeth that Garrick remembered from their younger, more carefree days when they would hunt and ride off to war together. A handsome and charming man, Strahan had no trouble winning the hearts of many ladies. His looks and sense of adventure appealed to most—though not to Morgana.

"I trust you, cousin," Strahan said, draining his cup before clasping Garrick's hand firmly.

"And I you."

"If anyone on earth can find Logan, 'tis Morgana." Again he flashed his grin before releasing Garrick's palm.

For the first time in days, Garrick relaxed. A hot bath, a filling meal, and he would be ready to deal with Morgana again. At the fleeting image of her, he felt desire speed through his blood. Mayhap he should find a woman . . . but he knew instinctively no other would do. He closed his eyes and willed his lust away. He had no time for seeking the pleasures of wenches or for silly fantasies about Morgana. There was simply no time to waste. He must find Logan and the traitor who had taken him.

Morgana settled into the tub of hot water and couldn't help sighing. After three days of riding, her back and legs were sore and every muscle in her body ached.

"Is it not lovely here?" Springan asked, handing her a chunk of scented soap and gazing upon the guest chamber that was to be Morgana's. Twice the size of the room she had shared with Glyn, this chamber was warmed by its own hearth. Several windows were cut into the whitewashed walls, and bright tapestries hung near the bed. The rushes on the floor smelled of lilacs and lavender, and the carved wooden bed was piled high with pillows and fur coverlets.

"Aye, 'tis lovely," Morgana agreed, though in her heart she would rather have been at Wenlock with her family. This grand room with its own antechamber for dressing lacked the cozy familiarity of her own home.

She dressed with Springan's help, stepping into a gown of crimson damask that buttoned to the neck with tiny pearls. The sleeves were gathered wide at the shoulder and tapered to thin bands at the wrist, and her hair was braided to the nape of her neck, where the black curls fell in wild abandon. Springan approached with a wimple, but Morgana waved it away.

"But, m'lady—" Springan said.

"I'm no longer my father's daughter, obliged to do as he wishes." She watched Springan put the wimple back on a shelf in the antechamber. In truth, her father hadn't insisted upon the bloody wimple at Wenlock, and she wasn't going to change her ways. "I'll wear my hair as I choose, and no one will much care, as I am considered a witch by most."

Irritated by Springan's awe of Abergwynn and her constant fussing, Morgana was anxious to get rid of the girl. "Go now. You must have other duties."

"Aye, but I promised Lady Meredydd that I would look after you."

"And you have. 'Tis time for you to get ready for the feast, for there is sure to be a celebration now that Garrick has returned. Besides, you probably have much to do to settle in yourself."

Springan argued no further, as she was eager to meet the other servants and find her own quarters.

Garrick came for her. Grim-faced as usual, he, too, had bathed, and the beard stubble that had sprouted from his jaw had disappeared. His surcoat, the color of a verdant forest, was thick and decorated with strips of leather, his mantle a rich sable brown.

" 'Tis time you met the household and took your place near Strahan," he said when she opened the door.

Her eyes met his, and for an instant she noticed a glimmer of something deeper than his usual disinterest in his silvery gaze. "Must I?"

He cocked a thick black brow and caught his lower lip between his teeth. "You are not anxious to meet with your betrothed?"

Morgana hesitated, but then decided that she'd best say what was on her mind. "I'll not marry Strahan, Lord Garrick. Know this now: I'll do what I can to find your son. Aye, I'll stay here and learn the lessons that my father insists I have, but I'll not marry anyone so vile as Strahan of Hazelwood."

"Vile? Strahan is my cousin, one of my finest knights."

"Then I despair for your army."

He rubbed a thumb beneath his jaw thoughtfully, and Morgana's eyes were drawn to the seductive movement of the pad of his thumb scraping his skin. "Strahan has time and time again proved himself in battle—for Abergwynn and for England. He saved my life not once but twice and has demonstrated his allegiance to Edward. He has even offered to go with Longshanks to fight the Scots if need be, and as we both know, there's always trouble brewing to the north."

"Aye, I have seen so."

"Ahh, the vision," he said stepping close to her. "The vision wherein I strike down all that you love." She trembled at his words, though his tone was soft. "They think I've lost my mind, you know. My servants and men. Even my family. They think I'm daft to have gone for you. Some believe that you are a witch and will bring a curse upon Castle Abergwynn. Still others consider me a fool, charmed by a beautiful woman who is leading me on a merry chase. Others claim your powers don't exist at all, that you are a fraud—"

"I've never claimed—"

"And yet still others think you actually talk to God."

"But I have not—" she began to protest.

He held up a hand to silence her. "Most of my people—yea, and even my own kin—think I should bury my son's memory and accept that he is dead." He paced between Morgana and the window, where he stared into the gloaming that crept across the forests and fields. The sky was a hue of deep purple, the land beginning to lie in shadow. The tension in Garrick's shoulders was a physical pain as he thought about his child. "But I care not what others think. And I cannot accept that Logan's dead." His fingers curved over the stone sill of the window until his knuckles showed white with conviction. "For I believe in my heart that my son is alive. I do not believe in your powers, sorceress, for I've seen no evidence of your magic." His brows drew down over his eyes. "But I will take the chance that you may have a gift, and I will suffer the humiliation of gossip by my men, and I will not give up until I know the answer. You," he ordered, casting a look over his shoulder, "you will do what you have to do to help me."

"My marriage to Sir Strahan will not bring back your boy."

"You insult me and my castle."

"As you've insulted me by keeping me prisoner!"

"Why can you not accept your fate?"

"For the same reason that you cannot accept yours!"

His hands opened and closed in frustration. "You try my patience, woman."

"As you try mine, m'lord," she tossed back, her green eyes flashing with emerald fire.

Without another word, he grabbed her hand and yanked her to him, drawing his face so close to hers that his breath, hot and smelling faintly of ale, fanned her skin. "We have a bargain, m'lady, and I'm holding up my end. Now you must honor yours. As for marrying Strahan, you should consider yourself very fortunate. Many a lady would love to be his bride."

"Then find him someone else," she retorted, trying not to notice the hands binding her and the silvery sheen to his eyes.

"Should I break my promise to your father? I've already left him some of my best men, and your sister and brother will be at Abergwynn soon. I promise to do Wenlock no harm, as long as you fulfill your obligation."

"As I said, I'll willingly try to find your boy."

"And you'll marry Strahan. I'll hear no more about it."

"Does he still want me? I did, after all, sleep with his lord," she jeered.

"I touched you not! Besides, Strahan trusts me," Garrick stated, the back of his neck staining red, his eyes glittering with a deadly fire. "I doubt you would lie about your virtue to Strahan, so don't threaten me."

It was all Morgana could do to keep from kicking the blackheart as he grabbed her elbow and propelled her toward the stairs. The sounds of merriment and music already drifted up the staircase, but at the top of the circular steps, Garrick paused, his mouth compressed. At the landing, his gaze swept her face, and his eyes narrowed as he studied her for what seemed forever. Then, cursing under his breath, he turned her back the way they had come, his long strides eating up the corridor as Morgana's skirts swept the floor. "What're you doing?" she demanded, suddenly frightened. Did he mean to punish her?

"Before we join the others, you must visit Logan's room," he said, deciding that the guests would wait. He was impatient and did not care much for festivities to begin with. The sorceress was here for a single purpose, and there was no reason not to start. She struggled against him, pulling back, as she was forced to half run to keep up with him.

At the door of his own chamber, he growled at the guard, "We are not to be disturbed," and Morgana's face turned ashen.

Silly girl. Did she think that Garrick was ruthless enough to have his way with her now, in this very castle where her intended was waiting, to rob her of her virginity, then pack her neatly into the arms of Strahan? The thought made him smile, for though he loved his cousin, he also loved to best him, for Strahan was forever competing against him—in the hunt, at tournaments, even in battle. As boys, Strahan had always been triumphant, winning every bet and race. However, as Garrick had grown older, he'd become stronger than Strahan, taken more chances, been more daring. He'd also grown taller than his cousin by a few inches and had become more agile, his reactions quicker, much to Strahan's disgust.

Now, as Garrick stared down at Morgana, whose razor-like tongue, for once, was frozen in fear, he couldn't contain his amusement. He touched the side of her face gently when he saw her eyes stray to the curtained bed he'd shared with Astrid.

Astrid, with her red-gold hair and amber eyes, the one woman who had captured his black heart and turned him away from a life of wenching and warring. The only woman he would ever love, the mother of his child. His heart wrenched painfully when he thought of the plans he and Astrid had made, the delight they'd taken in the coming of the baby, and then the horrid tragedy of Astrid's death on the night Logan was born. Clearing his throat, he caught Morgana staring at him, as if she could see into the depths of his soul.

"His things are here," he said gruffly, walking to a large antechamber where Logan's clothes still lay folded neatly, his few toys placed on shelves near his felt boots.

Morgana, insides churning, followed Garrick, then reached forward and touched the tiny shirts and breeches, her fingers running over the rough fabric as she tried to concentrate. She touched the boy's toys—a tiny bow, some arrows without heads, a wooden horse and knight, a small castle carved of wood. But as her fingers grazed Logan's belongings, she felt nothing of the lad, no current of life passing through the objects of Logan's affection. Oh, Lord, was the boy truly dead? If so, how would Garrick survive the loss of his child?

A lump settled in her throat, and her eyes grew moist.

Garrick's gaze was fastened to her back; she could feel its weight against her neck. She closed her eyes, willing some vision of the boy to appear, but knew that the effort was useless. No life force lingered in the dark closet.

"Well?" Garrick demanded.

"I—I cannot hear or see anything."

"Why not?" he asked, and when she turned to face him she read the scorn on his face—scorn that hid a dozen deeper emotions.

If only she could ease his pain. Though she felt no fondness for this man who would destroy everything she loved at Wenlock, she could not bear to see him in agony. "It takes time," she whispered, licking her lips at the lie. Giving him false hope was no better than inventing a falsehood. She swallowed against the thickness in her throat. "May I take his shirt?"

He seemed about to question her, but motioned impatiently instead. "Take everything. His clothes and toys are without meaning to me."

She reached for a shirt that was soft and felt as if it had been worn often, perhaps loved, and also took a tiny pair of soft boots. Tucking the items under her arm, she followed Garrick back to the main chamber where the baron slept. The room was larger than her father and mother's chamber at Tower Wenlock, and the stone walls were painted white and covered with tapestries in rich hues of green, gold, and scarlet. The rushes on the floor were piled thick and smelled of roses and cowslip. The hearth, opposite the bed, was built into the wall, and was tall enough for a man to walk beneath its stone arch. Great andirons held split wood ready to be lit for the evening fire.

Castle Abergwynn was a keep fit for a king, she thought, and yet the man who was its monarch was unhappy and lonely. She sensed much pain in this room.

Suddenly aware of her thoughts, she looked up and found Garrick staring at her, his countenance thoughtful, his arms crossed over his broad chest. His expression no longer harsh, he was almost handsome in a savage way. His features were bold but even, his lips thin and sensual. His eyes, a flinty gray, bored into hers in such an intimate manner that her silly heart skipped a beat.

She couldn't help swallowing, not from fear but from a restlessness she felt deep within her heart and soul. The silvery sheen of his eyes and the firm set of his jaw caused a lightness in her head, and her breath came in shortened bursts. "There was someone with the boy when he was last seen," she said, as much to break the awkward silence between them as to find an answer.

"Aye. His nurse, Jocelyn."

"She has not returned?"

"She was with Logan that day and disappeared with him," Garrick said, his brow furrowing again. "Come." He again took her arm, but this time his grip was less punishing, his expression far from angry. She felt the warmth of his fingertips, but no longer sensed fury flowing through his blood as he guided her through the antechamber to a small room that held two beds. "This was Logan's chamber," he explained, motioning to the smaller bed. "The boy slept there."

Morgana felt a chill in the room, as if a cold breeze off the sea had stolen in through the cracks in the castle walls and settled here in this empty chamber. Her skin prickled slightly as she approached the larger bed.

"Jocelyn slept there. Close by, in case the boy needed anything," Garrick explained.

"She was fond of Logan?" Morgana asked.

Garrick nodded, his eyes still trained on his son's empty bed. "I would not entrust my son's safety and upbringing to anyone else. Jocelyn, though only a maid, had been with my wife since she was a child. They had grown up together, and Jocelyn was Astrid's choice of a servant when we were wed. Jocelyn grieved sorely when my wife died. She would not have harmed the boy. She loved Logan as if he were her own." His voice had grown quiet.

Morgana closed her eyes for a second and felt the icy breath of death against her face. She lifted the coverlet of Jocelyn's bed and shivered from deep within.

"You've seen something," Garrick guessed when Morgana's eyes flew open and she dropped the fur blanket.

"No . . . no vision," she admitted, though *something* wasn't right here. Something within these cold stone walls was very, very wrong.

Morgana's heart thumped with fear, and her footsteps faltered as she crossed the short distance to Logan's bed, afraid of what she might feel as she touched the furs that were piled upon the feather mattress. Again the frigid cold swept through her, chilling her skin from the inside.

"What is it?" Garrick demanded. His eyes had become intense, as if he, too, felt the icy hand of death.

" 'Tis nothing. Just a coldness. As if something . . .

wrong . . . something evil . . . has happened," she said, her voice shaking.

He crossed the room and grabbed her shoulders. "By the blood of Christ, witch, tell me what you've seen! Is my boy alive?"

"I've seen nothing!" Morgana assured him. " 'Tis but a feeling I have that something is wrong. Very wrong."

His lips flattened, and he cursed the fates. "God's teeth, Morgana, I *know* something is wrong. My boy is missing. The maid is missing. But what I do not know is what happened to them. Tell me!"

"Would that I could!"

"Yet you suddenly fear for my son's life," Garrick surmised. "I see it in your eyes."

She rubbed her arms, trying to warm her cold skin. "I'm afraid that someone has betrayed you."

A sharp rap sounded upon the oaken door of Garrick's chamber. "M'lord?" the sentry called through the heavy wood, and Garrick crossed through the anteroom to fling the door open. Morgana followed him and watched as the guard and Garrick exchanged words.

As the sentry left, Garrick held out his hand to Morgana. "Come. We will finish this later," he said, his gaze resting for a second in hers. "But make no mistake, we *will* finish it. Now 'tis time we went downstairs." He wrapped his strong fingers familiarly around her smaller hand, and his eyes darkened with an unnamed emotion that was but a shadow passing quickly from his gaze. He tried to smile, but the grin faltered and for a second Morgana's breath felt trapped in her throat. With a strange premonition she knew that Garrick was about to lower his head and touch his lips to hers. A strange, not unwanted, anticipation stole into her heart, causing it to beat as quickly as the wings of a dove.

The seconds dragged out until a quiet cough caught Morgana's attention, stealing her gaze from the enchantment of Garrick's face.

"Morgana!" a low male voice exclaimed as Strahan of Hazelwood entered Garrick's chamber. He stood nearly as tall as Garrick, and above a hawkish nose his dark eyes moved from Morgana to Garrick and back again.

Morgana stiffened at the sound of his voice and tilted her chin upward. "Sir Strahan," she said, though her stomach roiled at the thought of this man as her husband. His skin was smooth, his stature that of a knight. He did nothing to offend her, and in a dark way he was handsome, yet the frigid current in the depths of his eyes curdled the contents of her stomach.

"What keeps you?" Strahan asked. " 'Tis time we went downstairs and announced our betrothal." He glanced meaningfully at his cousin.

"We will be but a moment, Strahan," Garrick assured him. "Morgana was trying to help me find Logan."

"In your chamber?"

One corner of Garrick's mouth lifted. "Wherever need be."

Strahan's lips became a thin, unbending line. "Lady Clare awaits you."

"We will be but a minute more," Garrick said, dismissing his cousin.

Strahan, his anger barely reined in, nodded stiffly, turned on a booted heel, and strode out of the room.

Shoving his hair from his eyes, Garrick wondered why he felt the need to bait Strahan. His cousin had every right to be offended to find his wife-to-be in another man's bedchamber, especially since Garrick had been about to kiss her. Yea, and if he were truthful with himself, he'd been bedeviled by thoughts of Morgana night and day, lustful thoughts that kept him awake at night and caused him to be surly during the daylight hours.

He'd been gruff with his men, barked orders, and expected excellence on the most mundane of tasks, all because of this woman and how she'd turned his head about.

Not since Astrid had he wanted a woman so fiercely. He thought about his wife and mourned her yet again. Why was he lusting after another man's intended?

He slid a glance at Morgana and found green eyes that held mystery and promise. If nothing else, Morgana of Wenlock was a free spirit, a woman who could enchant a man with a wistful look or flay his pride to ribbons with her whiplike tongue.

"Come," he said, pulling on her hand and following after his cousin. "Strahan is right. 'Tis time you took your place by his side."

"I'll not—"

"Don't argue with me, woman," he growled, angrier at himself than at her protest.

She yanked back her hand and glared up at him. "You would not so easily accept marriage to one you distrusted, m'lord."

"I would do as my king asked."

"Then pray that Edward is a kind man who will not ask you to marry an ugly, barren Scottish lady who would hate the very sight of you and would rather slit your throat than lie with you."

He grabbed her then and forced her up against the wall.

"Perhaps you'd best send up a prayer of thanks that you are to marry Strahan and not me, for I swear that if I were wed to a woman whose tongue was as cutting as a butcher's blade, I'd find a way to tame her!"

"What if she would not be tamed?" Morgana asked, barely daring to breathe, her back rigid against the stone wall. Her breasts were rising and falling, their peaks pushing against the cloth that separated his body from hers, and yet her breath came shallow and fast. She knew she was being willful and defiant, arguing with a baron much more powerful than her father, a man known for his black moods and vengeful ways, a lord who had the king's ear, and yet she could not stop the challenging words from spewing from her mouth.

"I would find a way," Garrick insisted, his body pressed hard against hers. "Now, no more arguments." Taking her roughly by the elbow, he again started for the stairs. "Come," he whispered as his breath caressed the shell of her ear. "Your beloved awaits."

Eleven

emember," Garrick muttered to Morgana as they started down the stairs, "everyone here knows you claim to be a sorceress—"

"I make no such claim!"

"—so be on your best behavior." He cast her a look then, a kinder glance than any he'd offered her so far. The hint of a smile flashed against his dark skin, and Morgana caught a glimpse of the man he'd been before tragedy had robbed him of all that he held dear. She wondered what Maginnis would have been like if his wife had not died and his child not vanished. She couldn't help but think that buried deep behind his fierce exterior was a gentler, more thoughtful man.

As they climbed down the stairs, Garrick's touch was warm. The hand on her elbow seemed possessive, though she knew she was imagining that thought, just as she had imagined that he wanted to kiss her in his chamber. He was guiding her to her betrothed. And to her doom.

In the great hall bustling servants carried trays laden with cups of ale and wine. Musicians played their lutes and pipes, and pages attended the raised table where household members and honored guests were already seated, drinking wine and talking among themselves. Morgana caught Strahan's eye as he lifted his cup, then drank slowly, his throat working. His gaze, over the rim of the cup, was almost mocking as he stared at her.

Morgana resisted the urge to flee—not that she could have with Garrick's firm grip on her arm. She tossed back her hair and took in the surroundings, purposely avoiding Strahan's smoldering gaze.

Garrick introduced her to his sister, a tall, regally built woman with large gray eyes that seemed to stare into Morgana's very soul. Her tunic was gold brocade, and an elegant necklace of emeralds encircled her long neck. Clare's smile was warm, and though she cast her brother a look of disapproval that Morgana didn't understand, the smile she offered Morgana seemed genuine. There was a pride in Clare's bearing, and Morgana guessed that though Garrick was lord of the manor, his sister ran the household.

Garrick's younger brother, Ware, was seated beside Clare. A striking boy with black hair and eyes the color of the sea, he blushed when he was introduced to Morgana, and from the stubborn set of his mouth, she guessed that he and Garrick were often on opposite sides in an argument. Ware's eyes lingered a little too long on the swell of Morgana's breasts before he forced his gaze back to the musicians at the far end of the hall in the minstrel gallery high over the screens separating the corridor from the great room. Music rose with smoke and laughter to the lofty ceiling and everyone, save Garrick and Morgana, seemed in a festive mood.

Strahan stood as she approached. His smile dazzling, his brown eyes gleaming as if with mischief, he took her hand, kissed it, and offered her a seat next to him. "You're more beautiful than I remember," he said, his voice soft and pleasant, before shooting his cousin a hard glance. But Garrick was already seating himself, as if he cared not about Strahan and his bride to be.

They drank of the wine set before them, and to Morgana's ultimate humiliation, Garrick announced to all the others in the great hall that she and Strahan were to be wed.

Though she forced a smile, her innards withered and she visibly cringed. Strahan grinned broadly and leaned close to talk to her as a trumpet sounded and the first course was carried in on silver platters: boiled mutton served with a pudding and spiced sauce, a pike stuffed with almonds, pheasants, and a baked custard in pastry. Strahan was a gentleman, sharing his trencher and cutting the meat before offering her the choicest morsels, but Morgana could barely swallow.

She suspected that beneath his manners and courtly charm, Strahan's heart beat as black as a raven's wing. There was no gentleness about him, only a honed manner that hid the cruelty in his soul. She closed her eyes, sending up a prayer for divine intervention, hoping that God would see fit to untie the knot of the matrimonial noose Lord Garrick had strung about her neck.

"A prayer, m'lady?" Strahan asked, his thin lips twisting in amusement. He knifed a joint of pheasant and wiped his fingers on his bread.

"Of thanks," she lied, hoping God wouldn't strike her dead for lying just yet.

"So you are pleased by my offer of marriage?"

"Pleased?" she repeated, then decided the truth might be the best measure. Strahan was a prideful man. Perhaps he was vain enough to think that any woman would want him, including her. There was a chance that, knowing her feelings, he would decide to call off the wedding. "Nay, I'm not pleased."

Slowly he licked the edge of his knife, and she wondered if he might cut his tongue. "Many women would kiss the ground should they be chosen to be my bride."

"I am not many."

"Aye. And that is why I want you for my wife. Because you are different, Morgana of Wenlock." Sheathing his blade deliberately, he turned to look her full in the face. "You have nothing to fear, little one. I will see to all your wants as well as your needs." He touched her lightly on the arm, and she tensed, forcing herself not to recoil from him.

"I do not want to be wed," she said flatly, though over the noise of the minstrels' songs, clattering tableware, and conversation, no one but Strahan heard her.

The ghost of annoyance crossed his handsome features, but he quickly locked the phantom away. "You will be happy, Morgana. I will see to it."

Morgana started to argue, but the murderous look he sent her caused her heart to freeze, and she forced her traitorous tongue to be still. She had no idea why Strahan wanted her to be his wife; she had not a large dowry, nor would she make a great lady. Yea, she could learn the art of running a household, but she knew that her skills were more suited to becoming a knight or a huntsman—hardly qualities a man would want for a bride.

Or a spy, she thought dismally as she remembered her escape from Tower Wenlock and her father's punishment. But Strahan would have no use for a traitor—or would he? She swallowed a thick chunk of pheasant and nearly choked.

To avoid the worrisome turn of her thoughts, she tried to listen to the songs and watch the jugglers and acrobats as they performed, but the knowledge that Strahan was there, so close, nearly touching her, caused her to be anxious.

Once, while trying to force the food past her lips, Morgana looked up and caught Springan peeking through the curtain. The maidservant's face was pasty white, her eyes nearly black with ire as she glared at Strahan and Morgana. Then, upon meeting Morgana's gaze, her expression again became pleasant and she quickly disappeared behind the curtain, leaving Morgana to wonder if she had imagined the hatred glowing in the servant girl's eyes.

Somehow, while the musicians and poets entertained, Morgana managed to pick her way through the meal and reply when spoken to. The festivities continued, but she was able, by pleading excessive weariness, to break away from Strahan and make her way back to her chamber. She nearly ran from the hall, aware that not only Strahan but also Garrick and his blasted family were watching her slip away from the loud room.

The rest of the household was still making merry, celebrating their lord's safe return. Music and laughter and a few bawdy jokes trailed after her as she climbed the staircase. Morgana could stand the confines of this rich man's castle no more. In her room she bolted her door, then tore off her fancy clothes, her mind coming up with a hundred ways of escape—all of them impossible. "Curse Abergwynn," she muttered between her teeth as she dug through the wardrobe for her favorite black tunic and gratefully slipped it over her head.

Sheathing her dagger she waited, pacing the bedchamber anxiously until, as the hours passed and the moon rose higher in the sky, the noise from the great hall dwindled. She heard footsteps pass by her door and imagined that they hesitated, but fortunately no one knocked or disturbed her. For that, at least, she was thankful. Eventually the castle was silent, and she assumed most of the guests and servants had at last fallen asleep.

Good. She could stand the confinement no longer. Hardly daring to breathe, she took Logan's tiny tunic and opened her chamber door. Well-oiled hinges hardly let out a creak as she slipped through the opening and closed the oaken door behind her. Holding her breath, she crept along the corridor close to the shadowy walls, out of the glow of the rushlights and candles, and made her way down the steps and through the door to the inner bailey. She felt guilty about unlocking the door, but told herself she would be out for only a few minutes—long enough to breathe in the sea air, which would help her fight the feeling that she was to be held captive the rest of her life.

Outside, the moon was a fat crescent in the ink black night. Clouds drifted across the sky, obscuring the few stars that dared wink in the heavens. A breeze blew over the castle walls, smelling faintly of the brine of the sea as it played through the vines and fruit trees near the kitchen. Morgana moved quietly, not wanting to wake the dogs and horses that were kept in the outer bailey or disturb the sentries positioned on the thick walls of the castle.

Somewhere in the distance a wolf howled, and Morgana thought of the dog she'd left at Wenlock. Her heart ached to think that he was chained near the stables, tethered and never allowed to run free. *Just like me,* she thought, her skin prickling a bit as the wolf cried again.

Not far from the armory, a fishpond reflected a silver swath of moonlight as the breeze danced across the shimmering surface, sending ripples through the water. Morgana knelt on the bank of the pond, closing her eyes and feeling the sigh of the wind against her face.

She heard the gentle lap of the water, the flap of the wings of a night bird stalking prey, and far in the distance, again the muted cry of a wolf.

"Help me, Lord," she prayed as she touched the neckline of Logan's tunic. "Help me find the boy, Logan. Guide me to him and keep him safe," she whispered into the breath of the wind, listening for the voice. "Please talk to me. . . . Let me know how to find Garrick's son. . . ."

Garrick stood in the shadow of the scullery, hidden by an empty cart, watching as the witch knelt, holding Logan's tunic in her hands. He'd followed her down the stairs and into the moonlight, silently observing her as she fell to her knees by the pond, her black hair blowing free, her face turned toward the moon. Soft words caused her lips to move, and she closed her eyes, calling up some magic—or praying to a heathen god. Her fingers twisted in the folds of Logan's tunic, and Garrick stayed in the shadows, his heart beating an unfamiliar rhythm as he observed her ritual.

He heard no chants. He saw no sacrifice. No blood was spilled, nor were any candles lit. Perhaps she talked to the wind, but she spoke as if in prayer. Indeed, had he stumbled upon her and known her not, he would have thought she was kneeling to worship.

From the distant hills he heard the cry of a wolf, and the hairs on the nape of his neck lifted one by one. One hound in the outer bailey offered a quick reply, but the wolf was silent, and aside from the creak of a bucket as it swung in the well and the incessant pounding of the sea against sand a hundred feet below, the night was quiet.

Morgana placed one hand in the water and moved it from side to side as if she could see into the pond's clear depths. Then she slowly rose and, with a hasty glance over her shoulder, hurried along the thick stone walls of the inner bailey and past the blacksmith's hut. From his position near the cart, Garrick watched her open the door of the stables and hurry inside. He looked up at the gatehouse where two sentries were posted, but neither they nor any of the other guards had noticed a mere slip of a girl moving about the castle as if she had every right to steal through the keep.

As he followed her, he thought of her foolishness at Tower Wenlock, the home she loved so dearly, and how easily she had escaped the fortress's walls, letting down Wenlock's defenses for the sake of a spell.

Here at Abergwynn, where she felt no such loyalty, she might prove dangerous to the entire castle's safety. Garrick had considered posting a guard at her door, but he'd decided to treat her like a guest, not a prisoner. And in truth, he'd been mystified by her, wanting to see for himself how she would go about practicing the black arts. Aye, she was unlike any other woman he'd met, and yet he was unconvinced that she was possessed of magic and spells and power.

The stable door was still open a crack, and he slipped inside. The smell of horse dung and dust, dry straw and leather, sweat and urine, mingled in the air. A horse snorted and pawed against its tether as Garrick passed. Slowly his eyes grew accustomed to the darkness. The sound of Morgana's voice, soft as the murmur of leaves turning in the wind, floated toward him.

"You see, Phantom, I've not forgotten you," she whispered, rubbing the mare's neck fondly and burying her face in the horse's coarse mane. The little mare nipped at her hand, and Morgana laughed quietly. "Ahh, you know me so well, don't you? Well, here you go, taken right from the lord's table, stolen from right beneath his nose, mind you." She offered Phantom a bit of apple she'd hidden in her sleeve, and the mare's soft lips swept the tasty prize from her palm.

"So now you're a thief as well as a witch." Garrick's voice resonated in the darkness. Morgana nearly leapt from her own skin, and several horses snorted and neighed, tossing their heads and rolling eyes that suddenly showed white.

"What the devil are you doing here?" she said, trying to keep her voice steady while she stared into the darkness. The only light in the long building came from small, high windows that had not been shuttered and allowed fresh air and moonlight into the dusky interior. Still, she could not see his face or even his form, though from the sound of his voice she knew he was close.

" 'Tis I who should be asking you why you are in the stables so late."

"I could not sleep."

"Neither could I."

He was closer now, his voice nearer. The horse next to Phantom shifted and minced as a boot scraped the hard dirt floor. All at once he was standing next to her, pinning her between himself and the mare. Phantom tried to shift away, but because of her tether she could not. "Think you of escape, Morgana?" Garrick asked, and in the moon's silver glow, seeping through the open door, she could see his chiseled features set in vexation as he stared down at her. He stood nearly a foot taller than she, but she refused to be intimidated by the sheer size of him.

"Escape the thick walls of Castle Abergwynn?" She almost laughed at his question. "Even I am not foolish enough to think I can steal away." Ah, but she would leave this castle—aye, even this land—far behind her if she could. They both knew it, as they both knew there was no escape from a fortress so strong as this keep. Mayhap, should she live here for years, she would find a way to flee these high stone walls, but she couldn't think in terms of months, let alone years. No, she could not escape, though living here as a virtual prisoner would surely kill her before she could make plans to depart. "I was restless and came to check on my mare," she lied.

"But you stopped at the pond." Garrick had plucked a piece of straw from the manger and twirled it between thumb and first finger, and even in the darkness Morgana saw the motion.

"Aye, to see the moon's reflection."

"You had Logan's tunic with you."

Her heart dropped. He wanted so much, and if only she could tell him anything about his child, she would. "I tried to see his image in the water. I prayed God would show me how to find Logan."

"And did you get an answer?" Garrick asked, dropping the straw.

"Nay, but sometimes God is long in replying. We must be patient."

"*I* have been patient," Garrick replied harshly, and a horse in the next enclosure began to snort. "Are you finished here, or are you planning to take your mare for a midnight ride?"

She knew that he was jesting, yet the thought of riding astride Phantom, her hair blowing free, the air rushing past her face, was a pleasant one. "Tomorrow, if you have the time, I would like to follow the trail where your son was last seen. If I am to find the boy, I must be able to go where he went, to walk in his shoes."

"He was but a child; he did not go where he pleased."

"But neither was he a prisoner, and though he was always accompanied by his nurse or a guard, he had freedom."

He heard the irony in her words. "You're a guest, not a prisoner."

"A guest?" she threw back at him. "Do you force all your guests to visit you and have them do your will by threatening their lives and the lives of their families?"

"I have not done so."

"Did you not, in the chapel at Wenlock, vow that you would be the death of all who lived within the tower if I failed to find your son?"

He didn't respond, but the leather of his boots creaked as he shifted his weight.

Morgana went boldly on, though her palms had begun to sweat and her heart was hammering with dread. "Well, Baron of Abergwynn, if I am to find the boy—and God have mercy on my soul and the souls of my family if I fail—I must be able to go where I will, to follow my heart, to listen to the wind. You say you want your boy back, and though you believe not in my powers, you expect me to make Logan appear to you. I will try to find him, but you must help me in my quest."

"Anything—"

"Then grant me the freedom to go where I please."

Garrick had no reason to deny her the request, except for a suspicion that she might escape him. But as he stared at her, he believed she would stay. She would never put the lives of her family in jeopardy, and though he would not hurt them if she failed, he allowed her to think him ruthless in order to compel her to do what he wanted. "I will let you have your freedom," he said at length, "but you must be accompanied whenever you leave the castle—to ensure your safety as well as to make certain that you stay put."

"I'll not endanger my family."

"I believe you," he said, surprised at the admiration he felt for her bravery. It took courage and perhaps a little foolishness to stand up to him. Few had the nerve. But Morgana of Wenlock continued to amaze him. He held open the stable door and took her hand, guiding her through the shadows so that the sentries would not take notice. However, as they dashed along the walls of the keep and through the door near the kitchen, he was all too aware of this tiny woman with her warm hands and wide eyes. He doubted she was a sorceress; in truth, he thought her just the wayward, spoiled daughter of a rich man who had not the power to mold her into a proper woman. Daffyd, for all his loyalty, was not a strong man; his three headstrong children were proof enough of his weakness.

And yet Morgana was truly different from any woman he'd ever met. Outspoken to the point of being insubordinate, free-spirited, and delighting in the earth and nature, she seemed harmless and enchanting. But a witch? Nay. He could not see her practicing the black arts or weaving spells.

Because of her eccentricity, she was considered a sorceress by some, and Garrick didn't doubt that she, too, thought she could talk to the wind or to any other force of nature. Had he not seen her chanting spells, lighting candles, and communing with the fates on that first curious night by the sea beneath the cliffs supporting Tower Wenlock? So surely she thought she possessed some powers.

Whether that was true or not remained to be seen.

Garrick, not wanting to be caught alone with her, was careful to sneak along the inner curve of the wall, avoiding the moonlight that pooled on the ground and cast the night in shades of pale gray. He felt a fool. He was master of this castle, and no one save the king himself could order him inside. Yet he felt, probably for Morgana's sake, that he had to hide.

Perhaps it was his own impure thoughts that made him so careful. Since spying her at the edge of the pond, he'd felt desire sing through his blood, and this wanton lust that filled his mind with thoughts of lying with her would not disappear. Now, in the darkness, her hand in his as they tried to elude his own sentries, he felt a youthful excitement that he'd long ago forgotten.

They paused at the doorway, taking in shallow breaths, and when he turned to face her, the moon caught her white skin in its luminescent glow, and her eyes seemed rounder, deeper green, and filled with a wondrous innocence that caused his gut to twist. Before he could think twice, he gathered her into his arms, and his lips captured hers with a rising heat that frightened him more than any soldier raising a sword against him. He'd sworn on Astrid's grave that he would never love again, vowed to live a life devoted to her memory.

Though he'd known he would not—could not—remain celibate, he'd promised that he would never again be tangled in a web of emotion from which he could not break free. But this girl, Morgana of Wenlock, caused all his pledges to slip from his mind, and he was caught up in the feel of her lips, trembling and unsure, against his and the weight of her bosom flattening as he pressed her against the wall, his desire sprouting like a young sapling, his body filling with an ache so vast that Garrick wasn't sure it could ever be relieved.

She didn't struggle, and her arms, reluctant at first, wound slowly around his neck. He became bolder—perhaps she was no virgin after all—and his tongue rimmed her lips, flicking against her teeth, probing the velvet-soft recesses beyond.

Morgana moaned, low in her throat, wishing to stop this assault on her senses, but unable to protest. Garrick's strong arms surrounded her. The feel of his muscles, hard against hers, with only the thin hindrance of their clothing, created in her a blinding need to explore further, to return his kiss, to let this tingling sensation go on and on. The smooth stones near the doorway were wedged against her back, but she cared not, felt nothing but the sweet pressure of his lips against hers and the provocative flick of his tongue mating with hers.

She knew, deep in a faraway part of her mind, that what she was doing was dangerous. Men could not be teased. She'd heard from her very own mother how a man, once aroused, was not to be denied. And yet, all Meredydd's warnings seemed to spin away, caught in a useless whirlpool that slipped away from her.

Garrick's breathing was as ragged as her own, his hunger evident in the part of him that pinned her hips to the wall. His fingers tangled in her hair, pulling her head back, and when he drew his mouth from hers, he let his lips trail down her neck, causing a chill to scamper up her spine. Gooseflesh appeared on her skin where his tongue pressed hot and wet against her.

Her knees felt weak, and she would have sagged to the ground had it not been for Garrick's rigid body supporting her. As it was, she was wedged between the wall of the keep and his own hard muscles. He kissed her again, more slowly this time, sucking on her lower lip, and her heart raced so quickly she thought it might burst. Desire, like a nest of butterflies breaking free, fluttered through her blood, and she found herself clinging to him, her hands wound high over his neck.

New sensations assailed her, and her skin quivered for his touch. He groaned and buried his face in her hair, as if trying to restrain himself. When at last he lifted his head, she opened her eyes and saw the smoke of desire still drifting through his gaze.

Studying her features, he could not restrain himself. He knew she was pledged to his cousin and would do anything to break free of the betrothal—perhaps even lie with another man so that Strahan would want her not—but Garrick could not help himself. It had been too long since he'd been with a woman, and his body cried out for this little sorceress with such hunger that he could not stop stroking her smooth skin and kissing her neck. His manhood ached to be set free, and he imagined the warmth of her tight body as he delved deep into her.

He knew that he was playing with fire, that becoming emotionally involved with Morgana was more than dangerous, but though he fought his passion, he was a prisoner to it. He imagined the sight of her breasts, two white globes, full and firm, peaked by dusky pink buds that would beg to be kissed, to be tasted, to be suckled from.

With a groan he gave in. His body was strung as tight as a crossbow, and he reached for the ribbons at her neck, but her small hand stayed his. "Nay. We must not," she whispered, her voice as ragged as his heartbeat. "Someone watches."

What kind of deception was this? Garrick made a derisive sound. "Who?"

She shook her head, but shivered, and the fear in her eyes was real, as if she were certain that unseen eyes were observing them. "I know not."

"No one but the sentries is about."

From the forest there came the cry of the wolf, closer this time, and Garrick felt a cold sliver of fear slice into his heart. Was she but playing a game with him, or did she really believe they were being observed?

Morgana took advantage of his hesitation and slipped through the door. She was careful as she mounted the steps to her room, her felt boots making not the ghost of a noise. She hurried to the door and slid inside, her heart thundering with a painful beat. Oh, she'd been so foolish! What had she been thinking, kissing the beast that was Garrick of Abergwynn? He cared not for her, though his desire was evident enough. Nay, he was used to having women, whomever he chose, and expected them to indulge his whims—even a woman he'd unwillingly betrothed to his cousin!

But her own heart was betraying her. She was beginning to care for the dark lord who had brought her here, though why she felt anything for him, she had no idea. She reached for the bottom of her tunic, intent on stripping and slipping between the covers, when she realized she was not alone. Her heart slammed to her throat as Sir Strahan, leaning against the wall near the hearth, pushed himself upright.

The fire in the hearth had burned low, and the room was lit only by the coals that glowed scarlet, reflecting against the walls and floor.

Morgana swallowed with difficulty and hastily smoothed

her tunic, inching up her chin to meet the darkness of his gaze. "You frightened me. What are you doing here?"

Strahan shook his head. "Just making sure that you were well."

" 'Tis indecent for you to be in my chamber—"

"As it was for you to be in Garrick's room earlier this evening?" Strahan asked, rubbing his chin. "I was worried about you, and I knocked at your door. When you did not answer, I called out. Again you didn't reply, so I opened the door to find that you had not yet slept." He crossed the room slowly, and Morgana's blood turned to ice. Clucking his tongue, he stopped bare inches from her. "Lady Morgana," he said in a voice so low she could barely hear it over her own heartbeat, "up so late and creeping about the keep. Where, I wonder, have you been?"

Twelve

She was with me!" Garrick shoved open the door and stepped inside Morgana's chamber.

"With you, m'lord?" Strahan's voice was scornful, and Morgana, grateful for the darkness, blushed at the thought of just how intimate she'd been with Garrick, though she felt no obligation to Strahan. As despicable as Lord Garrick was, she knew instinctively that he was a better man than his cousin.

"We were trying to find Logan," Garrick explained evenly.

"Now? In the middle of the night?" Strahan couldn't hide the sneer in his voice. His eyes, glowing with cold jealousy, reflected the dying embers of the fire. "And tell me, cousin, did you find him?"

"Not yet," Garrick said, "but I've been told we must be patient." He cast Morgana a look, and she managed a wavering smile. "Patience is not known to be my strongest quality."

"Yea, it well may be your weakest," Strahan agreed, but the doubt did not leave his tone. "However, I've always known you to be true to your word, Garrick, and I would not believe that you would do anything dishonorable to me or to my bride."

The unspoken accusation hung on the air like a bad smell.

Morgana was glad for the darkness and swallowed with difficulty.

But Garrick managed a grin. With a hollow laugh, he threw an arm around his cousin's shoulders, guiding him out the door. "Come, Strahan. Let us find a glass of wine and a game of dice before we rest."

Morgana closed the door and sagged against it. Her heart was racing, and a sheen of sweat moistened the back of her neck. In all of her dreams she would never have imagined that these two men she detested would be arguing over her. Closing her eyes, she slowly let out her breath and tried to calm down. In the darkness, her face was suffused with color and her cheeks were hot to the touch of her fingers. To think she'd kissed Lord Garrick, the brute himself, and behaved like a common wench! She'd *wanted* to feel his hands upon her. She'd opened willingly to his kisses, wanting more, feeling tingling sensations that seemed to center deep in her womanhood. It had taken all her strength to push his hand away when he started to touch her breasts. Even now the thought of his flesh against hers brought a tide of warmth to her skin. *Lord help me!*

She had to forget his kiss, forget the wanton heat that had swept through her blood. Mayhap it was just the night, the fear and excitement of being alone in the bailey with him. But deep in her heart she knew, she *feared* that this one passionate kiss was just the beginning. Angrily she pulled her tunic over her head and climbed between the linen sheets. But as she lay in the darkened room, she wondered what it would feel like to have Lord Garrick in bed beside her. Would his kiss forever cause flames to lick through her bloodstream, or had she responded more from surprise than from desire?

She pulled the covers over her head. How could she conjure up such vile but strangely pleasant thoughts? Squeezing her eyes shut, she willed sleep to come and denied that she felt any attraction to Garrick of Abergwynn. But her wayward mind spun free, and she imagined herself kissing Garrick as they lay in a fragrant field of clover, their bodies without clothes, perspiration molding them together, their arms and legs entwined, the warmth of the Welsh sun on their bare backs and legs.

The vivid picture disturbed her, for it was so like a vision that for a moment she thought she'd seen her future. Her breathing stopped at the thought. A future? Here? With the baron? Was her gift playing tricks upon her? Hadn't her grandmother foretold that she was to marry Strahan of Hazelwood? Startled, her heart suddenly thundering, she opened her eyes and sat bolt upright. As she stared at the moon through her window, she wound a finger in her hair and swallowed nervously. Nothing good could come of her attraction to Garrick, and yet a small part of her decided that being a guest within the walls of Abergwynn was not such a curse after all.

The next day she expected to see Garrick at dawn. She thought that before she could wake and climb into her clothes, she'd be roused by a tremendous pounding at her door. She would find Garrick, his black mood consuming him again, impatient and demanding that she find his son or suffer the consequences.

However, Morgana spent the morning at Mass under Lady Clare's watchful eye and at breakfast, where once again Clare was nearby. Garrick was seated far away, as if he wanted to keep her at a great distance. After the meal, Lady

Clare walked her through the castle, showing her the buttery, pantry, and scullery and introducing her to the servants in each of the quarters. The maids and pages were more than polite, curtsying and smiling kindly, but Morgana caught the glint of amusement in their eyes, the curiosity in their glances. The hefty cook crossed her bosom as if to ward off evil spirits as Morgana left the kitchen and followed Clare upstairs. Only a large, silent woman named Cailin, who seemed to be in charge of the rest of the servants, gave her so much as a kind but grudging "Hullo."

They passed two servant girls carrying laundry on the stairs. " 'Tis bad luck to have a witch in the castle," the tall one whispered loud enough for Morgana to hear.

"Mayhap she's not a witch," the second servant, a buxom girl with slanted eyes, said.

"Then she's a heathen. Same thing, if you're askin' me."

"Enough!" Clare ordered, whirling at the top step. "Now, mind your duties and quit wagging your tongues. This is Lady Morgana, and you're to treat her as you would any lord or lady who is a guest in this castle!"

"Yes, m'lady," they said in quick unison.

Clare turned again. "Come, Morgana."

Morgana gritted her teeth and held her head high as she climbed the remaining steps.

In the sewing room, women skilled with needle and thread were cutting, sewing, and embroidering gowns and linens. Ells, great lengths of cloth, were being cut and sewn into tunics, mantles, and cloaks. Morgana had never seen so many different fabrics in rich hues of scarlet, saffron, and purple. At Tower Wenlock there were only two skilled seamstresses and never more than four or five ells of cloth.

A tall, thin blond woman named Mertrice was working

on a mantle trimmed in ermine, and behind her, rabbit, beaver, and fox hides were piled carefully in the corner and kept under the sharp eye of the head seamstress. Again, the girls working so effortlessly with needle and thread were polite upon meeting Morgana, their smiles of greeting seemingly sincere. But as they resumed their work, Morgana saw the sly looks cast from the corners of their eyes.

Morgana was thankful to leave the room and sweep down the stairs after Clare. Outside, the sun was shining, and only a few clouds floated across the sky. Morgana felt a small sense of freedom as Clare pointed out the dovecote and beehives, in which she obviously took great pride. They stopped at a bench in the garden between the mulberry trees and climbing vines. Roses were beginning to leaf while gillyflowers and marigolds were promising blooms.

"Garrick tells me I am to make you into a lady," Clare observed. Her brows were drawn together as if the thought was perplexing. "He also mentioned that I'm to do the same with your sister."

Morgana brightened at the thought of Glyn. As miserable as Glyn was, at least she was kin, and Morgana missed her sister as she missed all of her family. "You'll have less trouble with Glyn," Morgana predicted.

"Why is that?"

"Glyn wants nothing more than to marry a wealthy baron and run a large keep of her own." A shadow played on the bailey, and Morgana watched a hawk circling overhead before it turned and dived swiftly to the field on the other side of the castle walls, away from her view.

Clare brushed a tiny gnat from her sleeve and frowned. "And this—marriage to a baron and running a castle—is not what you want, Morgana?" Clare's large gray eyes were kind, her expression more worried than disapproving, and yet Morgana was not sure she could confide in the sister of the baron.

"I am to marry Sir Strahan," she said quietly. "It has been arranged by my father and Lord Garrick."

"Had you no say in the matter?"

"I was told my own wants were not important." She lifted a shoulder as if accepting her fate while inside she burned at the injustice of it all.

"Strahan is a good man," Clare pointed out. "He does need a little straightening out, but a strong woman will guide him well—as long as he does not realize that you are guiding him." She frowned thoughtfully as if she understood Morgana's reticence. "He, of course, thinks only a man can make decisions—he is much like his father. But my aunt was a wise woman, and though Uncle Henry thought he made the decisions and ran the estates, it was her hand that was gently pushing him to make the correct choices. When she died, he married a foolish younger woman who knew no more about running a castle than she did about drawing a sword. Eventually they lost everything. Had Aunt Ellen lived, Uncle Henry would never have lost Castle Hazelwood to Osric McBrayne." Clare rubbed her fingers together. "Strahan will treat you well. He will see that you are provided for and kept safe and that you want for nothing."

Except love, Morgana thought, for love was a notion of the foolish. Troubadours and minstrels could sing of love, and poets could spin tales of lovers whose hearts beat as one, but, in truth, did love really exist? No, she decided, there was no true love, not in real life.

Clare sighed, and her gaze was focused beyond Morgana

and over the grass of the inner bailey toward the chapel. Her hands fidgeted nervously in the wrinkles of her skirt. "I've heard the most important reason you returned here with Garrick. Aside from marrying Strahan, you're here to help my brother find his son."

Morgana felt suddenly uncomfortable. She watched the bees circle and buzz near the hives. "Aye, but so far I've not helped him much."

"It may be an impossible task."

"He needs to know what has happened to his son."

"Does he?" Clare shook her head. "I wonder. There's a good chance that something horrid has befallen the child, and what good would come of Garrick's knowledge of his boy's fate?" She touched Morgana lightly on the arm. "When Astrid died, Garrick was beside himself. He wouldn't eat for days. Had it not been for the child, I do not know that he would have kept his mind. He loved his wife more than any man should love a woman. He was planning to marry someone else when he met her, but Astrid turned his head, and he would have done anything for her. He survived her death, I fear, only because of Logan."

Morgana's heart seemed to stop. She had just denied to herself that true love existed, but it seemed that Garrick had once found a love so pure that he could never forget it. She ached a little, for she felt a small current of jealousy of the woman who could elicit such deep emotions from so powerful a man.

Clare smiled sadly. "Sometimes my brother is not as strong as he thinks he is," she said. She drew a line in the gravel with the toe of her boot and said thoughtfully, "If he uncovers the truth about his son, and if that truth is unpleasant, I know not how he'll survive."

As if deciding she'd confided too much, Clare suddenly stood and walked along the gravel path, her hands in the vast folds of her rust-colored tunic, and Morgana followed her. "There is a rumor of trouble to the north, with the Scots. If Garrick is called away to fight for Edward, he'll need all his strength, all his wits. He cannot be worried about the fate of his child." At Morgana's horrified expression, Clare placed a hand on the girl's arm. "Of course it is natural that he wants to know. But . . . I am told you have powers, unearthly powers that give you visions. If the vision of Logan will upset Garrick before he readies for war, keep it to yourself."

Morgana thought of Garrick's wrath should he ever find out that she had withheld information about his son's fate. His vengeance would be swift and sure, and all who lived in Tower Wenlock would suffer. Morgana was sure of it. "I promised the baron as well as God himself that I would help Garrick find his child. I cannot go back on my word."

Clare's expression changed slightly, her lips pursing. "Do what you must, Morgana, but please think of the consequences. Castle Abergwynn and all that belongs to Abergwynn, even Llanwynn and Wenlock, are subject to Garrick. What would happen to all of us if he became so wrapped up in vengeance that he disobeyed the king or cared not for the townspeople? I've seen it happen before, Morgana. Vengeance can be a man's undoing."

Hours later Garrick sent his vassal, George, to find Morgana. Clare gave her leave of her lessons, and she followed George through the castle and outside, past the gate to the outer bailey where Garrick was waiting. His charger and Phantom had been saddled and, bridles jangling, were trying to pluck some of the spring grass.

"You said you wanted to be taken to the spot where Logan was last seen. We'll go there now," Garrick ordered.

She caught the look that passed between a thatcher working on the roof of the stables and a carpenter who was shoring up the walls, which had begun to lean. She didn't pause to wonder what the men who worked for Garrick thought of her. Mayhap there were many rumors concerning her powers as a sorceress and her relationship with the baron. She spied young Tommy Jackson shoveling manure from the stables. His friends were beside him, muttering under their breath, filling a cart with dung, and, upon seeing Morgana, throwing her hateful looks as they bent to their work.

Tommy's nose was wrinkled, but he put his small shoulders into his task. He, too, glanced up at Morgana, and she managed a smile. His response was to spit on the ground between the gap in his teeth. The hatred on his small face was all too visible, and Morgana knew in an instant that the boy blamed her for his smelly punishment.

"Come." Garrick wheeled his great horse around and, with a signal to the guard, rode through the double-towered gate and beneath the two portcullises. Morgana, upon Phantom, followed Garrick's lead, and her little mare's steps were quick, as if she, too, were anxious to shed herself of the high stone walls of Abergwynn.

As Phantom passed the final gate, she broke into a trot. Sensing a challenge, Garrick's charger flicked his black ears back, and his sleek hide quivered. Morgana leaned forward, and Phantom took off, moving easily into a gallop. The gray mare was quickly beside Warrior, but the stallion wasn't to be outdone and with a smooth stretch of sleek muscles, he exploded into an easy stride and quickly outdistanced Phantom.

"Come on," Morgana whispered, leaning forward, her hair blowing free, her tunic billowing out over the dappled mare's rump. Laughing, tears welling up in her eyes as the wind streamed past her and tangled in her hair, Morgana felt freer than she had since her first terrifying vision of Garrick astride his black steed. "We can best them," she whispered as the mare's strides flattened out and the grassy field swept beneath them in an expanse of green. She couldn't help but laugh, though there was no way Phantom could catch the black destrier.

Garrick pulled up at the edge of the woods, and for once his craggy face was relaxed, a smile, more dazzling than Morgana would ever have imagined, slid from one side of his mouth to the other, rising in crooked mockery as Morgana pulled back on the reins and Phantom tried to nip Warrior's flank.

"Your horse is spirited."

"But foolish, I fear," Morgana said with a laugh as Phantom sidestepped a kick from the larger horse.

"Like her mistress."

"Do not taunt me," Morgana warned, though she couldn't help grinning. Here at the edge of the forest with the sun warming the crown of her head and the smell of the loamy ground filling her nostrils, she couldn't be less than happy. Even the grim prospect of searching for the boy did not weigh down her spirits, so glad was she to be riding free.

"The guards who were with Logan said they took this path," Garrick explained as he pointed to a trail that wound through the thicket and into the gloom. He nudged

Warrior's great sides, and the horse entered the forest, following a trail that seemed, from the tracks of horseshoes embedded in it, to have been traveled by many men on horseback, probably in search of the lad.

Garrick was forced to duck beneath low-hanging branches as he studied the undergrowth. His merry mood soon disappeared, as if the dimness of the forest darkened his spirits. The trail curved suddenly and broke free of the thicket, into an open field where early spring flowers were already in bloom.

To Morgana, the grassland sprinkled with daisies was nearly as gorgeous as the rolling countryside near Llanwynn and Tower Wenlock, but Garrick seemed unaffected by the beauty of the landscape. Instead, his mood darkened even further, and his scowl became fiercer. "Logan was last seen hereabouts," he explained, climbing off his war-horse and studying the ground. Angrily he glared at the ocean and pointed to a finger of land that jutted out into the sea. "See those ruins? That was where Abergwynn was to have been built many years ago. 'Twas already started when the baron changed his mind and built the keep where it stands today. The baron felt that this land was too low, ofttimes thick with fog. The new site provided a better view of the surrounding lands and would be more easily protected."

Morgana studied the ruins and the grounds that stretched between the forest and the headland, but the beauty of the landscape seemed to fade as she realized she stood on the very ground where Garrick's child had last walked. She bent down close to the grass and placed her palm against the cool ground. She pulled the grass aside, scooped some dirt into her palm, and flung it high into the air. "Protect him," she whispered, thinking of Logan's boy.

"What sorcery is this?"

"Shh," she murmured, closing her eyes as she felt a cold shiver of dread tingle between her shoulder blades. The sun passed behind a cloud. A breath of wind teased her hair and brought a chill to her heart. She touched Logan's felt boots, which she kept in a pouch, and a tingle of fear skittered up her fingers and arms. "Holy Mother," she whispered, closing her eyes. Within her mind she heard a scream, but not a child's wail—no, something more fearful and terrifying. The back of her throat tasted of metal as she felt betrayal, as cold as a snake's skin, twist through her mind. *Beware,* a whispery voice rasped in her mind. *Treachery, betrayal, and bloodshed hover within the walls of Abergwynn.* Stunned, Morgana dropped the tiny boots and let out her own silent scream.

Strong hands surrounded her arms, shaking her, and Morgana, already frightened, jerked back. Garrick leaned over her. His face was ashen, his eyes filled with dread. "You've had a vision."

"Nay, only a feeling that something terrible has happened," she said, licking suddenly dry lips.

"Logan," he said, his voice strangled. "He's—"

"I don't know!" She placed a finger on his lips, not wanting him to utter the horrid words. "I saw nothing, but I heard a woman scream."

"There was no sound."

"No, only in my mind." She swallowed hard and let her finger fall from his lips. " 'Tis how it starts—with a voice and then later a vision."

The hands gripping her arms were punishing. "This scream," he said, and skepticism tainted his words. "It belonged to . . . ?"

"I don't know. Perhaps the nursemaid who was with

your son." Morgana's voice was breathless, her insides still cold with fear.

Garrick stared long and hard at the woman in his arms. She had every reason to lie. He'd brought her here against her will, threatened to harm her family if she didn't do as he ordered her, betrothed her to a man she despised, and demanded she find his son against great odds. Why wouldn't she conjure up some sort of tale to appease him? Clever, she was. She'd kept Logan out of immediate danger in her vision, yet bought herself some time. All his instincts told him not to trust her, and yet he felt her tremble in his arms and saw the fear still lingering in her sea green eyes. If she was not telling him the truth, then she was a damn good liar.

"What else did you see?"

Morgana swallowed. "I saw nothing, and yet I *felt* that there was treachery everywhere. There are those whom you trust who would harm you, Garrick," she said, forgetting that he was a baron. "They have betrayed you already—with Logan—but that was just the start."

"A voice told you this?"

She nodded mutely, wishing she knew more.

Garrick released her suddenly, and his eyes searched her face. "If you're lying to me, Morgana, I swear—"

"I'm not! You must believe that someone—someone, I think, who is very close to you—means you harm."

"It's not myself I care about," he threw back at her. "I care only about my son." A rustle in the bushes caught his attention and in a flash of gray-brown fur a wolf bounded from the shadows. Garrick's charger reared and whistled in terror.

The wolf streaked toward Morgana.

Garrick's face drained of blood. He drew his sword and lunged at the beast.

"Nay!" Morgana screamed, throwing herself onto the ground between wolf and man. " 'Tis my dog!" she yelled frantically. "Please—no!" she cried, but Garrick's blade flashed in the sunlight and she turned to yell at the dog. "Wolf—run!"

Wolf wheeled and snarled, his gold eyes glinting with hatred of the man who would slay him, but he turned and, tail between his legs, dashed into the underbrush of the surrounding forest.

"How dare you attack my animal?" Morgana demanded as she climbed to her feet and dusted her skirt.

"*Your* animal!" he thundered in disbelief and motioned to the woods. "*That* beast? I thought he was charging—"

"Alone? Have you ever seen a lone wolf attack a person in broad daylight?" She glared at him as if he were truly a fool. Then, as he lowered his sword, she turned and whistled toward the woods. Slowly, head low, Wolf emerged, his liquid gold eyes focused on Garrick. "It's all right," she assured the dog. When he reached her, she fell to her knees in joy. Burying her hands in the thick fur on his back she buried her face in his neck. "How are you, friend?" she whispered, her throat thick with tears. "How did you find me?"

He licked her face and wagged his tail, and tears of happiness spilled from Morgana's eyes. Oh, how she'd missed this big dog—her companion, her friend! "It's so good to see you," she whispered, her arms circling his neck. Wolf reminded her of home and of all that she had left at Llanwynn. She blinked hard and cleared her throat, all too aware of Garrick. Dashing her hand against her eyes, she slowly stood and smiled from the joy of having the animal with her again. "He must stay with me," she said, motioning to the wolf dog. "He has traveled long to find me and, no doubt, raised my father's anger. He must stay at Abergwynn, Lord Garrick. I will take care of him and make sure that he causes you no trouble."

Garrick eyed the dog thoughtfully and was rewarded with a black-lipped snarl. "This will only add fuel to the gossip against you."

"I care not! He's mine, and he's journeyed hard to find me. I will not turn him away."

With a heavy sigh, Garrick threw a hand into the air and shook his head. "Why not?" he asked the surrounding forest. "First a witch and now a wolf. Why not? Now no one will *think* I've lost my mind, they will know it!" He climbed upon his nervous horse and stared down at Morgana. "Make no mistake, Morgana, the first time there is trouble with him, he will be turned out or slain. If he frightens the children, kills the sheep, or sneaks scraps from Cook's table, he cannot stay within the castle walls!"

"He won't!" Morgana argued with far more confidence than she felt. For Wolf, bless and curse him, had more than his share of faults. But she'd keep her eye on him, and now, finally, she felt she had a friend at Abergwynn. "Come," she commanded the dog, but recalling her vision she felt the footsteps of doom climb up her back.

Thirteen

The voice had been right. There were many who were not as faithful to Lord Garrick as they would have liked him to believe. Morgana, in the next few days at Abergwynn, tried to ignore her own changing feelings for a man who had forced her to leave her family, betrothed her to a knight she couldn't stomach, and then kissed her so passionately that her entire world had seemed to turn upside down. She tingled each time she thought of that one wonderful, hateful kiss.

Within the castle walls she sensed the unspoken thoughts and the traitorous glances cast between some of Garrick's knights. She told herself she was imagining the tension that seemed to simmer in the air, and yet she could not shake the feeling that more than a few of Abergwynn's knights would plot against their lord.

To begin with, she did not trust Strahan, but after observing him with Garrick she had no reason to believe he was less than loyal. Though he was far from kind, he seemed to genuinely respect his cousin, and whenever they were together he placed Garrick and Abergwynn's best interests at heart. In truth, Garrick had been more than generous with Strahan; the castle and lands that were to be bestowed upon Strahan and his bride were valuable and well established. So why would Strahan rebel against a man who was so good to him?

As for the others, most of the knights and servants were outwardly fond of Garrick and prided themselves on being in the command of so able a leader. Only a few appeared discontented, but whether their animosity was directed at Garrick or at her, Morgana wasn't certain. She caught the disdainful looks cast her way and saw the hidden sneers when Garrick ordered the men to accompany her. She decided that the treachery she saw in a few of the men's eyes might exist because they considered their lord to have gone mad to bring into their midst a woman with so dark a reputation. Perhaps those she felt were disloyal were merely superstitious men who questioned Garrick's judgment in dealing with a witch. It could be that the tension she felt crackling between the castle and the bailey wasn't directed at the baron so much as at her.

Even the men she distrusted—Sir Randolph and Sir Charles and a few of their friends—never disobeyed an order and were quick to do Garrick's bidding. Sir York, though grim, did nothing to defy Garrick. Nor did Sir Hunter or Sir Joseph, and yet they made her uneasy with their uncompromising stares and their laughter at her expense. The smug turn of Charles's pinched lips and the lustful gleam in Randolph's eyes made her nervous.

Cailin, the heavy servant, had insinuated that Sir Charles was neglectful in his duties, and Randolph had made more than a few cruel jokes at Morgana's expense, but she'd seen no evidence that either of the men was plotting against Garrick. She wondered if baiting Randolph when she first met him had created a dangerous enemy she would never be able to trust.

As each day passed, Morgana tried to tell herself that the strain in the great hall was due to Garrick's black mood and worries over the fate of his child. Morgana studied with

Clare, became more familiar with the castle, and learned a little of the man who was baron. Most of his servants respected him. Even Cailin, who was often out of sorts, would smile at the mention of Garrick's name.

"Aye, and he's a sad one, that he is," she said, clucking her tongue as she counted the sacks of flour and sugar the provisioner had brought to the kitchen, for she didn't trust the man, and the steward, Cailin was convinced, drank too much to know what he was doing. "This loss of Logan, well . . . I don't know if Lord Garrick will ever recover. First his wife and then his son . . ." Sighing, she moved on to smaller sacks of rice, almonds, and pepper, touching each bag and moving her lips as she counted. "Well . . . he's got it right this time," she said, brushing her fingers on her dusty apron. "But that little twit has been skimming off some of the supplies," she said. "I'm sure of it. I just can't catch him." Vexed, she frowned and cast Morgana a curious glance. "I don't suppose you could work up some of your magic and cause whoever the thief around here is to be covered with a pox or have his hair rot out, could ye?"

Morgana, despite herself, had to swallow a grin. "I don't think so." She'd already quit denying her powers; denial did no good. People, including Cailin, would believe what they wanted to believe, be it good or bad, reasonable or foolish.

"Well, I'll have to find another way to catch him, then, a way that the provisioner isn't clever enough to notice," Cailin muttered to herself. "Mark my words, I'll not be blamed for a loss of wax or vinegar or soap or anything else that snake slithers away with."

"Have you talked to the baron about this?"

"I spoke to the steward, Sir Charles. A lot of good that

did. Charles said he was in charge and would handle any problems, and that, m'lady, is the last I've heard." She ended with a disgruntled snort.

Morgana silently agreed with Cailin. Sir Charles, who continually sent severe, self-righteous glances to follow the path of his hooked nose, made her uncomfortable. She was reminded of a lazy hawk. Even his mouth, pinched into a perpetual frown, added to the beakish appearance of his nose.

Morgana, as she had every day, was attempting embroidery. She pierced her finger with the needle. "Damned sewing!"

Wolf, from a corner, growled.

A horn sounded the approach of guests. Morgana tossed the hated hoop and needle aside and ran to the window where, over the walls of the outer bailey, she spied a double column of riders approaching. Guests! At last, some excitement.

With Wolf on her heels, she dashed into the hallway and started down the stairs where servants were bustling between the partitions. She stopped for a second, silently commanding Wolf to halt. "Shh," she whispered and heard bits and pieces of the excited chatter. From her position on the steps she couldn't help but overhear two of the women servants.

"Is it news of Master Logan?" Mildraed, a laundress with stringy brown hair and huge eyes, asked as she hastened toward the kitchen with a basket piled high with soiled sheets. Waif thin, Mildraed had a keen nose for gossip and could spread a rumor as quickly as she heard it.

"Nay, I think not," Cailin replied, dusting her fingers together.

Mildraed paused to catch her breath. "Who, then?"

"Could be Osric McBrayne, that blackheart, or some other scoundrel."

"Aye, or his daughter again." Nodding sagely, Mildraed balanced her heavy load on her hip. "Since poor Lady Astrid's death, she has been seeking marriage to the baron."

"Hmph," Cailin muttered. "Well, there's no sounding of the alarm, so my guess is that it's not McBrayne, thank the saints!"

Mildraed wasn't about to be turned away from gossip. " 'Tis no secret Sheena McBrayne sought Sir Garrick years ago." She leaned closer to Cailin and whispered, "You know, 'tis said that Sir Garrick was about to ask for Sheena's hand when he met Lady Astrid. Sheena and her father have never forgiven him for breaking the engagement."

"McBrayne's a scoundrel. Just remember it was Osric himself who stole Baron Hazelwood's land." Cailin grunted and started for the kitchen again. "I doubt Sheena would show her face here without her father, and if Osric were about, the knights would stand ready. Mayhap it's word from the king. Those Scots are making trouble again. Mark my words, 'twon't be long before those pagans start a war." She crossed her heavy bosom, and the rest of her words drifted away as she disappeared through the doorway.

Morgana knew the party that was approaching was no war party. No warrior would be so stupid as to plod along in full daylight to attack Abergwynn. With her skirts bunched in her hands and Wolf at her heels, she ran to the front door and nearly collided with Garrick.

She slid to a stop, and he reached out one strong arm to stop her from falling. Glancing down at her, he scowled. His gaze didn't drift away but touched hers with an intimacy that stopped her cold.

For a second her breath was lost in her throat, and she felt the weight of her breasts spilling across his forearm.

"Are you in such a hurry to see your sister?"

"Glyn? Glyn's here?" she said, her voice barely a squeak. Was the beast joking with her?

"Aye, and your brother, too."

"Cadell!" She felt a happiness well up inside her, and to her surprise Garrick's stony countenance broke.

One dark brow quirked in amusement. "Your father led me to believe that you and your sister could not get along— fire and water, he called you."

"Oh, but I've missed her," Morgana admitted, surprised that she could feel such emotion for Glyn. Beautiful, prideful Glyn with her false sense of piety and perfect sense of duty. " 'Tis true that we fought like hens in the yard at times, but . . ." Her throat clogged up a bit, and as the amusement died from Garrick's eyes, she felt a deep pain at the thought of her family and her father's cruel words.

"But . . ." Garrick encouraged softly.

"But she is my blood, and I . . . I've missed her," she repeated, swallowing the thick lump in her throat. She felt a dozen emotions deep inside, and though she didn't want to think about the fact that this man who had once kissed her so wantonly was now restraining her again, she couldn't ignore the heat from his body, so close. She had to bite her tongue to keep from licking her lips in nervousness.

Garrick, too, seemed suddenly aware of her nearness. He released her suddenly, as if her mere touch burned him, which, indeed, it did.

Morgana nearly stumbled, but she caught herself, and with one last glance over her shoulder, she whirled away. In a cloud of purple damask she hurried out the door.

Garrick couldn't help but smile. The excitement in her round green eyes had replaced the torment he'd seen brewing so often in her gaze. For the past few days he'd wondered about her silent agony. Was it just that she missed her family, or was she worried that she would not be able to locate Logan?

Logan. If only he could find his son. As each day passed with no news of the boy, his frustration grew. He was impatient and angry, and since Morgana's "vision," he seethed all the more.

What if she could not lead him to Logan? His eyes slitted. Rubbing the back of his neck, he remembered threatening her in the chapel at Wenlock. Well, she'd asked for it, hadn't she? Baiting him and belittling his men. But his words had been harsh, and she didn't know that he would never attack Tower Wenlock. She'd pushed him, and he'd struck back.

"God's blood," he muttered as another thought assailed him, a thought much more worrisome. Was the darkness in her gaze because she, too, had been tortured over the unbidden passion that had erupted between them that night when he found her in the stables? He'd only kissed her, for the love of Mary, but ever since, he'd spent many sleepless nights dreaming of Morgana, imagining what her soft curves would feel like against his own harder lines. Aye, he'd wakened with an ache in his loins so hard that he'd thought he might burst.

He'd been tempted to go to her, to kiss her again and see where the kissing might lead. But he had not. By his own code of honor he was forced to keep his hands off her. She was Strahan's. He himself had made it so. This black lust that crept into his blood was his own punishment for betrothing her to a man she so obviously despised.

And his desire for her could never be quenched. He'd considered lying with another woman, but the thought of taking a wench or a servant girl left a bitter taste in his mouth. He knew instinctively that he wanted Morgana not only for her body but because he needed more than the feel of her limbs entwined with his; he wanted to reach her spirit, to meet the challenge that she threw at him every time she tilted her chin upward or tossed her hair off her shoulders or gazed steadfastly into his eyes, daring—no, *defying*—him to touch her. Even now the image of her running down the steps caused a hardness between his legs that no other woman would satisfy. *Oh, little witch, why do you torment me so?*

"She's beautiful, is she not?" Strahan's voice brought Garrick up short, and he shifted quickly, hoping that his cousin would not notice the swelling that caused his breeches to bulge. Strahan cocked his head toward the steps down which Morgana had flown.

"Beautiful, aye, but dangerous."

"Dangerous?" Strahan barked out a laugh as they headed into the bailey. "Don't you know? I like my women dangerous." His eyes flashed with a dark flame. "It adds fire to the coupling. A little resistance, a little pain, makes the taking all the better."

Garrick's reaction was quick. His fist tightened, and he nearly hit his cousin, prodding him into a fight.

Strahan glanced at him from the corner of his eye. A cold smirk curved his thin lips. "We have guests," he reminded Garrick.

"Just be careful, cousin," Garrick warned. "The wife you've been promised is not a common wench. She'll need a gentle touch." With all his effort, he uncurled his fingers.

Ignoring the tightening in his gut, he walked swiftly across the spring grass to greet the new arrivals.

Morgana nervously shifted from one foot to the other as Glyn slid gracefully from her saddle and hopped nimbly to the ground. "Isn't it grand?" she whispered to Morgana as she stared at the towering hall rising at the far end of the bailey. "I've never seen such a castle!" Glyn's voice was filled with awe, and her eyes positively shone, until her gaze drifted downward to land upon Wolf. "Oh, no! Did that horrid mongrel actually find his way to you?"

"Aye. Thank God." Morgana rumpled the thick fur at the back of Wolf's neck.

For a second Glyn's smile faltered, but she forced it in place again as she glanced up at the battlements of Abergwynn. "I do believe this is heaven."

"Heaven? It's a pain in the arse if you ask me," Cadell commented under his breath as he leapt to the ground from his mud-splattered mount. However, he managed a thin smirk as Garrick strode up and greeted his guests.

Glyn, dressed in a white and gold tunic and an emerald green mantle, smiled up at him. Her blond hair was braided into thick plaits and coiled at the back of her head. The golden strands were sleek and gleamed in the sunlight. "Lord Garrick, your castle, it's . . . breathtaking," she said, sounding as if her breath had indeed been stolen from her throat. When Garrick kissed her hand, Glyn blushed and sent Morgana a knowing look.

Morgana stood frozen, her blood at once hot and cold with jealousy. Why should she care if Glyn flirted with the baron, and why should it matter that he offered Glyn a kind smile instead of the dark, hostile looks he trained on her? Glyn and Cadell were here, and that was all that mattered.

Glyn slipped her small arm through Garrick's, and they started toward the steps leading to the castle.

"Looks as if Glyn is set upon becoming mistress of Abergwynn," Cadell whispered to her as George ushered him away.

Morgana was left in the bailey, Wolf whining anxiously at her side. "Shh!" she scolded the dog before she noticed that Strahan was watching her intently.

"You're happy that your family is here?" he asked, flashing her a handsome grin.

She nodded, not trusting his charm.

"So am I." He nodded toward the doorway through which Garrick and Glyn had disappeared—the very doorway where Garrick had kissed Morgana with a hunger that had seemed to melt her very bones. "It seems your sister can make Garrick smile. It's been a long time since he's done so." Thoughtfully, he rubbed his chin. "It would be a great relief to me to see Garrick happy again," he said with surprising candor. "Since Astrid's death, he's not been himself, and now the tragedy with Logan . . ."

"Tragedy?" she asked quickly. "But he's only been lost or kidnapped."

For a second a shadow darkened Strahan's eyes. "Come, bride, let us talk of other things. A wedding must be planned."

Fourteen

arrick didn't sleep a wink. He lay in his large empty bed, thinking of Morgana, his body hard and wanting.

Though the night air sweeping through the open windows was cool and damp enough to extinguish the coals in his hearth, sweat trickled down his spine. And he ached. God in heaven, how he ached for her.

In frustration he'd thrown off the covers twice, climbed out of bed, paced to the window, and prayed that his lust would subside. It hadn't. In fact, as dawn drew near, he was nearly crazed with desire, his erection a stiff rod that embarrassed him. He'd spent half the night plotting ways to end Morgana's betrothal to Strahan and the other half cursing himself for wanting the witch. What was it about her he found so fascinating, so damned challenging? Again he sent up a prayer, and he imagined God laughing at him.

"You're a bloody fool," he growled at himself as the cock crowed and the first morning light began to filter softly through the windows, bringing with the grayness of dawn the sounds of the servants rustling about, making ready for the new day. For the past few days Strahan had encouraged him to plan for the wedding, but Garrick refused to allow it until Logan was found.

Garrick dressed hastily and was downstairs before many in the castle had stirred.

Outside, the soldiers were waking, and some of the servants were moving about the yard. In the outer bailey chickens began clucking as a plump servant girl threw them handfuls of grain from a basket. The hens and roosters gathered around her, feathers flying, clawed feet scratching, heads bobbing to snatch up each kernel or fine piece of oystershell. When the basket was empty of grain, the heavy girl crawled into the hen house, rummaged in the nests, and filled the basket with eggs for the cook. Another girl, burdened with large buckets, hurried to the shed to milk the bawling cows. The smith was busy adding wood to his fire, and two half-grown boys packed kindling to the kitchen, where Cailin was already barking out orders.

A laundress carried a huge basket of linens to the trough. She drew water from the well, and the chain creaked and groaned. A boy whom Garrick recognized as the smith's son was skimming fish from the pond with his net. Mornings at Abergwynn continued at the same pace they always had, despite the fact that Astrid was dead, Logan was missing, and a useless witch had started to enchant him.

The gates rattled open, and several of the town children grudgingly ambled inside as the gatekeeper let them pass. The boys and girls headed directly to the stables, and Tommy Jackson, looking barely awake, his hair sticking out at odd angles, joked and laughed with the rest. He noticed Garrick, and his expression changed from gaiety to a scowl. Casting a glare over his thin shoulder, just to show the great baron that he was not intimidated, he followed a well-worn path to the back of the stables where shovels and pitchforks were waiting.

Two creaking wagons followed the boys and girls into the bailey. The first, a new wagon pulled by a sleek horse and driven by the fat tailor, was filled with cloth and furs. The second, rougher wagon rolled slowly into the yard. A sway-backed animal that looked dead on its hooves was yoked to the cart, and a farmer flicked a whip over the beast's ears. The man was rail thin, and his face was bruised. Sacks of grain were stacked in the cart and shifted with each creaky turn of the muddy wheels. Cursing under his breath, the farmer slapped the reins over the bony horse's rump.

Sir Randolph had been speaking with the gatekeeper, but he spotted Garrick. "Halt there, farmer," he said and motioned to Garrick. "This man"—he gestured to the man seated on the sorry-looking wagon—"claims to know something of Logan."

Garrick's gaze landed on the man with a force that caused the farmer to visibly wince. "Is this true?"

"Aye. At least I think so, m'lord." The man scratched his arm nervously before climbing down from his cart and snatching off his hood, displaying in the process a face that was slightly swollen and discolored. Several of the man's teeth appeared to be missing as he bowed at Garrick's feet.

Garrick's muscles tightened, and he hardly dared to hope that the man was speaking the truth. "Tell me. Who are you?"

"Will Farmer. I live three days' ride from here to the east, at the edge of hills."

"And you saw my boy?"

The farmer cast a frightened look at Randolph. "I saw *a* boy, m'lord, in the company of a maid."

"When?"

"Seven—no, eight days ago."

"Describe the boy."

"Red-gold hair with a few freckles, m'lord. Blue eyes, I think. Barely a toddler. Two, mayhap three years old." He went on to describe Logan's clothes and Jocelyn as well. Garrick's teeth clenched, and he wanted to shake the farmer to make the words spill out faster. Feeling a rush of emotion so great that he nearly fell to his knees, Garrick silently thanked God that the boy might still be alive.

Will Farmer nervously rubbed his nose. "As I said, I'm not sure it's your boy, but . . ." He shrugged, letting the rest of his thoughts trail off.

"How did you come upon him?" Garrick asked, trying to keep his hopes from soaring out of control. For all he knew, this man could be lying for his own benefit, though there was an honesty about his weathered face and the calluses on his hands showed that Will Farmer was used to hard work. Garrick found it difficult not to trust him. "What happened?"

"I was robbed. A band of thugs who stalk the hills to the east attacked my cart on the way to market and took my sacks of wool. The maid and boy were with the group—kept prisoners, I'd guess, though I was so frightened I paid little attention and was grateful to get off with my life. The brutes left me for dead, but it takes more than a few punches and kicks to take the life of Will Farmer." He ended his talk with a little bit of pride, but then hung his head. "Had I guessed the boy was yours, m'lord, I would've fought to the very death to save him. But I knew not. . . ."

A thundering rage galloped through Garrick at the thought of Logan and his nursemaid being held by low-life robbers and thieves. Involuntarily, his fingers curled tightly, as if they were already circling the throat of one of the thugs. He turned angry eyes on Randolph. "Tell the steward to buy whatever Will Farmer will sell us from his cart. See that he's fed and rested. Then bring him to my chamber. Tell

Strahan I want twenty of my men ready to ride by noon today." Garrick rested his hand on the farmer's thin shoulder. "Thank you, Will Farmer. Now rest a bit and then tell me again what you know of my son. Should I find Logan by acting on your words, you will be rewarded."

Finally! Word of his son! Garrick tried to calm the eager beat of his heart and the rage that mingled with hope as it pulsed through his veins. This farmer's story could be false, or it might be yet another worthless bit of news that led to nothing. Garrick couldn't allow his hopes to soar, lest they be dashed again.

Morgana, standing at the bed, slid a glance at her sister. Glyn was pale, her throat worked, and she kept her eyes averted from the gash on the leg of the armorer's son. "This is important," Clare was saying as she washed the wound with a clean cloth and warm water. "Many times after battle you will be in charge of ministering to the wounded. Your knowledge and your ability to work swiftly will determine whether your husband's best soldiers live or die."

The boy, no more than sixteen and in too much pain to be embarrassed that his thigh was exposed to the women, moaned and squeezed his eyes shut. He tried to writhe in agony, but Clare's sharp tongue and the heavy armorer himself forced the boy's shoulders back against the sheets.

"He's a foolish one," the armorer gritted out, though there was concern in his dark eyes.

"He'll be fine," Clare assured the father.

Looking at the size and discoloration of the gash, Morgana wasn't so sure. The lad, known for his particular lack of brains, had been playing with a sword he was supposed to have been cleaning and had cut his leg nearly clear through.

Clare worked carefully, touching the torn flesh as she stanched the flow of blood from the wound. She slid a glance at Morgana's sister. "Now, Glyn, help here if you would. We have to bind the muscle together before we sew. Morgana, grab that silk thread and the small needle."

"Mayhap I should pray instead," Glyn said tightly, her complexion a greenish shade of white.

"There'll be time for prayers later. Right now God would want us to work quickly so that the boy loses no more blood."

Glyn groaned and looked sicker than before. "But there are bloodletters who believe that the loss of blood—"

"Enough," Clare snapped. "Bloodletters are fools! Now do as I say."

A sharp knock sounded on the door. It was flung open and Ware strode inside, his boyish face set and grim. "Garrick wishes to see Morgana," he said crisply.

Clare wasn't about to be bullied when she was giving a lesson. "She'll be finished in about—"

"Now. It's about Logan."

Clare dropped the bandage, and all eyes in the room, including those of the wounded boy, were focused on Garrick's younger brother. "Then he's alive?" Clare asked.

"Garrick seems to think so. Some farmer has reported seeing the boy with Jocelyn."

"Where?"

Morgana's blood grew cold. A premonition as dark as midnight eclipsed her soul. The images were vague and shadowy, but she was sure that something was dreadfully wrong.

Ware was motioning toward the windows. "To the east, near the mountains. Three or four days' ride. Logan may have been captured by robbers."

"Oh, dear God," Clare whispered, and Morgana felt fear for a child she'd never set eyes upon. "On Rowley's land?"

"Could be. Come," he said and started for the door.

Morgana followed swiftly. They climbed the staircase to Garrick's chamber and found a group of men inside. Garrick, Randolph, Strahan, and a thin man with lank gray hair were seated around the hearth. There was tension in the room, and distrust mingled with the smoke that rose from the fire. The stranger had bruises on his face and winced a little as he shifted on his chair.

Garrick's gaze sought Morgana's. His gray eyes were dark with a storm of emotions. "I thought you should hear Will Farmer's story," he said. "Will claims he saw Logan. Tell me if his tale is true."

"But how would I know—" she began, then held her tongue. Obviously this was another of Garrick's tests.

The farmer told of seeing a young boy and his nurse-maid in the company of thugs; of being robbed, beaten, and left to die; and of returning to his farm and learning of the disappearance of Garrick's son. He'd left his wife and five children to bring his news to Abergwynn himself.

"They robbed me of half a year's earnings," Will said, shaking his head. "I don't know how me and the missus and the children will get on. . . ." He cast a hopeful glance in Garrick's direction.

The room grew silent, only the crackle of the fire disturbing the peace. Morgana felt the weight of every man's gaze upon her. She knew Garrick expected her opinion.

"Well, witch," he said, "what think you?"

Morgana swallowed hard; she had no choice but to say what she felt. "I don't know if Will Farmer tells the truth, but I see no reason for him to travel so great a distance and risk angering you with a lie."

"He could have been paid to tell this tale," Garrick replied.

Morgana studied the farmer. The lines on his face had been drawn by long, honest hours of hard work in the elements. His hands were strong, bony, and callused. The bruises on his cheeks and jaw were still green and swollen. "If he came here for money, then he is a fool, for certainly he would know the extent of your wrath," she said, and the man didn't flinch. Facing Garrick, she continued. "You know I've had no visions, but . . ." She glanced around, unsure of herself, not wanting everyone in the chamber to hear what she had to say. "May I speak with you alone?"

"I have no time. I'm riding soon. If you have something to say, woman, say it," he snapped, his patience obviously worn as thin as the soles on the farmer's boots.

She squared her shoulders. "Will Farmer is the one man in this castle that I trust."

"The one man?" Strahan asked, obviously amused.

Morgana couldn't back down now. She felt the gaze of everyone in the room resting heavily upon her. Inching her chin up a little, she said, "I think there are many who would betray the baron."

"At Abergwynn?" Strahan laughed, but Randolph did not. His bony face grew quite grim, his features even harsher, and the look he cast Morgana was murderous.

Ignoring the fear that settled like ice between her shoulder blades, Morgana plunged onward, addressing Garrick. "Many of your soldiers are Welshmen—Welshmen who have never been loyal to the king. As you're Edward's vassal, pledged to defend the English crown, the Welsh would quickly betray you should they find a leader."

"You are Welsh," he pointed out succinctly.

"Aye, but—"

"And you have some reason to hate me."

Licking her lips nervously, she nodded. Lord, this wasn't going as she'd hoped. Why did the man have to be so bull-headed? She knew he intended to leave the castle to search for his boy, and with that knowledge came fear—dank and smelling foul.

Garrick leaned back in his chair. "Yet you tell me of others who would deceive me—men I grew up with, men I have been to battle with, men who have saved me from more than one of death's arrows?"

" 'Tis not farfetched," she said vehemently, and she felt the hatred in the room. It seemed to grow and pulse around her. How many of these very men would betray the man who trusted them with his life?

Garrick eyed her and thoughtfully rubbed his chin. "What do you propose I do, witch?"

"Just be careful, m'lord," she said a trifle breathlessly, and their gazes touched briefly, intimately, before Morgana looked away and Garrick, obsessed with the need to save his son, swung his gaze back to the farmer. "Why would robbers steal my son and send no one to demand ransom?"

Will gingerly touched his swollen jaw and shook his head. "I know not, m'lord. But unless I'm a blind man, your boy was with that band of ruffians."

"These outlaws, have they a name?" Strahan asked, obviously disbelieving the stranger.

"We didn't get 'round to introductions," Will said through two broken teeth, "but my guess is they were Newlyn's men. They roam Nelson Rowley's land, and some say they are actually rogue knights who pay homage to Osric McBrayne."

"I've heard this tale," Randolph interjected. "That Osric McBrayne hires men to torment Rowley in the hope that Rowley's servants and villagers will someday turn against him and join McBrayne in his quest to control all that Rowley holds. Eventually, some think, if McBrayne can get enough power, he'll start a war with you, Lord Garrick."

"Is that so?" Garrick whispered. "Where did you encounter this band of thugs, Will Farmer?"

At that point the bruised man crooked his thumb toward the east and told of the road on which he was attacked. It ran along the base of the mountains, he said, and followed a stream only half a day's ride from the village near his farm.

As she listened to Will's directions, Morgana watched the firelight play upon the leather of Garrick's boots and glint in red highlights in the dark strands of his hair. His gaze was centered on the glowing coals in the hearth, but clearly his thoughts were elsewhere. Her heart ached for him, and for once she longed to soothe him, to smooth the lines of worry from his brow, to tell him things would be fine. But she wasn't one to lie, not even for Garrick's peace of mind.

"We ride at once," he said as he shoved back his chair. The farmer glanced up expectantly. "You, Will Farmer, will return to your home with an empty cart and full pockets. We'll buy all you've brought here and give you a decent horse as well; that old nag of yours looks as if he's ready to draw his last breath. I want you back at your home with your family, should I need to speak with you again."

"Thank you, m'lord. You're most generous—"

But Garrick didn't have time for the man's gratitude. "Strahan, tell the steward to pay Will and add a little extra for his long journey. However"—Garrick leaned closer to the farmer, his features harsh and angular—"if I find that you lied to me, if this is just a ruse, I swear on the life of my son that you'll regret it for the rest of your days."

"I would not lie to you, m'lord," Will said, his Adam's apple bobbing indignantly.

Morgana believed him. The man was no liar, and yet she felt that parts of his story didn't make much sense. Why no ransom? Why keep a child and his nurse if not for money? Were they planning to sell the boy—or get rid of him by some other means? Morgana shuddered and once again prayed that her visions would come and she would be able to help Garrick find his son.

The men exited, but Garrick took hold of the crook of Strahan's arm. "You are to stay and guard the castle," he said, and Strahan's spine visibly stiffened.

"But why?"

"Because Ware is not strong enough."

Strahan's eyes narrowed suspiciously. He didn't like being left behind on any war party. "I'm the best archer you've got, the best swordsman. Why would you not want me at your side?"

"I need someone to take command of Abergwynn. My family is here, as is your bride. You'll stay and protect—"

"But I'm going with you," Morgana protested, cutting him off. "That's why you brought me here. To find Logan."

"He's been found. There's no point in putting your life in danger." Garrick, seeing the protest forming on her lips, let go of his cousin and advanced on Morgana. "I'll not have any Wenlock blood spilled over this. I made a promise to your father, and I intend to keep it."

"But—"

Strahan's nostrils flared ever so slightly. "Do as the baron wishes," he ordered.

"Make no mistake, Morgana," Garrick said, his eyes blazing. "You are to stay here, take your lessons from Clare, and begin planning your wedding." Behind him, resting a shoulder in the doorway, Strahan had the nerve to smile.

Morgana wanted to scream. She'd been cooped up in this castle for far too long, and this was her chance to be free and to help bring the boy back to Abergwynn. The thought of preparing for a wedding to Strahan—oh, Mother Mary, her knees nearly buckled.

"You'll be wed a fortnight from the day we return," Garrick said.

She thought there was a flicker of sadness in his gaze, but it quickly disappeared and she wondered if her own foolish heart had tricked her into believing that he regretted her marriage to his cousin.

"What if you don't find your son? What if I have a vision and know him to be somewhere else?"

Garrick's cruel lips lifted at one corner. "Your visions come conveniently, don't they, witch? For over a week you see nothing, but now, when a simple farmer swears he's seen my boy, you're jumping at shadows, seeing a traitor around every corner in this castle, thinking you'll see a vision of my son's whereabouts." He touched her lightly, his fingers curling in one dark strand of her hair. "You know, Morgana of Wenlock, I don't believe in your powers at all. I don't think you're a sorceress. I think the stories about you have been embellished over the years. Yea, perhaps you found a person, maybe even felt a storm brewing. But your witchcraft is a pitiful thing and probably doesn't exist."

"I don't believe in witchcraft!" she cried, heat rising in her cheeks. What was he doing?

"Good. Neither do I. I was a fool to let Strahan talk me into bringing you here. If he wants to marry you, well enough, but I don't need a woman muddying the waters while I ride to battle."

With that, he turned on his heel and strode out the door. Strahan, after casting a bemused glance in her direction, followed Garrick, and Morgana was left fuming, her fists clenched in rage, in the middle of Garrick's chamber. Blackheart! Fool! Beast of Abergwynn!

The vision came less than an hour later. Still angry, she stormed outside, talking to no one, not even bending down to pet Wolf between his ears. She was too furious. In the bailey she lifted her face, allowing the salty breeze to touch her skin and tangle her hair. Flint-colored clouds were beginning to gather, and the laundress, muttering beneath her breath, ran from the castle and began snatching the linens from the ground.

The farmer's old nag pricked up his ears and whinnied, his dusty hide quivering in fear. Wolf began to pace restlessly around her skirts, a series of low growls rumbling in his throat.

"Shh," Morgana said instinctively, but she, too, felt the change in temperature, the gathering of the storm. Crossing her arms over her breasts, she held herself and closed her eyes for only a second as the wind whipped her tunic close to her body. In that brief instant she saw death. Cold and black and shadowy, death was stalking. Who or what she could not tell. The vision was blurry and filled with vague images. Her insides froze as, within her mind, she observed a small hand—a child's plump hand—reaching into water where golden silk lay under the ripples.

"Please, God," she whispered, knowing the hand belonged to Garrick's son, "let me see the boy." She fell to her knees. "Tell me that he's safe—" But as quickly as the vision had appeared, it vanished, and she blinked against the sunlight, trying to peek through the ominous clouds.

Desolate, she climbed to her feet. What good were her visions if she could not help the boy? If she could not ease Garrick's troubled mind?

In the outer bailey the soldiers were gathering—Garrick's war party. A wagon was loaded, the horses saddled, and weapons clanked over the jokes and laughter of men about to partake of an adventure. For as serious as their mission was, they were excited and eager to get on with it.

The first few drops of rain began to spatter the ground. Morgana turned toward the castle and saw him. Dressed in dark leather, impatience radiating from his every movement, Garrick strode across the inner bailey and toward the gate.

"Wait!" she cried, dashing across the grass, disregarding the drizzle that ran down her face and neck. "Please, Garrick, you must listen to me!" She didn't care who saw her, and she ignored the stares of the carpenters and gardeners who gaped at her. She wanted to fling herself into Garrick's arms and beg him to take her with him, to wrap her arms around him and hear the steadying beat of his heart, for she feared that the death was meant for him. She didn't know how this vision fit with the first image she'd had of Garrick as the warrior from the north who would bring the downfall of Wenlock, she knew only that she cared for him, more deeply than she should, perhaps, and that she was sick with worry for his safety as well as for the safety of his child.

"What is it now?" he demanded harshly, though a ribbon of tenderness floated across his face.

"You must let me come with you. I—I saw something . . ." Her words were tumbling out too fast, and she was holding on to his sleeve, her wet face upturned to his.

Garrick's gut knotted, and before he knew what he was doing one of his fists knotted in her hair. He nearly drew her head to his and kissed those passionate red lips, but before his lust took control of his mind, he restrained himself. "You had a vision."

"Aye."

"Now?" he asked skeptically. "After all this time?"

"I cannot control when it will happen."

His eyes narrowed thoughtfully, and he let loose of the silken rope of her hair. "What did you see, witch?" he taunted, his mouth turning suddenly cruel. "Another vision of death?"

"Yea, and—"

"Whose death was it?"

"I'm not sure, m'lord," she admitted, horrified that his gentleness had faded so quickly and been replaced by a scoffing mockery that glittered like hard gems in his gaze.

"Now you want to come with me."

"Yea!"

"So that you can escape?"

She felt as if she'd been slapped, but she swallowed back her pride and clung to him. "Nay, Garrick, please. Listen. I want only what is best for you and Logan. I could help. I can ride and hunt, and I'm as good as your men with a bow and arrow. Mayhap I'll have another vision. One that's clearer.

One that will lead you to your son and will help you avoid a trap."

His fingers surrounded her arm, and she felt the leashed strength in his grip, as if he wanted to crush her bones to dust. "You have been here a fortnight, Morgana. In all that time you have been nothing but grief to me," he whispered harshly. "Now that I finally might find my boy, you want to ride with me and set all my men on edge."

"I wouldn't—"

"I never wanted a witch to scare my men, and I don't need a woman to take their minds off their duty. You stay here with Strahan. You're no use to me now."

She stumbled backward as he shoved her aside, and she felt wounded to her very soul.

He strode swiftly to the outer bailey where his men waited. Without so much as a look over his shoulder, he mounted his steed, galloped to the head of the procession, and rode away, his small band of soldiers riding fast behind him.

Morgana wanted to crumple to the ground, but she felt the gaze of Strahan upon her, knew he was watching her every move. She stiffened her spine and marched back to the castle, past Strahan and Ware, and through the great door where Springan, her mouth a tight little bow, swept her a knowing look.

Trying to hold on to her pride, she hurried up the stairs, feeling a fool, and all the while Garrick's taunting words floated on the wind behind her: *You're of no use to me now.*

The words reverberated through her head like a chant, over and over, hurting her more each time she remembered them.

"Damn you, Garrick of Abergwynn," she whispered, kicking at the rushes and plotting her escape.

fifteen

"Fool," Morgana muttered, but she couldn't still the traitorous beating of her heart as she watched Garrick and the column of riders disappear into the forest. Even when he was out of sight, her heart thumped a trifle recklessly as she leaned against the smooth stones of the windowsill.

She was glad there was news of Logan, and she prayed that the boy was safe, but as for Garrick, she was furious with him. He'd left her with strict orders not to leave the castle, and she felt more like a prisoner than ever. As the last of the column disappeared into the copse of oak and pine, Morgana again felt a premonition of doom race up her spine. Her skin crawled, and for a second she saw Garrick's death as surely as if an arrow had pierced his heart.

"Talk to me," she entreated the wind. Closing her eyes and emptying her mind, she waited for words to echo inside her head.

The voice was as soft as the drizzling rain falling gently from the sky: *There will be death. It comes to the House of Wenlock from the north.*

Perturbed, she responded, "This I already know. But why now? Why does the death come now?"

Because of the brave one's impatience.

"What of Abergwynn? Will Abergwynn suffer, too? What

of Garrick—is he friend or foe? And his son? Where is Logan?"

Again the vision of water—a brook with a bed of slick black stones and the gurgle of the current as the stream splashed and pooled. There were trees and voices—men's voices—and deeper in the shadows of the brook, where the current eddied and flowed, a scrap of yellow cloth floating under the ripples.

"What's the meaning of this?" Morgana whispered, feeling the breath of the wind against her cheeks. "Please, tell me—"

"Talking to yourself again?"

Morgana started at the sound of Glyn's voice. Wolf growled, and Morgana gritted her teeth, trying to hold on to her patience. Her fingers curled over the stones of the windowsill. Didn't Glyn know this was serious? Didn't she realize that Morgana was only trying to help Garrick? Turning slowly, biting back her anger, she found her sister standing in the chamber doorway, her expression bemused, a forgotten mirror in one hand.

"Oh, don't tell me you're still trying to call up some witchcraft." Walking warily into the room, never letting her gaze stray too far from the wolf dog, Glyn rubbed her arms as if suddenly chilled by the dampness of the rain that seeped through the window. "It's a little late for sorcery now, don't you think?" Yet her eyes betrayed her nervousness as she glanced rapidly from the dog to Morgana. She couldn't resist teasing her sister, but obviously she was uneasy.

"I'd just like to help the baron," Morgana said, glancing once again at the woods into which the war party had disappeared.

"Ahh." Glyn moved her hands, and the mirror, catching the light from the fire, bounced flashes of brilliance against the thick stone walls. "You've had a change of heart. I thought you considered the baron some horrible terror from the north, the death of all of us or some such nonsense." Before Morgana could respond, she added, "Well, I shouldn't wonder, I guess. He's . . ." Glyn paused, biting her lip as she searched for the right word.

"He's what?" Morgana couldn't help asking.

"He's so . . . so powerful and strong. It's hard to watch him suffer over the loss of his son."

Morgana agreed, but she didn't say so. This was a new side to Glyn, a side that noticed other people's troubles, a side that pushed her own vanity and ambition aside. Glyn was actually concerned. A fine line of consternation developed between Glyn's blond eyebrows, and though she still held the small mirror, she only played with the glass and didn't bother to stare at her own reflection.

"I've been praying for him, you know," Glyn admitted, stealing a peek at herself, frowning prettily, and stuffing a stubborn golden lock into her braid.

"That's good. I'm sure Garrick would appreciate any prayers—"

"That's not all." Glyn glanced a little guiltily at her sister. "I've also been asking God, begging him, to make me mistress of Abergwynn."

"You what!"

Glyn smiled at that thought. "It's just so wonderful here. So big—as big as a king's castle, I'll wager." She clutched the mirror to her breast and sighed dreamily. "I just wish Lord Garrick would find his boy and come back to me. However, if the lad has met with some horrible end and passed on, I hope Garrick will accept the boy's fate and forget about him."

"Glyn!"

"Well, he can't spend the rest of his life in mourning."

"I don't think it's so easy to forget a child," Morgana replied, stunned at Glyn's reversal. For a few minutes Morgana had thought her sister capable of caring for someone other than herself, but she'd been mistaken. Glyn had shown her true self once again.

Glyn made an impatient gesture with her hand. "I know, I know. And of course he loves the boy. It would be a terrible loss to think that your child was kidnapped or worse. But Garrick can have more children, many more children." Her eyes took on a naughty gleam.

"He'll never forget his firstborn," Morgana said stubbornly. To think she'd actually *missed* Glyn while she was here alone at Abergwynn!

"Of course he won't forget him. Not really forget. At least not at first, but when time passes and he sees his next son or daughter, Logan's image will fade and—"

"Oh, you stupid girl!" Morgana cut in. Her own visions of death had been so horrible she could barely think of anything else, but Glyn's vain self-interest was getting on her nerves. "How can you even think such things? The boy is alive, and Garrick will find him." *Especially if I help him.*

"Well, if Logan still lives—"

"He does!" Morgana said with more certainty than she felt.

"Garrick will still need a bride," Glyn insisted, lifting a delicate blond brow in silent reproof. "What is all this concern? Don't tell me, sister, that *you* fancy the baron—"

"Of course not!" Morgana cut in, though a rush of heat

invaded the back of her neck. She had to help Garrick, whether he wanted her assistance or not. Now that her visions had returned, she was certain that she could help him, if not in locating the boy, at least in warding off the evil she felt was luring the baron away from Abergwynn.

"Wolf, come," she said, snapping her fingers.

Glyn sidled a few steps away. "What—"

"Wolf needs to take a walk and stretch his legs." She offered her sister a meaningful look. "He gets restless and angry if he's cooped up too long. Want to come along?"

"Nay. I, uh, I have to work with Clare this afternoon. She wants me to learn all about those awful herbs she uses to treat the sick." She glanced nervously at the dog, and Morgana smiled. For once she'd bested Glyn and knew the herbs and their uses by heart.

Leaving Glyn with her mirror, Morgana whistled to Wolf, slipped down the hallway, and checked the corridor to see that she was alone. After sending Wolf downstairs she crept into Garrick's chamber. When the door closed behind her she felt the clammy shroud of death again. "You're imagining things," she told herself, but couldn't shake the feeling that Garrick was in danger. She hurried through the connecting chamber and entered Logan's room. There the temperature was cooler, as if winter had settled in this silent, tomblike chamber. Treachery seemed to lurk in every shadowy corner. Her pulse began to beat a frightened rhythm. She sat on the edge of the child's bed, and the vision came again—water and yellow silk, men's shouts, and a child's cry.

"Logan? Are you there?" she whispered, but the vision, as it had in the past, faded quickly, rippling away from her mind.

Morgana was left with a dread as deep as the sea. There

was little time to lose. Garrick and his son were in grave danger. Morgana would first ask Ware's permission to leave, and if it was denied, which she fully expected, then she would take off against his orders, defying him, defying Garrick, defying the very fates that had brought her here!

Ware drew back the arrow, pulling the bowstring so taut that the muscles in his forearm trembled from the strain. Taking aim, he set his jaw, then suddenly let loose. His arrow sliced through the air with a hiss. *Thwack!* It plunged into the heart of the target, a tarpaulin painted with a picture of a wild boar and mounted over thick straw bundles. He imagined that the target was the blackheart who had stolen Logan and that the surprised man was now pitching forward, clutching the arrow's shaft and screaming in agony.

"You should have taken me with you, brother," Ware muttered, as if Garrick could hear him. Ware's skill as an archer and swordsman was improving. Aside from Garrick and Strahan, Ware was the truest shot at Abergwynn. Yet he was treated like a child, forced to stay in the castle with his sister, told he was in charge, when in fact it was Strahan who ruled in Garrick's absence. Simmering with the injustice of the situation, Ware reached for another arrow, sent it streaking through the air, and killed yet another imaginary enemy.

Didn't Garrick know how Ware itched to do battle, how he longed to feel the charge of a lightning-swift war-horse as it galloped into a clattering melee of swords and beasts and sweating men? He longed to hear the clang of metal, the thunder of hooves, the battle cries and screams of death. He could almost smell the smoke from the campfires and the sweat of men who hadn't washed for weeks. He imagined the laughter and bawdy jokes and exaggerated tales of warring and wenching as the men, after conquering a rival castle, gathered around the enemy's hearth, drank the man's finest wine, lay with his wenches and servant girls, and felt a camaraderie and a bond like no other on earth. Ah, war would be glorious, and he would come back victorious, a hero, able to make the women—especially Morgana—sit up and take notice of his prowess as a warrior. Yet Garrick denied him.

The fool!

"Bloody damned idiot!" Ware strode to the target and yanked his arrows from the straw that was packed beneath the target. Blasted stupid prideful Garrick. Just because he was a few years older . . .

From the corner of his eye Ware spied Morgana. A small smile crept across his lips, and his chest puffed out with pride. She was indeed the most beautiful woman in all of Abergwynn. Though she was pledged to Strahan, Morgana obviously cared little for his company, and personally, Ware didn't blame her. Strahan could be a self-important pig when he wanted to be. As for Garrick, well, if Garrick was so smart, why had he gone to all the trouble of bringing back this so-called sorceress who hadn't helped him at all? True, she was the most intriguing woman Ware had ever seen, and there was an unearthly quality about her. He half believed the stories of her magic himself. However, the fact that her hair was as black as a raven's wing, her eyes were the color of the sea, and her lips were soft and pink gave Garrick no reason to drag her here using her supposed magic powers as a feeble excuse.

Squaring his shoulders, he walked back to his mark and fired another straight-on shot, one that would surely impress her, before he turned his attention in her direction again. "What is it?" he demanded when she didn't speak. Perhaps she was awestruck by his skill.

"Now that Garrick's gone, you're lord of the castle."

Ware lifted a shoulder and took aim at the boar again. He couldn't hide the touch of pride in his voice. "What of it?"

"I wish to leave."

"What?"

"I'm asking your permission to follow Lord Garrick."

He had just drawn back his bow. At her words he released the arrow and scowled as it barely nipped the target's edge. "Garrick ordered you to stay here."

"I know, but—"

"You'll do as he said," Ware ordered, shaking his head at her stupidity. Was she daft? Defy Garrick in his current mood? In Ware's opinion, she might as well ask for a death sentence. Some of his cockiness drained away. "For the love of Christ, Morgana, you're asking for more trouble than either of us could handle."

"I can help him."

He plucked another arrow from his quiver, took aim, and smiled grimly in satisfaction as he hit the boar dead center, near the heart. "You'll help him by staying here."

"Ware, please—"

He whirled on her, his bow taut. "Don't argue with me!" Angry that he had to defend his brother's rash decision, he kicked at a muddy stone and sent it flying toward the bailey wall. Had it been up to him, he'd have let Morgana go where she wanted, for he knew she was as restless as he. They were kindred spirits, held prisoner behind the castle walls when all the adventure, the thrills, the excitement in life, lay out there somewhere. . . .

She laid a hand upon his shoulder, and Ware nearly came

undone. His gut wrenched up, pressing hard on his abdomen, and he was more aware of her than he'd ever been. She smelled of wildflowers and soap, and her black hair gleamed in the pale rays of sun, which had managed to break through the gloomy clouds. "Garrick needs me."

"You?"

"There is trouble. I can feel it—"

"Enough, Morgana! If I let you leave Abergwynn, Garrick would have my head. You're my responsibility, and so you'll stay here, where you're supposed to, and I won't hear another word of it."

Ware knew she wanted to argue. He caught the flash of defiance in her eyes, the petulant curl of her lips, the strong, disobedient thrust of her small chin, but she bit back whatever words were hovering on the tip of her tongue.

"Look, Morgana, would that I could let you go wherever you bloody well pleased, but I cannot defy Garrick's orders, nor can you. Just wait. He'll return, and when he does, if he has his son, he'll be more reasonable."

He saw the clouds gathering in her clear eyes, and the sight pained him. Ware had never been in love and had sworn he'd never let a woman make a fool of him. But if he did allow himself to fall, if he let himself trust any female, it would surely be Morgana. Bloody damn, maybe she was a witch after all. She certainly managed to turn his thinking all around.

"How long must I wait?" she asked, seeming to agree.

"Just until he returns. I doubt he'll be gone more than a week—a fortnight at most. Be patient, Morgana," he heard himself say. He could easily have given that advice to himself, for he knew the torment of impatience, how it could tear a man up inside, make him do foolhardy and rash things. He supposed women felt it, too, though probably not the same way.

Women were strange creatures, as was proven by Morgana and her sister, who were as different as night and day—one beautiful and coy, a woman easily understood, the other as mysterious as a sea goddess, her beauty a sensual creeping being that seemed to grab him by his heart as well as his loins. Aye, he'd spent more than one sleepless night imagining what she would feel like against him, how her soft body would encase his as he thrust into her . . . He pulled himself up short. Already his manhood had sprouted to life, and a wave of embarrassment washed up his neck and cheeks. He was grateful that she'd already turned away and hadn't—please, God—seen the bulge in his breeches.

Morgana left Ware practicing his archery, his face flaming, his eyes averted. She stepped through the mud and decided that when she could not accomplish her goals honestly, she was left with no choice but to stoop to deception.

Will Farmer was pleased. Things had been looking up ever since that fateful night when he'd taken a wrong turn and been attacked. The men had robbed and beaten him, but in the end he was better off than he had been before. Discovering that the lad he'd seen might be the son of the baron had propelled him to Abergwynn, and as he'd hoped, Maginnis had been more than generous with his reward.

He slapped the reins over the sleek haunches of the horse he'd been given at the castle—a prize, this one, a fine brown stallion sired by one of the lord's prized war-horses. Luck, Will had decided to call him.

Luck clipped off at a fast pace, dragging the wagon and the old nag behind him. Will was counting the money he would make by hiring such a fine animal out to stud while being able to till twice as many acres each year as he had with the lazy gray beast.

He whistled to Luck and snapped the reins again. Aye, the robbery and beating, which had seemed so bleak a week past, now seemed a blessing.

He drove his wagon for several miles. The sun, weak though it was, was sinking, and he thought he'd better stop and make camp. No more nighttime journeys for Will Farmer. He'd learned his lesson and well. He glanced at his pack and considered the tasty rabbit stew that the fat cook at Abergwynn had given him along with hard bread, cheese, and ale. Today at the castle he had eaten better than he had in a long, long while, and tonight's dinner would be no different. His mouth watered.

He reined Luck in at the edge of a clearing, built a fire, and heated his supper. With a belly full of ale and food, it didn't take long for him to fall asleep.

He didn't see the she-devil hidden in the straw of his cart, didn't know that she quietly untied his new horse and climbed onto the stallion's broad back. With soft words, she nudged the animal forward, away from the warm circle of light cast by the dying flames and into the woods that were as foreign to her as the Holy Land. Yet she couldn't be afraid. Not now. Not when her escape had gone so well.

Morgana had waited until the last moment, until the farmer was in deep conversation with Cailin about the stew she was giving him. He had left his cart unattended near the stables. Armed with her dagger, Morgana had crawled inside, hiding beneath the straw and the empty bags that had held Will's produce, and praying that Clare wouldn't see fit to start another lesson and come searching for her. It had seemed to take forever before she heard shouts of good-bye and felt the creak of the cart's old wheels as it rolled slowly forward. Praying she was invisible to the guards in the tower, she'd listened as the farmer whistled off-key. His tune was accompanied by the steady beat of his horse's hooves.

Dust had clogged her nostrils and she'd held her breath, hoping not to cough or sneeze, hardly believing her luck.

Luck. Aye, the stallion was aptly named, she thought now as she guided the horse with her knees. She felt more than a passing twinge of guilt for stealing the old man's gift from Garrick, but he had another nag, and Morgana planned to return the stallion as soon as her mission was accomplished.

She only hoped that Garrick wouldn't see fit to punish her for disobeying him by leaving the castle and taking the gift he'd bestowed upon Will. She worried a little about that. Garrick would surely have to mete out some sort of punishment, lest he look weak to his men. She cringed inwardly at the thought, but still rode on, sending up a quick prayer asking God to forgive her for being disrespectful and a thief as well. She whispered a much longer prayer that Garrick would be forgiving as well, though she knew in her heart he would be furious at the sight of her.

Well, that was just too bad. She'd agreed to help him find his son, and she couldn't very well accomplish her duties by sitting on a stool at Abergwynn learning to read or spinning wool, or keeping an eye on the steward to see if he was taking his duties to heart. No, she had to find Garrick and risk his wrath in order to help him locate his boy.

The thought occurred to her that not all of her intentions were honorable. For there was a selfish side of her that wanted to be with Garrick, that craved to be a part of the expedition, and she felt an unlikely maternal instinct that caused her great concern for Garrick's boy.

She could no longer lie to herself and had to admit, albeit reluctantly, that she wanted to spend more time with the man she'd so recently thought of as the beast of Abergwynn, the man who she'd thought would bring death to her family, the man whose black heart all but beckoned to her.

"Saints in heaven, you're as foolish as Glyn," she reproved herself, for she was pledged to another man. Her stomach soured at the thought of marrying Strahan, and she knew she would never willingly become his bride. Curse the fates that had brought her to Abergwynn, to Garrick, and now to this dark, unfriendly forest.

The night was black. Only a few stars winked through the clouds, and the moon, a sliver of opalescent light, gave little illumination. But Morgana, driven by fear for Garrick's life and by a will as strong as iron, followed the directions she'd heard from Will Farmer, and urged the horse forward.

She pulled her cloak tightly around her to keep herself warm as fog seeped through the black trees and onto the road that wound through the woods. Her eyes adjusted to the darkness, for she'd always been comfortable at night, and she used the North Star to judge direction.

The undergrowth near the road rustled, and for a second Morgana feared she would be attacked by a marauding band of robbers. Her right hand tightened over the hilt of her dagger, but she saw no one and told herself that she'd heard a mouse or a rabbit scurrying away from the sharp eyes of an owl that was hooting softly in the distance.

Luck galloped onward, his hoofbeats in rhythm with the cadence of her heart. Her fingers curled over the reins, and she fought off the ever-present cold, hoping that she would find Garrick before she met the band of thugs who had stolen his child.

No more visions came to her that night, and she rode until she was exhausted and her mount weak. Convinced she had put as many miles as possible between herself and the farmer, she stopped at last and dismounted, leading the horse away from the road and into a thicket, where, after tethering the stallion in a meadow, she lay against the mossy bark of an ancient oak. Within minutes she was asleep. She didn't wake up until well after dawn.

Without even pausing to eat, she climbed astride the horse again and headed east toward the mountains. By midafternoon she'd ridden alongside hilly fields of tall grass and wildflowers. She'd found evidence of a large group of horses traveling on the road, and she wondered if she'd nearly caught up with Garrick or had run into the robber band.

An icy hand gripped her heart at the thought of what might become of her should she be captured by outlaws. The sight of Will Farmer's black-and-blue face and broken teeth filled her mind. She'd considered the possibility of becoming a prisoner of the thugs before, and she'd told herself she would escape by her wits, her magic, and her skill with weapons, all of which would surprise most men. However, now that her horse had turned toward the mountains and the gloom of the forest that grew on the banks of the creek, her worries intensified. The damp smell of wet earth filled her nostrils, and fog settled in the valley near the creek. Mist gathered along the banks and seemed to catch in the fronds of ferns and cling to the mossy trunks of older trees. Will had only been beaten—the men had had no use for his body—but there was a chance that the thugs would try to force themselves upon her. What good would all her spells and chants do then? She'd heard stories of men with voracious appetites and cruel hands. . . .

Morgana felt a fear unlike any other she'd experienced in all her seventeen years. She wished she could talk to her grandmother and that Enit's wise words would guide her, then shoved the thought aside when she remembered her grandmother's prediction that she would marry Strahan. Shivering, she urged the horse forward.

As dusk settled and the forest grew darker around her, she gripped her dagger more firmly and rode onward. Tonight there was moonlight to guide her. Tonight she would find Garrick.

Or come across the robbers.

Sixteen

What do you mean, she's gone?" Strahan thundered, his fist crashing into the table. Silver rattled, and wine from the half filled cups sloshed onto the old stained planks. The hounds growled, startled from their naps, and Ware bristled a bit as he stared at his cousin. After all, he hadn't made up the story; he'd just passed on the news of Morgana's disappearance.

To hide his embarrassment, Ware propped one foot against the bench and shrugged a shoulder, as if what the witch did wasn't all that important. "The servants have searched everywhere. Morgana of Wenlock is not at Abergwynn."

"Holy Christ, Ware, she didn't just walk out of here!" Strahan swore roundly as he shoved his chair away from the table. His face was knotted with anxiety, and his boots were restless against the rushes as he began to pace. A page, who had heard only part of the conversation, scurried down the hall, and several knights, drinking and tossing dice near the hearth, paused for a second before turning their attention back to their game.

Strahan's jaw slid to the side. "She probably just went riding—that's it."

"Her horse isn't missing. In fact, *none* of the horses are unaccounted for."

"What about that bloody wolf of hers?"

"Frantic," Ware admitted, feeling a fool. Morgana had duped him, pure and simple. "The dog was in her room and whined and scratched at the door. When we let him out an hour ago, the damned beast bolted across the bailey, trying like the devil to get out. The stableboy caught him and it was all Roy could do to restrain him. The animal nearly bit the boy's hand off."

Strahan squeezed his eyes shut, his patience wearing thin. "Bloody damn." His jaw ticked anxiously. "I can't believe that she was kidnapped. I have enough trouble thinking that Logan and Jocelyn were snatched away from our guards, but Morgana, too?" He snorted in disbelief and disgust, then reached for his mazer of wine and, finding it empty, snapped his fingers and pointed at the cup. A second later a white-faced page snagged the cup from the table and hurried off toward the kitchen.

"I doubt she was taken," Ware admitted. He didn't want to tell Strahan about his conversation with Morgana, but couldn't lie. So he explained about her request to leave and watched Strahan's emotions play across his chiseled face. At first anxious for Morgana's safety, his expression changed with the color that rode high on his cheeks. His muscles coiled, and he suddenly seemed primitive and savage, all signs of his English civility stripped away. There had always been rivalry between Strahan and Garrick, a rivalry that had worsened when Strahan's family lost Castle Hazelwood to McBrayne and Strahan had to bow to Garrick, a man he'd always considered his equal. The situation with Morgana only made things worse, for it was obvious to everyone in the castle that Garrick was attracted to the witch and quite possibly Morgana of Wenlock felt the same way toward the baron. Once again, Strahan came in a short second to his cousin.

Ware, too, understood Morgana's allure. Didn't he want the witch's attention? "My guess is she took off with the farmer—either paid him to hide her or deceived him as well."

"Bah! The girl is no fool! Why would she chance defying Garrick?" Strahan demanded.

"She is . . . stubborn."

"Or in love?" Strahan asked, the question catching Ware off guard.

"That I couldn't guess," he lied, though he, like anyone with eyes at Abergwynn, could guess at the silent passion in the witch's eyes as she glanced at Garrick. He flushed scarlet and buried his nose in his near-empty cup.

"Don't lie to me, Ware," Strahan said in a voice that was low and angry. "Everyone in this damned castle pretends not to notice what is happening between Garrick and Morgana. Aye, even I tried to tell myself I was seeing things that weren't there, but I was deceiving myself." He cursed softly under his breath and shoved his dark hair from his eyes. Until that moment Ware wouldn't have thought Strahan capable of caring about anyone but himself, but he'd been wrong. Apparently Strahan was very much taken with his bride to be.

There was a rustle behind the curtain, and Springan, Morgana's woman servant, appeared with a tray and two fresh cups of wine. Ware hadn't heard her approach and wondered if she'd lingered on the other side of the curtain, listening to their conversation. "Cailin thought you might want these, m'lord. The page said you were thirsty." She smiled at Ware and placed the cups on the table. Her face was flushed, her eyes bright, and Ware wondered if she'd been holding back tears. But why?

Strahan glanced in her direction, and his thin lips turned down, as if she'd done something to displease him. A shaft of agony cut across her features, but she quickly looked away. "Is—is there anything else?" she asked of Ware.

"No, this is fine."

"Be off with you, woman," Strahan ordered, and a spark of anger flared in the girl's eyes. Her fingers tightened around the rim of the tray. She turned, as if to do Strahan's bidding, but Ware wasn't finished.

"Wait a minute. You know that Lady Morgana is missing?"

"Aye," Springan lifted her small chin in a mimicry of regal defiance as she turned back to face Ware again. Her gaze swept to Strahan and landed for a blistering second before cooling as she spoke to Ware. "I reported her absence to Lady Clare."

"Have you any idea where she might have gone?"

One of her elegant eyebrows arched maliciously, as if she were savoring the conversation. "The lady told me nothing. But she would not leave her dog unless she left against her will . . . or unless she was in a hurry."

"You think she might have been taken from Abergwynn?"

"No," she said swiftly. Again a hot, furtive glance at Strahan. "I think Lady Morgana defied you as well as Lord Garrick and then escaped Abergwynn, either to return to Wenlock or . . . to follow her heart." Her fingers worked nervously around the edge of the tray, and she shot Strahan a biting, scornful glance. "I think Lady Morgana left to search out the baron, as she was afraid for his safety."

Strahan sneered, "You think she's in love with him."

"What I think, *m'lord,* is not important," Springan said

through clenched teeth before whirling around and marching stiffly out of the great hall.

"Bloody wench," Strahan muttered before taking a huge gulp of wine and wiping his sleeve across his mouth. "She knows how to service a man well, but she can't stop using her tongue as a damned whip." His eyebrows were knotted as he studied the hallway where Springan had disappeared. "If she were my servant, I'd beat her within an inch of her life."

Ware's stomach turned as he pictured Strahan, leather whip raised, sweat beading his brow while Springan lay across a bed, biting her lip to keep from screaming, the snowy white skin of her back marred by ugly red welts. "She was only speaking her mind."

"She's a servant, Ware; she has no mind. Besides, she beds any man who'll have her. For a kind smile a man can do what he will. She'll lift her skirts and spread her legs or, if you say just the right words—you know, whisper some ridiculous flattery—she'll use her tongue to . . . well, to do whatever you have in mind." He was looking at Ware strangely, as if the thought of bedding Springan was as appealing as watching her writhe in pain from a beating. "So don't worry about Springan. That little whore can take care of herself."

"Servants are never beaten at Abergwynn," Ware reminded him.

"Unless Garrick thinks they might be hiding his son."

"The guards who were in charge of Logan—"

Strahan waved off Ware's excuses. "They lived. Now what're you going to do about Morgana?"

Ware felt too heavy a burden resting on his young shoulders. "There is nothing we can do. Garrick told us to stay here and protect Abergwynn. That's what has to be done."

He drained his own glass as if his decision were final.

"Ha! So you *are* gutless." Strahan smirked. "I always thought so."

"Gutless?" The word cut deep. Ware flattened his lips against his teeth at the insult. Strahan would not have spoken so bluntly if Garrick had been present.

"Aye. You're a coward, Ware. Afraid of battle. You let Garrick make all your decisions for you, and because of that, you're soft—the stupid younger brother being bullied by Lord Garrick. What does it get you? Nothing."

Ware drew in his breath to stem the anger that ran hot and wild through his blood. Never before had he wanted to take a man by the throat and slam him against the wall. Strahan was talking nonsense, though in truth he was voicing all the self-doubts that Ware fought each and every day. Hadn't he just concluded that Strahan wouldn't be so bold if only Garrick were here? Well, Garrick wasn't here, and Ware was in charge. It was time Strahan understood that very important bit of information.

But Strahan wasn't finished. His thin lips curled in a sudden display of contempt. "I see you don't believe me. Well, let me prove it to you. Why do you think Garrick insisted that I stay at Abergwynn? It's simple. I'm his best and strongest knight, and he knew that I was needed here to watch over you. To protect Abergwynn."

Ware's throat worked. "I don't believe—"

"Of course you do. Contrary to what Garrick might think, you're not stupid—"

"Stop it, Strahan!" Ware yelled, causing the men who were playing dice to glance up. Near the table, the hounds growled. Ware pointed a long finger at his cousin. "We're going to stay here as Garrick told us—"

"Listen to me, Ware!" Strahan took a step forward. "To Garrick you're just a snot-nosed lad who needs looking after. Lucky me, I get to do the honors!" Strahan glanced at a few of the men playing dice in the hallway. "Well, I'll not sit here while Morgana is out in the wilderness alone. I'm not going to stay here and play the fool while Garrick goes about seducing her." Quick as lightning, he turned and started for the door.

"But you can't—" Ware said to Strahan's back.

"Don't you see, man? My honor is at stake here!" Strahan muttered harshly before turning to face Ware again. His nostrils flared in fury, his lips pulled hard against his teeth. "*I* can't take a chance that she wasn't taken by force, and I have to find out for myself if she's gone to meet Garrick. If she has . . . if they are lovers . . ." His eyes gleamed with a hatred so intense that Ware felt the footsteps of fear climb up his spine.

Instinctively, Ware drew his sword. Furious at Strahan's disloyalty, he growled, "You will not leave the castle. I won't allow it! Garrick left me in charge, and both *my* honor and *his* are at stake."

"Oh, Christ!" Strahan snapped his fingers, and three of the knights, who had seemed so absorbed in their game, jumped lithely to their feet. Their hands were on the hilts of their weapons, and they stood ready to do battle. "Don't make me do this," Strahan warned Ware. "Don't make me spill your blood."

But Ware's pride had been battered too much for him to worry about his safety. He advanced on Strahan, and the knights unsheathed their swords.

"Don't," Strahan said again, his face growing less harsh as if he realized that Ware, in all his boyish foolishness, was quite prepared to die. "Don't hurt him," he ordered his men, "but make sure he doesn't interfere with my plans."

Sir Joseph advanced. Huge, with a black beard and a scar beneath one eye so that his eyelid drooped a bit, he grinned at the smell of battle. One of his teeth was already missing and he didn't look as if he worried about losing another.

Ware shored up his courage, and with indignation as his shield, he lunged at Joseph, ready to draw blood in defense of Abergwynn. He had never trusted Strahan, and, frustrated at being left behind by Garrick, he found this battle exhilarating. No one would ever dare call him a coward again. With his heavy sword he slashed wildly in the air, swiping at the huge knight's arm. Blood sprayed the whitewashed walls, Joseph roared in pain, and from somewhere near the stairs a woman screamed and the dogs began to bark madly. Feet pounded the castle floor as Joseph jabbed, only to have Ware move quickly, hack again with his weapon, and sidestep a blow. Whirling swiftly, Ware swung hard and hit the big knight's sword with all the power in his sinewy body. Joseph's blade flew from the dark knight's hands and, clattering, skidded uselessly into the rushes. Ware whipped around, slashing the air and heading for the second knight, who was advancing as servants and soldiers entered the hall.

"What the devil's going on here?" the steward demanded.

"For the love of Jesus!" Mertrice cried.

"Lady Clare! Lady Clare!" Cailin's strong voice rose above the shouts of men and servants. "Holy Mother Mary, Sir Strahan, stop this nonsense!"

A man possessed, Ware spun and whirled, jabbing his sword, forcing the second knight backward against the wall as yet another of Strahan's men unsheathed his weapon and stepped forward, anxious for battle.

"Saints preserve us and our wretched souls!" Cailin cried as servants and knights, the friar, Cadell, Glyn, and Clare hurried into the room.

"Stop it!" Strahan snarled. He snatched the fallen sword and faced his younger cousin. "Don't make me hurt you, Ware." But Ware, intent on maintaining control of Abergwynn, paid no attention. Strahan called for more guards, and they, dodging Ware's wild swings with the sword, grabbed hold of the young lord of the castle and physically restrained him. Several knights hesitated, as if unsure whom to follow, but more than ten had no trouble showing their allegiance to Strahan.

"What's going on here?" Clare demanded. Striding regally forward, she glared at Strahan and his disloyal band.

"It's none of your business, Clare."

"It is if it has to do with Abergwynn and my brother!" Clare had buried a husband and a child, and she wasn't afraid of anyone or anything.

"Stay out of it, Clare," Strahan ordered, but Clare's expression changed from anger to disbelief as she took in the situation.

"You really think you can start a rebellion?" She laughed. "For God's sake, Strahan, you'll never be able to turn Garrick's men against him."

Strahan hesitated and then, to Ware's ultimate humiliation, said with quiet authority. "Already done, I'm afraid. I'm in charge here now. What I say goes. If you go along with me, Clare, everything will work out—to everyone's benefit. If not, then you can spend the next week or two, until I return, locked in your chamber, as Ware will be in his."

"I'll not—" Two guards, Andrew and Gilbert, immediately restrained her. "No, Gilbert, not you—"

A sword rattled. Peter stepped forward. "Let Lord Ware and Lady Clare go, or by all that's holy, Strahan, I'll slit your throat my—"

At a nod from Strahan, Sir York, the knight next to Peter, moved as swiftly and silently as a cat. Peter twisted as he was grabbed. The curved blade of a dagger glinted hideously in York's meaty hand.

"No!" Ware cried.

"Take this, you bastard." With a sickening thud, York plunged his dagger deep into Peter's chest. Scarlet blood spurted, raining over the walls and York. Clare screamed. Glyn fainted, though Cadell caught her before she hit the floor.

Strahan, staring hard at Ware, said, "It's your choice, boy. Are you willing to spill more blood?"

Ware glared with hatred at his cousin. From the corner of his eye he saw the slumped body of Sir Peter, blood trickling from the corner of his mouth to mat his beard, the dagger wound staining the dead knight's tunic red.

"This is madness!" Clare insisted. "Stop it at once! There'll be no more bloodshed!"

"Quiet, bitch!" Sir Andrew hit Clare across the face, sending her spinning and stumbling backward. Had it not been for Gilbert's strong hand on her arm, she would have fallen.

As quick as a hawk striking, Strahan flew at Andrew and placed his blade at the knight's throat. "No harm is to come to her, Andrew. None."

The stout knight's throat worked. "But—"

Ware saw his opportunity and kicked the knight full in the groin. Sir Andrew doubled over in pain, and Ware lunged for Strahan. His fingers tightened around his cousin's throat, and he held firm, like a dog on a bone. Gilbert let go of Clare and, taking vengeance on Ware, doubled his fist and swung his arm quickly, aiming for Ware's nose. With a sickening crack, pain exploded in Ware's face, blinding him. His grip on Strahan faltered. Blood poured from his wound, and he cried out. The knight kicked him savagely in the gut. Ware dropped to the floor.

"Damned fool!" Strahan growled as Ware held his hands over the pulp that had once been his nose. Blood trickled through his fingers, and agony ripped through his brain. "Now, Sir Ware, you will be held prisoner in your quarters, and you, Lady Clare, will be locked up as well."

From somewhere in his consciousness, Ware heard Clare protest. "Strahan, think. Garrick will kill you. You can't do this. It's madness."

"Maybe, but this is how 'twill be."

"When Garrick returns—"

"He won't," Strahan said with a note of finality that turned Ware's blood to ice. He tried to struggle but was kicked once more, this time in the temple. Pain splintered through his brain before merciful darkness engulfed him.

Garrick took the first watch, as he had the night before. He was too restless to sleep, too anxious to rout out the damned band of thugs and take Logan home with him. He glanced into the shadowy copse of trees and listened to the wind sigh through spring leaves in the oak and yew. At times like this he felt melancholy, afraid that the farmer's story was false or, worse yet, that the boy was dead.

Standing outside the glow of the fire, his eyes searching the darkness, he whispered a sincere, though long overdue, prayer for his son. He didn't fall to his knees—he was still too prideful a man, who had all but renounced God at the death of his wife and the kidnapping of his boy—but he did pray, hoping that the simple plea for guidance would quiet the raging demons within his soul.

He stared at the burning wood as the fire, which had once spit flames and sparks into the night sky, slowly died. He added more wood to the blaze and resumed his watch. As he did, he felt a strangeness in the forest. The skin on his scalp rose. He heard a twig crack and turned in the direction of the noise, squinting hard into the murky thicket, grabbing hold of his sword.

In the feeble moonlight a horse and rider appeared, and Garrick wasted no time. He slunk through the trees until he reached the solitary horseman and then, without so much as a sound, lunged upward. The horse was startled. It squealed and reared, but not before Garrick had grabbed the would-be attacker and pulled him hard off his mount.

As the horse bolted, Garrick wrestled with the rider, a strong, wiry man who kicked and bit as if possessed. He forced the smaller man to the ground, lying atop him, his arm at the attacker's throat.

"Let go of me, you bloody brute!" A flash of silver and Garrick barely dodged the blow from the knife as he recognized Morgana's voice.

His heart, already pumping with fear, now beat a new song as he half lay atop her. The clouds allowed enough eerie moonlight through their frothy veil to show Morgana's face, white as alabaster, and her eyes, dark and furious. Though a part of him was glad to see her, he was instantly angry. She'd disobeyed him, nearly killed him, and now was going to make him a laughingstock in front of his men. Much worse, she had put her life in jeopardy by following him. For he'd either strangle her or make love to her until morning. Teeth clenched hard together, he pinned her to the ground and leaned close to her face. "I thought I told you to stay put, Morgana of Wenlock!"

She stiffened at the sound of his voice. "I couldn't," she cried, as if suddenly realizing with whom she was dealing.

"Ware and Strahan and Clare were given direct orders—"

"I disobeyed them all," she said hastily, her breasts rising and falling rapidly, pressing up against his crotch only to fall away with her breathing. Garrick tried and failed not to notice that he was straddling her, that her body warmed his inner thighs, that he was growing as hard as steel with each teasing touch of the points of her breast against his legs. "I—I asked Ware to let me leave, but he would not."

"So you took it upon yourself to . . . what—steal a horse and leave my castle vulnerable, as you did with your father's keep?"

"Nay!" she cried and then bit her lip anxiously. She struggled a bit, and the movement of her body between his legs drove all anger from his head. What he was feeling and fighting now was lust, heady, mind-spinning lust. His member ached to be stroked, and he had to drive all thoughts of her sex from his mind. Though he burned to be touched, to have her hands and her lips on him, he had to resist her obvious charms. His body was hard and wanting, crying out for the hot pleasure that her fingers and mouth could bring.

It took every bit of concentration to keep his mind on the task at hand. "Why are you here?"

"I thought I could help. I . . . I had another vision, and I fear for you—"

"For me?" His voice had grown husky, and Morgana swallowed hard.

"Aye, m'lord."

He leaned closer, his breath fanning her face, his eyes searching every shadow and crease in her skin. The stiff arm at her neck relaxed, and his hand moved slowly inward to touch the base of her throat and trace the circle of bones surrounding her pulse. "You shouldn't be here," he said softly, and her insides turned to jelly, for she knew that he was speaking not of her disobedience but of the fact that he and she were alone in the wilderness, nothing separating them but a few thin scraps of clothing and a quickly shredding code of honor.

"I couldn't stay at Abergwynn when I knew that you were in danger."

His dark gaze penetrated hers, and the callused finger that had been circling her skin moved lower, to the neckline of her tunic. "I thought you wished me dead."

"Often," she admitted, though she was having trouble thinking clearly as his hand worked wondrous magic on her skin, creating concentric circles of warmth that started at the apex of her legs and moved ever outward, radiating to her extremities, causing her flesh to tingle and her breasts to ache and strain against her tunic.

"Yet you think you can save me."

"I hoped—oh!" Her breath swept inward as his fingers dipped beneath her collar to brush the top of her breasts. She knew she should stop him now, stay this madness before it went much further, but when his lips slanted swiftly over hers, she didn't protest. Her lips parted willingly, accepting the gentle thrust of his tongue and the hard pressure of his mouth. Her resistance, scanty though it was, collapsed, and she wound her arms around his neck.

He kissed her with a possession that swept through her

and turned her blood as hot as fire. His lips were eager and hungry, as if he'd not tasted of a woman in a long, long time. She answered his plundering kisses eagerly, returning his fever, unaware that she was squirming beneath him, that the white-hot fire in her center was matched only by the burning in his loins.

His hands were everywhere—caught in the thick strands of her hair, stroking her rib cage, pressing hard against the small of her back, and dragging her hips even closer to his. She felt his swelling hardness pressed into her abdomen, and instinctively she rubbed herself against him, moaning softly as he kissed her again, his lips trailing along the curve of her neck and lower still as he shoved the tunic over her shoulder and exposed more of the white mound that was her breast.

"Damn you, Morgana of Wenlock," he whispered between kisses. His hands surrounded her face for an instant, and she thought he might stop his fevered exploration of her, but he paused only to look into her eyes. Their gazes touched, his demanding, hers all too willing to yield. She watched as he hesitated, his hands on the hem of her tunic as if he intended to strip it from her.

Instinctively she arched upward, inviting his plundering hands to do more than tease.

He groaned and slammed his eyes shut, fighting the fires that consumed him, battling against the hunger that roared through his blood. He wanted her—oh, Holy Father, he wanted her in such a way as to make a decent man blush. "Christ's blood!" he growled, her tunic bunching in his fingers. "Why do you torment me, woman?" Angrily he yanked the hem back into place and muttered low oaths at himself as he rolled quickly off her. "Why couldn't you stay put?"

So angry he was shaking, he forced himself to his feet, shoved his hands through his hair, and muttering an obscenity, kicked the ground. "This is no good, Morgana. You should have stayed at Abergwynn."

"I could not." Picking the twigs from her hair, she struggled to her feet, and when he faced her again he found her chin tilted defiantly, her shoulders braced for whatever cruel words he might hurl at her. Holy Mother Mary, if he had any sense at all, he'd tell her to stay out of his sight, that she was no better than a street wench, that he wouldn't dishonor his cousin by lying with her. If he mortified her and wounded her harshly enough, she might have the good sense to stay away from him. Yet he couldn't summon up the words. He'd hurt her enough already, and though she was betrothed to Strahan, it was Garrick's responsibility to keep away from her—not by vicious words but by his own code of honor. So he gritted his teeth and, instead of demeaning her, took her hand and led her into the circle of light by the fire.

A few of his soldiers had awakened and were standing, swords drawn, as they approached.

"Oh, m'lord, thank the saints, 'tis you!" Calvert said, sheathing his weapon. A short man with a huge nose, he was obviously relieved at the sight of the baron. His gaze rested on Morgana for a minute, and the flicker of a smile teased his lips but was quickly hidden in the shifting light from the fire.

"We thought you might have seen the robbers," Hunter added, casting Morgana a glance that said more than words. She felt a blush steal up her neck, but refused to lower her eyes.

"As you can see," Garrick explained, his expression

unreadable, "Lady Morgana has taken it upon herself to join our search, though I instructed her to stay at Abergwynn. I'm not pleased that she disobeyed me, and she will be punished when we return, but I shall let her stay on with us, on the condition that she not wander off and that she stay within our ranks. You are to give her every consideration and yet keep an eye on her."

Morgana bristled at the thought but held her tongue. So far she was getting off with little punishment.

"Now let's all get some sleep."

"I'll take the next watch," Hunter offered, and Garrick motioned Morgana forward to his tent.

When she started to protest, he placed a finger to her lips. "Since you spent the last two days searching for me, I'll trust that you won't disappear in the middle of the night. I'll sleep with Calvert." His lips twitched a little. "He snores and smells of horses and ale, but at least I won't be tempted to do anything dishonorable."

Morgana blushed again, and Garrick's jaw hardened, his smile forgotten as he glared at her. "You've already made a fool of me by disobeying me, Morgana. Don't make that mistake again. The next time my punishment will be swift and harsh."

"What would you do, m'lord?" she said defiantly. "Betroth me to a man I detest?"

Before Garrick could respond, she slipped into his tent and threw herself down on his pallet. The man was horrible. And wonderful. And prideful. And handsome. And a bully. And . . . Oh, damn his black soul, she couldn't help thinking about him and the wonder of his touch.

If she thought of him still, she could feel the sweet, hot vibrations that had seeped through his blood to hers when he kissed her. To force her thoughts away from his kisses, she bit her lip, nearly drawing blood, hoping that pain would chase away her willful fantasies.

They broke camp, and Morgana, astride the stallion she'd "borrowed" from Will Farmer, rode behind the baron in the company of his soldiers. Garrick knew that the men were sniggering behind his back and that they expected him to punish this woman who had openly defied him. Punish her he would, elsewise there would be hell to pay, as his men would no longer respect him.

But he wasn't going to bend her over his knee and humiliate her, nor would he strike her, nor was he about to banish her to a tower or any other nonsense just to appease his men. No, her punishment would have to seem harsh to the men, while not injuring Morgana in the least. God's teeth but he felt as if he were standing in the middle of a river. On one side was a beach strewn with burning coals, on the other an icy bank so cold it would pull the skin from the soles of a man's feet. Yet he had to choose, because the river was steadily rising and if he didn't move, he would surely drown.

But drown in what? His love for Morgana—for that was what it felt like, as if he were falling in love with this witch-woman with her beguiling green eyes, her cutting tongue, and a stubborn streak that would break the patience of any man.

But *love?* The word caused him to scowl. He'd loved once, and he'd vowed never to love again. Astrid had been the love of his life. But Astrid was gone, and since he'd met Morgana, Garrick had thought less and less of his wife. It seemed that Astrid was finally and truly buried.

Now what was he going to do with Morgana?

Seventeen

The next two days brought nothing. Will Farmer's robber band, if it had ever really existed, seemed to have vanished into thin air. Morgana was beginning to wonder if the man had lied or dreamed up the whole chain of events.

Garrick, too, seemed to doubt the farmer. With each passing uneventful hour, the baron grew more grim. His jaw became set and uncompromising, his neck and shoulders more rigid. He barked orders at his men, and he was impatient with anyone who dared to cross his path.

The knights rode for endless hours, from dawn until dusk. They stopped often, and each time the company paused, one of Garrick's best men, the knight called Hunter, searched the ground for tracks. Once they passed a fire pit with ashes that were still warm to the touch, but they found no evidence that the people who had recently camped in the glen were part of the band of thugs who had attacked Will Farmer.

Whenever the search party stopped, Morgana climbed off Luck's broad back and touched the soil, feeling the texture of the moist earth, rubbing it between her fingers while she tried to conjure up a vision of the men who had traveled this road before. She drew runes for safe passage on the ground and caught Randolph watching her, smirking at her foolishness. But she wasn't about to be stopped by a fool's silly grin. Often she tried to speak to the wind, but the breeze was silent, and she was soon as frustrated as Garrick.

Most of the knights gave her wide berth. She didn't blame them. Obviously they thought she was either mad or possessed or both. Not that it mattered. She'd rather have them leave her alone and laugh at her behind her back than have to deal with their bawdy jokes and lust-filled stares.

Near twilight Garrick ordered the tired soldiers to make camp near a stream. Morgana watched as he dismounted with a creak of saddle leather. He tended to his horse, as she did hers, and then while the knights built a fire, he disappeared through the trees, presumably to relieve himself.

Morgana, too, left the growing light of the fire and found a path through the thicket of saplings guarding a creek. Ferns and vines grew along the bank, and the air smelled dank in the coming darkness. She washed the dirt from her face and hands and was still kneeling near the shore when she felt the first tickle of the wind against the back of her neck. Like an icy finger the breeze stirred the leaves overhead and touched her skin, causing gooseflesh to rise on her arms.

"Please," she whispered desperately, squeezing her eyes shut as she instinctively turned to face the current of air. Water dripped from her hands. "Tell me of Logan."

She strained to listen, but heard only the rustle of leaves, the flapping wings of an early-rising bat, and the soft, steady gurgle of water splashing over stone.

"Help me!" she whispered again, her wet fists clenching in frustration. "Give me a sign."

A low moan of air streaming through the undergrowth was the only sound that reached her ears. The voice, stubborn old thing, had decided to fall silent again. Morgana ground her teeth in frustration. What was she supposed to do? Garrick wanted her to help him by using her powers, but so far her gift seemed able only to play games with her and tie her insides into knots.

With a sigh she opened her eyes. "Stupid, stupid voice," she grumbled, kicking at a stone. "Go ahead, be obstinate, but I don't know how I am to find the fierce one's son without your help!" When the wind didn't answer, she scowled. "You started this, you know. Telling me of some danger to the north! Ha! So here I am . . . oh, Lord."

She sank to her knees again and finished washing, unaware that Garrick was standing in the undergrowth not ten feet from her, observing her with a mixture of incredulity and amusement. The witch rose and walked to a wet spot of earth, where she knelt down, and with the sharp blade of her dagger began one of her nonsensical drawings, taking painstaking care as she worked.

"What is that?" Garrick asked, and she started, raising her large eyes until their gazes touched. Staring into her night-darkened eyes, Garrick felt his abdomen shove hard against his lungs. Holy Mother, she was beautiful. Even in the dusk, her eyes shone a verdant green, her hair fell around her face in tousled disarray, and her mouth, pinched at the corners, was a succulent pink blossom.

Without answering, she turned her attention back to her scratches in the dirt, completing the sketch. "This is a rune for safety—ours as well as Logan's." He snorted and stepped forward. The toe of his boot nearly touched her work. Craning her neck, she stared up at him again, and this time her tunic gaped open, allowing him a quick glance at her breasts, round and full. "You asked for my help, remember?"

The back of his throat went dry. He forced his gaze away from the view of her flesh. "And you think some lines in the mud will ward off our enemies?"

"I don't think they will hurt." She tossed her head, and once again, his gaze shifted and he was captivated by the fullness of her breasts. Firm, white, and supple, they swung free. Beneath his breeches he grew hard, and it was all he could do to pretend that nothing was amiss, that the ache in his loins wasn't so hot and straining that he wanted nothing more than to throw her onto her back, rip off her clothes, and plunge into that magic between her legs. The mossy bank would do for a bed, and their bodies would mesh intimately together. Over the thunder of his heartbeat and the hiss of her breath, he would listen to the cool trickle of water and the hoot of owls while he was joining with her, feeling her velvet warmth surround him, pushing deep inside her, hearing her pant and moan while he tasted those sweet and perfect breasts.

He swallowed hard, using all his willpower to stave off the fire running rampant through his bloodstream. She was promised to Strahan—promised by his own traitorous tongue.

Morgana seemed to notice the change in him. As the night deepened around them, lengthening the purple shadows and closing about them like a private cloak, she stood. The glow from a half-moon pierced the canopy of leaves overhead and shone in her eyes. She glanced down to the bulge at his crotch and bit her lower lip.

He swallowed hard, hearing the muted sound of insects. He and Morgana were not touching, but they were standing so close they could have embraced each other if either had reached out. The air seemed to crackle with unspoken emotions, and Garrick burned for her. She licked her lips, and he stifled a groan, yet neither he nor she was able to take the first step.

"We—we should get back," she said, but made no move away from the creek.

"Not yet."

"But I . . ." She let out a whispering breath, and her eyes begged for the truth. "What is it you want from me?"

He wanted to lie, to say that she held no fascination for him, but he wasn't a man who dealt in untruths. "I want you," he said simply, and it seemed as if all the sounds of the night disappeared. He heard her quick intake of breath, noticed the widening of her eyes, watched her glorious breasts rise as she gasped in surprise at the boldness of his words. Oh, if he could but touch her.

"You've betrothed me to your cousin."

"Aye, and I was a fool to do it," he said, cursing loudly as he threw back his head and stared up at the pale moon. "Have you bewitched me, Morgana? Is one of those drawings in the ground a plea to God to torment me? Because that's what you've done. I tried to get away from you, to come on this journey alone, because I knew I couldn't . . . wouldn't be able to restrain myself."

He turned back to her, and she looked so beautiful in the starlight, so innocent and pure, that he damned his wicked thoughts of taking her right then and there. By rights he could do so. He was the baron. He could force himself upon her despite her protests. He could claim her in that most primitive of ways. But he had never taken a woman by savage means, and he was certain that Morgana wouldn't fight him. No, she would willingly lie with him just to rid herself of the shackles of marriage to Strahan. He could see it in her eyes—a flicker of something akin to desire. So why not?

He reached forward slowly. Twining his fingers in that thick mane of black hair, he drew her head back. She didn't protest. He sampled further, pressing his lips against the curve of her throat. Her skin was cool, and she trembled. From fear or passion? Or both?

The hardness beneath his breeches strained to life, and he slowly licked her throat, starting at her jaw and moving with deliberation, tasting every inch of her, his tongue sliding down the satin smoothness of her skin to the fragile circle of bones at her throat, her pulse jumping wildly within that delicate ring.

"You want me, too," he said in a voice raw with lust. His tongue dipped lower, past the neckline of her tunic, near the ribbon that laced her bodice together.

"I—I want no man," she whispered, but he didn't believe her. His knees buckled, and he dragged her to the damp earth with him.

She didn't protest, and he kissed her, long and full on the mouth, feeling her open to him as a flower might open to the sun. His tongue rimmed her teeth and found its mate, glorying in the sweet, soft pleasure of her mouth.

Slowly he untied the ribbon that held her tunic together, exposing more of her skin. He kissed her lips again, and when the fabric gaped open, he moved lower, his lips teasing and tasting as he slid against her body, letting her feel the need that was hot and hard between his legs.

" 'Tis wrong," she whispered, though she didn't resist, but seemed to yield even more to the gentle pressure of his body against hers. Her eyelids fluttered down, and she gave herself to him, body and soul. As surely as the wind rustled in the leaves overhead, she let go of her doubts.

He closed his eyes, bent on releasing her, but he couldn't stop himself. The smell and feel and taste of her were too inviting. He pressed his face against her soft flesh and kissed the top of each rounded breast.

She moaned low in her throat and arched a bit, though her hands had moved to his shoulders and her fingers dug into the muscles of his arms.

"Garrick, please," she cried as he slipped the tunic off her shoulder and her breast, bound only by her chemise, spilled into the night, white and full, peaked with a round button of darker skin that begged him to kiss her, to taste of her, to suckle like a newborn babe. He kissed her through the soft fabric, his tongue wetting the lace, and she quivered in his arms, growing warm and impatient.

"So you do want me, little witch?" he said in wonder, and when she didn't deny her desire, he kissed her again, his lips melding with hers while one hand found her breast, touching the nubile flesh, teasing her nipple to a proud point that begged him to suckle again.

"M'lord?" a voice, remotely familiar in Garrick's dazed mind, called through the trees and cut into his fevered thoughts. His desire cooled instantly, and he scrambled to his feet.

"Get up," he ordered, through tightly clenched teeth. He yanked her to her feet and helped her smooth the wrinkles from her tunic.

"Lord Garrick?" the voice—Garrick now recognized it as Hunter's—inquired again.

"Over here, near the stream," Garrick yelled, straightening his clothes and feeling a deep flush burn its way up his neck.

With a crashing of branches Hunter joined them and

came up short when he saw Morgana. "Oh, I . . . uh, I didn't mean to disturb—"

"You disturbed naught. Morgana was just showing me what her sketches in the earth mean."

Hunter's gaze dropped to the smudged rune, only partially visible in the darkness, but he didn't comment on it. Nor did he say anything about the untied ribbon at Morgana's neckline or the glimpse of breast he no doubt caught. But he seemed disappointed. "Just letting you know that Giles is opening the mead and Fulton's killed a buck. We'll be eating well tonight." Then, as if he knew he was intruding, Hunter returned down the path from which he'd come.

"Come," Garrick said, nettled at the intrusion and wishing to God that his desire for Morgana would just go away. "Our absence will be noticed."

"And that bothers you?" she asked.

"Among other things." He looked meaningfully at her partly exposed breasts and felt a little pang of pleasure at her response. Her mouth grew round, and she had the good grace to seem embarrassed as her fingers fumbled with the ties. He pointed impatiently at the ground. "I don't see that your sketches are doing anything to help us find Logan."

"And nearly bedding me did?" she threw back, unable to hold her tongue. Anger sparked in her incredible eyes. Brushing a twig from her hair, she glared at him, waiting for a response.

His jaw grew hard. "Why do you mock me?"

"Because you mock me. Do not make light of my gift just because you are as angry as a boar that wants to rut and cannot. I'm only trying to help you, *m'lord,* and the way I see it, we need all the help we can get, be it from God himself or from magic."

"You talk in circles!" Garrick scowled darkly. In truth it wasn't the silly lines in the dirt that bothered him; it was the woman. He couldn't get her out of his mind, or his heart. He wanted her, and he'd nearly taken her right here and now. He was a man who was used to taking what he wanted. The fact that she felt desire for him only made self-restraint more intolerable. Even now, seeing the embers of anger in her sea green eyes caused his gut to tighten. His gaze dropped from her face to the swell of her breasts and the curve of her waist. He imagined what it would feel like to span that small waist with his hands and plunge into her velvet warmth. Closing his mind to such willful and sinfully luscious thoughts, he grabbed her hand and drew her roughly through the trees and into the circle of reddish light cast by the fire. He couldn't consider her charms. He had to concentrate on finding his son.

Morgana yanked her hand away from his touch and held her head at a defiant angle as she half ran to keep up with his long strides, but Garrick tried to take no notice of her. God's teeth, she was more trouble than he'd bargained for when he rode to Wenlock to fetch her for Strahan's bride.

That thought curdled like bad milk in his stomach. Strahan's bride indeed! Christ, he was a fool.

Garrick tried to hide his irritation with the witch. Already some of the men were gathered about the fire, sampling the mead, joking together, their stomachs growling as the buck roasted and sizzled over the coals. A few of the braver soldiers cast knowing glances toward Garrick, but no one commented on his whereabouts with Morgana. Only Randolph seemed to smirk at her, while Hunter, obviously embarrassed, avoided her gaze. No doubt the poor knight, too, had fallen for her charms, though seeing her half undressed while she was alone with Garrick had probably destroyed his fantasies about having her for himself. Even if Hunter's lips remained sealed, word would no doubt get back to Strahan that Garrick had been found with the witch and she'd been half undressed. Damn and double damn. Garrick shoved the hair from his eyes and only hoped to talk to his cousin first. Obviously Strahan wouldn't marry Morgana now. Bah, what a mess! True, she was still a virgin, or so she seemed, but she'd been willing, *willing* to give her virginity to him.

He poured himself a cup of mead. Somehow he'd find a way to appease his cousin while allowing Morgana her freedom. That settled in his mind, he turned his thoughts to the present. If he could keep his breeches on and his desire at a level he could control, he could concentrate on finding Logan. Lifting the cup, he swallowed a long draft of the warm mead and felt the familiar heat that inflamed the back of his throat and scorched a path all the way to his belly. He would drown himself in mead, if need be.

The witch and her sorcery be damned!

Garrick didn't touch her again. In fact, he barely spoke a word to her or acknowledged her the next day. He drove the small company without a respite, and by nightfall the men were grumbling among themselves and the horses were lathered, muddy, and dead tired.

Morgana tended to Luck, offering him an extra handful of grain, which the stallion munched greedily, his thick lips brushing her palm for every last kernel. She brushed him long and hard, content to tend to the animal rather than join the men. Never had she felt more alone—a single woman among men with blood in their hearts.

"You're a good one," she told Luck, fondly patting his muscular shoulders. The horse nickered softly, and Morgana smiled for the first time that day. The night was warmer than last, and the first stars were beginning to wink above the trees. Clouds drifted lazily across the sky. "Aye, better than any other destrier or palfrey bred in that wretched Abergwynn," she added, enjoying her scathing comment about Garrick's home. She threw the brush she'd been using into an empty pail. It clattered against the metal, startling some of the horses. "Damn Abergwynn," Morgana swore.

At the mention of Garrick's castle, the wind picked up, dancing feather light and ice cold through her hair despite the mild night.

Morgana shivered and heard the lonesome cry of a wolf. Was it an omen—her thoughts of Abergwynn and the response of nature? Or was she imagining things, putting too much belief in the magic everyone else assumed flowed through her veins? She thought she heard the crack of a whip and the sharp cry of a soul in torment, but when she stood perfectly still, she heard nothing other than the swish of horses' tails, a soft nicker now and again, and the muted laughter of the men drinking at the fire.

They'd camped in a glen where the hills gently sloped down to the valley floor. Some of the men were becoming disenchanted with Garrick's quest. She'd heard the murmurs and whispers behind his back, and yet no one dared broach the subject that wasn't far from anyone's mind: how long would they be asked to follow a trail that was colder than a dead fish—if there was any trail to follow at all? More and more the men were beginning to believe Will Farmer to be a fool who had risked Garrick's wrath for a few silver coins and a horse that the witch had easily stolen from him.

Sir Randolph muttered that they were on a fool's mission, and Sir Henry only shook his head sadly, as if he felt concerned for his baron's state of mind.

She ate alone, barely tasting the leftover venison before she slipped between the furs of her makeshift bed. She was tired, her bones and muscles ached, and she welcomed sleep, since she'd spent the previous night remembering Garrick's embrace, seeing it over and over in her mind. She'd tossed and turned for hours, her body on fire. Deep inside, she ached, feeling an emptiness she'd never known existed.

But tonight she'd have no more of those wickedly wanton thoughts. No, by all that was holy, she'd sleep and keep her mind pure, she told herself. But try as she might, her mind continually strayed to Garrick. She knew he had taken the first watch again and wasn't yet sleeping. Though she'd spread her blankets far from the fire, beneath the protective branches of a willow tree, she felt as if Garrick were staring at her.

Eventually all the men had rolled themselves in their robes and settled down near the fire. Snores and groans replaced their loud jokes and hearty laughter. The campfire burned steadily as one or two of Garrick's men stood guard.

Morgana, from sheer exhaustion, fell into fitful slumber, her mind not yet settled, though her body craved sleep. She tossed and turned as images filled her brain—vivid and dark pictures that would not let her rest. Golden silk rippled beneath the surface of moving water, and a small child's cry echoed through her dreams. Morgana chased after the boy's screams. She ran through a blackened forest, and her feet caught on the gnarled roots of ancient oak trees. Hoisting her skirt so that she could run faster, she nearly stumbled, and the trail gave way to a wildly thrashing river where gold streamers floated beneath the surface like gilded eels. She heard the boy and caught a glimpse of him on the far shore. But in gazing at the boy, she caught sight of the countryside beyond him, where Castle Abergwynn, charred and skeletal, stood, its banner no longer showing the colors of the House of Maginnis. A new flag snapped loudly, waving bright colors against a steel-colored sky. Blood red, the banner bore the emblem of a black sword and triangle pointing toward the center of the earth, as if it could burrow straight to hell. Morgana screamed and tried to run. Despite the symbol of death on the flag, she plunged into the icy depths of the river and tried to reach the boy. Strips of gold silk knotted around her wrists and ankles, pulling her down beneath the surface. Her lungs burned for air. She struggled against the gold ribbons that wound tighter and tighter, like a fisherman's net, as she tried to reach Logan. Her head broke the surface and she gulped air, screaming to the child. "Logan!" she cried, hoping her voice wasn't drowned by the rush of water and praying that he could hear her as the golden cords drew her down to the black bottom of the river.

"Morgana!"

Her eyes flew open and she started to scream. A huge hand covered her mouth. "Shhh!" Silvery eyes glittered over her.

Relief flooded through her, and she let out a sigh as Garrick slowly withdrew his hand.

"Quiet, witch," he whispered against her ear.

She nearly cried. The dream was so real, so vivid, her terror so complete, that she threw herself against him and clung to his neck in gratitude for being awakened. She held back sobs and fought the sting of hot tears.

Garrick's breath ruffled her hair. Strong arms surrounded her, and she was calmed by the steady beat of his heart. He smelled of leather and smoke and musk.

"I saw Logan. I heard him crying."

His muscles tightened. " 'Twas only a dream."

"Aye, but so real." She felt as if a ghost had just crawled up her back, leaving feather-light footprints between her shoulder blades.

Garrick let his hands fall to his sides. "Tell me."

As she caught her breath and her heartbeat slowed to the point that she could speak without gasping, she described the nightmare, the stark images of the boy, the burned castle, the golden ropes, and the death flag.

Garrick, on his knees beside her, listened quietly. His visage was grim, his eyes betraying a pang of grief. "You think my son's dead," he said, the tortured words sticking in his throat.

"I think he's in danger."

With a snort of impatience, Garrick said, "I know that much."

"And you," she said quietly, more certain of the meaning of her dream than before. "You're in danger as well."

He snorted. "Is that the only song you know? First you were afraid of me, sure that I was the danger from the north. Am I right?"

She couldn't deny it and didn't bother trying.

"Then you said my son was in danger, which is a known fact. Now you expect me to believe that I, too, am in some dark jeopardy?"

"Not only you, Garrick," she said, using his given name freely. "But all of Abergwynn. I told you of the symbol of death in my dream."

"Ah, yes, the sword and the triangle. Well, rest easy, witch. Strahan and Ware are guarding Abergwynn," he said, rubbing the back of his neck. "As for me, I have no fear for my own life."

"Then, *m'lord,* you are a fool."

He glared at her for a second. "Another fact that can't be disputed. I came for you, didn't I?"

He was about to leave, but Morgana, still shaken by her dream, grabbed hold of him. Before he pushed aside the veil of willow leaves, she murmured a quick spell for his safety. Her words stopped him short.

"You don't have to whisper silly incantations."

" 'Tis not silly."

" 'Tis against the church," he pointed out, starting to leave her again.

"Only a prayer to nature. I don't think God would disapprove," she replied sharply. "Can't you see that I am trying to do as you asked?"

Garrick sighed, and the night was filled with his great sadness. He didn't disguise his torment, and his broad shoulders sagged a bit. Over his shoulder he said, "I asked you to find my boy, and you've failed."

"Not yet. There still may be time— Oooh!"

He had spun quickly and grabbed her, both hands digging into the soft flesh of her upper arms. "How long, witch? How long before we find my boy?"

"I know not."

"That's right. You know nothing! Nothing!" He spat out the words, his anger and frustration igniting as he glared down at her.

For a second Morgana knew fear—a cold, deep terror that nearly stopped her heart. But then he drew her to him and with the same punishing grip as that on her arms, he kissed her—hard and hot and savage, as if in pressing his mouth possessively to hers he could somehow drive away his desire, as if he could turn an act of love into an act of hate.

Morgana, blast her weakness, responded to him. Her body yielded even as her mind rebelled, and though she tried to push him away, to pry his hands off her arms, her own lips surrendered to his in a kiss that caused a shudder to rip through her body, creating an answering response in his.

"Why do you do this to me?" he rasped, his fierceness replaced by wonder. "This can't be."

Morgana knew it was true. Any silly hope that she and this powerful man could become more than a subject and her liege, died a quick and painful death. He was the baron, the man who still grieved openly for his dead wife, the man who had sworn she would marry another, the very man who had vowed to harm all that she held dear if she didn't obey him. Yet she had let herself feel something for him, some unnamed emotion that caused her to think irrationally, to risk her life, to do anything to be at his side. Oh, she was a goose! As silly as Glyn!

She didn't hate him as she once had, though in truth he scared her more than a little. But she cared for him much more than she should have.

With a groan he took her into his arms again, and this time his kiss was gentle, his tongue probing, his hands splayed against the small of her back. Through her clothes she felt him trace her spine with the tip of one finger, moving lower and lower until he found the parting of her buttocks. She squirmed when he stopped, and the finger rested at the apex of that sensitive cleft. Deep inside, she pulsed, moisture beginning to heat between her legs. She shifted, hoping he would draw those intimate lines against her skin again. A delicious warmth crept through her, and she pressed her eager, hungry lips to his. Her breasts were crushed against the great solid wall of his chest, and her blood thundered in her brain.

"Morgana, sweet, sweet witch," he whispered against her ear, and she knew that he was losing his control again, that all too soon they would be lying on the ground, their fingers clawing past clothing to find bare skin, their breathing as ragged and panting as that of mating beasts. "Stop me," he begged in a voice torn with agony.

"I—I can't." She closed her eyes and her mind to all that could happen—to the past that divided them, to the present that had thrust them together, to the future that was as bleak as any of her visions.

He grunted, low and primal in his throat, and one hand cupped her breast, feeling its weight, massaging the firm mound through her tunic until her nipples stood erect and ready. He kissed her again, his famished lips eager and wanting.

Her breath was lost, as was all reason, and only when he drew back his head, holding her face between warm palms that trembled, did she find the strength to pull away.

"I've never wanted another woman—not since Astrid, not like this," he said, his voice faltering over the name of his wife. "I thought and I hoped that I would live the rest of my life never feeling this way."

"And now?"

His lips twisted into a sardonic smile. "And now you're betrothed to my cousin, by my own choosing. It seems as if your fates have played a trick on both of us." He started to turn back to his own pallet, but Morgana touched his arm.

"Listen to me, Garrick!" she commanded, her voice a rough whisper. "I wouldn't lie to you. There is grave danger! I've seen it! Castle Abergwynn could be under siege at this very moment."

He snorted and shook off her hand. "I think the only thing under siege, Morgana, is my mind."

"Nay, please, listen—"

"Leave it be, woman. Tomorrow we rise early. We have a mission: to find Logan. And this—this distraction of love-making must be forgotten."

She felt the silly hope within her begin to wither and die, though she knew he spoke the truth. The child had been gone for many days. Time was running out.

As if Garrick could read her very thoughts, he let out a long, slow breath, and his eyes glittered with fury. "God be with me when I find the bastard who stole my son."

Eighteen

"I'll kill them all," Ware swore through his pain. His mind was hazy from the beatings, his eyes bloodshot and blackened, his nose still squishy, but Strahan's men hadn't been able to break his spirit. As he attempted to sit, he spat blood into a bowl Clare had begged from a servant. He winced when she tried to clean his wounds. "Leave me alone," he growled, ashamed, for he had lost control of Abergwynn. Garrick had been right: he wasn't man enough to protect the castle. He'd failed miserably, and his pride ached more than the pain in his face and ribs. Now he and a few others who were assumed loyal to Garrick were locked in the baron's chamber.

"Hold still," Clare admonished him, cleaning his wounds as best she could.

He suffered the indignity of her ministrations in silence, and he ignored the other people who had been confined with him, for their fate was his fault. Miserable and feeling sorry for himself, he wanted nothing more than to curl up in a ball or, better yet, to end his own life with his dagger. No! Even better, he would find a way to kill Strahan. No matter that he would die along with his cousin, at least he would avenge his pride and leave this world without losing all of his dignity.

He stifled a groan. His entire body ached, and blood had

clotted in his nose and throat, making eating and drinking nearly impossible. Clare lifted his tunic and began to treat the wounds on his back. Carefully she applied the cool cloth to his skin. He sucked in a swift breath through loosened teeth as the water touched his flesh. His back was striped with burning welts from a whip, yet he would take another ten thousand lashes before he'd kneel to his Judas of a cousin.

"This may hurt."

He remained stoically silent as she applied ointment to his back. His muscles quivered from the sting as the tincture of barks seeped into his bruises and gashes. He gritted his teeth and drew away from her. He had no time to think of wounds.

"Don't move!" she reprimanded him.

"I don't need medicine; I need to find a way out of here," he growled, angry at the world in general and specifically at himself for trusting Strahan.

Clare frowned at him and sponged his face yet again. "You know the castle as well as I. There's no escape but from that window, which is too far above the ground to jump from, the window in Logan's room, which is even higher, and the two doors, both of which are locked and guarded. So quit spending your time thinking useless thoughts and let me—"

"For Christ's sake, Clare, no!" He shoved her hand away, and her bowl of healing mash—made from the bark of pine, wild cherry, and plum—clattered to the floor.

"Oh, Ware," she sighed, staring at the dripping concoction that clumped in the rushes.

Ware didn't listen. His body throbbed, and his head pounded so that seeing was difficult, but he wasn't about to sit here and be tended while Strahan and his band of rebels were holding Abergwynn, not while there was a drop of blood in his body. "We must escape."

"I'm with you," Cadell agreed. Morgana's brother was young and green, but he thought himself ready for battle. He jumped to his feet and stood in a mock battle-stance, whirling and punching and pretending to fight off three attackers at once. There wasn't an ounce of common sense in the boy. However, Cadell's sister appeared to recognize the gravity of the situation. Glyn sat white-faced on a corner of the bed, her head bowed in prayer, her lips moving with the quick rhythm of one who had spoken often to God.

"No one would like to get out of here more than I," Clare whispered, "but escape is impossible."

"Never," Ware swore, and Cadell grinned broadly, the poor simpleton, Ware thought. The boy hadn't a clue that Strahan's men would gladly run him through with their swords if he so much as opened his mouth. "Surely most of the men are loyal to Garrick."

"Are they?" Clare asked, bending over to clean up the mash from the floor. "I wonder . . ."

"Of course they are. They wouldn't follow Strahan blindly. They've *pledged* themselves to Garrick's service."

"Words are easy. What choice had they? Either join Strahan or die. When a man's life is threatened, it's simple to find reasons to change loyalties."

"The bastard. The bloody no-good bastard of a traitor!" Ware bit out, still stung by the fact that he had failed Garrick. He'd been duped and beaten like a silly puppy. Holy Father, he'd been a fool!

But he wasn't going to give up. There had to be a way. He just hadn't thought of it yet. But he would. In time. And he'd wrest control of Abergwynn from Strahan again, proving to Garrick that he was worthy of his own castle and soldiers.

Footsteps sounded in the hall, and with a creak the large timber bolt was lifted. Old hinges groaned as the door opened, and Strahan, dressed in full armor, and Sir Joseph entered. To Ware, his cousin looked evil, his dark eyes shining, his sneer neatly in place.

Strahan swept a contemptuous glance over his captives before his dark eyes landed on Ware. "You look awful."

"Thanks to you."

"None of this would have been necessary if you'd only complied with my orders," Strahan pointed out. "Believe it or not, Ware, I don't enjoy having my own flesh and blood whipped."

"Except for Garrick."

A mean glint lighted Strahan's eyes. "All I want is Garrick's loyalty."

"Do you think he would ever kneel before you?" Ware spat. His stomach roiled, and he thought he might get sick all over Strahan's freshly oiled armor.

"I think there are ways to persuade him."

"He would never . . ." Ware's voice trailed off as the truth hit him full in the face. "You bastard! *You* stole Logan." Ware lunged forward, but Strahan pushed him easily against the wall. "Where is he?"

"The boy is fine."

"And what of Will Farmer?" Ware demanded. "The gang of robbers who—"

"Will was just a pawn. I used him to get the news to Garrick. The thieves and cutthroats, they are my men now," Strahan bragged, apparently enjoying the horror on his cousins' faces. "They were easily bought. For a few pieces of gold and the chance for free amusement with Jocelyn, they gladly took the boy and his maid and kept them on the run, hiding them in this place and that."

"You bloody devil!"

"God in heaven," Clare whispered, "how could you?" When Strahan didn't respond, she advanced upon him. "Why would you torment a man who has done naught but help you?"

"Ha! Help me? Has he ever once tried to wrest Hazelwood away from McBrayne?" Strahan demanded, his lips curling. "Nay. Never. And why? Because he enjoys being my lord and master and would never allow me to be his equal."

"You're daft!" Clare said, still walking bravely forward.

"I think not."

She stopped just short of him. "Let us go, Strahan," she demanded. "For the love of God, let Logan and Jocelyn go free and give up this sinful vengeance against a cousin whose only fault is that he trusted you. You have no right to take this castle—"

"Shut up!" He backhanded her, and Clare staggered backward toward the wall, catching herself with one hand, though she nearly fell to the floor. A throbbing red welt appeared on her cheek as she regained her balance.

"You cowardly bastard!" Ware lunged, but Sir Joseph, his arm still bandaged, lifted his sword, ready to slay the young whelp who had wounded him.

"Don't!" Strahan commanded, and Joseph, with a growl, stopped advancing. "Now, Ware, if you know what's best for you and your family, you won't cause difficulties while I'm gone."

"You're leaving?" Ware couldn't hide his delight.

"To find your brother. We've spent two days searching

the forests and villages for Morgana. She's vanished, and unless I miss my guess, she's fled to Garrick." His face had turned into a mask of hatred, and he clenched his teeth as if trying to keep back vomit that rose in his throat. "It appears that my intended has become your brother's lover."

"Garrick would never bed another man's woman," Clare stated. She rubbed her cheek but stood tall, silently daring Strahan to strike her again.

Strahan lifted a skeptical brow. "Cousin Garrick is used to taking whatever he wants. I doubt he feels any sense of honor where Morgana is concerned. He's stolen from me all my life; he won't stop now."

"That's a lie!" Ware growled.

"Anyway, you're to answer to Joseph and Sir Charles now."

"The steward was in on this?" Clare demanded, unbelieving.

Strahan lifted a shoulder. "Most men's loyalty can be bought—with either gold or women or fear for their lives. Charles was one of the easy converts."

"You bastard Judas!" Ware muttered, and Glyn began to pray again. For the first time Joseph noticed her kneeling on a pillow by the bed, her blond hair pulled away from her face as she whispered prayers for deliverance.

Joseph's eyes gleamed for a second, and he licked his fat lips. Strahan, reading his thoughts, placed a restraining hand on the huge knight's shoulder.

Glyn stiffened as she caught the lust in Joseph's glittering stare. Understanding the sudden tension in the room, she stumbled over her prayers, and her face drained of all color.

"You cannot have her," Strahan said to Joseph.

The knight's dark brows drew into a black knot. He

grunted and rubbed his belly with anxious fingers. "But, sire—"

"She's promised to someone else."

"I—I'm what?" Glyn demanded, and then, hearing her own voice, she bit her lip and looked as if she might faint.

Clare snarled, "You'll burn in hell for this, Strahan."

"My men will be rewarded, all of them," Strahan said with a cruel grin as he turned to Morgana's trembling sister. "You, Glyn of Wenlock, are a prize."

"No—oh, please."

Ware wanted to vomit. He lunged forward, but Clare held on to his arm, restraining him. "Nay," she whispered, before turning her swollen face to Strahan. "You can't pledge women's lives to your men—"

"I can and I have. Glyn is spoken for, and so, dear cousin, are you."

Ware leapt forward again, but Joseph gave him a swift, hard kick to the groin that sent him sprawling on the floor. Clutching his crotch and fighting back tears, he stared up at Strahan with hatred. "You lying black-hearted bastard. I'll rip your throat out!" Fighting the pain, he found his footing and charged again, only to be shoved backward by Joseph. He hit the floor with a thud, his head landing in the rushes, his pride in tatters as he still held his groin.

"Stop it, Ware. It's no use," Clare ordered, but her eyes were trained on Strahan. "I'll not lie with any man unless he's of my own choosing. I'll die first."

"I don't think so," Strahan said, and Joseph, his attention torn between Ware and Glyn, grunted.

"You've got your woman," Strahan reminded the lusty soldier. "Be satisfied."

Joseph frowned. "But, sire—"

Ware cringed at the term.

"I said, be satisfied. As for you"—Strahan pierced Ware with his evil glare—"I've left instructions that if you cause any trouble, you're not to be killed, but you will be chained and forced to watch as your sister and Glyn are raped and beaten. Now, you can save them a lot of trouble and pain by setting an example and doing as you're told. If you do not, Joseph here will carry out my orders."

From the corner of his eye Ware saw his sister step forward, tilting her face upward to meet her cousin's black glare. "God will punish you without end, Strahan."

"I think not. You see, even Friar Francis, after searching his soul, has seen the light and accepted me as the new baron of Abergwynn. He will absolve me of all my sins, cousin, so don't worry about my soul."

Clare spat on the man who was her cousin. Ware scrambled to his feet, determined to pummel Strahan should he attempt to hit Clare again, but this time Strahan restrained himself. "You'll regret that, Clare. I'll see to it personally." He turned and strode to the door. Joseph sent Glyn one final lustful glance and followed the new baron of Abergwynn from the chamber. The door swung shut with a thud that echoed through the stone halls and seemed to mock Garrick, wherever he was.

The sun was high and pale. Shafts of light filtered through a thin layer of clouds and thick spring leaves as Garrick's tired party followed yet another road. This path was overgrown, little more than a deer trail, which was no longer used, as a larger, more traveled road lay only half a mile east. The horses plodded through the undergrowth, and insects, excited by the sunlight, droned and flitted in the air.

Morgana was cold. Deep inside, she felt the wintry hand of death wrap itself around her heart. Hunter had ridden ahead to scout the area and to slice through the vines and brambles that blocked the road. Garrick rode at the head of the column, leading the rest of the weary band. Morgana, astride Luck, was wedged in the middle between Sir Giles and Sir John.

As the company made its way deeper into the copse of saplings and gnarled oaks, the sunlight became dappled, mere patches of light that pooled on the ground. Morgana felt as if a sliver of ice had slipped down her spine. Gooseflesh rose on her skin, and she wondered if the devil himself resided in these woods.

"You're being silly," she told herself, but even smooth-tempered Luck was nervous. His ears flicked forward and back, and his steps sometimes minced, as if he were afraid of laying a hoof down too long for fear some snarling beast would charge out of the dark shrubbery, claws and fangs extended.

Some of the men felt it, too, the change in the air. They looked anxiously over their shoulders. From the corner of her eye, Morgana saw Sir Adam make a hasty sign of the cross when he thought no one was looking. Others kept their free hand on the hilt of their swords, ready to slay whatever beast or man came rushing through the brush.

She heard a snap. Luck trembled. Pulling back on the reins, Morgana eyed the dark undergrowth. Something was wrong here. Very wrong.

"Ho!" Hunter called, his voice ringing through the woods and startling birds and rodents. Pheasants and quail were flushed out of their hiding spots in an eruption of feathers and a fluttering of wings that caused even the calm war-horses to dance and neigh. "Lord Garrick, over here!"

Garrick spurred his horse forward, and the rest of the knights followed. They joined Hunter in a clearing that had been trampled by several horses. A fire pit was filled with coals, now cold, and yet Morgana sensed that people had been here not long since.

Upon entering the clearing, Morgana felt death, and her throat grew dry. As the men studied the broken undergrowth, she dismounted and followed a narrow path to a brook slicing through the wet ground. Heart in her throat, she knelt at the water's edge and splashed a few drops on her face. She reached into the brook again, and her fingers touched a fragment of cloth. Her breath stilled in her lungs as she looked into the shallows and saw a scrap of gold shimmering just below the surface. *Just like her vision!* "Holy Father," she whispered, trying to stay calm.

The fabric was caught on a sharp root that extended into the stream. She reached into the frigid water and retrieved the scrap of silk.

"It's Jocelyn's." Garrick's cold voice startled her.

She jumped, startled. Looking up, she noticed fury mingling with fear in Garrick's eyes. He took the wet fabric from her hands and swore under his breath. "This is what you saw in your dreams, isn't it?" he asked, dangling the dripping silk in front of her nose.

"Aye." A feeling of impending doom settled over her shoulders.

"There was more to your vision and you chose to keep it secret. Now, tell me," he demanded, his eyes narrowing suspiciously as he grabbed her upper arms and drew her to her feet. His nostrils flared in anger, and the rage in his soul was mirrored in his eyes.

He clutched the scrap of silk in a death grip, as if in so doing he could conjure up his son. "This"—he held up the soiled fabric in his hands—"was Clare's. It is from a showy belt that Clare gave to Jocelyn because the girl fancied it. Clare had a fondness in her heart because Jocelyn was so good with Logan." Garrick's voice nearly broke and his anger disappeared as he thought of his son. He twisted the wet rag in his hands, and water dripped through his fingers. "What does this mean, witch?" he asked, his face taut with torment.

"I don't know."

"But you saw the vision. Can you not interpret it?"

She swallowed hard and averted her eyes, wishing she could hold her tongue and knowing he deserved the truth. "Yes, I saw this and more—the sword and triangle of death as I told you before."

"For Logan?" he asked, pale as a ghost.

She shook her head. "I know no more than you."

He gripped her so hard she thought she might faint. "Tell me, woman! I need the truth."

Her heart ached that he would think so little of her. Forcing herself to meet his eyes, she said evenly, "I would tell you all, Garrick, if I knew more. I swear it. I would never, *never* trifle with a child's life. As soon as I learn more of Logan, I'll tell you."

His eyes searched her face, as if expecting deception to show in the curve of her chin or the tilt of her head or within her steady gaze. "I swear to you, Morgana, by all the saints and God himself, if you do not tell me everything—"

"Lord Garrick! Over here!" Randolph called through the brush.

Garrick released her. Quickly he followed the sound of

Randolph's voice, moving upstream along the bank, holding back the branches for Morgana until they saw a small group of Garrick's men clustered near the creek.

"What is it? Why are you all . . ." His voice drifted off as he looked at the stream. The blood drained from his face. Morgana followed his gaze and suppressed the urge to scream, for there, face down in the water, lay the bloated body of a woman. Her blond hair billowed around her, and her tunic, too, swayed with the current, though the body didn't move; it had become wedged between the tangled roots of a willow tree.

"M'lord, I'm sorry," Hunter said, but Garrick's jaw tightened and he motioned to one of his men.

"Get her out of there."

Randolph, his bony face twisted in disgust, dragged the woman from the stream and turned her face up.

Garrick grew rigid, and the men murmured sounds of dismay. Fulton, usually a clown, dropped to the ground and, kneeling, offered a prayer over the blond woman's body.

"It's Jocelyn?" Morgana guessed, and Garrick, grim-faced, nodded stiffly.

All the hope soaring in Garrick's chest was suddenly hurled back to earth and dashed against cold, hard stones. He examined Jocelyn, and a horrid anguish filled him as he noticed the black-and-blue wounds on her back and legs and the scratches on her face. Though the water had washed her wounds, he guessed she'd been raped and beaten before she drowned—whether by her own hand or that of another, he could only speculate.

But there was no sign of Logan. Garrick's heart was as black as the clouds that gathered steadily overhead. Where was his child? Was he safe? And who was the bastard who had done this treachery? He vowed to avenge Jocelyn's murder—for what was done to her had either killed her or driven her to take her own life—and when he caught the beasts, he'd see to it that they suffered as she had. A quick death would be much too easy.

He ordered his men to bury Jocelyn, and then, leaving Morgana and two knights to make camp, he and a small band rode in ever-widening circles around the campground, looking for any sign of Logan or his captors.

Garrick rode alone. Astride his war-horse he mourned the woman who had raised his son as if Logan were her very own. He remembered Jocelyn's easy laughter, her lighthearted spirit, the joy she received when Logan ran to her and buried his head in her skirts.

A pain, deep and raw, tormented his soul. His body ached from the inside out, and his mind was vivid with horrible scenes of the torture of the woman. And what of Logan? What horrible fate did the boy face? With a blinding pain he realized that he was but a man, a mortal, and his son's safety was not in his hands. "Please, Lord, keep him safe," he said over and over, chanting the words as a litany and knowing that only the power of God could protect his boy.

As the men continued their search, Garrick reined in his horse by a giant oak tree. He climbed from the saddle and bowed his head. Laying his sword on the ground in front of him, he knelt, and thus, unarmed and repentant, he whispered, "I've been prideful and stubborn, Lord, refusing to accept you and your mercy. Please be with Logan. I offer you my kingdom, my soul, and my life for the sake of my son. Please, God, hear my prayer. If anyone should suffer, it is I, not the boy. He is but a child." Garrick felt the unfamiliar sting of tears, hot against the back of his eyes, thick in his throat. He sucked in a ragged breath and refused to cry, for there was still a godless streak of pride within him that would not allow him, even alone in the presence of the Almighty, to weep. "Please take Jocelyn's soul and protect my boy."

With that singular prayer, he stood, stared up at the darkening heavens, and finally mounted his steed. Jaw clamped tight, he jerked hard on the reins and urged his horse forward.

He searched until dusk and finally returned to camp. Morgana was by the fire, her face illuminated by the golden flames, and for the first time that day, he felt a whisper of joy. The witch was beautiful and headstrong and often at odds with him, but he was beginning to love her, and right now, as desperately as he needed God's forgiveness, he needed her love. The comfort of her body would ease his, and though he knew it was a sin and that God was watching, he couldn't help but think of the wonder of lying with her, of melding his hard body to hers, of claiming her with a primitive force that would bind them forever.

He smiled bitterly as he handed the reins to Sir Randolph and gratefully took a cup of mead. It seemed that no matter how good his intentions, he was destined to sin.

nineteen

You'll do us no good by starving yourself," Clare observed as she paced from the window. Her back was rigid, her face more lined than Ware remembered. Still, he shoved away the trencher in front of him. His face was beginning to heal, and his pain had lessened to a dull ache that pounded through his skull.

The chamber was dark, lit only by a few sconces and the fire glowing in the hearth. Ware thought of grabbing some of the burning embers and hurling them at his captors when they came close, but each time they had entered the locked chamber, the soldiers had been careful. They had grabbed Glyn and held a dagger to her throat. She'd screamed, but hadn't struggled, though she nearly fainted each time. No, Ware could not risk her life.

"I can't eat," he told his sister when she pointed at his trencher of untouched stew.

"You have no choice."

But Ware wasn't to be won over. Strahan had left two days before, and nothing had changed. There had been no chance of escape. The door was continually barred, except when a servant or guard brought in water, food, or slop pails.

Everyone in the room was listless. Glyn had given up on her prayers and often sat weeping in the corner. Cadell, his bravado ebbing with each day, was picking through the rushes, searching for mice, and Clare, though she walked as if an iron spike had been driven up her spine, was losing her spirit as well. Her words sounded hollow, and Ware knew that all of the prisoners were counting on him to set them free.

But he was failing. The hours passed and he had no plan of escape, no way to free them. He tried to pretend that he was Garrick, for his older brother, he knew, would never be kept hostage.

The door opened, and Springan slipped through with a pitcher of water. She moved slowly, her gaze lowered, her gait unsteady.

"Hurry, wench! I've not got all day, and I have other duties I wish you to perform. Duties much more pleasing." From the open doorway, Joseph's voice boomed through the room before he slammed the door and threw down the bar. Springan visibly shuddered.

Ware felt sick. So Springan had become Joseph's woman. From the looks of her, she was hurting. He watched as she poured water into the cups, and as she turned toward him he saw it—the bruise discoloring her face. Though she'd tried to cover the purple-tinged skin with her hair, the welt was visible, and Ware's guts tightened at the thought of her pain.

"Springan, wait!" he said when she started for the door.

"I'm wanted, m'lord."

Ware was on his feet and crossed the room quickly. "Stand still." He brushed back her hair. She winced at his touch, and her face suffused with color. "Joseph did this to you."

She wouldn't look at him, dared not answer.

Ware felt a wave of self-loathing. Not only had he failed

his brother, but he'd failed the servants as well. He touched her lightly on the chin, forcing her to lift her gaze up to his. "Springan, I'm sorry—"

"Wench!" Joseph called through the closed door.

"I must leave." Panic rose in Springan's eyes. "He doesn't like it if—"

The door flew open to bang against the wall. Sir Joseph weaved into the chamber. He smelled of sour mead, and his face was flushed. The leather thong holding his breeches together was undone, and his manhood bulged against the partially opened fabric. "There you are," he snarled when his gaze landed on the servant girl. "Not giving it to Sir Ware, are ye? Y're my woman now!"

"Leave her be!" Ware ordered and felt all his youth and impotence wash over him in a pitiful tide.

"Shut yer mouth. Y're not lord of the castle anymore," Joseph pointed out. "Not that you were before. Git over here," he yelled at Springan.

Eyes round with fear, Springan approached him and he laughed. "Not so saucy, are ye, wench? Not since ye've been warming my bed. *I* know how to handle a woman." His arm snaked out, and he grabbed Springan's hand. She dropped her tray, and all the cups clattered to the floor as he pulled her roughly to him. "Look at the mess you made, you stupid woman." He shoved her hard to the floor. "Pick it up! But mind ye kneel as you do it."

Springan's jaw tightened, but she did as she was bid, and Ware watched in horror as Joseph stood behind her, his legs spread, his hands planted on his hips, his gaze on her rounded rump.

"That's a girl," he cooed, wiping the back of his hand over his lips. His eyes slitted into lusty stones, and drops of sweat beaded his eyebrows. His thin tongue snaked around his bearded lips. "Just the way I like to see you—on all fours with your arse in the air."

"That's enough!" Furious, Ware kicked a burning log from the fire. It rolled toward Joseph, and the big guard's eyes left Ware for an instant. Without thinking, Ware sprang forward, catching Joseph off guard. His fingers slid around the bigger man's throat, and he clutched with all his might. With a scream of rage, Joseph nearly lost his balance and clawed frantically at the hands closing around his massive neck.

But Ware was a man possessed, and his fingers were like the springs on a trap, tightening, tightening, threatening to cut off the flow of air to Joseph's lungs as the bigger man bellowed and stumbled, trying to dislodge his attacker. In desperation, he groped for his sword, but Springan was quick and she leapt upon Joseph, biting his hand before he could unsheathe his weapon.

Footsteps pounded in the hallway and five men, guards posted by Strahan, rushed into the room. "Halt," the largest man commanded.

"You halt," Ware ordered, still hanging on to Joseph like a hungry dog on a bone. "I'm still lord of this castle."

The soldiers hesitated, and that was all the time Clare needed. She stumbled over Springan, yanked Joseph's sword from his scabbard, and swung it wildly. "Stop, all of you!" she commanded.

Cadell kicked the burning log at the soldiers. Embers exploded, raining fire and threatening to ignite the tapestries and rushes.

"Lady Clare—" Sir Guy beseeched her, but Clare lunged, cutting his arm with the sword.

"I said halt," she commanded, her eyes ablaze.

Ware and Joseph tumbled to the floor, and Springan rolled away from the wrestling men. Joseph still clawed frantically at the hands around his throat, his legs kicking wildly, connecting with Ware's already bruised midsection. Still Ware clung to him, desperate to redeem himself. He would either reclaim the castle or die trying. Joseph was losing strength; Ware felt the lifeblood draining from his enemy, saw the bulge of Joseph's cruel eyes.

The men raised their swords again, but Clare commanded, "Drop your weapons. I will kill you. One at a time."

" 'Tis you who will be killed."

"Is it? What would happen if Ware and I died at your hands?" she asked. "Are you foolish enough to want to be responsible to Lord Garrick for the death of his family? Unless you want to face him when he returns, unless you want to explain that *you* killed his brother and sister, you had better lower your weapons now!"

"That's right!" Cadell chimed in, ready to do battle.

Still Joseph struggled, making a last vain attempt to save himself. He kicked and twitched, but Ware only tightened his grip, and the bigger man's face turned an ugly shade of blue. Spittle collected in his beard, and he gagged repeatedly, gasping for air that he couldn't get to his starving lungs.

Ware pressed harder, cracking Joseph's neck. The big man convulsed as a shudder ripped through his body. His hands fell away from Ware's wrists; his legs sagged. His body twitched in Ware's death grip, but Sir Joseph was dead. In a hiss of stench, the last breath left his lungs, and his eyes rolled back in his head.

Silence followed, broken only by Ware's tortured breathing.

Sir Guy was paralytic as he gazed at the pile of flesh that

had once been Joseph. He glanced up at Clare. "What if Strahan kills Lord Garrick?"

Clare said evenly, "Are you, Sir Guy, willing to take that chance?"

From the open door of the hallway, a low, horrible growl rumbled into the room.

"The wolf!" the soldier nearest the door whispered nervously. "Who the devil let him out?"

"No one did," Cadell said as Sir Joseph expired. "I had but to call to him and he came. He is, after all, the beast of the witch. Come, Satan!" he said, whistling sharply.

Again the wolf growled, causing the hair on the back of Ware's neck to lift in fear. He struggled to his feet, the blood and spit of Joseph's death throes still staining his hands. Beyond his own fear, he admired Cadell's presence of mind. " 'Tis true. The dog is from the depths of hell. I heard Garrick say as much," Ware lied, thankful for Cadell's vivid imagination.

Two of the knights dropped their weapons and crossed themselves. Ware grabbed one sword; Cadell picked up the other.

Glyn looked stricken, but she didn't, thank God, utter a word.

Gold eyes blazing menacingly, the thick hair behind his ears raised, Wolf slunk into the chamber. His black lips were pulled back, and he snarled and paced, looking as if he might pounce at any minute upon anyone unfortunate enough to be in his path.

Glyn nearly swooned.

"Now, listen," Clare commanded, as if talking to children. "This castle belongs to my brother. You have pledged your fealty to him, and yet you betrayed him by rising against him with Strahan. Now is the time to prove your-selves." She lifted her sword a little higher, as if she intended to cleave into two bloody halves anyone who approached her. "What say you, Sir Guy? Are you loyal to Garrick or will you follow that swine Strahan straight to hell?"

Guy glanced around the room—at Ware, who had killed the bravest of Strahan's knights; at Clare, regal and self-righteous with her sword upraised; at pitiful, pious Glyn and daft Cadell. His gaze wandered to the wolf dog, and the beast crouched, his unblinking gaze focused on Guy's soft throat. Swallowing with difficulty, one eye on the dog, Guy knelt, his head bowed, his neck vulnerable, should Clare or the wolf attack. He placed his sword on the floor before him. "I shall serve Garrick," he said in a voice hardly more than a rasp. "I shall pray for God's forgiveness as well as Garrick's. Would that his justice be merciful."

"Aye." Sir James knelt as well, laying his sword on the rushes before him. Soon all five of the men had cast aside their weapons and pledged their loyalty to Garrick of Abergwynn. For this, Ware stripped them of their knives and imprisoned them in the very chamber in which he and the others had been held captive.

"We can't trust them," Clare warned him, and Ware agreed.

Sir Guy and the rest were too easily swayed, their alle-giance either bought or bartered. Better to hold them here until Garrick came back. He could deal with the traitors.

"Take everyone into the hallway and wait for me," Ware ordered.

Clare, after scooping up the weapons lying on the floor, did as she was bid, shepherding Glyn and Cadell outside. But Springan refused to follow them outside the chamber. Instead she hung back with Ware and the knights. Ware started to tell her to leave, but noticed the silent plea in her gaze. He decided she had been through enough and should be allowed to make up her own mind.

Still holding a sword, he wiped the blood from his free hand on his tunic. The men shifted, and Ware eyed the disloyal lot of Garrick's soldiers. "Try to escape and you'll die," he warned. "Mayhap, if you do as you're told, Garrick will be easy on you." The soldiers cast each other worried looks, but no one dared utter a word. Satisfied that they wouldn't rise against him, Ware said, " 'Tis done, then. We'll have someone come for that"—he motioned to Joseph's body— "and bury it." He glanced at Springan, "Let's go."

Springan hesitated, eyeing the hated body of Joseph. "May the dogs of hell forever gnaw on your bones, ye bastard," she said, spitting on Joseph's bloated upturned face before whirling swiftly and marching through the door.

Ware doused the fire, then took the candles from their sconces. "You followed Strahan into darkness and therefore shall you dwell without light," he said, proud of his words. Leaving the knights, he barred the door behind him.

Springan stood like a soldier in the hallway and offered to stand guard at the door. "Trust me," she said, her voice bitter, "I will let no man escape."

"God be with you," Glyn intoned, her voice shaky. "My father will see that you're rewarded."

"My reward will be Strahan's defeat." Springan's face twisted with a hatred so intense that her beauty was suddenly lost and she looked like a scarred old woman.

Ware offered her a knife he'd taken off Sir Guy and wondered at the reasons for her malice.

With Wolf at his heels, Ware led Clare, Glyn, and Cadell

along the upper hallway and down the stairs. His heart nearly stopped with every creak of the old timbers, but no more knights were lingering in the hallways. Except for a few servants, Ware met no one.

"Saints be praised, m'lord!" Cailin said, her eyes growing misty when she spied Ware at the foot of the stairs. She and Mertrice were carrying huge baskets piled with filthy tunics, shirts, and breeches.

"Shh, woman!" Ware hissed. "Tell us where the guards are posted. If we're to reclaim Abergwynn from Strahan, we must overpower his small army."

"There ain't many," Mertrice chimed in. "Sir Strahan took most of his men. But there's two sentries on the battlements, the steward's in the cellar, and two or three knights are still sleeping it off in the great hall."

"We'll take them first," Ware said, a cunning smile playing upon his lips.

"Are any of the servants loyal to Strahan?"

Cailin snorted loudly and Wolf growled. "Nay. He's a cruel one, he is. He has nary a kind word for anyone, and he's often as ready to cuff you as not. No, there's not a servant in Abergwynn who doesn't yearn for Lord Garrick's return." She offered him a toothless grin and chuckled. "Who do you think let the dog go free?"

"Good," Ware said, pleased that the servants had started their own quiet rebellion against Strahan. "Now, you, Mertrice, go to the stables and talk to the stable master, also the thatcher and the carpenter, the armorer and the smith. Send them back here, but one at a time, so as not to alert the guards. Everything must appear as it was."

" 'Twill be me pleasure." Mertrice hurried out of the great hall.

"Cadell, you and I shall take the guard in the east tower, then the guard to the west. Are you game?"

"Am I!" Cadell's eyes lit up with the fire of challenge. "I'll run 'em both through."

"Nay. We capture them and hold them with the others, if we can," Ware ordered. "You, Clare, deal with the chaplain. See where the loyalty of our man of God lies. But whether he be true to Garrick or has pledged himself to Strahan, he is to be imprisoned with the others."

"But he's a man of the church—" Glyn said, and Ware whirled on her, his temper snapping.

"Then God will protect him, won't he? As far as I'm concerned all those who allied themselves with Strahan, except for the servants, are traitors. It's that simple. Got it?"

Glyn swallowed hard. "I'll pray for your immortal soul," she whispered, crossing herself quickly.

"You do that," Ware shot back. Then, moving swiftly, he and Cadell mounted the stairs leading to the east battlement. Cadell carried a dagger between his teeth and lugged Joseph's huge sword while Ware was armed with Sir Guy's weapon. They pressed their backs to the wall, keeping to the shadows, until they came upon Strahan's guard, standing watch, his head nodding. Silently Ware stepped behind him, placed his knife at the man's throat, and said, "One word and it will be your last, Sir Ivan."

The old knight didn't even reach for his sword. "God bless you, Lord Ware," he whispered, but, though he seemed relieved that Garrick's brother was back in control of Abergwynn, Ware didn't trust him.

Within the half hour, both tower guards and the two men sleeping in the great hall were locked into the temporary prison with Springan at the door.

Ware assembled the men—servants and freemen who worked for Garrick. They were a strong lot, but they were used to wielding hammers and pitchforks rather than weapons. "We have no choice," he told the small group. "Cadell and I will take the fastest horses in the stables and go to warn Garrick. The rest of you will stay here and protect the castle. Let no one inside the gates. Clare is mistress of the castle. You, armorer, will be the leader of our new soldiers and the man responsible for the weapons. The women will guard the great hall, and the men will keep watch over the gates. Is that understood? All of you are to answer to Lady Clare."

The smith slid an uncomfortable glance at Ware. "Beggin' your pardon, m'lord, but is it wise to let a woman run Abergwynn?"

"We have no choice," Ware said swiftly and caught the flicker of indignation in his older sister's eyes. "Clare is as smart as any soldier and twice as brave."

The smith worried his hat in his hands. "I know, m'lord, but she's so small."

"One doesn't have to be large to be strong," Clare reminded him. "Think of Sir Joseph—a big man who fell easily."

Several of the servants mumbled their agreement. They had already performed the disgusting task of burying the brute outside the castle walls.

"All right, then," Ware said, satisfied that Abergwynn was as secure as possible. He turned to Morgana's brother. "Cadell, we ride!" He noticed Wolf, sitting apart from the hounds that lay under the trestle table. "We'll take Morgana's dog," he said, wondering if Wolf would not better serve Garrick here. "He'll lead us to his mistress and to

Garrick." Ware's eyes met those of his sister. "Be safe," he said to Clare, and then, with Cadell beside him and Wolf trotting behind, they hurried to the stables where two of the strongest mares were already saddled.

He could not stop himself. The witch was too enchanting. Garrick stared at the moon and wondered if she had cast a spell upon him, for it seemed that every night his desire for her was so intense that his insides were on fire. He tried to douse the blaze that seared through his blood, but just a glance from her or the hint of a smile caused a yearning so intense that he lost his ability to reason.

He took the first watch, standing on the outskirts of the firelight, his eyes narrowed against the dark woods. Oh, he'd been a fool, a prideful, useless fool. What right did he have to rule others? He thought of Jocelyn, who had been a happy, faithful servant. Jocelyn had taken to loving Logan as if he were her very own babe. How many times had Garrick stumbled upon them, she playing a silly game with the boy, the child, enchanted, giggling merrily. Now she was gone—killed, mayhap tortured and raped—because of his stupidity, his trust.

He didn't deserve his castle or his servants. Guilt constricted his chest, and he wondered again where Logan was this night? Without Jocelyn, the boy, if he was still alive, was no doubt scared to death.

Garrick's blood pounded at his temples. If he could but find his child—

"Lord Garrick?"

Her voice was soft, as dark as the night. "I thought you were asleep," he said, turning to find Morgana standing only a few feet from him. The moonlight pooled around her and touched her raven-black hair with traces of silver. Her skin was white, her eyes luminous.

"I couldn't sleep." She walked to a tree and laid a slender hand on a low branch. Her brow knotted, and she chewed her lower lip thoughtfully. "It's Abergwynn. Something is wrong," she said. "I fear—"

"You fear what, woman?" he demanded, his patience snapping. The witch was driving him out of his mind with her hazy visions. Yea, she had told of the gold cloth in the water, but she was unable to give him a single hint as to Logan's whereabouts.

"I sense trouble at the castle."

"What kind of trouble?"

She thought for a moment as he compressed his lips anxiously. "I know not," she admitted. "But the trouble is deep and dark and growing"—her worried gaze shifted back to him—"and I fear that you are in danger."

"I have no time for this, Morgana. I must find Logan. Can't you conjure up some magic and tell me where he is?"

He was mocking her. When the worry in her heart was so great that she couldn't sleep, he had the nerve to scorn her! "I never thought you a fool."

"No?"

"Your stubbornness and your pride will be your undoing!"

"Mayhap they already are," he growled.

"Then trust me when I say we should return to Abergwynn, to face the danger there."

"When we are so close to finding my son?" His nostrils flared in the darkness. "You should be happy. Your vision came to pass. Jocelyn was here, as was Logan. We will not return to Abergwynn."

"I am never happy when death is nearby," she whispered.

The knots in her insides twisted painfully, and the visions danced in her head. It was as if she were standing on the very pinnacle of a mountain, on one side a dark, looming abyss, on the other a murky, deep stream. Should she take a step the wrong way, everyone whom she held dear would fall, and yet she knew that she had to choose.

Garrick cast her a withering glance and wondered aloud, "Tell me, is it possible to change the course of the future, witch?"

"Aye."

"And I, in going to Wenlock to find you, could have changed the course of my destiny?"

"I don't know."

"Don't you?" He glared down at her and his eyes were lit with an inner torment that caused her to shiver. "Could it be that you're the reason the fates have turned against me?" he asked slowly. "The very reason that God has seen fit to punish me?"

"Your son was taken before you came for me," she answered woodenly. His words had cut through her pride to wound her heart.

"Aye, that is true," he admitted, reaching out to trace the curve of her jaw, "but since you returned to Abergwynn with me, my luck seems to have turned for the worse."

"You think you're on Logan's trail."

"Aye, but at what cost? Jocelyn's life? The danger you claim exists at Abergwynn?"

Abergwynn. At the mention of the castle a tingle of fear cast a cloud in front of her eyes, and she wasn't aware of Garrick any longer. The trees seemed to part in the moonlight, and like the nighthawk she had a vision so keen that she could see as far away as the castle, whose stone walls crumbled. She was swept back to Garrick's chamber, where the cold stone floors reeked of blood and death and Glyn's fear was nearly blood congealing as it flowed into Morgana's spirit.

"Oh, God!" In her mind's eye, she saw Wolf pacing, heard his cry, and watched as blood flowed down the tower steps.

"You saw something?" a voice in the distance asked. Rough hands shook her. Morgana blinked and found herself staring up at Garrick. His face was a mask of determination, and his silvery gaze drilled into hers. Her throat was dry and wouldn't work. She licked her lips as Garrick shook her again. "Speak to me, woman!"

"Blood has been spilled at Abergwynn."

"Blood? *Whose* blood?"

"I know not."

"For the love of God, Morgana, why do you torment me with half truths?" he demanded, his strong fingers digging into her flesh. "You tease me with only partial visions. You make up stories that have only a trace of truth. You—"

"I do not lie," she said slowly, her anger beginning to boil.

"Nay, you just give hints of trouble and danger."

"You must believe me!" she cried desperately, grabbing hold of the sleeve of his tunic. "Why would I lie?" Looking up, her face twisted in terror, she whispered, "My family is there, too, Garrick. My brother and my sister."

"Who would dare attack me? Who would know that my army is split?"

"Someone who knows you well," she said quietly. "Someone whom you trust."

He studied the lines of her face, the worry planted deep

in her eyes. "I might be close to Logan here," he argued, but she shook her head.

"Jocelyn has been dead for several days. The murderers are far away."

Shoving an impatient hand through his hair, he weighed his choices. He couldn't let go of his obsession with finding Logan, and yet he couldn't dismiss the witch's premonition. Not entirely. Had she not foreseen the golden ribbon floating in the water? Now, if truly there had been bloodshed at Abergwynn, he would never forgive himself if he ignored her advice.

"We ride back to the castle at dawn," he said, "and if there is nothing wrong at Abergwynn, witch, I will hold you responsible."

"I understand."

"Do you?" he asked, his voice low and threatening.

She shivered before him. "I've seen your justice, m'lord. A boy who openly thwarts you is forced to clean the stables; a brother who disagrees with you is left to guard the castle; a cousin who makes the silly suggestion that you search out a witch to help you find your son is given that very witch as a bride and a large parcel of land as a reward. Even the silversmith who is accused of killing a buck in your forest is allowed to keep the meat and has to pay a fine of two silver cups. Aye," she mocked, "your brand of justice does not frighten me."

His eyes searched her face. "You have no fear of me? Am I not the death of all that is Tower Wenlock?" His voice was softly mocking, the hands on her arms tightening ever so slightly. Morgana couldn't breathe, couldn't think. Her gaze centered on his lower lip—so close. "Eh, witch? Am I not the danger from the north?"

"A—aye," she whispered, her blood stirring. She watched as a crooked smile twisted that slender lip.

"But you would taunt me?"

"Nay . . . just tell you how I feel," she said. Forcing her eyes upward to meet the sizzle in his gaze, she swallowed with difficulty and licked her suddenly dry lips.

"How do you feel?"

"Frightened for Abergwynn and Wenlock, but not . . . not frightened of you."

Noticing the lines of strain near the corners of his eyes, she watched as one of his thick eyebrows arched. A strong man, a powerful man, a man used to taking what he wanted, he was nearly felled by the loss of his son.

"I could destroy all that you hold dear," he said as a nighthawk circled overhead.

"Aye. But you will not."

"I'm not a good man, Morgana."

"No?" She touched the side of his face with the palm of her hand. "Then why am I not frightened of you? Why do I sense this great hurt you bear? Why do I feel that you are not the beast I first thought you were?"

"Because you're a foolish woman!" He jerked his head away from her touch, yet he restrained her still, flexing his hands in his anger.

"Nay. I think not," she argued. "I think you're a kinder man than you pretend to be."

Unmoving, his eyes dark with the night, he stared down at her. Her breath was lost, her heart pounding an irregular beat as she tilted her face upward and the wind tangled her hair, blowing some of the dark curls in front of her face.

"Aye," he whispered, his countenance grim. "You're a witch, that you are. You've turned my thinking all 'round,

Morgana of Wenlock." He lowered his gaze from her eyes to her mouth, and she had to bite her tongue to keep from moistening her lips.

His jaw tightened, and he drew her swiftly against him. Her breasts were suddenly crushed against the wall of his chest, and his mouth captured hers. He groaned and pressed his tongue hard against her teeth, urging her lips apart so that he could plunder the wet velvet recesses of her mouth.

Morgana's thoughts swirled crazily as he cupped her buttocks and held her abdomen against the hardness of his manhood. "I want you, Morgana. As no man should want a woman, I want you. Is this some magic you've cast upon me?"

"Nay, Garrick, I—"

His lips crushed hers yet again, tearing the breath from her lungs, robbing her of any thought of protest. She felt the sweet pressure of his hand against the small of her back, forcing her to feel him, all of him, muscle to muscle, flesh to flesh.

One hand caught in her hair, and he raked his fingers through the long black strands, gently forcing her head back so that he could caress the arched column of her throat. His lips and tongue were wet and hot against her skin, and the female beast within her, a fiery but long dormant creature, began to yawn and stretch, sending flames of lust through her veins. Her blood pounded, and her skin quivered as his mouth delved lower still to the neck of her tunic.

Her breasts began to ache, and her nipples hardened in expectation. Slowly, with his weight, he drew her to the ground. His mouth found hers again, and one hand cupped her throat, gently touching the pulse, causing the female beast within her to break free. As the creature moved inside her, creating a hot, dark void deep within her center,

Morgana arched upward, silently begging for more of the bittersweet rapture of his touch.

Garrick complied, drawing her tunic down over her shoulder and kissing her exposed skin. He groaned against her, and again she bucked upward. "You are so willing?" he rasped as a large hand scaled her ribs, one at a time.

"I want— Ooh."

His hand cupped her breast, feeling its weight, rubbing the soft fabric of her tunic over her taut nipple. "Tell me what you want," he said, but before she could answer, he stretched out beside her, and covered her breast with his mouth. His tongue, held at bay by her clothes, sought to taste and stroke her. He groaned, and his muscles strained. The fabric of her tunic became wet and hot. Damp fibers grazed her nipple until she cried out with frustrated desire.

He didn't waste any time, but stripped her of the clothing and lay atop her. "Ahh, witch," he whispered in awe as he stared down at her breasts. She wanted to cover up, but didn't move as his eyes roved across the firm white skin with only a few veins showing through. Her nipples rose proudly—small, hard buds that puckered beneath his stare. He touched her tenderly, almost reverently, massaging her breasts while he, still dressed, straddled her. "You are Strahan's woman," he whispered in a tormented voice that trembled. His entire body shook, and she knew that he was fighting a losing battle with desire.

"I'm no man's woman."

"But I promised—"

"Tonight I am my own woman," she said boldly and rose upward, clasping a hand behind his neck, feeling the brush of his hair against her knuckles.

With a groan of surrender, he slid down her body, his

legs still surrounding her, lowering his head until his mouth found her naked breast. His tongue darted forward, flicking her nipple, and she arched upward again, wanting more . . . so much more. Lying with him was dangerous, she knew, but she couldn't stop herself. His breath was a fan to the already rampant fire of her desire. He suckled at her breast hungrily, like a starved babe. Again she cried out, closing her eyes against the stars shooting across the sky. He massaged her rump with one hand, holding her close to him so that his hardness, through his breeches, was pressed deep into the yielding flesh of her abdomen. Desire flowed through her veins to moisten the cleft between her legs. She could feel her female parts, awakened as they were.

He lowered himself further, his tongue darting in and out of her navel, his fingers creating a sweet magic against her buttocks. She gasped as he prodded her legs apart and probed deep into her womanhood. Her eyes flew open, and she stared up at him as he touched her. His eyes were glazed, and sweat collected on his upper lip. "Stop me," he whispered, but her hands found the hem of his shirt. His gaze was tortured, but his eyes burned with a desire so hot that she knew he was fighting vainly against his passion. "You're a virgin."

"Aye," she murmured, her voice a faint whisper.

"You should save yourself—"

"Aye." But she pulled his lips back to hers and kissed him like a wanton, her tongue seeking his. He growled deep in his throat and then returned her kiss with a hunger so raw that he shook. He yanked off his clothes, ripping seams as he made himself naked, his muscles gleaming in the moonglow.

She had never seen a naked man before, and the sight of him was an aphrodisiac. Sinewy muscles, some bearing scars, moved fluidly, his eyes glittered with unbridled passion, and an animal musk scented the air. He straddled her briefly and she saw his manhood, hard and erect, as he poised himself over her.

He pressed her knees apart with his own and, after only a second's hesitation, plunged deep into her waiting nest of moist black curls.

Pain knifed through her, and she cried out, her eyes flying open as her maidenhood was ruptured. Panic streamed through her blood, but Garrick held her close, folding his arms around her as she caught her breath. "It will hurt for but a second, little one," he said against her ear, and slowly the pain subsided.

He kissed her, molding his lips to hers as he began to move within her, slowly at first, until she began to respond, her hips catching his rhythm, her fingers digging into his shoulders. The heat within her swelled, and she closed her eyes against the pressure that was building deep inside her. This was Garrick, her foe, her lord, her lover. Her breathing was short and shallow, her mind spinning in circles that blurred the stars and moon.

An explosion, like the very earth shuddering, ripped through her, sending shooting stars into splintering fragments behind her eyelids. She felt him stiffen before throwing back his head and calling her name as he plunged into her one last time, spilled his seed, and collapsed upon her body.

"Morgana," he whispered over and over again. "Morgana, Morgana . . ."

Instinctively she wrapped her arms around him and buried her face in the sweat-dampened crook of his neck. He smelled of the earth and musk, and he held her as if he were afraid she would escape him. Great convulsions rocked her, and she felt warm and dreamy in his arms. It was as if all the elements had come to this very spot—earth, air, water, and fire, swirling about them, wrapping them in a protective shield.

"Holy Christ, Morgana!" His breathing was ragged and hot. Propping himself up on his elbows, he gently pushed the tangled strands of her hair off her face. "Did I hurt you?"

She shook her head and couldn't stop the smile that teased her lips. "Do I look wounded?"

"No, but you were a virgin. . . ." His eyes darkened, and his voice was edged with torment.

"Aye."

"And I took that virginity from you."

"Nay, Garrick, I gave it to you." She stared up at him honestly, with no hint of regret.

"But you are promised to Strahan."

She felt the warm afterglow surround her like a cozy coverlet that would protect her. "You can change that, Garrick. You have but to say the word and I shall be free of Strahan."

He stared at her, his pride hardening his expression. "I do not go back on my word."

"But—"

"I will not, Morgana," he said swiftly, and her heart cracked. "I hope you did not lie with me in an effort to persuade me to change my mind and break my vow to my cousin."

"No, but—"

Again he caressed her face, but this time she rolled away, not wanting his hands or his glorious body to touch any part of her. She felt suddenly soiled and dirty. He'd lain with her and had no intention of ending the betrothal! "I trusted you!" she said, shivering and rubbing her arms. Her dignity shattered, she searched the ground for her clothes. What a fool she'd been—a silly, lovesick fool! Her eyes burned with unshed tears as she hurriedly pulled on her tunic.

Garrick watched her, his eyes troubled. "As I said before, I'm not a good man, Morgana. I lusted after you. I wanted you as I've never wanted a woman, even though you were forbidden."

"By your own tongue!" she cried, discovering one of her boots and yanking it onto the wrong foot. "Curse it all!"

"This—this lovemaking—'twas a mistake," he said, and the words seemed to echo through the forest and pound in Morgana's brain. She dropped the second boot. One of the slumbering horses, tethered near the camp, stamped a hoof and snorted while the creek gurgled and rushed nearby.

"A mistake," she repeated dully, knowing that her betrothal to Strahan was sealed and that the love she'd felt stirring in her breast wasn't returned. As her grandmother had predicted, she would become the bride of Hazelwood. Discovering the missing boot again, she pulled it on her foot, cramping her toes. Oh, she'd been a twit all right, a ninny, to think Garrick of Abergwynn could care for her.

He touched her lightly on the shoulder, but she drew away from him as if his very touch repulsed her.

"Morgana—"

She didn't answer him, didn't look over her shoulder. Tears washed from her eyes and clogged her throat. She heard him behind her as he struggled into his clothes, but still she stared away into the forest. Even when he grabbed her and spun her around, forcing her chin up with his fingers, she avoided his eyes.

"There is no other way," he said.

"Of course not, Lord Garrick. 'Tis your way or no way,"

she declared bitterly. She raked her gaze over his disheveled clothes and shook her head. "So I am to marry your cousin. What will he say when he discovers I'm not a virgin, I wonder? What will he do?"

Garrick winced.

So Garrick knew of Strahan's cruel streak. And yet he would wed her to him! "Leave me alone, Garrick, and do not worry about tonight. 'Twas nothing."

A muscle worked in his jaw. "If I could change things—"

"You *can,* and yet you will not, because of some foolish sense of loyalty to your cousin. Let it lie, *m'lord,* for at least we now know where we stand with each other. And trust me, I will never breathe a word of this to anyone!"

Twenty

*bergwynn is lost, Abergwynn is lost, Abergwynn is lost . . .
lost . . . lost. . . .*

A chill wind, blowing low through the trees, tickled the back of Morgana's neck. She opened her eyes to see the light of dawn just beginning to chase the stars away. The moon was still visible, three-quarters full and sending light through the fog rising off the creek.

Somewhere in the distance, a wolf howled. Her skin prickled, and she heard a soft voice droning through her mind. Her throat closed for a second, and she rolled off the pallet to face the breeze. A cool current pressed itself intimately against her face and lifted her hair from her neck. Several dark strands blew across her eyes, but she didn't notice.

The fate of Abergwynn is in your hands.

"But how?" she whispered, hardly daring to believe the voice. Was it her imagination? Was her silly mind playing tricks on her? A foggy picture formed in her mind, and she saw the stone hallways of Abergwynn spattered with blood. Women screamed and men cursed and Wolf howled piteously. "Oh, God, be with them," she prayed, her throat dry with fear.

Morgana, why have you abandoned us? Glyn's voice rang with terror. *Help us please. Our Father, who art in heaven . . .*

Morgana fell to her knees as the vision faded. Tears rolled

down her face. "Glyn, oh, Glyn," she whispered, her fingers clenching in the dirt and grass. "Please be safe. God, please let them be safe!"

Only you can save the baron's son and his domain. The voice was cold and commanding. She lifted her face, expecting to find a messenger from God standing before her, but she saw only the trees of the dark forest.

"Logan? Where is he?" She asked the voice, but heard nothing. Then a vision, soft around the edges, showed her the face of a small boy, his hair matted, his face streaked with mud and tears. He was in darkness, and water dripped steadily down the slick stone walls of his prison. Morgana's heart beat faster. "Where is this? Logan, can you hear me?" she cried, but the vision started to fade. "No! Where is this dungeon that would imprison a child so small?"

Home, the voice whispered. *Home.*

Frantic, nerves strung as tight as a bowstring, she swiveled her head, searching, hoping to learn more. "Home? What means this?" she cried. "He is not at home!" Her insides churned, and she heard nothing save the frenzied beat of her heart and her own frightened breathing. "What say you? Please don't leave me now!" With all her strength, she forced an inner calmness to tranquilize her. From experience she knew that she couldn't hear the voice when she was overwrought. She had to remain calm, to coax the stubborn voice to answer her. She imagined the gentle roll of the sea, the feel of sand beneath her feet, the soft fur of a newborn foal, until her heartbeat slowed. "Tell me of the boy," she begged.

He is frightened.

"But safe?"

If you rescue him.

"Who holds him?" she asked, her teeth sinking into her bottom lip.

One with whom Garrick of Abergwynn would trust his very life.

But Garrick trusted so many! Why, oh, why, did the voice speak in these wretched riddles? "One of Lord Garrick's knights?" she asked, her mind clicking off the possible traitors. Ivan, Guy, Randolph, Marsh, Joseph! There were far too many to count.

One he loves like a brother.

"Not Ware!" She wouldn't believe it. No, Ware was young and mayhap impatient, but he would be true to Garrick to the very death!

The voice retreated as the wind picked up, and instinctively Morgana knew that the conversation was over. "Wait! Please. Tell me! Ware would never . . ." Her innards shook, and she trembled violently. "Ware! Oh, please, God, not Ware," she prayed, still on her knees, her tunic stained, her eyes wet with tears.

But the voice had not said that Garrick's brother had betrayed him. No—what were the exact words? "One he loves like a brother"—that was it. Not his brother. Not Ware! Another man or woman whom he trusted. But who? Clare would never . . . *Strahan!* Oh, God, of course! Morgana's entire world crumpled. Strahan! The very blackguard to whom she was betrothed!

Her shoulders slumped in shame and desperation. After last night, after giving herself to Garrick and trying to talk him out of forcing her to marry Strahan, Garrick would never believe her if she told him that she'd heard the wind condemning his cousin, the man she detested. Garrick would laugh in her face. He would remind her of how she had pleaded with him to revoke her betrothal. No, the great lord would assume she had made up a story that would release her from her obligation to a man she despised. Her small fists curled, and she wished she could find a way to escape. But she had no time to think. The blood-spattered walls of Abergwynn and Glyn's terrified scream convinced her that she had to make Garrick believe her.

The campfire had burned low; only a few embers glowed red in the gray dawn. A sentry, his back propped against a tree, was staring into the woods. Morgana ducked into Garrick's tent and found it empty. With no time to spare she quickly scanned the area, then entered the forest on the other side of camp, picking her way to the creek that gurgled and rushed through the saplings.

She followed a deer trail until she was certain the baron had eluded her and had perhaps wandered to the other side of the camp. Then suddenly she came upon him, kneeling on the creek bank and staring into the watery depths.

A branch snapped beneath her boot, and he turned quickly, his hand moving swiftly to the hilt of his sword.

"Nay, 'tis I!" she said quickly and emerged from the thicket. Just the sight of him brought hope to her breast. As her gaze rested on his broad shoulders, she knew that beneath his shirt, scars webbed his flesh. She'd touched those ribbons that had once caused him pain, kissed them with her lips. Now, as she stood staring at him, reminded of the passion that had burned between them, she blushed.

His scowl deepened, but he let go of his sword. "You shouldn't be creeping about—"

"I heard the voice on the wind at dawn," she said quickly, not wanting him to think she was a common wench hoping for another quick bedding. "There is trouble at Abergwynn," she said, lifting her chin a fraction. "A traitor has taken over the castle."

His eyes narrowed a little. "The wind told you this? Did it also tell you who the traitor is?"

"Aye."

He didn't say a word, just crossed his large arms over his chest and waited, impatience flaring in his eyes.

Her heart was thundering, her palms sweating. "The traitor is someone dear to you, someone you trust." She licked her lips nervously.

"There are many whom I—"

"Strahan has betrayed you, Garrick," Morgana rushed on. "He's spilled blood at Abergwynn and wrested command of the castle from Ware."

"Strahan," he said coldly, his stony, unbelieving glare cutting through her soul.

"Aye."

"The very man whose heart you would gladly carve from his chest rather than marry."

"Nay, I—"

He crossed the ground between them quickly, and steely fingers surrounded her wrist. "Do you take me for such a fool, Morgana? Did you think I would believe your silly story, that I would not see through your ruse to lull me into mistrusting my own kin?"

"Blood has been spilled," she said, her gaze clashing with his. She would not back down. In an instant she saw emotions surface in his eyes, emotions that seemed to echo her very own. Her throat grew tight, and she wished with all her heart that he would draw her into the safe circle of his arms and tell her that everything would be all right.

Instead, he stared down at her suspiciously, as if he

could read the guilt in her upturned face. "Go on," he urged.

"I heard screaming and cursing and saw blood discolor the stones of the great hall."

"Whose blood?"

"I know not."

"Logan's?"

She stopped, trying to bring the vision back into sharp focus, but it was gone, and she could not retrieve more than the vague impression with which she'd been left. "The wind says he is safe, that I alone can find him."

Garrick snorted. "Your wind serves you well, Morgana."

"I do not control it," she snapped.

"No, but your memory, like your vision, is not always clear."

She bit back a sharp response. If he wanted to be surly, so be it. She had only a message to give him. "The wind claims the boy is at home."

"At Abergwynn?" he scoffed. "The castle was searched from the highest battlements to the deepest well—"

"He is in a dungeon with slick walls. Water drips from the ceiling. I . . . I have seen him!"

"You have seen my son?" Garrick roared, his handsome features twisting into a mask of suspicion. "Now, after all this time, you have finally seen him? How convenient."

Morgana tossed her hair out of her eyes, determined to make him believe her. "His hair is light—a red-gold color that shines like the sun."

Garrick's mouth compressed into a hard line.

"He has freckles and his teeth are gapped, but his eyes are the color of the winter sky. He is small for his age but quick, and right now he is very, very scared!"

He blanched. "You have heard him described by the soldiers and the servants. Cailin knows not when to hold her tongue."

"I swear to you on the lives of my family that I have seen your son. He is safe for now, but the wind says he is in danger and I am the one to save him." The fingers around her wrist moved slowly, touching the pulse on the inside of her arm.

"Your wind seems to talk only when you want something from me, Morgana. I think you control everyone and everything you touch." He yanked her hard against him and forced her chin upward so that she could stare into the cold depths of his eyes. "I think you cast your spells and turn men against their brothers, all for your own amusement."

She blanched and attempted to ignore the warmth his fingers inspired. "I swear—"

"So you've said."

Dear God, why wouldn't he believe her? She yanked her hand free and stepped away from him. "If I am wrong, or if I have lied, you can punish me."

His lips curled. "Punish you? Has not your own father already banished you from Wenlock?"

Her shoulders slumped a little at that horrid memory. Would that she could see her home again, but that was not to be.

"So how am I to punish you, witch? By hurting your father—taking away his keep? By bending you over my knee?"

"You have already dealt out my punishment."

"By forcing you to marry Strahan?" he asked, his lips without blood. "You would go willingly to be his bride?"

The thought was repulsive, but she had no choice. Not

only Logan's life but now Glyn's and Cadell's hung in the balance. "Aye," she whispered, her insides growing as cold as the winter snow.

"You will be a true and loyal wife?" he asked flatly, his eyes showing no emotion.

In her mind's eye she pictured Strahan, handsome but cruel, a wicked leer playing on his lips as he took Springan on the floor of Tower Wenlock. He lifted her skirts, lay with her, poured his seed into her, sired her child, and then cast her aside and treated her with as little respect as he gave the rest of the servants.

"Well, witch?"

Morgana's stomach turned over, and she thought she might be sick. "Aye," she whispered, accepting the death sentence of her spirit.

"You'll be faithful and obedient and never give him cause for grief?" The skin grew taut over his harsh features. His eyes were filled with a private torment, his jaw set in stone.

"Aye, aye, aye! Did I not say it?" she fired back at him. "If this is what you want, Garrick of Abergwynn, lord and master, then so be it!" Tears threatened her eyes, but she held them bravely at bay. "I'll not remember last night. I'll pretend you didn't . . . we didn't . . . that it never happened, and I'll be a faithful wife to that black-hearted Strahan, but I will never, *never* go to his bed without shame!"

"Because of me."

"Because I despise him!"

He hesitated, swallowing hard, and for a moment she thought he was weakening to her, that he would pull her into his arms and kiss her and promise to love her forever, to marry her, to die for her if necessary.

"Tell me this is what you want, Garrick."

He ground his back teeth together and squeezed his eyes shut. "Aye," he said, forcing the word over his lips. " 'Tis what I want. 'Tis best for all of us."

Morgana had no choice but to accept her fate. Though her knees threatened to buckle, she would not weaken before him. She managed to stand proud and accept her destiny. She could deal with anything, she told herself, if only her family and Garrick's son were safe.

Ware's mount stumbled yet again. Though the mare was the best horse left in the stables, she was old, and the punishing gait was too much for the beast. The road was uneven and dark, and the animal tripped again. "On with you, nag!" Ware urged, but the huge horse heaved and shuddered, her lathered body glistening as dawn approached.

"You must rest," Cadell warned, drawing his own mount to a halt. "We cannot take a chance of losing our horses."

Angrily Ware pulled in on the reins, and the old bay immediately slowed to a walk. Cadell was right, he knew, but he couldn't ignore the sense of urgency that screamed through his brain: Faster! Faster! There was no time to lose. Any extra minutes spent tarrying might mean the downfall of Garrick and Abergwynn. If only he'd thought to bring extra horses, even palfreys or coursers or Clare's spirited jennet, any horse that could be ridden when these mares became tired. But he'd been anxious and impatient to find Garrick and had grabbed only a few provisions and weapons to carry with him on his quest. The night ride had been grueling and dangerous, and his whole body ached. Yet he rode on. If only he could impart his iron will into his tired mare's mind.

Beyond the horses and riders, loping through the thicket,

the wolf stayed with them, never too close, but always darting through the shadows of the trees just ahead. Ware found the dog disturbing but necessary. Three times already the beast had stopped, barked gruffly, and altered their course. Cadell had unerring faith in the half-dog, but Ware wasn't convinced that the beast wasn't on the trail of a buck or a boar.

"Wolf made it all the way to Abergwynn, didn't he?" Cadell had said when Ware voiced his doubts. "He'll find Morgana, all right. If you don't believe me, we could put down a little wager, but be careful of gambling with me, my friend, for I am brother to the witch and sometimes I think that I, too, can see through a window to the future."

Ware had refused to bet and had scoffed at Cadell's claim, but he continued following the wolf. What other choice was there? The wolf dog was following the very directions Will Farmer had given Garrick.

"Come—there's a clearing," Cadell said, squinting into the rising mists of dawn. We can rest for a few hours, give the horses time to cool off and drink, then be off again."

"And in that time Strahan will be up and after Garrick," Ware grumbled.

Cadell glanced at Ware's flagging horse, and Ware knew there was no point in arguing. The mare, if she kept up the gallop Ware demanded, would be dead by noon. Muttering under his breath, Ware slid from his saddle and led the old bay through the opening in the trees. The horse's ears pricked, and she drank long from the stream that rushed through a thicket of oak and pine.

Ware loosened the girth and breast straps and removed the saddle. His mare quickly found a patch of wet earth and rolled in the mud, grunting with pleasure, legs lashing the air.

Cadell, once his horse was free of saddle and blanket, plopped down near the water's edge and stared into the creek. "I don't know how she does it," he said, his expression perplexed as he watched the ripples. "But Morgana claims she looks into the water and sees what will be."

"You believe her?" Ware settled against the thick bark of a willow tree.

"There is something to what she does, all right. I've felt the twinges myself."

Ware didn't believe him. Cadell's imagination ran away with him at times. But all in all, he was a good lad, and Ware was grateful for his company—visions or no visions.

Finally, seeing nothing but stones, gravel, and fish in the stream, Cadell, too, propped himself against the tree.

"You think Garrick's near?" Cadell asked as he cut a length of willow branch and began stripping the new leaves from the supple ropelike stem.

"Nay." Ware glanced across the stream, where the dog sat, ears cocked, staring toward the east. "I think our friend wouldn't wait around if Morgana was nearby, and I'll wager my best sword that she and Garrick are together."

"That won't please Sir Strahan." Cadell used the branch as a whip, slicing the air.

"Nothing much does," Ware said bitterly as he ran his tongue around his teeth. Some were still loose, though the blood had dried and the cuts on his face were healing. Clare told him he'd bear a scar for the rest of his life and his nose would never again be straight, but he didn't care. His looks mattered not. Getting even with that lying, double-crossing bastard of a cousin of his did. 'Twas all that did matter.

He poured mead into two cups and drank heartily. His eyes felt heavy, and his muscles ached. Cadell was right; they all needed rest, though he doubted he could sleep. He yawned, then saw the wolf cock his head. The wild creature whined, paced quickly back and forth, then looked at Ware, as if to say, "Come on with you, man. We've got miles to travel before we rest."

"Soon," Ware said, finishing his mead and wiping his sleeve over his mouth. He felt the warm liquid slosh as it hit his empty stomach. Cadell was already stretched out and snoring in the grass, the willow whip lying on the ground near him. Such a boy. Again Ware yawned and let his eyelids drift downward. He would rest a few minutes, he told himself, just long enough to ease the cramps from his tired muscles. Then they'd ride again. He began to doze.

The dog whined anxiously, but Ware couldn't find the strength to open his eyes. "In a bit," he muttered, drifting off and not seeing Wolf's restlessness as he paced worriedly along the banks of the creek and growled low in his throat. With a sharp bark that barely touched Ware's consciousness, the wolf, as if frightened of the very devil himself, snarled and dashed into the protective darkness of the woods.

"Two men on horseback, m'lord," the scout, Sir Quinn, reported. " 'Tis Garrick's brother, Ware, and the brother of that witch. The wolf's with them as well."

Strahan grimaced. How did Ware and the boy sneak out of the castle? Lazy good-for-nothing guards! They would have to learn a lesson, as would Ware and Cadell—a lesson in obedience from the whip.

"Their horses are nearly spent. They rest now, by the creek." Quinn leered wickedly. " 'Twould be easy to sneak up on them and slit their throats. They wouldn't know what hit them."

"Nay." Strahan rubbed the crick from his neck, and his horse moved beneath him. He didn't like the idea of killing Ware, for, truth be known, he liked the lad. As for Morgana's brother, Cadell of Wenlock, heir to Daffyd, he could prove useful in the future. No, Strahan's fight was with Garrick, and should the baron resist him, Strahan would be forced to take his life. Too many years and too many contests had he given up to his cousin, the worst of course being that while Strahan's father had lost his lands to Osric McBrayne, the wealth of Garrick's family had increased. Strahan, who had been groomed to become a great baron, had been deprived of his inheritance and forced to settle for becoming a mere knight who pledged his fealty to his cousin. On the day of the ceremony, when he had knelt before Garrick, a bad taste had filled Strahan's mouth and he had barely been able to make the pledge. It had taken all of his willpower not to spit on the smooth leather of Garrick's boots. And that vile taste was with him yet. He took pleasure in the thought that soon Garrick would have to kneel before him.

Only one minor flaw marred his plan—a flaw as irritating as a dying fly in a bowl of broth: Strahan had been forced to ally himself with the very man who had robbed him of his birthright. But that didn't matter now. He could live with his choice. Osric McBrayne, lord of Castle Hawarth, had approached Strahan two winters past. Destiny's die had been cast. For Strahan wanted power almost as much as he wanted Hazelwood.

"If you can give me half the lands of Abergwynn and strip Maginnis of his power," Osric had said, his old eyes gleaming in the firelight from the hearth at Castle Hawarth, "then you shall have all your lands again and part of Abergwynn as well."

Strahan had at first laughed in the old man's face. Why would he trust McBrayne? Hadn't Osric brought him to Hawarth as a prisoner? But as the night wore on and Strahan drank more of McBrayne's wine, it became evident that Osric was determined to increase his estates by acquiring the vast lands of Abergwynn. In truth, Hazelwood was a much smaller demesne, but it was home, and by his birthright, Strahan should rule there.

Osric hated Garrick for the simple reason that Garrick had turned down Osric's daughter, Sheena, for another woman. Her humiliation had been public, her disgrace made known throughout the kingdom.

Old Osric had given Strahan the chance for which he'd been waiting. He knew that his power, once he defeated Garrick, would be great. For Morgana of Wenlock, the sorceress who talked to the wind, would be his bride. Since meeting her, he had wanted no other woman—at least not for a wife. Yes, he'd found many who had pleasured him, but only Morgana of Wenlock would serve as his wife—and serve she would.

Now, astride his horse, his loins began to ache. These days, when he took a wench to his bed, it was Morgana of Wenlock's face he envisioned. The hands that stroked him, the tongue that slipped across his skin, belonged to Morgana—at least in his very fertile mind. Oh, he had plans for their wedding night, plans that caused him to grow hard and long, and he had to shift in the saddle and turn his attention to Sir Quinn, who was still prattling on about how easy it would be to kill Ware.

"Mayhap he turned some of your men against you,"

Quinn worried aloud, obviously concerned for his own Judas-like skin. "Even now Garrick may rule Abergwynn again."

"Even if Ware did manage to take Abergwynn again, he has no one to protect it, and soon McBrayne will storm the castle. Fear not, Abergwynn has fallen." He felt a keen satisfaction at that thought. Soon he would be baron to the king himself, have a bride who could read the future so that he would be able to predict the downfall of his enemies—even old Osric McBrayne, the bastard. For eventually Strahan planned to seek his vengeance on McBrayne, though now he needed him as an ally. "We'll follow Ware," he said. "He can be of use to us." A plan formed in his mind and he nearly laughed aloud. "If the boy has bested my men and it's true that the gates of Abergwynn are closed to us, he will open them again. But we must lie back so that he's unaware that he's leading us to Garrick. Then our search will end and the battle will begin."

As they rode west, Morgana felt Luck's huge muscles shiver. His ears pricked forward, and he snorted as if in fear. "We'll be home soon," she said, patting the stallion's sleek shoulder, but she, too, felt the changes circulating in the currents of air swirling through the valley. The fates were stirring, and their search, which had gone on for days, had turned up naught.

The woods and the mountains seemed to loom close, to press inward.

The wind began to whine, whispering low as it turned the leaves of the yew and poplar trees. Gooseflesh rose on Morgana's arms, and rain, so cold it seeped into the bones, began to fall.

Luck pranced out of line, sidestepping and nearly kicking Sir Hunter's steed.

"Watch out," Hunter snarled, but the horses collided, and Morgana, in an instant of clarity, smelled death. Something was wrong—oh, God, what was it? She tried to ignore the image, but little by little, her vision altered and she was no longer riding in Garrick's company, but watching in horror as soldiers on horseback, weapons drawn, attacked. Blood spewed, horses screamed, throwing riders and trampling them.

Her heart thundered, and she twisted her fingers in the leather reins. "No," she whispered as she saw Cadell's face in the vision. Not her brother! No! Yet he was there, with a band of Garrick's knights! But they bore him ill will, and at the lead was Strahan of Hazelwood. "Oh, God, please no!"

She spurred her horse forward past two pairs of knights as she tried to reach Garrick. The horses kicked and bucked, and several knights swore loudly, but Morgana didn't care.

Hearing the ruckus, Garrick pulled up short and Luck nearly ran into Warrior. "What's the meaning of this?" he hissed when she reined her mount to a mincing stop.

"There's a trap," she said.

He rolled his eyes to the heavens, and she watched the cold rain drizzle down his neck, beneath the opening of his shirt. "What're you saying—that we should turn around once again?"

"I don't know."

"Christ's blood, woman! Make up your mind!" he growled and his horse tossed his great head and reared on thick black haunches. Garrick shifted his weight, and the stallion dropped down again. "You're making me look like a fool in front of my men!"

"There is trouble. It comes for you—"

"Don't tell me. Strahan is on the loose."

"I don't know—"

"Oh, for the sake of all that's holy!" He motioned to the forward scout, jerked hard on the reins, dug his heels into his horse's sides, and began riding again. The small company followed him, pushing at Morgana's horse as she realized that Garrick wasn't going to heed her warning.

She wouldn't give up. She kicked Luck hard and, catching up with Garrick, grabbed the reins to Warrior, stripping the wet leather straps from his hands. Both horses reared and whinnied.

"What the devil's gotten into you, woman?" Garrick roared. He snatched the reins from her hands, his face a mask of fury.

"It's Cadell. He—he's with Strahan."

"You're talking nonsense. I'll not be fooled by your silly visions. You wanted to return to Abergwynn, and we're nearly there. By tomorrow nightfall, we'll be at the castle. What else would you want?"

"Just listen to me!"

"No, Morgana! You listen to me! You forget who is lord here!" Furious, he leapt lithely to the ground. While his men watched, he reached up and yanked her from her saddle.

"What're you doing?" she demanded, her face turning scarlet, her eyes worriedly darting from Garrick to his men. Lightning sizzled in jagged white streaks over the hills, and thunder rumbled ominously. Rain poured down on them. "I'm teaching you a lesson you'll not soon forget, witch," he growled. "This is the last time you make a fool of me in front of my men!" He turned to the nearest knight, Sir Marsh. "Find a place to make camp. Lead the men there.

We'll catch up with you. The witch has had another vision, and I need to hear all about it."

Marsh's knowing gaze slid from Garrick to Morgana and back again. The hint of a smile showed beneath the stubble surrounding his mouth. "Aye, m'lord."

To Morgana's horror, the company moved on, leaving Garrick and her alone with their horses. Garrick waited until the last destrier had rounded a bend in the road. Then he grabbed her arm and dragged her through the puddles on the roadside and into a copse. "Garrick, please, I don't understand—" she said, half running and stumbling to keep up with him.

"Nor do I!" he nearly shouted, his face twisted in anger, his nostrils flared. "You're using your magic on me, Morgana—"

"I'm not!" she cried. "I'm not!"

"First you tell me to stay in the castle, then to leave, then to go back, then to turn around! My God, woman, you've made me a laughingstock. I follow your orders like a bull with a ring through his nose. All you have to do is pull and dream up some wild vision and I do what you command. Do you not see how this appears to my men? They think I've lost my mind—all because of you!" He threw up one hand in exasperation and swore loudly.

"Did I not see the ribbon in the water?" she asked, forcing him to stop.

The hand on her arm tightened a little. "You have not found my boy."

Silence yawned between them. Raindrops peppered the ground, and the wind clutched them both in its icy fist. "You must listen to me, Garrick," she pleaded, grasping his shirt in her fingers and twisting the woolen fabric until the fibers scraped her skin. "There is grave danger for all of us!"

"At Abergwynn."

"Aye."

"And here?"

"Everywhere!"

His gaze centered on her lips and then on the raindrops running from her forehead to her chin. Her eyes were round and dark, a deep green that was filled with fear and something else . . . something much more dangerous. He felt her fingers in the folds of his shirt, smelled the scent of rain in her hair. Swearing under his breath, he drew her into his arms, and his chilled lips met hers with a hunger so intense she nearly collapsed against him.

"You vex me, woman," he growled between kisses as he licked the drops of rain from her face. She wound her arms around his neck and felt the coldness leave her body. His cool lips began to heat as his tongue slipped easily between her parted lips. Desire claimed him, and he lifted her tunic, touching her breasts with cold hands. Her warm skin seemed to seep into his palms, and her nipples became hard and ripe, succulent. He fell to his knees, unmindful of the mud, and dragged her down. Then he tore her tunic from her and stared at her bare torso, her proud breasts wet from the rain, her black hair coiling in damp waves to her waist. His hands were large as they scaled her ribs, and he watched in wonder as he cupped both breasts. She sucked in her breath, her abdomen flattening, her flesh nearly blue with the cold.

The hardness between his legs screamed for release.

"I could take you right here," he said, his hands beginning to massage that firm, supple flesh that held so much fascination for him. Her nipples puckered prettily, begging for the bittersweet torment of his tongue.

"Aye," she said proudly, her chin still lifted, her breathing short and shallow.

"You would not stop me."

She closed her eyes as he touched her nipples, and a shudder ripped through her. "Nay, m'lord," she whispered.

"And what of Strahan?"

She stiffened. "Mayhap that is my question to you. Would you lie with his bride?" Her breath whistled past her teeth as he dipped his head and tasted her nipple.

"I cannot help myself."

"Is the great lord so weak?" she asked, barely able to concentrate as he began to tug and nip at her breast. The feminine beast within her yawned again, causing a hot need deep between her legs.

"Where you are concerned, aye, I am weak," he admitted, his hot breath fanning her cool skin. "You have made me powerless, Morgana. You have caused me to follow your visions when I could see none, you persuaded me to listen to your silly conversations with the wind, and you have turned my mind around so that I cannot help but want you—the very woman I promised to my cousin."

She saw his hardness, firm and anxious and straining at the strings of his breeches, and she wanted to touch him, to offer him the sweet magic that he'd given her.

"Would that I could forget you," he whispered, his hands winding in her hair, his eyes boring deep into her own gaze as if searching for her soul. He kissed her again, his arms around her.

She reached for his breeches, and he caught his lips between his teeth, as if suddenly trying to fight off the demons that drove him to lie with the woman he'd promised to his cousin. He told himself to stop, to leave Morgana alone. But passion sang through his blood, and when he felt her velvet touch, he shivered with desire. *Don't do this, don't go against your word, don't betray Strahan!* But as he lay atop her, felt her curves yielding to his own hot flesh, his reason fled. Her black hair spilled around her face, and her eyes, luminous and blue-green, were filled with sweet promise.

Ignoring his own code of honor, he gave in to the emotions burning in his breast. He plunged into her sweet warmth, for he had no choice but to make love to her. No other woman's touch felt so right, no other woman's mind was so quick, no other woman's body seemed so inviting.

After their last lovemaking, Garrick had promised himself that he wouldn't touch her again, and here he was making love to her as if she were *his* bride! He squeezed his eyes shut and closed his mind to the doubts raging in his heart. She pressed her tongue intimately to his chest and moved beneath him, whispering his name, digging her fingers into his arms. All his doubts disappeared, and he cradled her close against him as he stiffened and poured his seed into her. She cried out, and he collapsed in her arms. Rain dripped from the trees, cool against his back, and somewhere far away thunder pealed. Garrick buried his face in her neck and licked the drops of rain and sweat from her skin.

She smiled up at him, and he was undone. All his promises of self-denial seemed silly, all his mistrust a mistake. She would never lie to him, not this beautiful woman. He caught himself grinning back at her as he played with a coil of her damp hair. "My men wait for us," he said sadly.

"Aye. We must be off."

Neither moved. Garrick kissed her forehead and wondered at the swell of tenderness that grew within him. With one finger he traced the slope of her shoulder and, seeing her nipple pucker, lowered his hand to the point of her breast.

She laughed huskily. "Again, *m'lord?*"

"We have no time." But his thumb moved slowly across the nipple.

"None?"

"Mmm." He lowered himself and took her breast in his mouth, tickling her nipple with the tip of his tongue. Looking up, he watched as she threw her head back and closed her eyes, ready for yet another round of lovemaking. This time, he thought, he would take it slowly, show her what it was to want him so badly that she would lift her hips anxiously. He trailed a hand along the slope of her thigh and across her abdomen, his fingertips brushing the soft curls at the apex of her legs. She moaned beneath him as he touched her, feeling her hot moisture collecting again, though she was still filled with his seed. Her legs parted to his touch, and he stroked her, slowly at first, but more quickly as she began to respond. He wanted only to service her, to give her the best of lovemaking. He caressed her with his fingers and tongue, seeing her rapturous torment, watching as her eyes glazed over.

He had no intention of lying with her again—this time was for her—but she began to claw at him and tug him atop her, and his manhood was already hard again, thick and full.

"Garrick, please," she pleaded when he probed her more deeply, massaging the swelling bud. She bucked upward, tossing away his hand, and dragged him atop her.

"So you want me again, witch?" he teased, though it took all his strength not to delve deep into her.

"I want you."

"And I want you, my love," he whispered, unable to restrain himself or control the words that rolled so easily off his tongue. He wrapped strong arms around her, and his lips captured hers as he thrust into her again, harder than ever, as deep as he could, listening to her cries of pleasure as he withdrew only to plunge in again and again and again. She was on fire beneath him, clawing and kissing and writhing until, with a primal scream, she let go.

"Garrick! Oh, Garrick!" she cried, convulsing against him and holding on to him as if to life itself. Her body rocked, and he couldn't hold back any longer.

With a final thrust he fell against her and kissed her eyes, face, and neck. "Little witch," he whispered against her hair as afterglow surrounded him and he tasted the salt from her skin.

The rain had stopped and a few soft shafts of sunlight stole through the clouds, but as the afterglow faded, Garrick's heart grew heavy. He was falling in love with Morgana, and he hated himself for his weakness.

Weak he was where she was concerned, for he couldn't imagine a day passing without his lust for her driving him to desperate measures. He would meet her, lie with her, perhaps sire a child by her. Dear God, he'd betrayed his cousin, been a traitor to his own good word.

He didn't think he could live without Morgana. Without a woman who talked to the wind. Without a woman who drew meaningless signs in the dirt. Without a woman whose visions came and went at her whim.

"Come, get dressed," he said a little gruffly as he rolled away from her. "We have things to settle."

"Do we, *m'lord?*" she teased, though her eyes were sad. "I thought we settled quite a bit just now."

His face reddened. The nerve of the woman to ridicule him! "Nay. Things are worse than before," he bit out, tugging on his breeches and frowning at the mud stains thereon. Morgana's clothes, too, were wrinkled, wet, and muddy. It wouldn't take even the dullest of his knights long to figure out what he and the witch had been doing. Soon the word would reach Strahan. Garrick couldn't let the marriage take place, but he couldn't very well go back on his word.

Mayhap the best solution was to offer Strahan something more—a larger parcel of land, a woman with more wealth and status. Perhaps there was a woman in the king's family—some distant but beautiful cousin with a large dowry and the king's ear—who would appeal to Strahan.

As he tugged on his tunic and led Morgana back to the horses, he thought of Edward's relatives and knew that Strahan's chances of a marriage with royal blood were slim. Nay, he would want the bride he was promised, the bride he'd handpicked.

He would find out that Morgana wasn't a virgin, that she'd been sleeping with Garrick, that even now she could be pregnant with Garrick's child. Strahan would be furious.

And, with his black temper, there was little doubt that Strahan would demand a fight to the death.

Twenty-one

arrick's camp is within a day's ride from here," the scout, Sir Quinn, reported, finding Strahan in the forest. Rain fell from the sky and dripped from the trees.

Strahan stared at the shallow, muddy grave that no doubt held the body of the maid, Jocelyn. As he kicked at the fresh earth with the toe of his boot, he remembered the girl. It was too bad about Logan's nursemaid. Her death had been a waste. She was a beautiful creature, and had she not learned that Strahan was plotting against Garrick, she could have lived. Aye, he was as sorry to see her die as his men were sorry to see their source of entertainment gone. She'd serviced the entire band who had abducted her, trading sex for her life. Aye, 'twas a shame. Strahan did not like to see blood spilled without cause. Only when it was necessary. His cruel nature was not turned against the world as a whole, just against Garrick and Osric McBrayne.

"Garrick has but twenty men riding with him, and some of them are loyal to you. But his army has turned 'round. They are now headed back to Abergwynn."

Strahan's brow furrowed. "Why? They could not know that Logan—"

"Nay." Quinn shook his head. "But they will come across Ware and Cadell and the wolf soon."

Strahan's mind moved quickly, turning the situation to

his advantage. "We take Ware now," he said, his fingers stroking the hilt of his sword. "Then we return to Abergwynn and wait for Garrick."

"Why not just do battle with him here?"

Strahan motioned impatiently. "Here the battle is even. At Abergwynn we have more men."

"As does Maginnis. In fact, it looks as if our rebellion failed, elsewise why would Ware be free?"

"That can be easily changed." Strahan hesitated. He would have preferred to attack Garrick this very day, but he'd learned from past mistakes that patience would serve him well. Already he could see how to use this change of plan to his advantage. "We return to Abergwynn with Ware."

"What about the boy from Tower Wenlock?"

Cadell. Aye, he posed a problem. For Strahan had not planned to kill him but realized that if Cadell died, Tower Wenlock would fall to Morgana or Glyn. It was only a matter of getting the witch with a boy child and that would be no problem. He had sired four bastards that he knew of, three of which were male. So, once Cadell was gone and Strahan married to Morgana, Strahan's son would inherit Wenlock from old man Daffyd.

"We'll take the boy prisoner, then return to the castle," he said. "Garrick's looking for battle. I was anxious before and could not wait for him to return to Abergwynn, as I thought he might be gone for several fortnights. But now that I know he's returning, what better place to have the battle than in the very halls that he considers home?"

"Unless Ware has taken it from our soldiers."

Strahan stared at the scout through narrowed eyes. "No one will ever take anything from me again!" he decreed, thinking of Hazelwood.

There was a spark of mirth, an evil satisfaction, in Quinn's expression and it goaded him. "Of course not, m'lord," Quinn replied, then added, "Morgana is with Garrick." Again the flame of humor at Strahan's expense flickered in Quinn's mean eyes. Strahan knew the hateful truth: Garrick had bedded Morgana. His blood boiled and any kind thoughts that had lingered for his cousin quickly dissolved.

"Leave me be," he ordered gruffly. "Tell the men to be at the ready. I'll make our battle plans."

With a tiny smile Quinn bowed, then turned and strode back to camp. Strahan stood alone in the woods, his anger causing his skin to flush, his teeth grinding in silent humiliation. So Garrick, in his arrogance, had lain with Strahan's bride, robbing her of her virginity, possibly implanting his child within her womb. At Strahan's expense. The child, if it existed, would be a problem, for Strahan needed his own issue in Morgana's body. He would have to wait, for nearly a month if need be, until her cycle was complete and the bleeding began. If it didn't, if she was already carrying Garrick's child, then the wait would be much longer—until after the birth.

Fury raged through his veins. Quick as a cat pouncing, he yanked his sword from its sheath. With a powerful thrust, he lunged at an oak tree, burying the blade deep in the trunk. His arm was jarred by the impact, but he barely noticed, so hot ran his hate. Would that this yielding bark were Garrick's black heart! Where once he had hoped not to kill his cousin, his thoughts had taken a murderous turn.

All of Strahan's men knew that he intended to marry Morgana of Wenlock. Soon they would realize that the wench had lain with Garrick. Well, both she and Garrick would pay. She would be forced to watch as Garrick slowly died, but before his death, while he was helpless, Garrick would be given no choice but to watch as Strahan bedded the woman Garrick loved. A cruel smile curved his lips. At the beginning of this quest, he had wanted only to best his cousin, to steal Garrick's wealth. There had been fondness for Garrick in Strahan's heart and he hadn't seriously thought of doing his cousin physical harm. He wanted only for Garrick to kneel before him. But time passed and he slowly wanted more. Garrick's humiliation had become important, and Strahan had boldly stolen the boy from him, then suggested they locate the child through Morgana. He knew that if he kept changing Logan's hiding place the witch would have trouble finding the boy, but Strahan had wanted to see for himself how strong were her powers. He was now convinced. Her sight would prove most valuable. If Garrick had coupled with his bride, Strahan would find great satisfaction in making him suffer. He could almost imagine Garrick's roars of rage as he watched Strahan mount the woman he loved. He could envision Morgana's sea green eyes widening in horror. Oh, she would fight like a hellcat, but would eventually submit, for he would lead her to believe that by lying with Strahan, she could save Garrick's miserable life. He yanked hard on the sword and slowly the blade, wedged deep in the meat of the tree, began to wiggle free. Throwing his shoulders into his task, he withdrew the sword, made a mental note to have it sharpened, and sheathed the long blade that would bring Garrick's death—his slow death after Morgana had warmed Strahan's bed, pleasing him with her hands and tongue.

Absently Strahan rubbed his loins, feeling the swelling and imagining the sweet wet touch of Morgana's mouth.

Mayhap he would let Garrick watch as he gave the wench her first beating—nothing serious, just a few quick slaps on her rump and the light touch of a whip against the white flesh of her back.

At that thought he turned as hard as a yew branch and wished he'd had the foresight to bring along a servant girl— even Springan—so that he could relieve himself. Then again, maybe this pain was worthwhile. 'Twould make the taking of Morgana all the more pleasurable.

He hurried back to camp, gave the orders, and soon his men were riding. There was excitement in the air, and the storm rolling over the hills only added to the adventure of it all. *Soon, Morgana, you will be mine, and Garrick will die.*

"I tell you he's gone," Cadell said, whistling yet again and listening for the wolf's answering call.

"But he was here only an hour past!" Ware was vexed. He should have found Garrick by now, and every minute he was away from Abergwynn, his worries increased. He'd been certain that the wolf dog was on the scent. Earlier today, before the storm, the animal could hardly restrain himself, running through the trees, looking back over his shoulder as if urging the men and horses to a faster pace.

Cadell reined in his mount and whistled again.

Ware strained to listen over the steady drip of the rain. The horses stamped their hooves, and steam rose from their nostrils. It was cold—bitter cold—and the lightning that scorched the sky over the hills to the east seemed ominous. If only they could find Garrick.

"We'll split up," Cadell suggested, his eyes turning a darker shade of blue. His brow furrowed and he shook his head, as if trying to clear his mind. "I'll go after the dog this way, through the trees, and you take the road. We'll both head east and meet before nightfall. . . . Wait!" He lifted his head, and his eyes narrowed to slits. "Do you hear that—a voice?"

"No one speaks," Ware said, and Cadell frowned.

"You hear nothing?"

"Are you daft? There is no one here."

Cadell's eyes grew round, and his face turned white, as if he'd learned of his own death. "Holy Mother Mary," he whispered, yanking hard on the reins so that his mount reared and whinnied.

"What the devil's got into you?"

"Shh! Listen!" Cadell's color slowly returned, and whatever had scared him had apparently faded. His mouth stretched into a wide grin as he regained control of the horse. "I knew I wasn't going mad. Can't you hear it, man? 'Tis riders! Coming this way!"

Ware strained his ears, but he heard nothing. "I think not—"

"Yes! Wolf's found Morgana. That's why the beast left us. Now they approach!" With a slap of the reins against his steed's rump, Cadell wheeled the courser around and headed back toward the south. Dirt flew from the horse's swift hooves.

"Wait, Cadell!" Ware called, exasperated by the younger boy's impatience. Ware genuinely liked Morgana's brother, but the boy was so damned impetuous—ready to do battle at the snap of a twig and now taking off over some silly sound that Ware didn't hear. In some ways Cadell was as mysterious as his older sister. Now he, too, was hearing voices. Well, Ware had to save him from his own damned rebellious streak. "Ha!" he kicked his horse's sides and followed the lad, for he had no other choice. When he caught up with Cadell, he intended to make sure the younger man understood who was giving orders! As for the dog . . . Ware's skin crawled a little as the rain hit his face and slid down beneath his shirt despite the hood on his surcoat. Why would the beast take off? Unless he was near his mistress. Or unless he was frightened for his life.

Ware's heart turned to stone. Oh, God, this could be an ambush! The thugs who had taken Logan could surely be about, or worse . . . Strahan was somewhere within these hills and valleys. Though he and Cadell had passed their camp two nights before, there was a chance . . . Oh, sweet Jesus, please don't let—

As Ware rounded a curve in the road and yanked hard on the reins, he saw his worst fears crystallize before him. His mount slid in the mud, nearly throwing Ware, but he didn't care, for his eyes locked with the cruel black gaze of his cousin!

Strahan stood in the middle of the road, one hand pulling Cadell's hair taut, the other holding a wickedly curved blade to the boy's throat.

"Don't!" Ware cried.

"Run!" Cadell screamed. "Ware, turn and leave!"

Strahan smiled. "Yes, cousin. Show your true colors."

Ware had no choice. As he watched Cadell try not to tremble, he slowly dismounted, drew his sword, and tossed it at Strahan's muddied boots. He felt the arms of strong men surround and restrain him, and didn't bother struggling when a rope was looped over his shoulders and legs.

"You stupid boy," Strahan snarled as he threw Cadell into

the heavy arms of one of his men. His eyes never left Ware's. "Why couldn't you stay put? I left you at Abergwynn for your own safety!"

"You can kill me, but you'll never take Abergwynn again," Ware said bravely. "The castle belongs to Garrick."

"Does it?" Strahan seemed neither surprised nor worried. "But Garrick is not back at Abergwynn yet, and as for Clare . . ." Strahan looked Ware up and down and shook his head. "I'm sure we can persuade her to open the gates."

"Never."

"Your sister is willing to watch you die?" Strahan asked evenly. From the corner of his eye, Ware saw Cadell struggle. The guard holding him slapped him so hard the smack echoed through the trees. Cadell's head snapped back, but he managed to stay on his feet.

"Clare won't believe that you would do me harm!"

"No? Mayhap not. I suppose we'll have to start with Cadell, here. And we'll do it slowly, Ware, a piece at a time. A finger, an ear, maybe even an eye—just to make sure that Clare understands how serious I am."

Ware felt sick. His knees threatened to buckle, but he forced himself to stand and face the cruel man whom he had called his kin.

"You'll not cut off my fingers!" Cadell said, struggling against the man who was binding him. "Not unless I cut off your balls first!"

Ware shot the younger boy a hard glance. Why would Cadell be so foolish?

"Aye, I'll cut them off, then feed them to the wolf, that I will!" Cadell said, his tongue working more quickly than his brain.

"Will you, now?" Strahan walked to the younger man, his knife still in his hand. "Think before you speak, son, for you've given me an idea."

"No!" Ware cried.

Strahan ignored him and pressed his face close to Cadell's. "Let's start with you." Swiftly he raised his knife and slashed at the fabric of Cadell's breeches. The boy screamed and Ware struggled against his bonds, but no blood stained the severed fabric and Cadell's bare flesh showed through, white and without a trace of blood. His face drained of color, and he nearly swooned.

"For the love of God, Strahan, leave him alone!" Ware cried. "He's but a boy—"

"Next time I'll do it," Strahan snarled, and Cadell's lower lip trembled. Seeing that he'd finally gotten the respect he wanted, Strahan turned, his knife still in his hand, no hint of blood on the sharp blade. "You'd best keep your friend in line, Ware."

Ware held his head proudly, refusing to answer, his gaze holding Strahan's. He didn't blink. But in his peripheral vision, he saw a blur of black and brown fur streaking through the trees. Ware's gut tightened. *God be with you, Wolf,* he silently prayed, hoping that the animal could reach Garrick and warn him before it was too late and all was lost.

Garrick was relentless. Upon deciding to return to Abergwynn, he'd pushed the men and horses to the extreme.

Every muscle in Morgana's body ached, and she thought about a warm bath and clean clothes and a real bed piled high with fur coverlets. But she was worried. Though the storm had passed and the sun warmed the wet earth, she felt a tension in the air. Her visions had stopped again, and she was frustrated. Garrick asked her often if she'd seen into the future. Half the time he was teasing her; the rest of the time he seemed serious.

She was in love with him, she knew. This lighthearted giddiness she felt whenever he looked her way had to be love, though how her feelings had changed and how she'd come to care for the beast of Abergwynn, she knew not. Aye, he was handsome and powerful and his lovemaking caused a great tide of desire to rush through her blood, but there was more to the man than only these qualities. She'd seen strength in him, yet witnessed kindness; she'd observed his emotions, often held under tight rein, and knew that he would die to ensure the safety of his men. He was gentle with his horses, and he did not object to her dog being at the castle.

He was desperate to find his child. His love for his boy was all-consuming. That alone caused her heart to ache for him, and that ache had evolved into a love so deep she would do anything for him. Aye, she would even, if need be, become his wench. That thought wounded her deeply, for she was beginning to want more than just his touch. She saw herself as his wife, as the mother of his children, as the woman who would hold and caress him in bad times and good.

"You're as silly as Glyn," she chided herself as she rocked in the cursed saddle. She was still pledged to Strahan.

They were close to Abergwynn now, and soon the hours of riding would end. At the memory of Abergwynn she smiled. Aye, she'd come to love the big castle and the servants therein. She missed not only Glyn and Cadell but also Lady Clare and Garrick's impetuous younger brother, Ware. Never had she thought that any home other than Tower Wenlock would be hers, and yet . . . though she missed her parents and her grandmother, and the freedom at the tower, she had learned that she could live elsewhere, that she could become mistress of her own castle—if that castle was Abergwynn.

She patted Luck's sleek shoulder and thought of Phantom, her own little mare. Once they returned and she had bathed, she would snatch the largest apple in the kitchen and take it to the stables. "And one for you, too," she whispered to Luck, as if the horse could read her thoughts.

In a flutter of wings, two startled pheasants flew in front of the company. Garrick's horse shied and sidestepped. Another steed reared.

A wolf slunk into the road.

Morgana saw the dog and from the corner of her eye she noticed Sir Marsh draw back his bow.

"No!" she screamed, jumping off Luck and causing the horse to backstep into another animal. " 'Tis my dog!" she yelled at Marsh as she flung herself onto Wolf. The dog wagged his tail and licked her face and jumped all over her. She giggled and buried her face in his thick, somewhat foul-smelling fur.

Garrick urged his horse closer and dropped to the ground beside her. "I thought the dog was confined."

"He must've escaped," Morgana said, her joy pushing aside all her worries and fears.

"How?"

"I know not . . ." She glanced up and found Garrick frowning. "You think this is part of some trick?" she asked, her voice filled with disbelief.

" 'Tis unlikely, is it not, that anyone in the castle would get close enough to untie him?"

With a sinking heart, she understood the wisdom of Garrick's thinking.

"And there is no noose around his neck, as there would be if he had chewed his way through his bonds."

"Why would anyone turn him loose?" she asked, though she was still grateful that the dog had found them. She ran her fingers through his coarse fur and tried to avoid the pink tongue that continued to wash her face. "Stop it," she whispered, scratching the dog behind his ears.

"I know not why he would be set free." Garrick scanned the surrounding woods, his eyes narrowing, his hand on the hilt of his sword, as if he expected to be attacked at any second.

Morgana shivered, and her frivolous mood seeped quickly away. The tension she'd felt earlier returned, and though she was glad to have Wolf with them, she knew that Garrick was right. Had she not convinced him that danger lay behind every tree in these woods, that there lurked in the forest dark eyes silently watching them? Quickly making the sign of the cross, she stood and Garrick touched her gently on the sleeve. Their gazes locked for an instant. " 'Twill be all right," he assured her. "I will keep you safe."

"I'm not worried for myself."

"But for your brother and mine."

"Aye, Garrick, and for Logan," she said, remembering her vision and shuddering. She suddenly felt silly for letting the appearance of Wolf give her such joy, for surely Cadell was in trouble—serious trouble.

"Tell me of Abergwynn," she said, searching Garrick's face as she described for the tenth time the prison in which she'd envisioned Garrick's son.

"All the dungeons were searched."

"But could he have not been hidden somewhere else, then been taken to the dungeon later?"

"Someone would have seen or heard—"

"But you no have prisoners at Abergwynn and the walls are thick. If a traitor had gagged the child and hidden him away in the dark of night, no one would have suspected."

Garrick frowned. "I would like nothing better than to believe my son is in my fortress, witch. When we return, I'll take you to the dungeons and you can see for yourself."

"When we return, I'm to marry Strahan," she pointed out.

Garrick gave her a thin smile. "Only if he's not the traitor you've named him."

"Then I have naught to worry about," she quipped, but Garrick's grin faded. His eyes touched hers, and for an instant she saw his silent agony. For his son? Or for his honor—the honor he destroyed when he'd lain with her? Morgana forced a brave smile. She loved Garrick, and though her pride had seemed to flee, she cared not. She was glad she'd lain with him. If their time was to be brief, she would live on her memories. As for sleeping with Strahan, well, that would never come to pass. Garrick would soon discover his cousin to be a traitor.

Muttering under his breath, Garrick helped her onto Luck, mounted his war-horse, and gave the signal to move ahead. She watched him ride proudly, his shoulders square, no helmet upon his head. Morgana cast a glance at the sky and shivered. If the fates were with them, they would reach Abergwynn on the morrow.

Clare's mouth turned to sand. She stood on the battlement with Glyn and several of the servants as she stared down at the small band of soldiers—her cousin and his men. Strahan had come forward, close enough to the castle walls that an archer's arrow might reach his evil heart. However, he was holding Cadell prisoner by twisting one arm behind the boy's back. In his other hand he held a knife with a hideously curved blade.

The message was clear: either open the gates or Cadell would die. Ware would be next. He was forced to stand farther back, at a safer range. Bound with thick ropes, his face ashen, his shoulders stiff and brave, he waited his turn with Strahan's soldiers.

Clare's heart twisted. What was she to do? Why had so many men—brave men whom she had trusted—turned against Garrick, and how had they caught up with Ware and Cadell?

"Clare!" Strahan yelled, his voice echoing through the valley.

"I could shoot him, m'lady," the armorer said. A fistful of arrows was clutched in his big hand, and a quiver was slung over his broad shoulders. "Without hurting the boy, I could kill Strahan."

"But the others would kill Ware," she said, realizing that she had no choice but to open the gates and allow Strahan entrance.

"If we let them inside," the armorer argued, "do ye think he will be spared?"

"Mayhap," Clare said, though she saw the man's wisdom. "Yet there's a chance I'll be able to reason with my cousin."

The armorer's expression turned grim. He spat on the stone floor of the tower. "The chance is slimmer than that of a mouse in a roomful of cats, m'lady. Sir Strahan has gone this far. He'll not stop with your brother's life."

The words rang true, and yet she had to try. "If there is a way," she said to the man, "to sneak one of the servants out, send him to the abbot of the monastery. Tell him that Abergwynn has fallen and he must get word to Daffyd of Wenlock."

"I will—"

"But whoever leaves must be careful! Choose someone Strahan would not suspect . . . mayhap one of the children who work in the stables." The plan was flawed; some of the children lied so often that even their mothers did not believe them. But Clare had no other choice.

"I'll do it, m'lady."

"Clare!" Strahan's voice boomed again.

"Let him go!" she yelled, and Strahan moved quickly, slicing Cadell's ear. "No!"

Blood spurted. Cadell's agonized scream rang through the castle.

"No! For the love of God, no!" Glyn screamed at Strahan. She turned wide, terror-filled eyes upon Clare and clutched at Clare's sleeve with desperate fingers. "Please, please let them in," Glyn begged. Her face was the color of snow, her lips without blood. "I beg of you, please don't let Strahan kill my brother bit by bit."

"Clare?" Strahan's voice boomed. "Next time 'twill be his whole ear, and I won't stop there."

Closing her eyes, Clare made the sign of the cross and stiffened her spine. "Hold on, Strahan," she yelled hoarsely. "You may enter." She signaled the guard at the gate, and the chains of the portcullis began to rumble and clank. Clare's sad eyes met Glyn's frightened gaze. "You'd best go pray," she said, "because we will need all of God's help."

"But Garrick will be back soon," Glyn whispered, ever hopeful.

"Aye, that he will," Clare whispered, knowing that Garrick was riding to meet his death. He had to be warned . . . but how? *Holy Father, please deliver us!*

She watched in silent horror as Ware was prodded upon his steed and Cadell, bleeding from the earlobe, was pushed onto a waiting horse. Strahan's band of dirty soldiers began moving forward, holding the reins to Ware and Cadell's horses and leading them like prisoners of war inside the thick walls of Abergwynn.

Please God, warn Garrick, she silently prayed, then handed a small knife to Glyn.

"I don't want—"

Clare pressed the knife into Glyn's palm. "You may need it."

"Strahan would not harm me—"

Clare slapped her quickly. Her palm smacked hard against Glyn's face. "You saw what Strahan did to your brother. Do you doubt that he would have killed him?"

"Nay, but—"

"What of his soldiers? Do you not think they will be anxious to lie with a woman? Mayhap a lady?"

Tears starred Glyn's eyes. She rubbed the side of her face. Her voice trembled piteously. "But they would not dare approach me—"

"There will be no asking," Clare told her. "They will just take."

"But not me! Surely not me. I am a virgin and—"

Clare's fingers curled over Glyn's hand, forcing her to hold on to the small weapon. "I know. But you will not be spared. The knife gives you a choice. If you decide to endure what the soldiers do to you, then you will not need it. That might be best: suffer the humiliation and spare your life."

"Oh, dear God in heaven—"

"But if you can't lie with them . . . well, you could easily press the blade into the heart of a naked man."

"I couldn't kill—"

"You'll be surprised at what you can endure and what you will do," Clare replied, her own eyes dark, as if with painful memories. "But if the pain is too great, the humiliation too much for you to bear, the knife will offer you a way to end it all for yourself as well."

" 'Tis a sin—"

Clare closed her eyes as the first horse entered the outer bailey. "I know, but take the knife, Glyn."

Glyn gulped, but as Clare removed her hand, Glyn's fingers stayed wrapped around the knife's carved hilt.

Twenty-two

I'll not die a prisoner to the likes of Strahan of Hazelwood," Cadell sneered. His ear was crusted with blood and his body bruised as he lay in his new prison in the lowest level of Abergwynn. Dug deep into the earth, these rooms, barred and smelling of dampness, were seldom used. The hay on the floor was filthy and rotting. No one had set foot in here for years, except when the keep was being searched for Logan.

"How are we to break free?" Ware asked. He, too, wanted to escape, though he'd been told by Strahan that should he find a way to flee from the castle walls, the other hostages would pay. Clare and Glyn would surely come to no good.

"I am not afraid to die," Cadell whispered.

"Then you are foolish. For Strahan will make your death painful."

"I think not." Cadell offered a smile that was barely visible in the half-light. He glanced at the one small barred window high over their heads where daylight dared to filter in and pierce the darkness. "I'll let you in on a secret," he said in a voice so low it could barely be heard.

"What is that?" Ware was in no mood for Cadell's childish fantasies. He, too, was working on a plan of escape but as yet had come up with naught.

"Morgana is not the only grandchild of Enit who can see the future."

Ware's skin crawled. "I do not believe even she can."

"Then you're the fool, my friend. For I have seen her powers. But I knew not that I, too, was blessed with the gift of sight."

Ware snorted. He remembered Cadell's last vision—the voices that had led them into Strahan's trap. "Why have you not told me this before?"

"Because I hardly believed it myself. My visions are not so bright as hers. I had none until this winter past when my voice began to ring with strange notes and hair appeared on new parts of my body."

"So your 'gift' came to you as you became a man?"

Cadell's eyes shifted to Ware's, and they seemed to hold an eerie light. "Mayhap it was always there, but as a lad I was unaware of it." His expression was troubled. "I've heard no voices—no wind talking to me."

"Until today," Ware reminded him.

"As I said, my sight into the future is much weaker than Morgana's gift, and I have not been able to use it to my advantage." He rubbed a hand against the soft down on his dirty jaw. "But in time, I think, these visions of things to come will serve me well."

"If you live long enough."

"That's what I've been saying." Cadell scrambled over to the side of the cell where Ware was slumped against the earthen wall. "I have seen my own future, Ware, and I will not die—at least not by Strahan's hand. I will escape this dungeon, and I will prevail."

The boy was in one of his moods again. Letting his imagination run wild. He had no more sight of the future than did Ware.

Cadell's face crumpled when he realized that Ware didn't believe him. Glancing over his shoulder, as if he suspected unseen eyes in the darkness of the prison, he whispered. "Look what I found." He held up a small bone. "Left over from the last meal of some prisoner, I'll wager. Whoever was in charge of cleaning this place missed this."

" 'Tis only a bone."

"Nay, Ware," Cadell said with a smile bordering on evil. " 'Tis a knife, sure and true. Look." He ran his thumb along the curved edge of the bone. "Sharp enough, if rammed into a man's eye, to wound him."

"You are going to attack the guard?" Ware asked, but his heart was beating faster. It just might work.

"Aye. You call him over. Complain of an injury or something. Make him take his eyes off me. That shouldn't be too difficult, for he thinks I am but a boy, nothing serious to worry about. I will jump him, and as I stab him, you grab his sword."

"What if there are two guards?"

"Then take the man in front of you, and I'll handle the second." Their gazes met in the darkness. " 'Tis our only chance," Cadell whispered, and Ware knew the lad was right. Even though Strahan had promised not to hurt Clare and Glyn if Ware and Cadell remained prisoners, Strahan could not be trusted. Even now the women might be suffering torture or rape. Garrick's return wouldn't help, for he was walking into a trap—a trap Ware himself had helped to set.

They were half a day's ride from Abergwynn when Morgana pulled up short. The air around her stirred, then became still. Heart in her throat she waited for the vision she knew would appear.

"Hey! What's this?" Sir Randolph queried.

"Get on, Lady Morgana," another knight suggested.

But Morgana held Luck's reins tight and hardly dared to breathe. The hills and forest had disappeared, and again she saw the boy child crying, his face streaked with mud, his eyes round with fear. There was darkness around him and damp fog.

Without regard for the men, she slid from the saddle.

Garrick ordered the company to stop. Several men grumbled, for they were anxious to be home, but they pulled up obediently and Garrick told them to rest the horses and to eat.

"You see something," he said approaching her.

"Aye, 'tis Logan."

Garrick's throat tightened, and his lips thinned. "Alive?"

"Aye, but frightened and bound."

"I'll kill whoever did this." He grabbed her arm. "Come with me," he ordered, then commanded one of his men to look after his horse. Wolf snarled as Morgana half ran to keep up with Garrick's long, determined strides as he set off on an overgrown path through the forest. "It's time for you to earn your keep, witch," he said. "I'm tired of your visions, for they are unclear. They give me hope, but no true way of finding my boy. Now, sit there"—he pointed to the stump of a fallen pine tree and shoved her in that direction—"and tell me everything about my son first and then about Abergwynn. We'll wait here all day and all night if need be." He stood, arms crossed, and watched her. Wolf, sensing Garrick's anger, growled and paced restlessly in the brush.

Morgana understood Garrick's frustration and, for once, held her tongue. "The vision I have of Logan is unclear. As I said, he is being held prisoner."

"I know that. Where? By whom?"

Closing her eyes, Morgana called on her memory. "The chamber is dark and damp. Fog enshrouds him. He is tied and ofttimes alone. This scares him more than being with his captors." Her forehead wrinkled as she pulled hard on her memory. "There is the smell of salt—brine—and the dull roar of the sea echoes through the chamber. He must be near the ocean, and he's cold, though his captor has given him a fur coverlet . . . of rabbit and trimmed with ermine. He calls for you, Garrick." Opening her eyes, she found Garrick's face as pale as a new moon.

"How did you know the blanket was missing?" he demanded, his muscles rigid. " 'Twas Logan's favorite."

"I knew not."

"You think Strahan took my boy." He shook his head. "Then why did he not hold Logan for ransom?" He shoved his hair from his eyes, and his strong hand trembled. "What else do you see—about the castle and our brothers?"

She closed her eyes again and wound her fingers in the dirty folds of her tunic. She called up Ware's face from memory, but had no clear picture of him. The castle, too, eluded her, though she smelled smoke, and upon thinking of Cadell, her heart nearly stopped. His face was there before her, but he was wearing the mask of death.

"God help him," she whispered, opening her eyes. "Cadell faces death," she said, her throat thick, her eyes brimming with tears. " 'Tis my fault."

"Nay, Morgana." Garrick was suddenly beside her, holding her and kissing her temple. "Cadell is at Abergwynn because I came for you and your father bargained with his children's upbringing. Do not blame yourself."

"But we must save him. And Logan."

"Is there naught you can do?" he asked. "Can you not chant a spell for their protection?"

"You believe in my spells?" she asked in wonder.

He shook his head. "No, but I believe in trying anything." He motioned to the ground. "Do whatever you must to keep my boy and your brother safe."

"First we pray." Morgana knelt and prayed for the safety of her family and Garrick's. From the corner of her eye, she saw Garrick lay down his sword and bow his head, and she silently asked God to forgive him his arrogance. Once the prayer was finished, she used a stick to draw a circle in the earth, then sketched four crescents that overlapped in the middle of the full circle as they pointed outward, for the protection of Logan, Cadell, Clare, Glyn, and Ware.

"This is it?" Garrick asked, staring down at her rune. "Looks like a horse trampled the earth here."

" 'Tis the best I can do," she said, her shoulders stiffening in pride.

His jaw worked. "Then it will have to do." She stood, dusting her hands, and he was taken again with her beauty. Despite all the fear he faced, the desperation to find his son, he still noted the soft angles of her face, the black waves of her hair, the pride in the small point of her chin. Though he doubted her powers, she did give him hope, not only for Logan's safety but for his own future as well, for he knew now as he stared down at her that he could not go on living without her. She'd charmed him, this witch, turned his thinking around, caused him to forget his vow to Astrid that he would never love another woman, and caused him to revoke his pledge to Strahan, that Morgana would be his bride. Aside from Logan, Morgana of Wenlock was the driving force behind his existence. She'd given him back his passion in life, his belief in God, his ability to laugh, and she'd brought to his blood a fire that knew no bounds.

"Come, Morgana," he said, drawing her into the circle of his arms. He kissed her lightly on the forehead and ignored the hardness growing in his loins. He had no time for lying with her. Not yet. Not until Logan was found. " 'Tis time we went to Abergwynn. If, as you say, Strahan has taken my boy as well as my lands, then he must answer for his deeds."

Heavy footsteps lumbered down the stairway, and the guard, a thickset man with foul breath and a pockmarked face, opened the door. His name was Brodie, and he was known for his love of bawdy stories and gossip. Along with a burning torch, he carried a pitcher of water, an empty pail, and a trencher of old bread.

"Drink from the pitcher and piss in the pail," Brodie ordered, after unlocking the door and entering the dungeon. He was a huge man, twice the size of Cadell, and he stank of stale mead and garlic as he glowered down at the two boys. "So ye got yerself in a pile of trouble, didn't ye, Lord Ware? Ha, that brother of yours is a fool. If ye had a brain in that head of yers, ye would've taken up with Strahan. Ye'd be in a far better place than this." He set the torch into a holder in the wall.

"Would I?" Ware threw back at the man. He affected a thoughtful pose, though he knew that in an instant he would kill Brodie and think nothing of it. "Suppose I told Strahan that I'd changed my mind?"

"He wouldn't believe you. Just as I don't." Brodie dropped the empty pail, and it rolled and clanged against the wall. "You'd never plot against your own brother."

"I wouldn't want to, but I'm a practical man."

The guard snorted. "Man?" He let out a loud belly laugh. "Ye call yerself a man? Ye be but a boy yet. Ye probably haven't even had yer first maid."

Ware's eyes glimmered. "You'd be surprised, Sir Brodie. Many a maid has lifted her skirts for me."

"Bah! The devil you say! Y're but a lad."

"The women think not," Ware lied, seeing the older man lean forward with skeptical interest. "Not only serving wenches, but maids in the village and ladies as well."

"Yer talkin' too big for yer age," Brodie scoffed, but his eyes reflected curiosity in the torchlight, and he grinned, exposing yellowed and broken teeth.

"Big? Aye, I'm big," Ware boasted, touching his groin proudly as, behind the large man, he saw Cadell rise silently to his feet. "I've had no complaints . . . not even from Lady Fiona."

Brodie's eyebrows rose, and his tongue rimmed his lips. "Fiona? Nelson Rowley's niece? The beauty of Castle Pennick? The devil ye say—"

Cadell suddenly leapt upon the big man's back and ground the bit of bone into his eye. Blood spurted, and Brodie fell screaming to one knee.

"You bloody little bastard, I'll cut yer heart out!" Brodie roared, reaching for his knife.

Ware snatched the torch from the wall and set flame to the big man's tunic. Furious and afraid, blood dripping from his ruined eye, Cadell still clinging to his back, Brodie screamed. He fell to the floor and rolled in the hay. The rushes caught fire. Crackling flames burst all around, and thick smoke roiled upward.

"Get off him, you fool!" Ware yelled as Cadell jabbed his bit of bone into the guard's neck. Brodie screamed, fire licking at his limbs as Ware grabbed his sword and ran him through.

"Come on!" Ware grabbed the pitcher and flung the water on the growing fire. Then, clutching the younger man's shirt, he pulled him toward the stairway.

But Cadell wasn't quite through. He reached through the blaze and pried Brodie's dead fingers from his knife. Once armed, he followed Ware up the stairs and out the back entrance to the inner bailey. Smoke drifted upward, and one of the other guards started shouting.

"Hey, you!" a guard called.

"Blood of Christ, there's smoke!" a woman screamed.

"Fire!" the laundress yelled.

"Fire!" the armorer joined in, and soon everyone in the inner bailey was screaming. People ran to the castle, to the pond, to the well, each with the single purpose of dousing the blaze.

"Fire!"

"Where?"

"There—my God, it's the castle! In the basement—the prison! For the love of Mary, look at the smoke!"

"The prisoners! Oh, saints in heaven, Sir Ware and—"

"Get to work, woman! Bring me pails and every free hand in the house, and pray that the clouds drop rain!"

Men and women scrambled toward the source of the blaze. Carpenters, thatchers, huntsmen, and soldiers joined laundresses and serving girls at the well. They carried pail after pail of water to the castle while Ware and Cadell ran for the stables in the outer bailey. Ware grabbed the animals in the first two stalls while Cadell crept ahead to the gate. Only one man remained standing guard at the portcullis, and Cadell, with the aid of Brodie's sharp blade, quickly silenced him.

Mayhem prevailed in the inner bailey. Cadell and Ware mounted their sorry-looking horses. With a kick to his steed's sides, Ware led the way. He heard a shout behind him, realized that a sentry upon the battlement had seen them. "Come on, you nag," Ware said, spurring his little bay mare forward. The sky was dark, the wind cold, and the smell of rain was heavy in the air. Ware clung to the hack's neck and wished she could gallop as fast as his destrier.

There were louder shouts from the castle, and Ware guessed that the blaze had been doused and that Strahan's men were going to give chase. He glanced over his shoulder at Cadell and was rewarded with the boy's audacious grin.

"When this is all over," Cadell yelled over the wind that whistled against Ware's ears, "you must tell me about Lady Fiona."

Ware laughed and kicked his mare. Soon they would be in the woods, safely out of sight. . . . Then he heard it—the thunder of hoofbeats. He glanced over his shoulder, and his heart froze, for a war party of no less than twenty was following them. The men rode fresh, strong destriers and coursers, and as the distance between them lessened with horrifying swiftness, Ware recognized some of Strahan's strongest archers.

"Ride, Cadell!" Ware cried, "and don't look back! Hiiiya!" He slapped the reins against his own mount's shoulders and prayed that he and Cadell could lose Strahan's men in the woods.

They were close to Abergwynn and the wind was blowing from the north. Morgana smelled the air and watched the leaves of the saplings near the road, hoping the wind would turn. The north wind, her grandmother had taught her, was the wind of death. Dry and barren, blowing from regions of cold, the north wind blew hard, and Morgana shivered. The day had turned to night. Black clouds roiled overhead.

Even the horses knew they were near home. In the last hour, the pace of Garrick's band had picked up. Horses snorted impatiently, and men, once tired and grumbling, now began to smile and talk among themselves. There was much talk of hot baths, women, and mead. They began to joke and laugh, but Morgana's stomach was like a band of steel tightening with each step of her horse.

Would her visions prove true? Was there deception and betrayal at Abergwynn? And what of Logan? The poor child, where was he? She'd prayed and turned her face to the wind, hoping for some inkling of the future, but the voice had fallen silent again and she was left with a feeling of impending doom.

The road widened, and the horses thundered out of the woods and through the valley over which Abergwynn towered, the banner of blue and gold snapping in the wind. Garrick held up his hand and they reined in their horses to stare at Abergwynn. The castle stood proud, seemingly unharmed, and was far from the blackened ruins she'd seen in her dreams.

Garrick, from his war-horse next to her, glanced in her direction. "See you any visions?" he asked.

"Nay. But the wind is from the north."

When he didn't respond, she bit her lip.

" 'Tis a sign of death," she whispered.

He scowled. "So this danger you see—it still exists?"

Her fingers twisted around the reins. "I know only what I've told you before—that there will be death and bloodshed. And the feelings are strong—stronger, mayhap, because of the wind. She lifted her head and smelled the acrid scent of smoke drifting on the breeze.

"You once feared me. Did you not think I was the death from the north?"

"Aye, but now I follow you," she said, her heart open, though her visions were still terrifying. She would ride with Garrick wherever he took her.

"Think you that I shall bring death to Tower Wenlock?"

She swallowed. "Not to me," she said, thinking of Cadell, for all day long his image had been close to her, and several times she had tried to speak to him, to communicate with him over the miles. There was danger for everyone, but right now Cadell was in the gravest peril. She could feel it as she felt the mists rising from the sea to touch her skin.

Garrick frowned, his expression hard. "I must face Strahan alone," he said. " 'Twould not be safe for you. I'll leave Sir Bradford with you."

"But I must ride with you," she protested, panic rising in her heart. Her visions came together in her mind, and she saw death for all whom she loved. "Garrick, please. The wind said I am to help you. I am to find your son. Do not leave me—"

"Enough, Morgana!" he commanded. "I'll not have your blood on my hands. Stay here until I know 'tis safe in the castle."

Fear gripped her guts, and she reached out to touch him. "This is a mistake, m'lord," she begged. "Your very life may depend upon me."

"As yours depends upon my decision." He covered her hand with his in a moment of tenderness that squeezed her heart, and she knew that he expected never to see her again.

"Garrick, please," she begged, tears suddenly brimming her eyes. "I cannot bear to leave you."

" 'Tis best."

Her throat closed in upon itself. "You need me!"

"I need to know you are safe, witch. I've already lost my wife, my son—everyone I've loved. I'll not lose you by my own foolishness."

"But I can be of help!" Tears streamed from her eyes.

Garrick wiped one of her teardrops from her cheek. His gaze lingered on her face for a mere second before he turned to Sir Bradford. "Stay with Morgana. Her life is in your hands. I'll send for you both when I know the castle is secure."

"Nay, Garrick, please!" Morgana cried, but she watched in agony as he yanked hard on the reins and the huge war-horse whirled and galloped through the lush fields surrounding Abergwynn, carrying Garrick and leading a small band of soldiers to their fate.

Twenty-three

Garrick rode through the open gates of Abergwynn with the sour taste of deception in his throat. No guards stopped them. Was Strahan really a traitor or was there another Judas in the midst? It mattered not. Whoever had stolen his son would curse the day he'd lured Logan away from the castle walls.

His tiny band entered the outer bailey, which was as silent as death. No stableboys. No carpenters. No washerwomen. No workers of any kind. "Make ready for battle," Garrick commanded as the gate to the inner bailey opened and Strahan, astride a huge white horse, appeared. An army of archers and swordsmen stood behind him. Arrows were drawn, aimed at Garrick's heart. Some of the men were knights in whom he'd trusted. So Morgana was right. Her visions had proved true.

"Cousin. You returned," Strahan said, and Garrick wanted to strangle him with his bare hands.

"Where is Ware?" Garrick demanded. "He's in command here."

Strahan grinned. "I'm in command, Garrick. Abergwynn is mine. Your sister and your son are my prisoners and your brother is at this moment being hunted down after escaping."

Garrick's rage was deep and hot. He could barely remain astride his mount. "Logan is here?"

"Nay."

"Where, then?"

"Safe." Strahan's gaze roved through Garrick's small band of men. "Where is Morgana?"

"Safe."

Strahan couldn't help but smile. "So 'tis true. You've claimed her for yourself."

"She wants not to be your bride," Garrick said evenly, unsheathing his sword. "Unless you want your miserable life to end right now, I suggest you tell your men to put down their weapons and tell me where I can find my son."

Strahan snapped his fingers and, to Garrick's horror, two soldiers opened the door of the great hall. On the top step, a guard holding one arm wrenched behind her back, stood Clare. Her back was arched in pain, and her long mahogany-colored hair was missing—shorn from her head. Her pink scalp showed small bloodied scabs, and Garrick had to swallow back the foul taste roiling up his throat.

"Clare," he murmured, his heart heavy. He had brought this shame to her.

"Do not give in, Garrick," Clare said. "Ware's escaped and—" She sucked her breath between her teeth in a hiss as the guard twisted her arm harder. Tears streamed down her face from the pain, though she would not break down and sob. "He and Cadell will bring back forces. Do not back down, Garrick, for surely that would be our doom!"

"If you ever want to see your son alive again," Strahan said, "I suggest that you sheathe your weapon. I've given orders that if I'm killed, the boy is to be tortured until he dies."

Garrick's insides shook, but he held his ground. "You lying bastard, I'll kill you—"

"And kill the boy," Strahan said flatly, "as well as Clare, and Ware, too, when we catch up to him. It's only a matter of time." His dark eyes delved deep into Garrick's. "As for Morgana, I assure you that if you defy me, I will make her life with me so painful she will often wish for death."

Garrick's gut twisted.

"You see, cousin, you have no choice."

"Oh, but I do, Strahan." With that, he raised his sword high over his head. "I'll make your last hours on earth a living hell if you don't tell me now where the boy is."

A bloodcurdling scream filled the air, and Garrick turned to see Clare, blood flowing from a cut above her eye. The brutish guard leered and held the knife closer to her eye.

"Next time she'll lose her sight," Strahan said, and Garrick steeled himself to face the pain he'd brought upon his family.

He could not bring harm to those he loved. Already his pride had cost him too much. Slowly he lowered his weapon and cringed at the cruel satisfaction gleaming in Strahan's dark eyes.

"I wish to see all the prisoners, including my son," Garrick said. "Once I know that they're truly alive and you've assured me of their safe passage to Wenlock, I will surrender the castle and all my lands to you."

Strahan's tongue flicked over his lips. "Why should I trust you?"

"When have I ever gone back on my word?"

"When you chose to lie with the woman you promised was to be my wife!" Strahan's eyes glittered with hatred. "However, I'll accept your terms if you tell me where the witch hides. 'Twill save my men the trouble of searching for her."

"Morgana is to go free."

"She will be my wife."

"Never," Garrick said.

Eyes narrowing in anticipation, Strahan reached for his sword and ordered, "Capture the witch and bring her to me. We'll be married tonight!"

"I'll see you dead first," Garrick vowed hoarsely, praying for Clare's safety as he kicked his horse forward to battle.

An arrow hissed through the air, landing square in his shoulder.

Clare screamed, but Garrick stayed upon his charger, the steed galloping the short distance to meet Strahan straight on. Garrick's men spurred their horses behind him, but Strahan met him eagerly. Arrows sprayed the horses and men. Garrick felt the sting of wounds in his thighs and arms. Still he didn't falter, intent on reaching the traitor.

"You bastard," Garrick yelled, swinging his sword as their horses collided. The animals screamed and fought. Strahan lunged at Garrick, his sword slicing the air. Garrick brought his weapon down, striking Strahan's mail with a clang. Strahan's horse reared, and Strahan swung wildly, his blade hitting Garrick's arm and throwing him off his horse.

Garrick hit the ground with a thud and tried to roll away as his destrier's sharp hooves came downward. He felt as if his chest had caved in, and his breath left his body before blackness overcame him. "Morgana!" he cried, clinging to her memory as he lost consciousness.

The wind still blew from the north. Death surrounded her. Morgana stood deep within the forest, where Sir Bradford insisted they hide. Her thoughts were with Garrick, but she knew she couldn't save him. She and Bradford had watched as the portcullis rattled shut. There was nothing to do but wait. Yet she felt a restlessness, an irritation that she couldn't do anything to dispel.

The north wind touched her cheek, as frigid as the lands from whence it came. Sir Bradford was running a knife along the inside of his destrier's front hoof, trying to dislodge a stone the horse had picked up. Luck was grazing, his saddle propped up against a tree.

The wind shifted slightly, rolling through the forest, touching leaves and branches, moving the fronds of the ferns.

Morgana.

She started, looked over her shoulder, but Sir Bradford hadn't quit working on the horse. Nay, he had heard nothing.

Morgana, you must seek out the boy.

"Logan," she whispered, her heart hammering. "But where?"

To the north, where the sea is nearly a circle.

"Hey—what? What's going on?" Sir Bradford asked, looking over his shoulder. "Yer not makin' any of that devil magic, now, are ye?"

Morgana smiled inwardly. "I talk to the wind. It says I am to find Logan."

"Not now, ye ain't. Y're staying right here with me."

"But I must find the baron's son."

"I thinks not. In good time. What the devil?" He let his horse's hoof down and listened. Morgana could hear the noise, too. Men on horseback, shouting to each other. Wolf bristled and growled. Sir Bradford grabbed the hilt of his sword. "Be quiet, m'lady. Mayhap they are from Lord Garrick."

But Morgana saw the furrow in his brow and the set of

his jaw beneath his thin beard. "Strahan's men," she said, knowing as surely as if she could see into their faces that the riders brought death.

"You stay here. I'll have a look." Bradford stole through the underbrush while Morgana waited, her heart beating so loud she could barely hear the sounds of the forest. The minutes passed slowly, and she wondered how long she would have to sit beneath the trees not knowing if the riders were friend or foe.

"Who goes there?" Bradford's voice boomed through the trees.

" 'Tis I, Sir York," a voice replied.

"Be ye faithful to Lord Garrick?"

"Of course, Bradford."

"Ahh. All is well, then," Bradford assured them, though Morgana felt fear in her heart. York had been left at Abergwynn. Surely Garrick would not send a soldier whose loyalty was in question.

"Have ye seen two riders?" York asked. "We're looking for Sir Ware and the boy, Cadell, from Wenlock."

Morgana's heart nearly stopped beating.

"They've not been this way," Bradford replied. "I've been here nearly three hours."

"Then you're of no use to us."

"No use? What? York! Do you betray Lord Garrick?" Bradford asked. Then he let out a horrible scream and said no more.

"Come on. Let's be off!" York commanded, and hoofbeats once again echoed through the forest.

Please God, let him live, Morgana silently prayed as she followed a deer trail through the woods and searched for Sir Bradford. He was a big man, and soon she found him stretched out on the ground, his body unmoving, a bloody gash deep in his chest. Leaning over, she pressed her hand to his neck, hoping to feel a heartbeat. Sticky blood stained her fingers. His chest didn't move, nor did any breath escape his lungs.

She bit her lip as she stared down at him. "May your soul rest in peace, Sir Bradford," she said. Bending down, she closed his eyes and forced herself to turn her thoughts to Cadell and Ware and the men who were chasing them. She ran through the brush and climbed astride Luck's broad back. Skirts bunched up over her legs, she dug her heels into the stallion's sides and turned him toward the north, into the wind.

They'd eluded Strahan's men, at least for the time being. Now, as Ware led his lathered courser through the forest, he followed the overgrown deer trails he'd traveled in his youth and motioned to Cadell to keep quiet. Branches struck him in the face, and twigs snapped beneath his feet, yet he plowed onward, toward the north, keeping the sea to his left. Swallowing back his fear, he silently prayed that the muted pounding of the surf on rocks would cover the sound of their movement.

His plan was simple. He intended to keep moving until nightfall, hoping that the soldiers behind him would give up their quest. Then he and Cadell would circle back, intercept Garrick, and join forces with him.

And what of Clare and Glyn? What of the servants who risked their necks to stand with you? His gut twisted, and he knew darkest fear. "God be with them," he silently prayed as he shoved a branch from his face.

The moon was rising, offering light that filtered through

the forest and guided him onward through the ferns, brambles, and vines to the meadow overlooking the point whereon the first castle of Abergwynn had been started. Through the trees he stared past the field to the old fortress that had never been fully constructed. Blocks of stone and huge timbers were still stacked near the steep-sided motte that was now covered with bracken and grass. The base of a tower jutted upward into the night, and crumbling walls littered the ground. If he remembered from his youth, when he oft went exploring while he should have been hunting, underground rooms and passageways still existed wherein he and Cadell could hide.

He motioned to the boy, and when he was close enough, whispered into his ear. "We can stay here in the forest or hide in the ruins of that unfinished castle."

Cadell's eyes sparked with a devilish light. "What think you?"

"The forest offers a means of escape, but 'tis impossible to hide here without fear of being seen. The ruins will hide us and our horses well, but if we are found, there will be no easy way out. We could be trapped."

Cadell hesitated and Ware heard the snap of a branch behind them. They glanced at each other and knew they had no choice. Quickly mounting, they kicked their horses and raced along the edge of the cliff and downward toward the ruins.

Somewhere behind them a man shouted, and Ware's heart nearly stopped beating. "Come on, come on!" he urged his tired courser. "Move, will you?"

Cadell was near, his horse panting. The shouts followed them, and soon the army of men broke from the forest, huge looming shadows riding as fast as the wind. Down the hill toward the ruins Ware sped, holding his breath each time his nag stumbled, quietly cursing the rabbit holes and burrows in the uneven ground.

"Halt!" a voice yelled.

Ware kicked his horse.

"Halt, I say. Damn you!"

An arrow whizzed past his head, and Ware tucked his body low against the mare's neck. "Run, you bloody mule, run!" he yelled, whipping the poor animal as it sped forward. Another arrow sliced through the air, nipping the horse's flank before being deflected. "Bloody Christ!"

"Ware!" Cadell screamed. "Christ, Ware—"

Ware wheeled his horse around, and in an instant he saw Cadell, one arrow lodged in his shoulder, begin to fall from his mount. "Hang on." He guided his horse close to Cadell's and reached over to grab the boy. Cadell's hands clawed at his arm, but as he yanked him from his mount, a hot pain sliced through his thigh. Still he held on as the mare raced along the edge of the cliff. Riders seemed to come from every direction—across the grassland, from the forest— huge men with quivers and crossbows at ready.

"Holy Mother," Ware swore as Cadell's horse stumbled and fell. The boy swung free, all his weight on Ware. He let go of the reins, pulled Cadell with both hands, but the mare broke stride and Cadell lost his grip.

"No!" Ware cried.

The boy fell away from him, pulling him off the horse. Ware hit the ground with a thud and rolled toward the cliff. The shaft of the arrow in his thigh broke and drove the steel-tipped point even deeper into his leg. Ware ignored the pain. He reached forward, lunging toward Cadell.

Cadell slid toward the edge, but caught his balance.

Foolishly he stood up on unsteady legs. A final arrow pierced his chest, and he screamed in pain as he fell backward. His feet scrambled in the soft dirt, and suddenly he pitched over the embankment.

"No!" Ware screamed, crawling rapidly toward the edge of the cliff. Cadell couldn't die. He couldn't! Not after all they'd been through.

"Halt or die!" a voice commanded.

Ware disregarded the warning and reached the edge. He stared down at the rocks and sea below, but nowhere did he see Cadell's crumpled body. Hot tears streamed from his eyes, and his fingers curled into tight fists in the wet earth. "Cadell!" he yelled, his body racked with sobs, the pain in his leg blistering.

"He's gone."

Ware looked over his shoulder to find a huntsman astride a big war-horse, his bow taut, an arrow pointed at the middle of Ware's back. The man kicked his mount and moved steadily closer to Ware. "Do you wish to join him?"

"I care not," Ware snarled, spitting at the horse's hooves.

"Don't! Strahan wants this one alive," another rider called from the growing darkness.

"Strahan be damned!" Ware scrambled to his feet, drew himself up straight, and boldly faced the men's dark faces. His thigh burned, and his eyes were bright with defiance. "I'll not ride with you."

"You have no choice."

A strange smile split Ware's boyish face. "There are always choices," he said, his chin tilting mutinously upward. "I'll never bow to Strahan, nor will I be bound in his chains."

"Come, Ware—"

"Give my brother my best and tell Strahan . . . tell him I'll meet him in hell!" He turned around and jumped then, his body soaring over the rocky surf below. He closed his eyes to the fear that froze his heart as he hurtled downward into the swirling darkness.

Twenty-four

Morgana watched in horror as Cadell pitched into the blackness and over the cliff. "No!" she cried, but her voice was drowned by the rush of the wind, and all too soon Ware, too, leapt to his death. "God in heaven."

The men on horseback who surrounded the ridge did not see her hidden in the shadows of the forest. Tears streamed down her face, and she silently cursed the fates, cursed God, cursed Garrick, and cursed herself for the deaths of Ware and Cadell.

In misery she sat down on the forest floor and felt Luck's hot breath against the back of her neck. The horse nudged her head and nibbled at her hair, but Morgana took no comfort from the stallion. Even Wolf, who lay beside her and placed his heavy head in her lap, could not bring a smile to her face. " 'Tis my fault," she said softly, her heart breaking a thousand times over. "My pride brought me to this, my believing in voices and visions and thinking I was something that I'm not."

With deep trepidation, she watched the soldiers mount and head south along the ridge above the sea. These were Strahan's men, the very men who had killed kind Sir Bradford, and she knew in her heart that Garrick had fallen into his cousin's trap by returning to Abergwynn. All because of her visions.

Garrick, too, was probably dead, and she would never see him again. Bitter tears streamed down her face, and she fought the urge to break down and sob. Instead, she watched the soldiers through the shimmer of her tears.

Strahan's murderous warriors soon gave up their search of the rocky bluff and remounted. They rode through the forest, and followed the western trail that wound away from her hiding place. Not that it mattered. There had been a time when all she'd wanted was her freedom, but now, after seeing Cadell's death and Ware's as well, she knew she would gladly marry Strahan if only her brother would live. She could bury her love for Garrick and accept her fate as Strahan's bride if only she could see Cadell's face again.

Throwing herself face down on the ground, she cried until she had no more tears in her. Only then did she allow the dry sobs to rack her body. She buried her fingers in the damp earth and dug until her nails bled. "Help me. Help us all," she said, not even realizing that she was praying.

'Tis you who must help, Morgana, the voice, rolling softly over the sea, whispered into her ear.

"Go away!"

You have not yet completed your quest.

"And you are evil, aye, the voice of the very devil himself. No more will I trust in you!"

You must find the boy child of Abergwynn.

Logan! Oh, Lord, where was the boy? Through her pain she still cared for the child.

Trust your heart, Morgana of Wenlock.

"My heart has deceived me!" she screamed, stumbling to her feet. Blinded by tears she ran out of the woods and stood facing the sea and calling out to the dreadful voice. "*You* have deceived me! Cadell is dead! Ware is dead! Even now Garrick and Glyn and Clare might be dead! I have helped not!" She fell again to the earth and cried, great tears streaking her cheeks. The wind shifted, turning in the night, curling around her until the current flowed from the east, toward the sea. Morgana felt the change, the uplifting of the spirit that an easterly wind always brought. Yet she would not be swayed from her misery.

"The wind from the east is your friend," her grandmother had once told her, when Enit could still walk in the gardens of Wenlock. "It brings with it new hope and life. It is a powerful wind that comes from the point where the sun and moon rise. The mind becomes strong, for the power from the east is great. Use it, child. Harness this great breath of goodwill."

Morgana lifted her face to the east, letting the wind dry her tears. Slowly, as if pulled from above, she rose, and with the horse and dog following her, she used the moonlight as her guide. The wind seemed to push her onward to the bluff, until her toes touched the edge and she stared over the rocky precipice at the swirling black sea far below. White swells surrounded craggy rocks. No one could have survived the fall, she realized, her throat hot and tight. The rocks below were deadly, and the sea was a thrashing, icy dragon that would surely swallow any poor soul who slipped into its frigid depths.

"God be with you, Cadell," she prayed, "aye, and you, too, Ware. You were brave men and deserved not this. Forever will I do penance for your lost lives." She plucked a wildflower from the grass and tossed it into the air. In the shaft of moonlight the flower feathered down to disappear into the blackness.

She turned inland again, and the darkness seemed to

vanish. In the clear moonglow, mists appeared, and within the shifting fingers of steam she saw again the child Logan weeping, his soft sobs causing his tiny shoulders to shake.

Reaching out, as if she could touch her vision and soothe the frightened boy, she called his name. "Logan . . ."

He is near, the voice told her as the vision disappeared. In its place were the ruins—the rubble of what was to have been the first Castle Abergwynn. Morgana's throat turned to dust. In an instant she realized that Logan was there, captured by Strahan, moved about by a band of Strahan's outlaws, and finally hidden close to Abergwynn as a horrid joke. Her feet began to move of their own accord, and she ran over the uneven ground, stumbling, catching herself, and feeling an inkling of joy return to her blackened soul. If she could save Garrick's child, all would not be lost.

She was winded by the time she reached the crumbling walls. Moonlight caused shadows to play within the outer bailey and she picked her way carefully, listening but hearing nothing save her own breathing and the gentle pad of Wolf's paws against old stone.

But the feeling was stronger, and she was certain that the boy was hidden nearby. Wolf stopped suddenly, and the hair on the back of his neck rose as he stiffened in fear. His lips curled, and he stared straight ahead to a dark opening in one of the half-standing walls. "Shh," she hissed, entering what had once been a doorway to interior stairs. Slowly she descended, carefully placing each foot on the crumbling steps, holding her tongue as rats and mice and all manner of other creatures scuttled out of her path. She kept one hand on the wall and was comforted by Wolf's presence behind her.

Blackness surrounded her as the stairs turned. Not even a

hint of starlight pierced the interior. The stone walls felt damp, and the scent of the sea was strong. Somewhere deep in the bowels of this catacomb, she heard a soft whimper and saw a faint glow from a torch.

"Be quiet, ya brat," a thick voice muttered, and Morgana nearly slipped. Her boot scraped on the steps, and her heart clenched as a pebble rolled down the stairs.

"Hey! Who's there? Ivan, is that you?"

The boy wailed pitifully.

So Sir Ivan was a traitor as well! The light shifted, and Morgana, holding her breath, scuttled backward up the stairs.

"Bloody rats," the guard growled, and the light retreated.

Morgana's hands circled the hilt of her dagger, and this time, as she descended the curved steps, she was silent.

Holding her breath, she saw again the red-gold glow of a torch. Wolf crouched, ready and still. She trod lightly over the stone steps. The sound of the sea was closer now, a dull and constant roar. Rounding the final bend in the stairs, she witnessed her horrible vision come to life.

Logan lay in a corner of a rotting cell, and his guard leaned against the wall, drinking mead and belching. A torch, mounted near a narrow window cut into the cliff face overlooking the sea, gave off an eerie flickering light. The air was thick with smoke and smelled of burning wood, stale mead, and urine.

Morgana's blood boiled as she crouched. This was no place for a child. She only hoped she had the courage to kill the guard. Suddenly Logan saw her. He screamed, and the guard whirled, knocking over his cup. Mead sloshed onto the floor and splashed upon his filthy leggings. "What the bloody hell?" he growled, scrabbling for his sword. The dog growled and the guard's eyes shifted. "Saints in heaven, what's that?"

Wolf snarled louder, and the boy cried out.

"Holy Christ, 'tis the witch!" The guard's face paled.

"Leave the child," she ordered.

"Nay." His hand was on the hilt of his sword, but as he drew back, Wolf lunged, jumping and snapping at the man's throat. The guard screamed and fell, dropping his sword. His arms flayed uselessly at Wolf's hide, and his face twisted in terror. "Get this beast of Satan off me!" he shrieked.

"Will you leave us alone?" she asked.

White fangs snapped at his throat.

"For the mercy of God, Lady Morgana—" he rasped, still trying to throw the dog off him.

"Wolf! Back!" Morgana grabbed the man's sword and held him at bay.

Tears streamed from the man's eyes, and scratches bled at his throat. He shivered and sniveled, a weak coward who tortured a small boy. "Please do not curse me. I've got a wife, and we've a child on the way."

"Yet you treat Garrick's son this way?"

" 'Tis but orders I was following, m'lady."

"You disgust me! You are lucky I don't chant a spell that would kill the very seed within you so that you would never again father a child."

"No! Oh, m'lady—" he whined.

"Wolf, stand guard." While the dog's golden gaze remained fastened on the sentry, Morgana grabbed a length of rope and tied the man's hands and feet so that he could not move.

"You're not leaving me here?"

"Aye. Alone in the dark, where you and God can talk things over. Since you won't be needing this," she added, picking up a bow and a quiver filled with arrows, "I'll be taking it along as well."

"Just don't curse me. Please be merciful."

She paused, as if conjuring up some horror.

"Oh, please, m'lady, *please*," he begged, tears streaming down his red-veined face. "Do not chant a wicked spell."

"Very well," she said, as if she actually had the knowledge and the desire to dabble in the black arts.

"You'll send someone back for me . . ." he mumbled piti-fully.

Morgana strapped the quiver and bow over her shoulder. "Pray hard, man. Maybe God will hear you."

"Please, m'lady, have mercy," he cried, but Morgana ignored the wretched mass that was one of Strahan's men.

She walked quickly to the child, and her heart tore as Logan shrank away from her. Holding out her hand, she said, "I will take you to your father, Logan, for he is greatly worried about you."

"Nay!" the boy cried.

"Do you not want to leave here?"

Logan's eyes were round in the torchlight, and his little lips quivered. Morgana's heart bled for him. "Come, child, I will keep you safe."

His eyes moved to the dog, and Morgana smiled. "He will watch over both of us, little one. See?" She petted Wolf's thick fur and was rewarded with a wet tongue against her hand. "Come on." Carefully she cut Logan loose from his bonds and hauled him up. She grabbed the blanket she'd seen in her dreams and draped it over the lad's shoulders. He was stiff and unyielding in her arms, and she knew that only time and his father's love would heal his memory of the horrors that he'd lived through.

Carrying the torch and the boy, with the dog at her heels, she carefully climbed the steps. Over the steady roar of the sea, the guard's cowardly cries followed her up the stairs. Oh, she would send someone for him, but not until the man had learned a lesson about children. Would that she did know a spell to kill his seed so that he could spawn no more like himself!

As they emerged from the dungeon, the east wind again caressed her face and tickled the silken strands of Logan's hair. Luck was grazing in the moonlight, noisily plucking blades of spring grass. The boy brightened when he saw the stallion.

"Would you like to ride him?"

He didn't reply, just stared at the horse.

"Come. He's a great war-horse and deserves a rider like you." Morgana lifted Logan onto Luck's bare back and took the reins in her hands. She led the horse through the trees, away from the cliffs where Ware and Cadell had plunged to their death, and into the darkness of the forest.

Part of her quest was complete. She'd found Logan. Now she had to find a way to save Garrick and Abergwynn, and that would take time. If, indeed, Garrick was still alive. She ached to the very bottom of her soul, and she longed for vengeance against Strahan. "Hold on, child," she whispered, to herself as much as to the boy, "we face a long journey."

"I do not want him to die yet!" Strahan said, eyeing the bed where Garrick lay. Garrick hadn't moved all night, and despite the continual droning prayers of Morgana's sister, Glyn, he seemed to be worse. Even Clare's ministrations had no effect.

"If you didn't want him to die, you should have ordered your man not to shoot!" Clare snapped, her lips curled in disgust. "Your greed and treachery have led to this, Strahan, and if you are stupid enough to trust Osric McBrayne, then you deserve all the suffering that God will send your way." She rubbed some ointment upon the wound in her brother's shoulder and turned her back on Strahan.

"He must live," Strahan said. "Make sure he does."

"Then you'd better find Morgana of Wenlock." Turning toward him, Clare lifted her pointed chin defiantly. Even with scratches on her hairless scalp, she was a commanding woman, a woman Strahan sometimes feared. "For my brother needs stronger medicine than I can give him, aye, stronger than that of any physician or apothecary. Only Morgana can save him. Elsewise, I suggest you tell Father Francis to administer last rites."

"You lie," Strahan said.

Clare's eyes turned sad. "He is my brother, Strahan, my only brother still living, if your men tell the truth. I would do anything to make him well again, but 'tis out of my hands."

Strahan felt a rising panic. True, he had ofttimes envisioned Garrick's death, but always in a heroic setting. In his fantasies Strahan saw himself as a great leader of men who set others free of Garrick's rule. He wanted Garrick, before he died, to understand why he'd stolen Abergwynn and to watch as Strahan took the things he most valued—his castle and his woman. As for Logan, Strahan would not have hurt the boy—not truly hurt him. He only wanted to see Garrick stripped of everything he cared for. But now, as he stared down at the white face of his cousin, he felt an absurd twinge of guilt.

"M'lord." A soldier stepped haltingly into Garrick's chamber, and Springan slid past him, eyes downcast as she carried a bowl of chicken stew. She, too, was without hair, and Strahan felt a glimmer of satisfaction that her lush red tresses had been shorn from her scalp. Always a little uppity, that one. Well, the whore knew her place now.

"What is it?" Strahan asked the soldier.

" 'Tis the boy, Logan, sire. He's missing." Strahan's spine stiffened. "We searched all night, but found only this—" The knight motioned to the hallway, and a pathetic man stumbled into the chamber, bringing with him an odor so foul that Strahan wrinkled his nose. "Your guard, Kent of Hawarth."

"Where is the boy?" Strahan demanded.

The man, red-faced from too much mead, seemed to tremble. "The witch has him, m'lord."

For the love of God, the man was actually quivering! "You let a woman best you and steal the boy?" he demanded, as the heat of fury swept up his back.

"But, Lord Strahan, she swooped up from the very depths of hell with a beast from Satan that lunged at me and nearly took my throat. While the creature held me to the floor, she chanted curses and grabbed the boy afore she flew from the chamber and left me bound in the darkness!"

"You ass! Do you expect me to believe—"

" 'Tis true!" the man insisted, his beady eyes moving from Strahan to the knight who had brought him here. He fell to his knees, groveling for his miserable life at the toes of Strahan's boots. "Please, I beg of you, believe what I say!"

Strahan's stomach turned over. This man had been entrusted to him by Osric McBrayne. "One of the finest fightin' men Castle Hawarth has to offer," the old man had said, and Strahan, fool that he was, had believed him.

He glowered down at the sorry lump of flesh in front of him. "What I believe is that you were lazy, drank too much mead, and let a small woman scare you! You're lucky I don't curse you myself!"

The journey took all of four days, but at last, travel-weary and nearing exhaustion, Morgana guided Luck through the trees to see Tower Wenlock jutting upward to the cloud-strewn sky. Tears filled her throat at the thought of seeing her parents again. She knew her father would at first be furious, for she was still banished, but eventually he would listen to her. He had to.

"Come," she whispered to the boy sleeping in her arms. "'Tis time you had a warm bath and a fresh bed." She kicked the stallion's sides, and the game horse responded, ears pricked forward at the sight and sounds of the tower.

Morgana smiled as she heard the sentries shout. She threw back the cowl from her head and let her hair fly free. Wolf raced beside them, and a horn blasted, announcing her arrival.

Wenlock! Glorious Wenlock! For a brief instant her heart felt unbound. She rode through the open gates, and before Luck slid to a full stop, she hopped lithely to the ground, the boy in her arms.

"Morgana?" Daffyd of Wenlock's brow was furrowed as he approached. "Where is Lord Garrick or Sir Strahan? Don't tell me you've—"

"Father!" she cried, wanting to throw her arms around him. She licked her lips nervously, and tears threatened her eyes. "Please, Father, before you get angry, let me tell you all that has happened."

"You're as dirty as a forest dweller!" Daffyd said, his eyes dark with worry. "This child . . . is it . . . ?"

"Aye! 'Tis Garrick's son! Oh, Father, I have so much to tell you! We must make ready for battle—"

"Morgana!" Meredydd flew down the stairs of the great hall, her skirts billowing behind her, a smile brightening her smooth face.

"Mother!" Still holding Logan, Morgana embraced her mother. Overcome with relief, she was suddenly unable to speak, for how was she to tell of the horrors at Abergwynn? Responding to the warmth of her mother's arms, she wanted to cry yet again.

"You've found the boy. I knew you would!" Meredydd's voice rang with happiness. "But where is Lord Garrick? Tell me all. Glyn—is she learning her lessons? What of Cadell? He is not making too much trouble at Abergwynn, is he?"

"Oh, Mother," Morgana whispered, tears raining from her eyes. She blinked hard, trying to remain strong, feeling the curious gazes of the servants and sentries upon her. For Gwladys and Nellwyn, Berthilde and Cook, the smith and several huntsmen, the stableboys and carpenters, had stopped their work and gathered around to watch the reunion between father and wayward daughter. Even the provisioner had ventured out into the bailey. "I have sad news," she finally said, her voice barely a whisper.

Once in the castle, Morgana told her story carefully, and Meredydd upon learning of Cadell's death, could not be consoled. Grief-stricken, she screamed and cried, and only after the maidservants had taken her to her quarters and Logan to be fed was Morgana able to continue her conversation with her father. Daffyd, too, was grief-stricken, but he shed no tears. His eyes narrowed in fury and vengeance.

"We must hurry to Abergwynn," she told him, but Daffyd was immovable.

"No daughter of mine will return to that place of death—at least not until Garrick is lord again!" Daffyd pounded his fist so hard against the table that the silver rattled and several cups of wine overflowed. Wolf, from his position under the table, barked, and several of the dogs lying in the rushes next to Daffyd growled.

"But, Father—"

"Nay. I'll send a message to Nelson Rowley at Castle Pennick. We shall meet two days hence, and together we'll lead our armies onward and attack Abergwynn."

"What if Strahan decides to kill Glyn?" Morgana asked, cringing inside when she saw her father blanch. "Or Garrick? Or Clare?"

Her father glowered, anger snapping in his eyes. "Then I'll personally cut out his black heart. But I'll not have you sacrifice yourself!"

"Father, please," Morgana begged. "I must go back. 'Tis the only way."

"So now you are a soldier, eh?" Daffyd scoffed. "I think not. Stay here, daughter, with your mother. She needs you, as does the son of the baron. War is for men."

The discussion was over. Morgana knew that any further argument with her father would be futile, for Daffyd of Wenlock was a very stubborn man.

He intended to take all the soldiers Garrick had left at Wenlock, as well as some of his strongest men, and attack the fortress that was Abergwynn.

They didn't have a chance. Morgana knew that as well as

she knew that she loved Garrick. The only way to ensure that Strahan would spare the lives of those left at Abergwynn was for her to sacrifice herself and become his bride.

Daffyd insisted she eat, and she forced Cook's food over her tongue. After the meal, she hurried upstairs to her grandmother's room. A servant was just removing a tray from the bed where Enit rested.

"Ah, child, I heard you were back," Enit said, her wrinkled face filling with happiness. "Knew you were coming, too," she said. "You brought the boy."

"Aye, Grandmother, but I bring bad news as well."

"I know. I, too, have seen Cadell's face"—her cloudy eyes fell to her hands—"but there is hope, for the soldiers of Hazelwood have found neither his body nor that of the brother of Garrick."

"You think they live?"

Enit sighed. "I know not," she said sadly. "My eyes have grown dim, and my power, so vibrant in my youth, has all but seeped from my body."

"Oh, Grandmother, no!"

Enit held up a veined hand to silence Morgana. "I have had Cook bring up some herbs for healing, and Berthilde was kind enough to give me some candles. They are for you."

"Why?" Morgana asked, but she guessed the reason.

"Have you not a plan to save Abergwynn and the man you love?" Enit asked with a knowing smile.

"You know?"

"I have seen your destiny, Morgana," she said, settling back on the pillows. "You have within you all the good to make you a powerful wife, mayhap even a ruler one day, but you must prove yourself."

"I would do anything to save Garrick," she said simply, and Enit patted her hand.

"Then you know what you must do: sacrifice yourself and marry Hazelwood."

Injustice took hold of Morgana's tongue. "He is a vile, wicked traitor!" she spat out, appalled at the old woman's suggestion. "He killed my brother and Garrick's brother, and he has been cruel to those who trusted him."

"He is to be your husband," Enit said gravely. "For the sake of the child and for the sake of the man you love, you must marry him."

"I cannot!"

"Yea. Be a good wife. Trust in God. Have faith in the powers he has given you."

"A good wife?" Morgana repeated. She knew in her heart that her grandmother was right, and yet her spirit fought the very idea of being bound to a man she hated. She shivered and wished the fates had chosen a different path for her. The voice of doom seemed to echo through her mind.

"You are clever, Morgana," Enit said. "More so than Cadell. Use your power wisely, and take these herbs, the candles, and this." Her fingers slipped beneath the covers to a hiding place in the bed. Slowly she withdrew a white bundle. She carefully unwrapped the old linen to show Morgana a knife with a thin steel blade and a carved wooden hilt. "Take this, child. See how it fits in your hand."

Morgana did as she was told. The knife curved comfortably against her palm. Her fingers tightened easily around the wooden handle.

"This is not a weapon, Morgana. Understand that. This knife is for your magic and *only* for your magic. Keep it wrapped until the next full moon. After sunset on that day, take the knife to a wild place where you can be all alone. Upon a small hill with a stream running by, you must kneel facing north and plunge the knife blade into the earth. Leave it there for the count of thirty, and then pull it out of the ground. From the highest spot on the hill you will then face east, hold the knife aloft, and conjure up the winds. Afterward you must build a fire, face south, and thrust the knife into the flames. Finally, dip the blade into the stream and face west. Each time you use the knife you must ask nature to aid you in your practice of magic. Then you should wrap the knife in the linen for safekeeping. It will serve you well, as it has served me, but it is to be used only in the healing arts."

Gently Morgana folded the cloth over the knife.

Her grandmother's hand clamped firmly over hers. "All that I have, Morgana, is yours. All the powers of my sight are now vested in you. I thought that Cadell, and mayhap Glyn someday, would be able to see their destiny, but Cadell is gone and Glyn will never open her mind to the healing arts. 'Tis only you who is blessed."

Morgana felt her grandmother tremble and noticed the rasp that was each breath. Fear assailed her. "But, Grandmother—"

"You are the guardian of the magic now, my child. God be with you. 'Tis time I rested."

Morgana held on to her grandmother's hand as, with a sigh, the old woman slipped from this world into the next. "Grandmother, please, don't go, not yet. I have so much to learn!" Morgana pleaded. Tears streamed from her eyes as the last rattling breath left Enit's lungs and she lay still.

Twenty-five

ou'll not return to Abergwynn, and I'll hear no more of it," Daffyd declared yet again. His face was etched with grief as he studied the blade of his sword. They stood in the great hall, and several of his most trusted men had entered. Daffyd waved them off and said to his daughter, "There's been enough death in this family." He shoved his sword back into its sheath. "I've made many mistakes, I fear. 'Twas wrong of me to banish you, Morgana. God's eyes, but you know how to vex me, and I was too quick to punish you. But now that you are here and safe, you must stay. Leave the making of war to the men."

"But, Father, I could be of help," she insisted, touched by Daffyd's admission. 'Twas not easy for him to concede that he'd erred.

"You heard me, Morgana. Do not argue. Go to the chapel. Pray for the souls of your brother and grandmother and for the safety of your sister. I must think of war." He waved her away from him and ordered a page to serve wine to his most trusted knights as they made battle plans.

Morgana knew that he would not change his mind, for Daffyd of Wenlock was known for his stubborn streak. Morgana, however, had no intention of kneeling on a cushion for hours when she was the only one who could save Garrick's life. Daffyd had nothing to offer Strahan except bloodshed, but she could bargain with her wedding vows.

She hurried to the chapel, for she knew her father could see her, and she knelt before the altar and quickly crossed herself. Praying softly, she waited, half expecting Daffyd to send someone to spy on her. But the chapel remained quiet, and slowly, her heart in her throat, she stood. She wasn't going to kneel here trembling and chanting feeble prayers, like Glyn, hoping for divine intervention while Garrick and his family were fighting for his castle and their very lives! No, she would have to find her own way to help Garrick.

Escape would not be difficult, for there was a window above the altar. As for a disguise, several monks' robes hung nearby. She grabbed one of the scratchy dirt-colored cloaks and tossed it out the window. Searching quickly, she found a candle, an extra length of thick rope for the church bell, and a flint. She threw them quickly outside and heard them land with a thud. Whispering a prayer that she wouldn't be caught, and touching her pouch to see that her grandmother's knife and her own dagger were tucked safely inside it, she hopped lithely onto a table near the window and climbed onto the sill. The drop to the inner bailey was less than ten feet, and she slipped through the window, hung by her arms for a second, and then let go. She landed in the mud and grass and quickly snatched up the dull brown cloak. The rope was too heavy for her to carry, but she took the flint and candle. Then, before she was seen, she darted behind a hay wagon and donned the scratchy habit, raising the cowl to cover her hair and her face. In the pocket she found a small prayerbook. She pulled the hood lower over her face and waited for darkness.

*   *   *

As night fell, Morgana ran briskly through the outer bailey, her hands deep in the pockets of her robe. Clutched in one fist was her dagger, and with her other hand she rubbed the binding of the prayerbook. "Help me," she whispered as she hurried to the stables and sent up a silent prayer of thanks that her father had not come looking for her.

The stableboy, Robert, was still mucking out dung. She hid her face from him and approached Luck, glad the stallion was tethered close to the door.

Robert stopped his work and eyed her. Holding her breath, she untied the horse.

"That's Morgana's stallion, Father," Robert said as he leaned upon the handle of his shovel. "Ye know who I'm talkin' about—the daughter to Daffyd, the one they claim is a witch."

Morgana stiffened. She couldn't let the boy recognize her. She lowered her head, keeping the cowl over her face. "Aye," she replied gruffly. "I'm to bless the animal, I am. To make sure there are no devil curses upon him."

" 'E's a bloody ghost-horse! Just like that mare she used ta ride. Bloody Phantom—that's wha' the witch calls her."

"Back to your task, lad, and . . . and may God be with you." She made a quick sign of the cross and hoped her act was believable. If only Friar Tobias could see her now—all those years of lessons had not been wasted.

"You, too, Father, ahh!" Robert dropped his shovel and stepped back a pace. " 'Tis the fiend of Satan himself!"

His face was white in the half-light as Morgana heard a low snarl behind her. *Wolf! Oh, Lord, why now?* "Aye, I'm to bless the wolf dog as well," Morgana replied, keeping her voice deep as she quickly led Luck into the darkening bailey.

"Y're no priest!" Robert declared, following her. "Y're the witch 'erself!"

Morgana had to gamble. "That's right, Robert." She grabbed him by the front of his scruffy shirt and wound her fingers into the fabric as she dragged him close so that her eyes and his were level. "If you don't want warts all over your face or your toes to fall off or worms to cover your head, you'll keep your mouth shut. If anyone asks, swear that you saw me near the kitchen."

" 'Twould be a lie!"

"You've lied before, I'll wager, and this one will save you from the warts."

He gulped, and in the moonlight she saw the fear in his eyes. "I'm telling you now, go!" she said, pushing. She felt a stab of guilt for scaring the child, but she had no choice. The fate of Abergwynn was in her hands. Without wasting a second, she headed for the portcullis.

The guard at the gate was straining his eyes against nightfall as she passed. "Good night to you, Father," he said softly.

"And to you, my son," she murmured, hardly daring to breathe. She kept Luck's gait at a slow walk so as not to disturb the sentry and was nearly past the portcullis when she heard him cry out.

"For the love of Saint Jude! What the devil is that beast doing here? Father . . . ?"

Wolf snarled menacingly, and Morgana kicked Luck hard in the sides. The horse plunged forward as the warning sounded. "God be with us all," she prayed, thankful that Wolf had caught up with her and run ahead. They raced across the moonlit fields toward the forest to the north. The cowl flew off her head, and she stared into the dark stand of pine and oak. She prayed that Garrick was still alive. She would give anything—aye, even her own body—so that he could live!

He was sore and tired, so bloody tired. But he felt as if he hadn't moved a muscle in a fortnight. He heard the voices around him—voices he recognized. But her voice wasn't there. Morgana wasn't speaking to him. Morgana. Morgana. He had thought of her often since the blackness covered his mind, imagined he heard her, felt her warm hands on his stone-cold soul. But now, as he swam closer to the surface of consciousness, he prayed for her touch, for her smile, for her kiss. . . . He tried to open his eyes but couldn't, nor could he understand what was being said. There was trouble; that much he knew. Though his mind was blank when he tried to remember, he felt as if a heavy stone had been placed upon his chest and he couldn't shove it off.

Clare's voice again. She sounded worried, but hadn't she always? Even when he was a child, she had tried to tell him what to do, where he was making mistakes, what the proper course of action would be.

He tried to smile but could not. His throat was dry and tasted of sour vomit. A searing pain burned through him, almost as if his muscles had been severed by a white-hot sword. His stomach convulsed when someone tried to pour hot broth down his throat.

For an instant he thought of his son. Where was he? There was something wrong where Logan was concerned— the rock on his chest seemed to grow heavier, and the blackness started creeping over his mind again. He thought he heard Strahan's voice, and he went cold inside. Strahan, his cousin. Strahan . . . the evil one. Strahan would have to pay.

He would burn in the fires of hell! Garrick struggled toward consciousness only to lose the battle, and the blackness covered him like a soothing blanket as he dreamed of the beautiful witch.

The rising moon was full. A few clusters of clouds dulled the stars, and the air felt like rain and mist—the coming of a storm.

Morgana gathered her courage. After three days of riding, she was only an hour from Abergwynn, and she knew her father and his soldiers were not far behind her. She had heard them on the first day of the journey; then the thudding of hooves and men's shouts had disappeared. Today again she had heard them. Soon they would catch her, but not before she'd opened the gates of the castle. Not until she'd seen for herself if Garrick was alive or dead.

At the tormenting thought she let out a moan, and she herself felt dead inside.

Her horse was lathered and spent. She stopped near a stream, and as the stallion drank from the cool water, she made herself ready. As her grandmother had instructed, she unwrapped the knife and faced in one direction after another, touching the blade to each of the four elements. She closed her eyes, sure that her grandmother's voice rode on the wind, but she heard nothing save the lonely call of an owl, its hunt disturbed by her incantations. The wind was from the north, which was not a good sign, and yet she faced the cool breath of the fates. The breeze picked up, cold as death, whistling through the trees and moving heavy clouds across the sky. Morgana shivered as her hair was lifted away from her neck and tossed in wild waves around her face.

"Do not fail me," she begged.

When she'd finally finished her incantations, she doused her small fire with water from the stream, wrapped the knife again, and hid it inside her boot. Then she fell to her knees and prayed, not for herself but for Garrick and for God's help in her task.

She shivered inside at the thought of marrying Strahan; her guts roiled in rebellion. Yet she would marry him gladly if he would but spare Garrick's life!

Clouds slowly covered the moon. Luck quenched his thirst, then rolled in the mud and rested. The pounding of hooves and the voices of men sounded through the forest. She had no time to lose, for if her father caught her before she reached Abergwynn, all her plans would be for naught, and more blood would be spilled. Quickly, scurrying in the darkness, she remounted. Rain began to fall gently, and the moon was soon all but hidden. Morgana's heart thudded in a painful rhythm. More than once she questioned her wisdom in disobeying Daffyd. Surely her father knew more than she about taking a castle, but she was driven by an inner fire that could not be smothered. Only she could save Garrick.

The forest gave way to lush meadows above which Abergwynn rose, a cathedrallike fortress that commanded the countryside. Through the mist, the moon cast silvery shadows upon the land and illuminated the great towers and battlements of the castle. Was Garrick inside, even now dying from a mortal wound? Was he already dead?

There was a small chance that he had wrested the castle from Strahan, that her visions of death had been wrong, but she knew, deep in her heart, that her hope was false.

Steeling herself, she kicked her tired horse forward. Marriage to Strahan—the thought was like a hard, painful fist in her stomach. Her hands trembled, and she began to sweat.

A hundred yards from the castle she dismounted and quickly planted six candles in the damp earth surrounding her horse and her dog. Using her flint, she lit each taper and held one long white candle aloft, saying nothing until a sentry, probably roused from his sleep, finally caught sight of her tiny flames.

"Hey—wha'?"

"I want to speak to the baron of Abergwynn," she yelled, her voice carrying on the wind.

The guard in the southerly tower shouted gruffly, "Who goes there?"

Morgana swallowed back her fear. Her small fists clenched. " 'Tis I, Morgana of Wenlock. I need to speak to the baron."

"Holy Christ, the witch has returned! Halt where you are! Advance no more!"

Morgana did as she was told, waiting, sweat dripping down her spine though the night was cold and rain drizzled down her neck. She heard the rush of the wind and the battering of the sea against the shore. Cool breezes played with her hair and touched her cheeks, and the earth smelled damp. But she felt no joy in nature this night. Her heart pounded in dread, and she sent up prayer after prayer that her visions had been false, that the gates of Abergwynn would open and Garrick would appear. She trembled at the thought. Upon spying him she would run into his arms, confiding that she loved him, telling him she couldn't live without him. Her heart nearly burst with the thought of all the vows of love she would make to him.

What would happen if he were already dead? She groaned

inwardly and added another vow—a vow of vengeance. Enit's knife pressed hard against her calf, and she hoped that the voice of the wind was wrong.

She heard a commotion inside the castle walls—men's voices, horses whinnying, soldiers shouting, and above it all, with a loud rumble and clank of chains, the portcullis of Abergwynn rattling upward.

She braced herself, and yet when the outer bailey of the castle was visible through the open gate, her insides turned to ice.

Strahan of Hazelwood stood on the other side of the gate.

Morgana nearly fell to the ground. *No! Oh, God, please don't let me be too late!* Dread clutched her in its icy grasp.

Behind Strahan, torches held by a dozen huntsmen lit the castle walls. Smoke curled into the damp air, and red and yellow flames cast moving shadows on the ground. Strahan, thrown in relief by the fires, looked like the devil himself.

"So, Morgana, you've returned." He glanced at her circle of light and her monk's robe. "No doubt to bargain with your life for those you love," he guessed, his voice filled with scorn. "Dressed as a servant of God. I trust this was for my amusement."

Morgana thrust her hands in the pockets of the monk's robe. In one she touched the prayerbook; in the other she felt the hilt of her dagger. "I am here to beg you to spare Garrick's life."

"You bring his son with you?"

Morgana shook her head. "Nay. Never would I entrust a child to you."

"No? Not even your own children? *Our* children?"

She felt a rush of vomit climb up her throat at the thought of bearing Strahan's child.

"What if I told you that Garrick is already dead?" Strahan asked, adding to her torment.

Her heart cracked. Fear flooded through her veins. "I would not believe you."

"Would you believe his sister?" Strahan asked.

Oh, God, please, no! "If Clare says he's dead, then, yea, I will believe," she said, panic welling up within her. Was it possible? Could Garrick really have ceased to exist? Would she not have sensed his death? If he were gone, wouldn't a part of her, too, have left this world? Her heart shattered, and her knees weakened. All seemed to have been for naught . . . but as she stared at Strahan she saw the glint of pleasure in his eyes. He was but playing with her. Again she felt Enit's blade against her leg, and the knife was a comfort.

"What makes you think I want you still, after you've given yourself to another?" he asked.

She held her chin high with pride. "Mayhap you don't."

"Mayhap I want you only as my whore," he said. "Are you willing to give yourself to me without marriage, as you have given yourself to Garrick?"

No! "I will do what you wish if Garrick, his family, and mine are set free," she said evenly, though rebellion boiled in her blood. "However, if they are not, then know you this: I would rather die than lie with a cur like you."

He laughed aloud, the sound terrifying. "You're not in a bargaining position, I fear."

"Am I not?" Morgana asked, daring to match wits with him. He believed in her gifts, so why not see if she could cause him fear? She lifted her arms to the sky and turned her face to the wind. "Come all that is wild, all that is free.

Follow these flames." The sky seemed to boil as the clouds moved. Rain splashed against her eyes and cheeks. As the lightning charged the sky, she turned in a slow circle and chanted: "Master of the gentle rain, mistress of the storm, guard against the sinner's bane. Keep us all from harm. Shield the son of Abergwynn from the traitor's blade, and let the traitor know we shall not be afraid—"

"No spells, witch!" Strahan commanded sharply. "Come forward slowly. If you truly wish to save Garrick's miserable hide, you must prove yourself."

Morgana walked through the circle of light thrown by her nearly doused candles. Her heart was filled with dread as she stopped a few feet from Strahan. "Before I go into the castle, set them free," she ordered. "Garrick, Glyn, and Clare. They're all to be unharmed."

Strahan laughed. "Why should I bother?"

"So that I do not kill you," she said evenly, her eyes holding his.

"Think you that your spells scare me?"

She forced a cold smile. "I think you believe in my powers. Elsewise why would you want me?"

"Perhaps I want you for your beauty."

"Many women are beautiful."

He touched her wet cheek, and she shrank away from his hand. "Nay, not as beautiful as you. But beauty is only part of it. Garrick wanted you. He was tortured with desire when you were promised to me, and that made me crave you all the more. I have waited many nights for this one," he said. "Aye, I will set Garrick's family and your sister free, but only after we are wed."

"I believe you not."

" 'Tis the only way."

Though she quivered inside, she stood proud. She had her dagger, Enit's knife, her own hands, Wolf's sharp teeth, and her wits at her command. These she used now as she whispered, "Know this, Sir Strahan: I have seen your death. With my own eyes I have watched you lie on the floor of Abergwynn, your blood staining the rushes, your body writhing in pain."

"You lie," Strahan growled. "No one can stop me. McBrayne is on his way to help me defend Abergwynn."

"He's an old man, a man who has betrayed you before, and yet you trust in him. You are more a fool than I thought!"

The blood drained from Strahan's face, and he slapped her hard on the cheek. She stumbled and would have fallen if he hadn't grabbed her roughly by the arm. "Enough of your lies!"

Wolf let out a low growl, and Strahan froze. "Kill him," he ordered, motioning to the dog.

One archer stepped forward.

"No!" Morgana ordered. "Wolf, run!"

The dog ran into the shadows of the night.

"Lord Strahan! He awakes!" A burly knight, the one known as Ivan, strode through the ranks of the huntsmen. "Lord Garrick is stirring!" The archer lowered his bow after Wolf had darted away and hidden in the shadows.

Morgana couldn't disguise the relief that coursed through her. Not only was her dog safe, but Garrick was alive!

Strahan's fingers tightened in frustration. "Tell the chaplain to make ready the wedding Mass, and have the cook prepare a feast. Tonight Morgana and I will be wed. Come, my love," he cooed, his eyes as dark as the night, his fingers digging into her soft flesh. "You must prepare yourself. I promise that you will remember this night until the end of your days."

"I will not wed you unless Garrick and the others are set free."

" 'Tis done," he said easily, motioning to a servant. "Now, come."

Pain seared through his body as Garrick felt his pallet being moved. He groaned, shifting his weight, and groaned yet again. His head thundered, his eyes burned, and all around him he heard the excited voices of servants and soldiers—some he recognized, others he didn't. The smell of smoke and perfume, sizzling meat and baked goods, wafted around his consciousness, dragging him out of the black oblivion in which he'd dwelt. He felt stronger than he had the other times he'd tried to rouse, and yet he was much weaker than his usual self.

"Welcome, cousin," a voice, an ugly voice, greeted him.

Forcing his eyes open, Garrick found Strahan, dressed in magnificent gray velvet, staring down at him with dark, malevolent eyes. Garrick started to move, but a huge hand belonging to Sir Andrew held him down against the pallet, which had suddenly stopped moving.

"Oh, don't get up. You can watch from there."

Dizzily Garrick lifted his head and found that he'd been carried through the castle and was now in the chapel. Father Matthew was dressed in elegant vestments, and Morgana the enchantress stood nearby, her face ashen. Dressed in a white gown trimmed in gold, she looked at him and couldn't contain the joy in her eyes.

"You're awake," she said, but Strahan grabbed her roughly and forced her to kneel before the altar.

"Let her go," Garrick whispered in a voice that could barely be heard.

"I think not. We're about to be married. You can watch, just as you'll watch afterward, when I claim her as mine," Strahan said.

The gasp that escaped came not only from Morgana's lips, for Glyn and Clare, too, stood as witnesses in the small chapel. Glyn seemed frozen while Clare's face was a mask of harsh determination, as if she were enduring this mockery of a ceremony only until she could rebel.

"We had a bargain," Morgana reminded Strahan, but he laughed at her insolence.

"You cannot marry—" Garrick began, fury rising in his blood.

"As baron of Abergwynn I can do as I please," Strahan interrupted.

"You are not baron!"

"Oh, but I am! I have command of this castle, and I will marry Morgana of Wenlock. You have the privilege of watching, as you may watch the consumation of the marriage."

"Strahan, no!" Clare cried.

"Shut her up," Strahan commanded a guard. Then he turned back to the fury burning bright in Garrick's eyes. "Though my bride would as soon cut out my heart as say these vows, she's agreed to marry me so that you and your miserable family can go free."

"Nay!" Garrick tried to sit up again, and once more he was restrained. This time Sir Andrew's hand slapped him across the cheek, and he fell back to the pallet, pain exploding through his brain, his mind threatening to swim back into the comfort of blackness. Yet he forced himself to remain alert, for he had to find a way to kill Strahan before he placed a hand on Morgana, no matter what the cost.

"Do not strain yourself," Morgana said to Garrick, though she fought tears. " 'Twill be all right. Logan is safe, and you will be free to go with him."

Relief flooded through him. So she had found the boy after all. If for no other reason, Garrick would live, but he would not, could not, allow Strahan to marry Morgana. "I will never be free without you," he said to Morgana.

"How touching," Strahan cut in. "But you have no choice. The lady has agreed to marry me."

"Never!" Garrick's jaw tightened in anger, and Strahan laughed.

Closing his eyes for a second, Garrick wished the scene away. Mayhap this was all a bad dream.

But when he lifted his eyelids again, he was still in the chapel. The chaplain was at the altar, praying, and Glyn, Clare, and several soldiers were on their knees. Morgana and Strahan faced the altar, and Andrew kept his harsh eyes on Garrick. Another soldier stood guard at the door. Garrick clasped Andrew around the wrist. "You vowed your fealty to me," he reminded the tall knight.

"Aye, but I changed my mind."

"You cannot. You promised me, and Abergwynn and the king—"

"On with the ceremony!" Strahan cut in, and Andrew shook off Garrick's feeble grasp.

Never before had Garrick felt so helpless. Aye, he'd been proud, and true, he'd been raw with pain when Logan was stolen, but this—to watch as Morgana married the man she hated—this was too much. Rage kindled in his breast, but he feigned sleep, hoping to put Sir Andrew at ease.

The Mass was moving much too quickly, and his brain

was too thick to think clearly. But there had to be a way to stop this madness, to save Morgana before she gave herself to Strahan. He searched the room, his eyes moving slowly beneath his half-closed eyelids, rage pumping through his veins.

God help me, he prayed as he gritted his teeth and, with all his strength, threw himself off the bed. His body pitched forward toward the altar. Andrew reached for him and missed, grabbing the air. Glyn screamed, and soldiers reached for their weapons.

"For the mercy of Jesus," the chaplain shouted as Garrick landed on the altar, spilling the wine and toppling the candles. Wax dripped, and flames quickly ignited the altar cloth.

Glyn's scream curdled upward to the rafters.

"You idiot!" Strahan jumped back, grabbing for his sword. Several men raised their weapons. Quick as a cat, Morgana tossed one candle into the rushes, and fire swept through the chapel, flames crackling hungrily at the priest's vestments and Strahan's surcoat.

"Stop!" Strahan commanded.

Clare grabbed the chalice and swung it at the guard standing next to her. As he stumbled, she deftly relieved him of his sword.

"Morgana!" Garrick yelled.

Terrified screams and shouts filled the small room, and Garrick kept moving, his feet leaden as he tried to stay out of the guards' hands and away from Strahan's sword.

The priest quickly stripped off his alb, stamped at the flames, and grabbed the small font of holy water.

"Fire!" the guards yelled, and footsteps pounded in the outer hallways. Women shrieked, and the growling of dogs added to the terror of the crackling flames.

"As I predicted, Strahan," Morgana said, narrowing her eyes. "Here you will die." Swiftly she reached into her boot and withdrew the small knife with its carved handle. She ignored Enit's warning and swung at Strahan. He grabbed her wrist, pounding it hard against the altar. The knife fell to the floor.

"Stop, bastard!" Clare held her sword aloft, aimed at Strahan's head, but he ducked as she swung it down, and Glyn screamed yet again.

"Fire! Fire!" the soldiers shouted, still dancing around the flames, their hands on their swords.

Garrick was breathing hard, his entire body aching as he lunged for Morgana's knife. He found the blade, but the hot metal seared his hand. Again the knife fell to the floor. All around him smoke and crackling flames burned the air, filling the chapel with a horrid stench.

"Let there be no bloodshed in the house of the Lord," Father Matthew insisted, stamping out flames on his way to the door.

People rushed through the chapel in a panic, and Garrick grabbed a candlestick, the only weapon he could find. It, too, was hot, but he held it aloft and turned on his cousin.

"You miserable asp!" Strahan swore as he finally yanked his sword from its sheath. "Go now to Satan!"

"Let there be no bloodshed in the house of the Lord!" the chaplain repeated as he fled toward the door. "Please, save yourselves!" He threw the few remaining drops of holy water onto his vestments and ran from the chapel as the first servants carried in tubs of water.

Strahan swung his sword, but Garrick rolled away quickly. His body aching, consciousness threatening to fail, he dodged the sword by mere inches. The blade stuck hard in the wooden altar. With an effort, Strahan pulled his weapon free.

Smoke clogged the room. Morgana wrapped the hem of her skirt around her hands and searched the burning rushes, withdrew the white-hot blade, and held it aloft. "Stop, Strahan," she ordered, "or I will kill you myself."

"Morgana, no!" Garrick cried, for Strahan had whirled upon his new wife, wielding his sword. Garrick grabbed Strahan's legs, bringing him to the floor, and they grappled for the sword. Pain exploded through Garrick's chest, but he hung on and swung a fist toward Strahan's face.

His hand connected and sent a shock up his entire arm.

Strahan scrambled away, but Morgana still held her grandmother's knife.

"Think you could kill me with that?" Strahan asked, eyeing the small weapon.

Glyn fainted, and Clare swung her sword at a guard before bending down and slapping the girl into consciousness.

"She won't have to kill you," another voice yelled over the frenzy. Garrick twisted to find the servant woman, Springan, standing in the doorway. Her shaved head was red with anger, and her fingers were coiled tight over the handle of a pail. Her face was twisted, and tears streamed from her eyes as she cried, "Strahan of Hazelwood, servant of Satan, I now consign you to hell, for that is where you belong!"

"Kill her!" Strahan ordered, struggling to his feet.

A guard swung his sword in Springan's direction, but before the blade felled her, Springan threw the liquid from the pail at Strahan, and it ignited with a roar, crackling and spitting, smelling of animal fat.

Strahan let out a horrendous scream, and the knight's sword struck Springan in the shoulder. She fell, but her eyes stayed fast on the fiery mass that was the father of her child.

Morgana stepped back, sickened at the sight, while Strahan's men tried to douse the flames with tubs of water. But the grease had soaked into his clothes, and he had become a screaming human torch, clawing painfully at the skin on his face and neck, wildly running in circles as the fire swept over him, consuming the cooking grease and charring his skin.

"No! Holy Christ, save me!" he cried, writhing from the torment of the flames. Again the soldiers threw water on him, but still he was hideously blackened, his face destroyed, his hair a blazing halo surrounding his ghastly skull. His screams echoed through the castle as he ran crazily, as if he could escape the flames that were eating him alive.

"Father, help us," Glyn prayed, trying to swoon yet again. Springan lay where she had been felled, her life seeping from the mortal wound. Morgana ran to her while Glyn whispered prayers and Clare ordered the girl taken upstairs.

" 'Tis too late," Springan whispered, her voice barely a rattle as her eyes sought Morgana's. She clutched the sleeve of the dress that was to have been Morgana's bridal gown and begged, "Lind . . . please see that my boy is cared for."

"It shall be done," Morgana vowed.

"Forgive me for hating you. 'Twas my jealousy over that bastard Strahan," Springan said.

"Think naught of it," Morgana said as Springan's eyes glazed over and her soul departed. Morgana held her still, unmoving, until Garrick pulled her to her feet and guided her from the chapel where servants and soldiers alike worked to put out the flames.

" 'Tis over." Garrick held her close, kissing the crown of her head. " 'Tis the path she chose."

"But—"

"As I said, 'tis done." Despite his weakness, he gathered her into his arms and kissed her like a man who was starved, as if in holding her he gained strength.

She returned his kisses, and tears streamed from her eyes. Tears of sorrow. Tears of happiness. Tears of relief. "I thought I'd lost you," she whispered brokenly, her fingers curling in the coarse fabric of his shirt.

"I'm not easily lost," he teased, kissing her eyes, her cheeks, her throat, though he could barely stand.

"But Logan is safe at Tower Wenlock. My mother waits for word that he can be returned to you." Swiping at the tears in her eyes, she managed a smile.

"So you are a witch after all."

"Nay."

"A sorceress, then," he said, twining his hands in her hair before he buried his face in her dark locks. "I love you, Morgana of Wenlock," he finally admitted. "I've denied it for a long time, but I love you, aye, mayhap more than life itself."

Morgana stood on her toes and kissed his cheek. "As I love you, m'lord, though now I know 'twas not you but Strahan who was the danger from the north."

His footsteps were not steady, and she helped him limp through the great hall to the inner bailey, where servants and soldiers had escaped from the smoke and gathered in clusters. In a hoarse, little-used voice, Garrick ordered the wounded to be tended and Strahan's and Springan's bodies to be buried outside the castle walls. That done, he turned to the mass of people whom he had once commanded.

"Hear you now!" Garrick said as loud as possible, his

rasping voice ringing with an authority belonging only to the rightful baron of Abergwynn. "The fire is dead, as is the traitor who led some of you against me and the king. I am once again baron of Abergwynn, and anyone who betrayed me had best step forward now, for his punishment will be much less than later when I discover his treachery and lies."

There was a murmur of voices, a rustling and shifting of feet, but no one spoke. Still leaning on Morgana, Garrick scowled down at his men. "Know you this: I will marry Morgana of Wenlock. You are all to bow to her and treat her as the lady of Abergwynn, for that is who she will be!"

"M'lord," Morgana whispered, her throat thick with tears, her heart filled with love.

"Should I have asked?"

She smiled, and her eyes brightened a bit. " 'Twould have been nice," she replied with some of her old devilment.

"And what would you have said?"

"That I cannot wait. Will not the priest marry us now?"

He grinned, and his mouth hurt a bit as it stretched. "Are you so eager?"

"Oh, yea, m'lord," she replied saucily. Lifting a dark brow, she cooed, "I find it impossible to wait another night without warming your bed."

"Wench," he growled with a laugh and swatted her fondly on the rear. "We need not be married for bed-warming tonight."

She giggled and bit her lip, eyeing the man she loved with all her heart. *Lady of Abergwynn.* Wife to Garrick. Mother to Logan. Aye, 'twas all she could ask. The fates that brought her here she no longer cursed, but thanked Almighty God for the gift that had led Garrick to Wenlock so many weeks before.

Slowly the men in the yard stepped forward, and knight after knight laid down his shield and sword, swearing his fealty and accepting Garrick as his lord and Morgana as the new lady of Abergwynn.

Garrick was about to talk to the priest about a marriage ceremony when shouts rang out. "My lord!" a sentry yelled. " 'Tis soldiers!"

"Father!" Morgana cried. "He followed me here, and I fear he'll be angry with me."

" 'Tis as it always is," Garrick said with a chuckle, then yelled, "If the army belongs to Daffyd of Wenlock, open the gates!"

Within minutes the soldiers passed inside the castle walls and, upon spying her father, Glyn screamed joyously and ran toward him.

"What's this?" Daffyd demanded, spying her shaved head, as he dismounted.

"Oh, Father! Father! Thank God you are here!" She threw herself into his waiting arms and sobbed with joy against his shoulder. " 'Twas awful! So hideous!"

"There, there." He patted her scraped scalp and held her closer. " 'Twill be all right."

"Nay, never!"

Sighing, he looked over his trembling daughter's shoulder and spied his eldest. "Morgant!" Daffyd growled, eyeing his firstborn with quiet rage. "You have defied me for the last time."

"Aye, that she has," Garrick said, his arm firmly around Morgana's waist. "She has given me back my son and my castle, and I owe her my life. You'll have no more gray hairs from this one, Daffyd, for she is to become my wife."

"Your wife?" Daffyd said, his scowl slowly changing to a

smile of calculated pleasure at the thought of losing a willful daughter and gaining a powerful son-in-law. "Well, well . . ." With one arm still supporting Glyn, he crossed the inner bailey, moving past the kneeling peasants and knights. "This I will give my blessing, and I bring you good news: Osric McBrayne has turned back to Castle Hawarth. Lord Rowley and I convinced him it would best serve him to leave Abergwynn to you."

"You are truly faithful," Garrick said. "You shall be rewarded."

Daffyd's eyes narrowed a bit, as they always did when he contemplated gold.

"There are others who must be rewarded and some who will be punished. We will find out which of Strahan's thugs stole Logan, and they will be banished or beaten or worse," Garrick proclaimed. "The men who killed Cadell and Ware shall be punished as well. And as for Will Farmer, I think we owe him a horse."

"Not Luck," Morgana argued quickly. "For without him, I could not have returned."

"Then we shall give the farmer the pick of the stables," Garrick said, his arm slung possessively over the shoulders of his bride to be. "What say? A little food? A lot of wine? A marriage ceremony?" Garrick looked at his kneeling army. "Arise," he said. "Those of you who will stay, I shall speak with on the morrow"—he glanced slyly at the witch—"long after noon."

A hair-raising howl rose from outside the castle, and Morgana whistled sharply. Wolf streaked through the gate and into the inner bailey and wiggled his way into Morgana's waiting arms.

Morgana laughed and ruffled his fur before Garrick took

her arm again. "Come. 'Tis time for a wedding." He linked his arm through Morgana's, allowing her to help him climb the steps. With Wolf padding behind them, the lord and future lady of Abergwynn walked into the great hall that was to be their home forever.